TRIPLE CROSSING

Triple Crossing

Tom Kay

The Pentland Press Limited
Edinburgh · Cambridge · Durham · USA

First published in 2000 by
The Pentland Press Ltd.
1 Hutton Close
South Church
Bishop Auckland
Durham

British Library Cataloguing in Publication Data.
A catalogue record for this book is available
from the British Library.

ISBN 1 85821 767 9

Typeset by George Wishart & Associates, Whitley Bay.
Printed and bound by Antony Rowe Ltd., Chippenham.

To Joyce who sailed thousands of miles in the cold Scottish waters whilst this story was developed.

ACKNOWLEDGEMENTS

1. *Yachtsmen's Pilots to Scotland* by Martin Lawrence. Published by Imray, Laurie, Norie & Wilson.

CHAPTER I

IN THE GREY, DAMP, Edinburgh afternoon with an icy north-east wind knifing its way between the tenements of Easter Road towards the palace of Holyrood, he walked like a very old man, and the greying moustache and hair belied the thirty-five years. The Safeway bag contained a few groceries, milk, a small jar of coffee, cigarettes and a bottle of vodka. It was very obviously a major effort just to make his way along the street from the main road towards his flat in the old tenement block, but not so unusual in that district that it drew any special attention from the other occupants of the street as they hurried, head down, about their business. Neither looking right nor left he pushed open the battered black door and climbed the cold stone stairs slowly, resting every third or fourth step as the pains shot across his lower back, until he reached his first-floor flat. With a further great effort he forced his back straight, sighed deeply, put his key into the lock and turned it to open the door. Carefully dropping the latch on the Yale he shuffled his way through the dark hall, across a carpet so worn that all semblance of colour was long since gone, into the living room and over to the refrigerator under the stained worktop by the window.

The strain showed in beads of sweat on his brow although he felt cold. The pain in his lower back was increasing. He couldn't wait any longer. The bag of groceries was laid on the floor in front of the refrigerator and he dragged out the bottle of vodka.

Sinking back onto the settee he breathed a deep sigh and gulped a mouthful of the clear liquid straight from the bottle, quickly followed by another. He looked around at the faded wallpaper, the brown kitchen door with the peeling varnish and the scratched sideboard with the missing handles.

What has happened? He felt really ill, weak. The pains in his lower back and stomach would soon go. He should have phoned his mother. She would have come back. But she would have told him to go to the hospital or the doctor. He couldn't face that again. He would cut down. He still remembered his father's phone number. He

1

couldn't call him again after the last time; after cursing him because he wouldn't provide the money for another bottle. His father would speak to him, he knew, but it was too difficult to apologise yet again. He looked at the large belly hiding the thin legs that used to propel him at great pace. He looked at the pile of empty bottles lying in the corner of the living room. He looked at the photograph on the mantle. In it he was standing at the helm of his family yacht with his arm around his father. It was so good then. He could go back but he would have to stop drinking. Money was tight. He had failed to attend to 'sign on' for some time and even his housing benefit had stopped. His mother could not go on paying his rent forever. Yes, after this bottle he would telephone her and go to the clinic.

Another mouthful. The sweat was drying on him. The room was cold and he was too tired to light the gas fire. It was so tiring going to the shop. He had only bought the food to please his mother and as soon as she had driven off he had swopped most of the food for the bottle. The local Pakistani shop was very obliging. His mother didn't mind the cigarettes but she wouldn't allow him to have a bottle. He should have called her, though, when he felt so bad. He was so tired. A rest now and then call. He settled back and closed his eyes.

This was the third time the tall man had called to collect the rent. There had been no reply on the previous occasions, and the company liked to keep tabs on their least well clients. The cleaners they sent in once a month just to keep the properties habitable hadn't had any reply either and that was unusual. This time he had a key.

The key stopped. It would not turn. He tried again. No. The latch was down. Not good news. The occupant was inside and not responding. The tall man made his way back to his car and called the office. They would arrange for the police to be present when the door was forced.

It wasn't until 6 o'clock that evening that the rental company supervisor and the tall man, accompanied by two police constables, forced the door. As they entered the living room they saw the Safeway bag lying on the floor in front of the refrigerator. The contents had thawed out and a pool of water stretched from the bag to the edge of the frayed rug. The occupant was lying back on the settee, a half-finished bottle of vodka standing on the floor beside him. One of the constables immediately called for help.

The supervisor returned to his office and telephoned the only recorded relative of the client and broke the bad news. 'I am so sorry. I realise this must be distressing for you even though you have had so much trouble. I am sure that he passed away peacefully. I will help as much as I can. I will gather all his personal things from the flat and any papers or relevant mail, and arrange for you to have them.

'The police will call on you and explain procedures, but basically this is what will happen. Your son's body will have to be examined because he died alone and in due course, probably by tomorrow, the Procurator Fiscal's Death Enquiry Unit in Chambers Street will issue a report which is required before the Registrar can issue a death certificate. But don't you worry. As soon as you have been told the Fiscal's report is available, and the body can be released, call me and then you can leave the arrangements up to us. We will keep you informed.'

The elderly lady shook her head to fight back the tears. 'Thank you so much. You are so helpful. I'll let you know as soon as I hear anything.'

The tall man made one more visit to the flat, where, after a short search, he located what he had been looking for: a brown envelope tucked down the back of the settee. The envelope contained a birth certificate, a benefit card and a letter from Buckingham Palace in response to some youthful observation. The letter could be passed to the family.

The following day the tall man entered the Procurator Fiscal's building in Chambers Street and approached the security guards and the metal detector screens. He was dressed soberly and looked glum. 'Death Enquiry Unit,' he mumbled.

'Certainly, sir, take the lift on the left-hand side to the third floor.' The guards looked mildly embarrassed and turned away. They had no wish to further upset the bereaved.

The tall man followed the instructions and on reaching the third floor turned left and into the Enquiry office.

'Yes sir. What can I do for you?'

The question was posed by the typist sitting at the far end of the narrow room.

'I have come for the Release Form for Patrick Dougan.'

The brown envelope was lying on top of the small pile in the tray just inside the window. The receptionist made her way over to the counter and thumbed through the small pile even though the one requested was clearly visible on top.

'Here you are.'

'Thank you.'

The tall man swung round and left the way he had come. As he left the building it flashed through his mind that he could have been anybody. In fact, he was anybody. He returned to his office.

Three days later, one Patrick Dougan, alcoholic, was cremated whilst a small intimate group consoled a distraught mother. The forged death certificate was removed from the crematorium company's files and although arrangements were made for a small plaque to be installed to commemorate the unfortunate, no record of his passing would exist in the usual place of search, the Registrar's Office.

One week later a Patrick Dougan, with a light Irish accent, arrived in the Glasgow suburb of Newton Mearns where he occupied a large stone-built house. He took over a small transport logistics business and became a respected pillar of the community.

The Ecological Property Rental Company went about its business looking after alcohol and drug-dependent clients in whom no-one else took much interest.

CHAPTER II

T HEY MET REGULARLY for a sailing week. At least they met whenever they could all get the same time off, and as Craig and Mike were their own bosses, more or less, it wasn't too difficult. The situation had always been the same. Craig and Mike drove to Ardfern, loaded the boat with the food and booze, filled the water and diesel tanks, checked the gas bottles and switched on the battery charger, before making their way to the Galley of Lorn on the Saturday night. Progress to the local restaurant was often slow as much time was spent catching up with the news from the crews of other yachts just about to leave or just returned from their cruises. A few of these interruptions to progress necessitated the partaking of the odd dram or two.

Alan usually arrived about breakfast time on Sunday after an all-night drive from London and whilst he was fairly tired the other two were always fighting a significant hangover. The scenario was always the same: too much to drink on the first night and a later-than-planned start on Sunday.

There had been no exception this time. Craig and Mike had walked to the Galley of Lorn, ducked through the low, narrow doorway and crossed to the long bar, dined well and then returned to the bar. The old hostelry had to try to be all things to all men: a 'local' to the villagers, an hotel and lounge for the tourists and a refuge for the 'yotties'. Total success would always elude it because, despite valiant efforts of management and staff, and determined culinary endeavour, the odd local lout or resident hippie spoiled it for the tourists, the pseudo sophistication and cultivated accents of the tourists annoyed the locals, and the noisy yachtsmen spoiled it for everybody, but it had to go on trying as there just wasn't enough business from any one group to identify with them alone, and someone would always be seduced into believing that a fabulous opportunity existed in that strangely haunting place to develop the hotel and make their fortune. The failures of so many never seemed to daunt the newcomer and they tried again and again. The current owners, David and Susanna

5

appeared to have got the mix about right and had created conditions that seemed to please all of the disparate group.

The dining-room decor was an odd assortment of styles, colours and futuristic art, but compensated with fresh Jura prawns and spicy mayonnaise, wild salmon, lobster and sole goujons in a champagne and honey-flavoured white wine sauce, and fine, rare, Scotch fillet steak. The long bar aided the maintenance of order as it allowed enough space at most times for the diverse groups to find their own space without impinging too heavily on each others' nerves.

Often they indulged themselves with dinner at The Shower of Herring but that meant a drive and curtailed the drinking so it was usually visited by boat on the return journey at the end of the cruise. That way the superb cuisine and liberal hospitality could be enjoyed to the full without breathalyser worries, although the row back to the mooring was often fraught with danger; probably the greatest danger of the holiday.

Craig and Mike got up to date with each other's business, and Craig found Mike's relaxed attitude refreshing. Mike owned an hotel which specialised in the fishing and walking fraternity, convivial groups which suited Mike well. He had bought the hotel because his wife could not accept the lifestyle of a drinks salesman with a major brewery group, but only one year after buying the hotel, and four years previously, Mike had parted from his wife when she decided that she wasn't prepared for the sixteen-hour days, and seven-day weeks with separate holidays. Initially she moved in with her sister and although they still spoke occasionally, that ended when she moved in with a bank manager. Mike did not usually think much about the past and found that the constant involvement with the hotel problems occupied him without too many regrets getting in the way.

Mike liked meeting people; mixing with strangers and drinking with his regulars he had all the company he needed. He was very popular with women who loved the way he listened and never appeared to disagree with them, but he was only rarely tempted by the available fruits. The slightly rough male company of the boat appealed to him although he wasn't a devotee like Alan who was a perfectionist and studied everything in detail, sometimes at a speed that wasn't exactly electrifying, but he did enjoy the combination of excitement, company and booze.

Mike was a little older than the others, a little heavier, a lot less fit.

The 5-foot 10-inch frame wasn't portly but carried a good few more pounds than his fighting weight would allow. His round features, ruddy cheeks and greying hair confirmed his 'mine host' appearance and he was never at a loss for a tall story. It was rare to hear Mike express strong opinions and he was usually happy to idle along through life with an easy-going gait. He was a fund of stories like 'Did you hear about the Pakistani who went to work in an Irish builder's yard?'

Craig occasionally felt slightly embarrassed when Mike told his often risqué jokes in mixed company but they all laughed loudly. Mike had an ability to be popular with nearly everyone. He was a first-class listener, and with Mike no-one felt embarrassed if their own joke fell a bit flat. Being with Mike was comfortable. He was rarely radical.

Unlike Mike, however, Craig had very strong opinions about most things and although he occasionally exaggerated for effect or to stimulate a good argument, he often firmly believed what he said. Indeed, during a break-in at home Craig had returned to see the culprits still on the premises. Finding the front door locked from the inside he rushed around the side of the house only to fall over the waste sacks that the intruders had placed to cater for just such an eventuality. The steel fence support he picked up would certainly have been wielded, regardless of the possible consequences to himself had he reached the back of the house before the criminals escaped. He willingly helped others with their business problems but tolerated no obstructions to his own ideas and plans.

Business was paramount in Craig's life and he expected the same commitment from his associates and employees. He shared success generously, abhorred failure and could only tolerate it if he was allowed to assist the individual to correct the situation. He would never laugh off shortcomings in himself or others. To some degree this was mitigated by his ability to forget the bad things of the past. Only the best memories were at the forefront of his mind and he really had to work hard to dredge up past unpleasantness.

As usual he had migrated around the bar, talking to locals, tourists and yachtsmen. Indeed he talked to everyone except the noisy loudmouths living it up on daddy's yacht and money and their accompanying girls intent on doing as much damage to women's freedom as possible.

It was partly because the Ardfern Marina was also a working

boatyard that attracted him to the place and he enjoyed talking boats with the boatbuilders and engineers from the boatyard. It was while he was listening to one of the boatbuilders describing how he was refitting an old classic boat he had bought that he became aware that a woman standing back from the bar, and close to the fire and doorway to the pool room, repeatedly drifted into his vision. She particularly attracted his attention. Slim and firm bodied, with penetrating green eyes and fair hair, possibly not wholly her natural shade, and with a bearing emphasised by her confident head-high stance, she surveyed the occupants of the bar.

When she smiled at him, Craig was suddenly aware that he had been staring, blushed furiously and turned away, composed himself immediately, turned back and returned the smile even though the flush had not quite dissipated from his cheeks. As the disarming smile again curved her lips he stepped directly towards her.

'Hi. Are you on holiday here? I don't think we've met before, have we?'

She immediately held out her hand. 'Surely that's right. We are here to sail. I'm Mairread. Let me introduce Sean.'

She turned to her right and Craig was aware of a wiry individual of medium height and build with staring eyes that seemed to look right through him. The eyes had a yellow tinge to the grey and although he had a broad smile Craig felt no warmth in the welcoming, 'Just good to meet you, boyo.'

Craig shook hands, flushed again and apologised. 'My name's Craig. I am sorry. I didn't realise you were together. Please excuse me.'

A lovely, gentle, comforting laugh relaxed the tension and the woman put her hand on his elbow. 'Not at all. We were hoping to meet a local.'

Craig looked deeply into the green eyes and felt a ripple of warmth flow over him. 'I'm not a local. Just a regular. I sail from here.'

'That's great. That's what we are about to do, isn't it?' She turned and looked at her companion, who nodded and kept his gaze firmly and disconcertingly on Craig's face. 'We are here to sail for two weeks. Perhaps you can help us with details of all the good anchorages.'

'Gladly. I'd love to do that. Hold on just a minute. I'll introduce you to one of my crew.'

Craig found Mike, completed the introductions and within minutes Sean and Mairread had enthusiastically joined in the general conversation. Apparently they had chartered a yacht, the 'Atlantic Lord', for two weeks and Mairread, whose sparkling green eyes mesmerised Craig, explained that although she and Sean sailed regularly it was normally racing in Strangford Lough, and they were looking forward to their first long cruise in Scottish waters. To Craig's enquiry about how far they intended to range they were non-committal, merely indicating that they would restrict themselves to day sailing.

Craig, who was often outspoken enough to ask forthright questions, some of which could have been more delicately phrased, questioned Mairread about her occupation.

'Oh, it isn't very exciting. I'm a secretary to a political figure in Ulster; although obviously I can't say which.' She smiled as she replied but her eyes and posture conveyed quite forcefully that he shouldn't probe further.

Craig smiled to himself at the gentle but broad vowels in her soft Irish accent.

Sean's responses were restrained, and as Mike and the others became more boisterous he remained quiet without seeming to be aloof. Craig, twice, felt as though eyes were boring into the back of his head, and when he turned he found Sean staring at him. Although Sean reacted immediately Craig was aware of the yellowish eyes – like a cat, was the thought that flashed through his mind – but fair-haired, green-eyed Mairread soon distracted him.

Instead of the evening ending with a politely drunk 'goodnight' they had been invited back to the Atlantic Lord with Sean and Mairread for a nightcap. Mairread, who had been the centre of attraction in the Galley all evening, and Sean, whose eyes gleamed with a worrying intensity, enthusiastically set about serving up the drinks.

Most of the night was spent putting the world to right, arguing about the continuing creation of too many laws; ineffective policing; that the religious minorities and gays had too much influence on authorities; that nuclear weapons were essential; that life should be lived to the full, and generally making fairly worthless remarks that drew forth increasingly incoherent agreement. Craig had found himself sitting next to Mairread and was mildly thrilled to feel her hand resting on his thigh when she made important points. At one stage he took her hand and squeezed it. She smiled at him but said nothing.

Craig's reading extended to the *Scotsman*, *Financial Times*, and *Sunday Times* and he had a superficial knowledge of most subjects. He held strong views about the way business in Scotland failed to exploit all the best marketing methods and about the participation, or rather the non-participation of staff in matters about which they knew nothing. He could see no point in spending thousands of pounds training a Marketing Manager for him to be subjected to scrutiny by someone whose training and experience qualified him as a first-class bricklayer and, indeed, vice-versa. The Works Council only worked when it was strongly chaired otherwise hours were wasted in pointless chatter. He believed that people should stick to what they did best and that was also his view on business. There had been too much diversification just for fashion's sake and most companies would have to retrench sooner or later.

His knowledge was adequate to lead to a good discussion, especially when they were all just a smidgen inebriated, but during the course of the night he was regularly brought up short as Sean chipped in to the conversation. Craig was aware of critical remarks about Britain, the government, policing, social services and benefits. They were just remarks thrown into wide-ranging conversations, and no-one picked them up or expanded on them, but from time to time Craig felt himself bristle as disagreement surged up, yet somehow Mairread always made an appropriate light-hearted observation that disarmed the situation.

Mike, on the other hand, was relaxed and rarely got excited.

The last dregs were drained at about four a.m. when they staggered back to Wizard.

A fairly typical first night had ended, except that Craig's last thoughts before oblivion struck was that neither Mairread nor Sean seemed to have drunk very much, or maybe they just held it well, and of Sean's staring eyes which were uncomfortable to look at but difficult to ignore. It was almost impossible not to look directly at just one eye and that became embarrassing. In fact it wasn't possible to recall much about them at all; not even their relationship, and such enquiries that were made were met with a polite but positive 'heave to'. *Her faint, soft, Irish accent was lovely though!*

CHAPTER III

CRAIG AWAKENED to the sound of Mike greeting Alan and the rich aroma of coffee. His head hurt and when he bent forward to piss he felt slightly sick. He blushed momentarily when he remembered taking Mairread's hand and the unnecessarily extended goodnight kiss, but hoped it would be put down to an excess of alcohol. *I need a couple of glasses of orange juice and some Resolve.* He glanced through the window at the bright sunshine, decided on lightweight trousers and T-shirt; after some deliberation he chose a new pair of deck shoes and went to join the others.

Alan's arrival was a catalyst and resulted in an upsurge of activity. Mike and Craig hurried along the pontoons and after a passing 'Good morning' to adjacent yacht crews made their way to the toilet block, showered to blow the remaining mushiness away and returned to the yacht. Mike quickly organised the cooking and very shortly the smell of a traditional fry-up was drifting through the boat. Mike made sure that, as well as opening the bar on time each day, a filling breakfast was served up. If they ever had to make an early start he could be relied upon to produce the same just as soon as the gear was stowed and the sea state allowed. A yacht was like a business. Although it was necessary to have the right professionals and technicians, quality support staff kept the wheels oiled. Mike was quality and without command he could be relied on to produce food, snacks and drinks of the hot, cold, alcoholic and non-alcoholic variety as appropriate as well as getting himself fully involved with most of the more arduous of the sailing processes. In other words, despite not having a detailed knowledge of boats, and never himself owning more than a small dinghy, he was a vital member of the crew. Everyone else on board always relaxed with Mike's easy-going attitude.

Alan felt invigorated. Despite the long drive, the fresh West Coast air with its tang of seaweed and pine, and the warm morning sunshine were a great lift. He stared out across the anchorage, over the small island to the shimmering loch and thought of the Underground, the pushing crowds, the interminable board meetings, the worry as sales slumped, and the late arrival home each day just in time to watch the news and fall into bed. *Where has love, friendship and family gone? How much better would life be without the London crush? Why not retire now and come north? But can we manage without the income?* His tall slim frame slumped slightly. He remembered the pungent smells of garlic sweat, damp clothes on rainy days, and the acrid smell of ionised air from the electric sparking of the trains in the Underground. He recalled the nights in business hotels with nothing to do except write up the day's notes, eat too much of poor cooking and sit up late to watch a movie. The desire to succeed and the freedom of the Scottish seascape conflicted. He shrugged away his thoughts and laughed as Craig arrived in the cockpit with a glass of orange juice.

'I can guess what you were doing last night,' he laughed.

'Yes. Just one or maybe two too many. Still, I'm glad to see you are surviving the rat race. You do look as though it has been taking its toll. But never mind. This week will blow the cobwebs away,' welcomed Craig.

'I do hope so. I do hope so. It was a grim drive. Even at night we seem to be getting heavy traffic down South, and the food at these motorway cafes only gets worse.'

'And how are Sylvia and the family?' enquired Craig.

'Sylvia is fine. Her business is booming. Kate has a new job with a fashion house and Martin has opened up a computer systems business with a couple of mates. They are doing quite well and have had some business from Guardian setting up a database to co-ordinate the records of all their clients who have different types of investments with them.'

The late start didn't damp the enthusiasm and the warm, brilliant sunshine and clear blue sky of the quiet Sunday morning increased the feeling of well-being as they cast off, waved to the crews on boats yet to depart and headed down Loch Craignish. The fenders and warps were all stowed, and the morning G&T nestled comfortably in their hands. The Autohelm was engaged and once again they were underway. It had always been so.

'Did you see that our friends of last night had made a sharp start? No sign of their boat,' observed Craig.

Mike looked up. 'I don't think they have been away long. I think they were just disappearing round the end of the island as we were coming on deck.'

Alan peered quizzically at Mike. 'Who is this you are talking about?'

'Oh, an Irish pair we met last night. I thought they were an odd couple, if indeed, they were a couple. When we went back to their boat I thought Craig was going to have a spontaneous orgasm,' laughed Mike.

'Was she that good?'

'Shut up, stop exaggerating and do something useful,' grinned Craig. Alan hitched himself up onto the cockpit coamings and peered into the morning haze. 'On Friday I was tied up until late and had to go in again on Saturday, but things just panned out nicely around 4 o'clock and I got on the road at about nine-thirty. On the drive up here I often wonder if it is worthwhile, but just to sit here and see the Paps of Jura pointing up at those downy clouds drifting in that absolutely clear blue sky makes it all worthwhile.

'It hasn't been too good a spell recently. There has been a lot of talk about redundancy. However, I've just been asked to examine a new marketing projection so perhaps I will be OK. On the other hand, the redundancy arrangements are so generous that perhaps I should sell up and come north.'

'Perhaps they would transfer you to a store. The cost of living here is so much less than London you would manage on a store manager's salary, and your health would be much better,' observed Craig. He shrugged and continued, 'Of course, almost anywhere in the world would be cheaper still.'

'You are probably right, but it is a difficult decision to give up my income, and not only would I probably have to wait for a new store opening but I think a store manager job would bore me.'

'Well then. Just take early retirement.'

'It's worth thinking about, I suppose.'

Alan's family were grown up and working, and his wife ran a very successful business catering for board room lunches in small to medium-sized businesses. She delivered everything from hors d'oeuvre to dessert, including the wines, china, glasses and cutlery, and then removed everything on completion of the meal. She was busy. The high-quality service with minimal disruption to office time was popular, and it was an interesting, indeed very profitable, way to pass the long days that Alan worked.

There was a light south-easterly wind and progress down the loch was comfortable, but fairly quick, and they turned through the Dorus

Mhor, the great gate, with the start of the flood tide. The view through the Gulf of Corryvreckan always drew their gaze, and no matter how many times they sailed through there was always the memory of looking into the Gulf on winter flood tides after a westerly gale and seeing the huge wall of water and the white fountains that jumped twenty to thirty feet into the air. The thunder of the crashing water always caused a little churning even in experienced stomachs. Someone always mentioned the fear and fascination and this time was no exception.

Mike peered into the Gulf. 'Isn't it strange how it is always so calm and peaceful when you sail through, and yet you can't help being aware of how wild it can be? Even on a hot day there seems to be a cold wind current in the Gulf.'

'Yes. I always feel a chill when we go through,' agreed Alan.

A gentle jibe and the yacht surged forward through the swirls and boiling surges, swinging like a pendulum with the undertow and devious currents, between the guardian islands and into the Sound of Luing, then on to Fladda, picking up speed with the current and gently sweeping from side to side with the eddies with the same easy gait of the elephant as it swings along its way. The sun made the twin lighthouses gleam and look newly painted, although it was always a disappointment to find that they were uninhabited and, when close to, it was obvious that the paintwork was somewhat grubby and all of the surrounding walls were disintegrating. Gazing at the empty cottages and the old walled gardens it wasn't too difficult to imagine the lonely life of the keepers.

There was little banter or chat at this stage of each cruise as they all unwound, forcing their business concerns to the back of their minds, and allowing the rich sea air to permeate their lungs and feeling their bodies respond to the constant but random motion of the sea and yacht.

The current speeded up as they bisected the channel between the lights and there was a 'speedboat' feeling as the yacht rushed on with the flow, through the eddies which sweep across the rocky steps and across the slope where the stream flowed over the ledges at the lighthouses. On into the Firth of Lorne with Mull's cliffs stirring the first real excitement of 'heading for the ocean'. The office, the guests, the long hours, argumentative architects, bleating clerks of works and the dusty building sites were matters of another time. All that was important now was good sailing, fine whisky and good food, mellowed by the chameleon-like shading of the mountains, the clear blue water and plunging porpoises, the islands in the haze and a week of good company among friendly people.

Craig's eyes always turned towards the island of Belnahua, and his mind drifted off to form pictures of the old houses and mine workings wafting him back in time to bring forth vivid portraits of the people who toiled there. Part of the continuing fascination of island sailing was the ease with which he could return to the times of clans or Norsemen, warriors, maidens and kings.

Mike stopped in mid sip and said, 'Craig. Did you notice that neither Sean nor Mairread asked what we did? It was almost as though they knew or felt it would be embarrassing to ask. It is unusual for not one member of a group to mention his job.'

'Well, we usually manage to get through a week without talking shop. After all, we made it a rule years ago not to bore each other with our business problems.'

'That's not the same as other people asking. And what's more, they didn't mention what either of them did, did they?' He hesitated. 'What the hell. I wouldn't mind meeting up with them again. I enjoyed the evening.'

Craig did not mention his rebuff.

Mike was gazing towards Easdale and Inch Island. 'Is that Londoner who used to live in the cave on the island still there?'

'Well, he was last season and had fitted patio doors to the cave mouth. But I haven't seen any sign of him this year,' answered Craig.

Just then, Alan who had been looking towards Easdale through the binoculars pointed, 'Look. Did you say they had a Westerly Ocean Lord? Could that be their boat coming out from Cuan? Let's see if we can catch up. Any chance of hoisting the spinnaker?'

Craig had a quick look through the 'glasses' and confirmed that it was the Atlantic Lord. He looked up at the sky, down to the instruments and said, 'I think the wind will get up a bit later but we could certainly try right now.'

'Shit,' said Mike. 'This is when all conversation stops.'

'Go on,' said Craig. 'If we don't get the damn thing up now we'll find an excuse to avoid it all week. Anyway it will be good practice for West Highland Week.'

'Stuff that. I could do without West Highland Week too if I have to handle that great blanket,' niggled Mike, but he went below to get the bag.

With a technique distinctly lacking in polish Mike got the spinnaker on deck.

'I see we are doing it the easy way,' said Craig, as he saw that the sail was in the 'squeezer' that prevented the huge sail from filling with wind until it had been fully raised.

'That's the way it was left and that's the way I like it. With only three of us it's easier and safer.'

'Damn,' shouted Alan as he hit his head on the spinnaker pole. 'These catches are always fouled up with salt.'

After what seemed an eternity, the spinnaker in its sleeve was hoist, the sheet and guy run and the pole positioned.

Craig laughed but inwardly cringed at the sloppiness of it all. The muffled thump of the large sail filling and blossoming brought a smile, however, and they all stared up at the great conversation killer.

'They ought to have one of these in Parliament. It might just cut out a lot of the inane babbling,' murmured Craig.

The great pink and blue shimmering laxative swung gently but awesomely from side to side and three heads moved in unison with it. It looked like the reactions of the crowd at a slow-motion tennis tournament.

'For Christ's sake get that guy eased,' yelled Craig, and the bow wave increased to a hiss like a Sabatier slicing through paper. The boat dipped slightly down at the bow and with diverging waves of wake it left them feeling elated.

Mike disappeared below to reappear with three more gin & tonics, passed them round and then perched with Alan on the starboard coamings and visibly relaxed. Alan stared forward at the Atlantic Lord. 'She's still under genoa and main. With only two aboard that's probably all they can handle.'

'We'll see. They seemed a pretty enthusiastic pair,' said Craig. 'We'll be up with them in no time.'

'We should catch them before Black's Tower,' enthused Alan as he went forward and crouched to look under the sail at the approaching Mull coastline. He wanted to watch the gap closing.

The white of the Lismore light and Lady rock was easily visible and Craig asked Mike to take the helm. 'OK for fifteen minutes?'

'Yes. Fine.'

The smell of steak and kidney pie drifted up and shortly afterwards plates of mashed potatoes and pie, along with cans of beer were passed on deck. They took turns at the helm as they ate and drank, and Alan had just taken over when there was a sign of activity on board the Atlantic Lord.

'That looks like Mairread up forward, and she has a sail bag,' observed Craig. 'I don't think it can be a spinnaker.'

They watched in silence as the activity on the yacht ahead slowly blossomed into another large rainbow of coloured sailcloth. 'They've put up a second genoa, and poled out the windward one,' shouted Alan. The gap between the yachts which had been visibly decreasing seemed to be increasing again. Alan raised the binoculars and after some minutes looked back to the cockpit, 'We are still closing, but very slowly.' Alan looked at Mike who seemed intent on examining the Mull shore through the binoculars and hoping not to hear any commands that would mean any additional work.

'Mike, just check that the "jenny" sheets are clear, and call Alan back here,' ordered Craig. 'I want the genoa out.'

If Mike had spoken it would probably have been only four-letter words that came out, but he went forward to check and came back with a smiling Alan who said, 'I knew we wouldn't let them get away with that. Now we'll really catch them.'

The big furled sail rolled out without problems and the wind remained steady and light. The yacht handled easily in the calm sea and in the light wind and tide there was an opportunity to appreciate the mass of Ben Nevis to the north, the sweep of mountains rising to the sharp peak of Cruachan in the east, on to the Christian islands of the Garvellachs and west to the might of Mull and the shallow entrance to Loch Spelve.

By the time they had reached the Sound of Mull they were to windward and level with the Atlantic Lord. The two yachts rounded Duart point almost alongside and the visitors to the ancient castle, where the McLean standard soared dark against the sky, proudly proclaiming the presence of the chief, stared down from the battlements as the creaming bow waves slid from the hulls to create two fan-shaped streamers flirting with each other until their marriage was consummated astern of the yachts.

The Atlantic Lord closed to within hailing distance.

'A bottle of champagne says you can't beat us to Tobermory,' shouted Mairread.

'Right, that's a bet,' responded Craig, and looked up to see the spinnaker roll forward around the forestay. The wind shifts at Duart Point were notorious. They were being carried over to the Atlantic Lord very quickly. Mike realised that the guy had jumped free of its cleat with the rolling of the sail and he winched in violently. As the pole came round Craig eased the helm but had to come up to avoid colliding with the other boat.

As he looked round for Alan he saw the laughter on Sean's face. 'Sure they can be mean blighters, can't they?' he yelled through his laughter, and Craig just managed a smile in response.

Wizard's troubles were not yet over. 'Wind shifting to the bow,' said Alan. 'Isn't that good. They have got both "jennies" drawing on the same tack.' Craig ignored the technical misdescription and concentrated on trying to avoid the spinnaker being backed by sailing Wizard to the lee of the other yacht.

'Get the bloody thing down. Alan take the helm.'

'OK. Where do you want me to steer? We will be close to the rocks off Grey Island if we hold this heading.'

The little island with the light beacon had nasty reefs inshore of it.

'Head for Grey Island. We will see where we are once we get this spinnaker stowed.'

Mike did not usually respond quickly but could always be relied on to act like lightning when the spinnaker was being packed. He was ready to dowse the spinnaker with the 'bucket' and Craig quickly gave him the free sheet and halyard to do it. Craig could not help but grin as he observed that Mike was always more efficient at handing the spinnaker than at hoisting it!

Craig looked up. They were closing with the Atlantic Lord where they were having difficulty trying to drop the second genoa and the flailing of it was spoiling the set of the other one. The 'Lord' had almost stopped.

Craig shouted, 'Ease the sheet and main sheet. I'm going to fall back round his stern. We aren't going to make it past the island.' The response of Mike, Alan, and Wizard was immediate and they surged forward past the 'Lord'. Sean and Mairread had just about sorted the mess on the foredeck and were now too short of way to clear the island to their starboard or to tack through the wind to bear over to

Mull. They had no choice but once again to let the sails fly and drop back behind the stern of Wizard as she rounded the east end of Grey Island.

'Jesus, look out!' Alan stared as the bow of the 'Lord' came in astern of them. The anchor mounted in the bow missed the pulpit rail by millimetres.

'Ease that main sheet.'

'More, much more. Ease the genoa.' Wizard had opened a gap and was now clearing the east end of the little island.

'I could have gone on board for a drink,' said Alan.

'He is trying to come inside us. That wind is coming straight from the Mull shore. Come up a bit closer to the island. They are still coming up. Hold at that.'

The little interference from the island was just enough, and the 'Lord' dropped back as she lost speed.

'They are moving out now. Watch them, Mike, and let me know if they pick up speed on us again,' said Craig.

Wizard, indeed, picked up speed as, with more time, they improved the set of the sails, and a gap of a cable or more opened up, until the Atlantic Lord, too, steadied, picked up clean wind and moved after them.

Furrowed brows, large whiskies, and numerous casual, or not so casual, glances over shoulders over the next hours prevailed as they attempted to maximise the current and wind shifts all the way to the Fuinary Bouy and Green Island, halfway up the sound.

'This must be the only place in the world where no matter which direction you are sailing the wind is always on the bow,' muttered Alan.

Craig gazed over Salen Bay to the gap in the Mull shore reaching through to Loch Tuath which funnelled winds from south-east to west through into the sound and when combined with the circulating currents around the bend in the sound frequently created difficult sailing conditions. Often yachts heading west and those making their way east both appeared to be being headed by the wind for periods at the bend in the Sound of Mull.

As they closed with the knee of the bend in the sound the Atlantic Lord had taken the course over by the island and Craig had held to the north side to 'cut the corner' and it began to look as though it had been a wrong choice.

19

'He is just about abeam. Unless we get more wind he will pass,' said Alan, pointing the compass at the 'Lord'.

'I think they'll lose the wind shortly, especially if they hold the Mull shore,' muttered Craig. They continued to stare and Craig suddenly realised that he was tense. He dropped his shoulders and rocked his head from side to side, hearing the tension cracks in his neck and relaxed. 'For Christ's sake get me a whisky and American.'

Mike appeared almost immediately with a glass and offered one to Alan too. Both were taken, almost grabbed, and Craig settled down on the helmsman's perch and looked at the sails. As Calve Island off Tobermory Bay approached, Craig was still towards the mainland whilst Sean and Mairread had taken the 'Lord' close in to the island.

'We've got more wind. We've got more wind. Mike, sheet in the main.' Wizard's bow came up and headed straight for the entrance to the bay. 'Just a little in on the jenny.' The command was all that was said.

Alan watched the 'Lord'. He pointed the compass and pressed. He pointed again. 'We might just get him. I think if the wind holds we might just reach the corner first.'

'I bloody well hope so. After the work we have put in I just hope they were trying,' exploded Craig with feeling.

The gap was closing quickly. Wizard was still heading straight for the headland off the entrance to Tobermory Bay. There would be no room for Atlantic Lord to round the point unless she was clear ahead. Craig looked at Alan. 'Will we make it?'

Alan stared at the land and said, 'They are still losing ground. We should just do it.'

Mairread was standing by the mast and looking across at them. Craig almost instinctively bore away and then corrected. There was only 50 metres between the speeding yachts and Craig sensed that Sean was trying not to let him see that he was being watched. Craig looked under his cap brim at the 'Lord'. He could feel himself tense again. *Will he give ground? Can I hold this course? What will the wind do just beyond the point?* Craig looked at Mairread. She was laughing. *What is she laughing at? What have I missed? We're too close. He must bear away. Now.*

He tensed and had almost started to turn the wheel when Mike yelled, 'We are through. We are in.' Surely, Sean had eased the sheets and brought the 'Lord' round just enough to cut straight across the stern of Wizard. So little, but he was now most definitely behind.

The last of the sun was shining on the brightly coloured properties along the harbour road. The pier clock said 8p.m. The bay was like a mirror and there was just room to anchor between the ferry mooring and the shore. The local harbour committee had instituted a fairway from the fishing pier through the anchorage, supposedly to avoid the dust-ups between yachtsmen and fishermen as the fishermen raced their boats between the moored yachts. However the three or so unprofessional fishermen who operated out of Tobermory didn't give a damn and still continued to race through the yachts. Collisions continued to occur and 50 per cent of the most suitable depth for anchoring had been lost in the fairway. The attitude in Tobermory was, fortunately, not typical of many of the West Coast Scots. In Tobermory they would gladly take anybody's money as long as they didn't have to do anything for it or inconvenience themselves too much. In fact the general impression they created was that if you could just send your money it wouldn't be necessary to actually come.

'It doesn't matter where we have come from. Every time we arrive here I feel a great sense of relief,' said Alan. Alan looked at Craig. 'Shall I row over and ask if they are going to the Mishnish?'

Craig felt a flush of pleasure as he agreed. 'Yes. Tell them we're eating ashore and will be in the Macdonald Arms first and then the Mishnish.'

Alan and Mike inflated the dinghy and rowed over to the Atlantic Lord. Craig checked the windlass and chain, the spinnaker pole stowage and satisfied himself that the mainsail was covered, then went below with a feeling of satisfaction and poured himself a large Glenfiddich.

After a warm and satisfying dinner in a harbour restaurant, and a couple of drinks in the Macdonald Arms, they wandered along in the warm evening air to the Mishnish. It was unfortunate that the late evening sun did not reach the harbour because of the hill above the town, and although it remained warm and shirtsleeve conditions it became dark fairly quickly.

The mixture of West Highland tones and the Glasgow yap of yuppie yachtsmen was a familiar sound in the late Bobby MacLeod's bar. An Italian bus party added an international flavour to the gathering and Craig and the others managed to find a seat at the small tables around 'the floor', in front of the 'bandstand'. It was difficult to say why the Mishnish was the traditional drinking haunt of the sailing fraternity, but Bobby MacLeod's own love of the sea must have had something to do with it as the tidy bar, bench seats and back room couldn't have been the motivation for so many tired sailors to gravitate there, but descend in force they usually did. Mike had just bought drinks when Sean, resplendent in bright green trousers and a scarlet sweater with 'sailors do it in a hammock' embroidered on it, and Mairread with her hair gathered into a printed lemon and navy scarf, pale blue cardigan and navy trousers appeared and they too squeezed onto the settee seating. Mairread carried a bottle of Moet & Chandon and Sean had the glasses. 'I wish I could say the best crew won, but a deal is a deal,' she laughed.

'You were lucky today. If we had just followed you instead of the wind. In fact if we had come across towards you halfway up the sound, we could still have beaten you,' said Sean.

'Not at all. Skill and local knowledge triumphed,' retorted Alan.

'Sure, the local way of handing the spinnaker interested us,' beamed Mairread, and Craig blushed. He couldn't remember when he had last felt his face flush like that.

'Oh now don't you worry, boyo, you won,' said Mairread placing her hand on his knee, and Craig suddenly felt pleased with himself. 'Seriously though I think you could do with some foredeck lessons.'

'I don't mind where you give the lessons,' joked Craig, and felt the warmth rise in his face yet again. Mairread smiled.

Mike turned to Mairread. 'Do you sail together often?'

'About four or five weekends a year and often a week or occasionally two in summer, and sometimes we sail over to the Clyde for the weekend, but this is the first time we have sailed up in these waters, and if we have more of today's weather it is going to be really fantastic. Don't you find that the hotel business is a bit restricting of free time?'

Mike replied, 'Yes, but my trade is mainly walkers, anglers and folk up for shooting and they are a pretty predictable lot who come most years so I can have the right sort of staff to look after them.'

Craig started speaking to Mairread and Sean, and Mike found himself looking very closely at Mairread. Her oval features had sufficient lines around the eyes to suggest that age as well as laughter had created them. About 40 he thought, but pretty with it.

Just then the accordionist appeared and started playing, the crowd sang; the atmosphere became smoky and the whiskies went down more and more smoothly, until the interval. They were laughing and discussing the next few days' sailing when a tall, slim, young man in his twenties came over to them and spoke to Sean. When she saw him approach, Mairread's voice seemed to increase in tenor as she was asking if they could meet up again on Canna. Craig was about to reply, when he caught just a snatch of Sean's conversation. The young man was speaking 'We must assume . . . they know of the "Lord".'

Mike, who was nearest to Sean, couldn't catch Sean's response, and the young man went away.

Shortly after the man left Sean leaned over and said to Mairread, 'We must be going if we are to be up and about in time to chase this lot out to sea in the morning.'

Mairread laughed, 'Call us in the morning and let us know where you intend to make for.'

'We will do that,' was the chorused reply. Craig felt a youthful sinking feeling in his stomach as Mairread smiled at him and turned away.

Alan, who had managed to avoid some of the rounds by drinking tonic when he was buying, felt it was safest if he rowed, so Mike sat in the bow of the inflatable dinghy, smoking, and Craig sat in the stern. There were only wavelets in the bay but the perverseness of dinghies resulted in the inevitable soaking of Mike's backside, a fact he did not notice until he stood up to grab the boarding ladder of Wizard. The session had ended a little earlier than was often the case in Tobermory and there had not been the usual erratic progress across the bay to the boat. However, on going below they had to have the regular nightcap, a whisky big enough to ensure a good profit for Glenfiddich.

'Who was the chap who spoke to Sean?' asked Alan. 'Did you hear what they were talking about?'

'Not really,' said Mike. 'But I think he must have been a teacher or something as he mentioned Loyal Proctor and I think that is another name for a prefect.'

'What age do you think Mairread is?' murmured Craig.

'I thought you fancied her,' laughed Mike. 'Just because you have your own cabin we are not having any of that unless you look after the crew's needs too.'

Alan was miles away and didn't even notice when Mike topped up his glass with an even bigger Scotch.

Alan slowly straightened up and looked at Mike. 'Listen. Listen. Loyal Proctor is a Customs or Navy boat. We saw her in Arinagour last year. Why, do you think, were they talking about her?'

Both Mike and Craig looked up and frowned, but no-one answered.

'Where are we going tomorrow? I don't mind just as long as there is a pub,' said Mike.

'There is a pub on Eriskay and it is a very sheltered anchorage. Why don't we go there? It is a long time since we've been there and it didn't have the same attraction then.'

'The wind is due to stay southish so if it looks like a good day then that's what we'll do,' replied Craig. 'We will try to make an early start, Mike, unless you want to call the hotel and see how they are managing.'

'No. They can manage. We are fully booked with regulars and they will be out all day. It's all fishermen this week and they need attention only for breakfast, dinner and drinks. Not like bloody tourists wanting attention all day especially if it rains.'

Craig went below saying, 'I'm turning in. All this fresh air knocks me out.'

'It's too bad when even a good Scotch can't keep you up,' said Mike and reluctantly followed Alan below.

Craig retired and as he slipped into his sleeping bag he wondered what Karen was doing. Three times during the course of the evening he had tried to telephone after Susan had given him the number of the Liverpool hotel, but they were unable to obtain any reply from Karen's room. The whisky slowly took a firm hold and his puzzlement faded as he dropped off to sleep.

CHAPTER IV

CRAIG BURGESS had bought the yacht to ensure that he took a break. The building business had gone through some very difficult periods until just over a year ago when his firmly held belief that quality work and efficiency were paramount, even on the small jobs he had taken for years, paid off. He had always cajoled the foremen into making sure that all jobs started on time, continued steadily and even when there were the inevitable supply problems some men were kept on site to ensure that customers saw 'continuous' working. Apart from the efficiency of this, the competition generated a lot of annoyance with men turning up for an hour or two, sitting around, going for lunch or not even turning up at all. Craig wouldn't stand for that.

The four new contracts transformed life. The hours at work obtaining the business were unthinkable; the hours spent entertaining boring councillors were oppressive; and the volume of Chablis and smoked salmon consumed was enormous.

Craig had made sure that as the volume of business increased he had encouraged his personnel to develop their own knowledge and skills and as a result a clerk of works and an accountant had both worked hard at obtaining good general management experience, had become friendly with and understood the major customers and had developed a first-class profit sense. He felt very comfortable leaving the business for a vacation, something which had been impossible in the beginning.

However, there wasn't much time left for home, and with the children, John and Susan, now 18 and 16, and very independent, general family problems were unwelcome. The boat ensured that he did not have to spend too much of what little spare time he had at home.

As a young man he had impressed the girls with his wavy hair, his obvious strength, and believable exaggeration. He had known lots of girls around his own age but they always pretended to be so knowledgeable and he found that the younger girls often were more amenable to doing the things he wanted to do – boozing with the guys; going motor racing; meeting up after the rugby match to go for a drink and to a dance; and putting up with his occasional drunken outbursts without nagging.

He had grown a beard for a while to cover a scar which ran from nose to chin and resulting from a falling rivet, but that had been too pretentious for him and he had shaved it off. He had been a favourite at the rugby club as a Kamikaze forward but sport had not figured greatly in later years. He kept fit – just! Craig was just on 6 feet tall, and marginally overweight, but not enough to detract from his smart appearance. He was able to talk about most subjects with enough knowledge to stimulate interest in others and without being boring.

Craig had always leaned a little to the left, probably inherited from an upbringing in Port Glasgow, a father who had been a joiner, working much of the time in the shipyards, and long periods in shop-fitting, and the influence of his brother Eric who was a welder and spent long periods out of work, at the pub, the dogs, and in the local Labour party where he didn't lead but was good at supplying the ammunition. A real 'spurtle', he didn't appreciate Craig's new-found success, and Craig was never too sure if his brother's animosity arose from jealousy or deeply held conviction; but he favoured the former.

Craig had bought the business from the previous owner. He had joined the firm after leaving Technical College with an HND in Mechanical Engineering and old man Macallum made him the Estimating Department. The Old Man had been unwell for years and Craig took on much work that really wasn't his to do including a lot of ferrying and fetching for Mrs Macallum. When the old man died Mrs Macallum had been happy for him to buy the business, provided that he gave her an income for the rest of her life and life rent of the house which was an asset of the business. It wasn't difficult to agree to these terms and she set a very reasonable price.

Thirty years old at the time, he could not have afforded the money but Karen's father provided most of it as a wedding gift and as marriage had seemed the natural thing to do, everything seemed all right with the world. If he had held any doubts about the wedding, and he couldn't recall whether or not he actually had had any, they rapidly disappeared. Karen had only rarely been out with other men and then only to upset Craig when he had been particularly inattentive. It was a perfect match they, whoever 'they' were, said.

Karen enjoyed the company around boats and the hot days when lying back on the deck in a swimsuit was possible, but the hard days in the rain and wind, the long slog against the elements held little appeal. She liked to be fit and often swam long distances in the local pool. She could 'switch off' when in the water and found the exercise relaxing.

Karen's contribution to society now came with her involvement with the meetings of the Social Enterprise Committee, an organisation set up by middle-class Newton Mearnsians who felt a little guilty about their standard of living so close to the areas of Glasgow that had felt the brunt of the industrial decline. Nevertheless, the organisation did help to provide facilities and equipment for the pursuit of educational and leisure interests in the depressed areas and since all associated with it appeared to obtain some reward it had proved a useful venture. In addition Karen had spent quite a bit of her time looking after her father who lived about 10 miles away. The new-found income had allowed for the new red Golf GTi. Craig's Volvo Estate was really too big but seemed about right for the image of the business.

Karen had been perfect at accepting Craig's early foibles and although he had not been too popular with her father she usually got her own way and she definitely wanted Craig. Craig was happy to be seen with Karen as all his mates fancied her and saw her as something special. Her short neat hair, stylish features, brown sparkling eyes with a 'come on' glint, a nose that curved slightly upward and nicely shaped mouth gave her an attractive appearance, which was enhanced by well-proportioned breasts, a small waist, a bottom that was perhaps a little too flat, but beautifully tight, and legs that would look good in a Pretty Polly advertisement. She was a little too short to be described as a film star but men found her exciting to be with. She looked stunning in any casual and day-to-day clothes and smart rather than fashionable in formal wear.

She was an intelligent soul but had never found much satisfaction in exploiting her languages degree, and whilst initially she had enjoyed the travel associated with her Foreign Office job, she was just as happy at home, and went about the business of providing stimulating interests for the children.

Karen had for years been the perfect hostess, even with the vulgar approaches she experienced from fairly drunk councillors and surveyors. She always seemed approachable, but succeeded with a 'look but don't touch just now' projection that worked very well. They kept coming back for more and ensured that social contacts with desirable clients were easy to maintain.

Daddy giving a further £100,000 'to make sure Karen has the facilities she is used to,' confirmed their security. As the children had grown up Craig had been content to encourage Karen to take up interests outside the home. It eased his fleeting guilt feelings over his long periods away and long hours at the office.

John Burgess had left home for Aberdeen University to study Maths & Economics and rarely came home. John was a slimmer build than his father, had brown hair like his mother and was very intelligent. He was very fully occupied with campus life and involved himself in the various societies and social events of the University.

He was good-looking, fit and a complete sportsman and was much involved in rugby and athletics. Like his dad he was very popular with the girls and on the odd occasion when he came home he always brought an attractive female companion.

Susan, on the other hand was less outgoing. She was waiting for her 'Highers' results which would probably be OK. She wasn't at all sure what she wanted to do and alternated between 'being a vet' and 'being a secretary'. She had a similar build to her mother and was almost classically beautiful although she bemoaned her mousy hair for which she tried to compensate by careful grooming. Her features and perfect slim figure had boys always asking her out, but she usually refused although there was one boy with whom she would go to school and local functions. He would come home occasionally and they would study together. However it didn't seem to be that special a relationship – just a good friendship, and Karen approved.

For a while Karen was concerned that Susan took no interest in boys at all until she found some badly taken photographs of two boys from the school completely naked and 'excited'. They were, Karen thought, the sort of stupid things that get passed around at school and when the next day they were gone she forgot about it and felt mildly relieved.

Craig worked hard and encouraged Karen to take an increasing interest in the Social Enterprise Committee, a group purported to be apolitical, intent on ensuring that local government had its priorities right and allocated its resources to the needy areas. At least that was the objective. Craig was aware that his business had become something of a passion and that he was not devoting as much time as he might to his wife and home. He saw the SEC as a useful distraction and was pleased at her involvement. From time to time at functions organised by the group he met other members and had found some of these contacts to be useful. All in all it was a fairly satisfactory state of affairs.

Most meetings at the SEC were spent discussing hypothetical situations such as the means of encouraging youths to start their own businesses, the creation of a Palestinian homeland, and the rights of coloured people to educational establishments supporting their culture, or the justice of 'giving Ireland back to the Irish'. However, Karen took things more practically and kept pressing for a more viable response and for a long time she received little support from the committee members who had too many personal engagements to get down to 'charity' work – little support, except from Patrick Dougan who generally was encouraging, always listened attentively, and who also seemed to want to direct the committee to more constructive projects.

Afterwards they all usually moved along to the inn for a few drinks and a gradual return to reality. Karen regularly found herself next to Patrick and she was fairly sure that he manoeuvred himself to that position deliberately. She was pleased that he agreed with her attitude to the committee's objectives.

Patrick Dougan had started to attend the SEC meetings about a year before when he had arrived in the community and started a transport business. Most months she was pleased to find that he shared her views. She guessed his age to be around forty-five, with thinning brown hair, blue eyes and fine features and a nose that was slightly too big. He was a fit looking 6 feet tall, and dressed only moderately well, but the combination was attractive and reassuring and his own confident manner left Karen feeling that he was very good to be with. He didn't have the build of a truck driver, had small hands and although he was fairly deep chested he was obviously a businessman rather than a manual worker. From the club records Karen had discovered that he lived close to the Burgess household and they now alternated cars month about unless Patrick called to say he was not going to the meeting.

Patrick always made the correct responses, although sometimes he gave the impression of a man trying to think about several things at the same time. He was politely interested in the family and what they did, when they did it, where they went, and how often Craig was at home, their business, and vacation plans. His memory was remarkable and whatever they discussed he asked about at their next meeting. With Craig away so much, Karen found it comforting to know someone who took such a concerned interest, and he was an attractive man to be with. His Irishness came through only occasionally with only a slight accent but a real Irish humour. Like the Scots he often told stories against himself. Karen regularly felt a thrilling shiver as they spoke and many times she thought the laughter in his eyes spoke of more than just amusement.

It was difficult to elicit any positive information about his leisure interests, and when questioned he was vague and non-committal. 'I raise and lower my arm a lot, especially when I have a whisky at the end of it,' he would respond. As far as she could tell he wasn't a member of any clubs other than the SEC, expressed no strong political views, but he was an admirer of the achievements of Margaret Thatcher. Any enquiry about his background or his Irish past was deftly fielded with a response which went on at length but which when analysed afterwards had given nothing away and was totally non-committal.

Patrick's house, Wildwinds, was a stone-built property standing in about an acre of wooded grounds and difficult to see from the road. It was very much like the Burgesses' although it was rather nicer with turrets and shields and a few stained-glass windows, but somewhat faded white paintwork. In a blue grey shade, and well maintained, Karen thought her home looked just that bit smarter. The Dougan house always looked dull with only net curtaining obvious at the windows and a lack of female colour about the whole place. From time to time as she drove past she spotted cars in the drive but Patrick never expanded on any query or remark about them other than to simply acknowledge their presence with the suggestion that some friends had called in when they were in the area.

At the last but one meeting of the SEC, Karen had proposed that they consider raising money for the purchase of a sailing boat to encourage local children away from the arcades and pubs. 'Oh, a mini Malcolm Miller' was one response, and another thought it would be just as well to send the children to somewhere like John Ridgeway's

Adventure School. After much discussion and a surprisingly positive response from Patrick it was agreed that they should consider fund-raising activities. Patrick felt that the conventional 'coffee morning' approach would take too long to raise the £90,000 necessary and he said that if they all tried to encourage their friends and associates to use Thrufast, his transport business, he would donate 5 per cent of the value of all such work to the SEC project.

Karen smiled as she noted the degree of support from the middle-aged female section of the membership who stared rapt at Patrick as he offered his support to the motion. She was delighted that the idea had made progress so quickly, but appreciated that it may not have been so rapid without Patrick's twinkling eyes and forceful presence.

As they left the meeting Patrick suggested that she might like to have a drink on the way home, and although they drove past the usual watering hole, she said nothing, and was only moderately surprised when they turned up the driveway of Patrick's house.

Once they were indoors Patrick smiled and said, 'I thought tonight's success deserved a bit more than a vodka and orange. How would you like a glass of champagne to celebrate?'

'That would be lovely.'

Karen found the new freedom and achievement very satisfying, and the slight shiver when she was close to Patrick exciting.

Patrick returned to the lounge with a bottle of ten-year-old vintage Moet & Chandon and when the bottle was opened and they were sitting together on the large settee, Patrick said, 'I may have been a bit hasty with that proposal as I could well be short of drivers and the extra volume probably will not justify taking on a full-time man. On the other hand I don't want to go back on it when everyone seemed so keen on the idea.'

Karen, who saw her success slowly evaporating, jumped in quickly with, 'I'm not too busy most days and wouldn't mind driving a small van occasionally, if that would help.'

In view of the feature on the SEC that the local paper, the *Leader*, was going to run Karen thought that driving the van would produce a good interest angle as well as showing her involvement in the community.

'Thanks very much, but I'm not sure that would work as I need a driver when the business is there not just when it coincides with your spare time.'

A little put down Karen blushed and said, 'Well, keep me in mind. Give me a ring if you're stuck.'

Patrick stood up and left the room. Karen looked around. Everything that was necessary was there, and very much in keeping with the style of house. Large comfortable furniture with deep blue covers with peacocks; heavy co-ordinating drapes, and large yew coffee tables, bookcase and magazine rack. There were appropriate large paintings of gun dogs and mountain scenes on the walls, but something seemed wrong. She rose and walked through the doorway into the dining room. A beautiful yew table was surrounded by leather and yew chairs, a large drinks cabinet and a long sideboard. Everything matched perfectly, but the same feeling of there being something missing persisted. There were no personal items, no photographs of a family or even of himself, nothing emotional.

When she returned to the lounge, Patrick was already seated on the settee and pointed to a plate of crackers and two dips. 'Prawn and crab, and chicken and avocado,' he said.

Karen blushed. 'Sorry. I just wandered through. The furniture is really lovely.'

'That's all right. Feel free. I'm glad you like it. Here you are.'

Patrick handed her a crystal glass full of bubbling champagne.

Karen sat down at an angle and her leg rested against Patrick's. He was leaning back with his arm along the back of the settee. Talk ranged from the new project itself to the attitude, objectives and background of the committee. Karen noted that he was careful not to comment on either of their own objectives.

They ate a few of the biscuits but Karen found it difficult to concentrate. She felt hot, flushed, and couldn't quite think of things to say. She looked deeply into Patrick's blue eyes.

Although she hadn't said anything, Patrick leaned forward. 'I know,' he said, 'I feel the same way.' His arm came off the settee and round her shoulders as his lips touched hers. 'You are so lovely.'

Karen couldn't help her tongue probing into his mouth, and the feeling of the pressure of his tongue made her want to be even closer. She felt the back of the settee as Patrick's mouth roamed over her face with his lips kissing her eyebrows and her nose before floating on to her ears and neck. She ran her arms over his chest and down to his waist before enfolding him and pulling him hard against her. The shoulder of her dress and bra strap had been slid down her arm and she felt his hand envelope her breast and then felt his tongue and teeth on her nipple. Patrick moved his leg in between hers, and the sudden tightening of her dress as his knee became caught in the fabric brought her back to reality. She tried to laugh but it sounded like an echo, 'Stop. I must go home.'

Patrick nodded, kissed her slowly and slid her dress back on to her shoulder. Karen looked straight into Patrick's eyes, and saw only the sparkle, humour and warmth. Both her hands were against his chest and the urge to kiss him was overwhelming. Her hands cupped his face and she reached forward and kissed him, probing deep into his mouth with her tongue. They slowly slipped back against the settee and Patrick murmured, 'You are so lovely. I want to kiss you all over.' Unaware that she was actually lying on the settee Karen ran her hand over the front of Patrick's trousers, felt the firmness then quickly moved her hand under his sweater, and found a nipple. She felt his strength overcoming her as she ran her hands through the hair on his chest and back to the waistband of his slacks.

Karen felt only the warmth of his mouth as she became aware that her dress was round her waist and felt her small breast being drawn fully into Patrick's mouth. Her hands roamed over his back until she grasped his firm buttocks and pulled him towards her. She felt his hand caress the soft inner thigh and slip up over her stomach. She knew what was next but couldn't stop as his fingers curled over the waist band of her tights and pants and pulled downwards. She pressed down against the seat but there was enough freedom for him to lower her pants and allow his fingers to press down towards her secret place. She forced herself up on her elbow, and stared straight into his eyes.

'I love you. I really love you,' he said, and she relaxed. Her legs had opened slightly and she felt his hand reach down and felt him find the opening. 'Come for me. Come for me, my darling,' he whispered, and she felt herself thrusting against the heel of his thumb; the heat increasing until she felt a violent surge through her and she gasped out a loud cry. The heat, the surging in her stomach came again and again as Patrick's fingers touched all the sensitive places. Patrick must have been uncomfortable and as he moved position she suddenly felt the cool air on her inner thigh and sat upright. Patrick continued to kiss her gently, but she stared straight at him.

'This must never happen again. I've never been with any man other

33

than Craig, and I'm not going to start now. I'm not sure how I feel about you but it just can't happen.'

Patrick looked at her. 'I have never felt this way about anyone before. For the last few months I have wanted just to be with you more and more. Just being near you is the nicest thing that's ever happened to me.'

'Yes. I think I know. But it has to stop now. This was just a celebration. I must go.'

They went out to the car, and said very little on the short run to Karen's home. Karen could not understand what was happening but she did allow him to lean over and give her a long kiss before getting out of the car.

'Bye.'

'Goodnight.'

After the visit to Patrick's house Karen's thoughts ranged over every possible reason for her action, and every time she convinced herself not to see him again she got a tight, sick feeling in her chest which she couldn't describe but it left her with a feeling of helplessness. She thought of the children, of everything Craig had done for her, and how she couldn't let him down. He would be desperately hurt. Then she ranged over her feelings about Patrick. She loved to listen to him when he explained something or argued his point. She wanted to be with him, and when she was with him she just needed to touch him. Twenty years of giving everything for the children and Craig. Craig had always done everything just for her. *How can I do something which will hurt him so much? Why now can I not have some freedom; freedom to find myself; to find out what I want for the rest of my life?* It wasn't possible to consider the position rationally. Whenever she started to do anything her mind wandered off to Patrick. *Where is he? Is he thinking of me?* The words of tunes started to have meanings directly concerned with her. She started to play tapes that contained sentiments she felt reflected her feelings. She had never used the car tape player. Now she played tapes at every opportunity. She drove to the shops past Patrick's house. She didn't know where she was going. *What can I do?* The arguments went on and on. *What will Susan and John think? What will they say? They are old enough to understand; to make their own way without being too upset, aren't they? Will they be hurt, surely not? How will Dad react? Will friends stand by me? What the hell am I going on about? I haven't left home, have I?* Answers just would not gel.

The journalist from the *Leader* had just left the Burgess house. He needed to complete the feature on the SEC next week and had interviewed the other members. If she was to get into the feature she would just have to ask Patrick if they could have a 'photo' session at his yard with one of the vans. Karen wasn't really sure if Patrick would agree.

When Patrick phoned a few minutes later she was surprised and confused and really couldn't get a greeting out clearly and all that she said was 'Hello. Er . . . How have you been getting on?' and blushed. Her stumbles were ignored and she didn't hear his first few words as she rapidly tried to think of a way to broach the subject, and it wasn't until he said, 'If you'd rather not it's OK,' that she recovered and said, 'Sorry, I didn't catch all the details. Could you just say that again?'

'What I said was, "Could you manage a short trip with one of the vans on Wednesday?" It is actually an SEC load and a journalist from the *Leader* has suggested that you could be photographed sitting in it.'

'That will be super. What time?'

'Be at the yard at nine and we should have time to get organised. See you then, Bye.'

Karen couldn't believe her luck. The buzz of the phone had reawakened her. She was looking forward to it as a new experience and she liked driving anyway. It was only then that she realised that she must have sounded very odd. She had made no attempt at conversation at all. Although there was no-one present she blushed.

The photo session went well. Patrick had a new Renault Traffic van and had parcelled up some of the packages in SEC labels. She had a new green and blue overall and felt the part. She enjoyed the publicity over the following days, as people who had barely known her said 'Hello', came up to her and congratulated her on the charity effort. In fact it was all great fun. Over the next few weeks Patrick asked her to do a short run on Tuesday or Wednesday afternoons, until the week when Craig and the others were due to go off sailing.

Craig was methodical and had a detailed inventory for the boat and she said she would do the shopping on Friday afternoon so that everything would be fresh for him going north on the Saturday morning. When Patrick called on the Monday to ask if she could drive on Sunday, Craig was none too pleased. The thought of Karen driving around with strangers while he was away did not appeal to him but as he was about to disappear for a week he did not feel he could protest unduly.

There had been no difficulty meeting Patrick again. When they were alone he asked her how she was getting along. He said he was always finding her creeping into his thoughts. They embraced and kissed gently but she made no arrangements to see him although it was killing her.

Craig got away with all his boat stocks and his boyish enthusiasm had overcome his concern about leaving Karen. He had loaded up the car and never stopped talking about the sailing week and where they would go. As he drove the heavily laden Volvo out of the drive he leaned out of the window, waved, and shouted, 'Drive carefully.'

Karen was able to contemplate meeting Patrick again without too many qualms.

CHAPTER V

THE FIRST ACTIVITY that Monday morning was somewhat lethargic. Craig called the Coastguard, confirmed the forecast and had the orange juice poured when eventually Mike stirred and looked up all bleary eyed. 'What time is it?'

'About eight-thirty, and time you were up and about. You were the one with the bright idea of an early start and of heading for Eriskay.'

Just then the pumping from the heads announced that Alan was active and a few moments later he appeared. 'Did I hear Eriskay? That seems like a great idea. Just feel the warmth in that sun already.'

There was a warmth and stillness, very different to that of the hot dry countries, in air that carried the sounds and smells of the harbour town out over the bay.

Mike quickly made amends for his sluggish start and produced a breakfast of bacon, sausages, mushrooms, black pudding, tomatoes, potato scones and eggs and they all sat in the morning sunshine, drinking orange juice and large mugs of coffee and watching Tobermory coming to life.

The morning sunshine flooded the harbour making the windows flash, throwing shards of light on to the multi-coloured fascias of the waterfront shops and restaurants. The tourists began appearing on the harbour road dressed unseasonally in short-sleeve shirts, T-shirts, and in many cases, shorts. It was the type of weather which would have turned Scotland into a Mediterranean resort were it to be commonplace.

'Good morning. Sleep well?' Sean's voice rose from the yacht tender closing with Wizard. Mairread sat in the stern glowing with laughter in the warming air.

'Yes. Just fine. A slight hangover. How about you?' called Alan, looking down at the inflatable dinghy close alongside. He saw but failed to register the two large holdalls lying in the bow of the dinghy.

'Sure, but it's not so great this morning. We have a faulty water pump impeller and we don't have a spare so I don't think we'll be going very far today. Looks as though we could be stuck here for some time. We will have to get one from Ardfern or Oban.'

Craig was attracted to Mairread whose gold hair shone in the sun and he couldn't help noticing that she wasn't wearing a bra. The tight blue trousers, stretched taut by the awkward angles of sitting in an inflatable yacht tender, emphasised her fine ankles and thighs.

'I think your motor is the same as ours, he shouted, 'a Volvo 2003, isn't it? I have two spare impellers. Why not take one of ours?'

'Well, if it's not a problem for you that would be just fantastic. That will save us a lot of time.'

Sean tied up to Wizard's boarding ladder and they came aboard whilst Craig, followed by Sean, went below to open the spares box.

Mairread sat opposite Mike and Alan. 'Have you decided where you are going?' She looked enquiringly at Alan.

'Yes, I think so. We haven't been to Eriskay for years and since there is a pub there Mike fancies going back; plus the fact that the wind is in the right direction. No beating unless vital is our motto.'

'Yes, that's the way we would like to sail too. Unfortunately it's not always possible.' The accent was not so noticeable as Sean's. 'Have you told the Coastguard?'

'Yes. I think Craig called them first thing this morning.'

Craig looked up through the hatch. He did not smile and his reaction to the presence of the Irish couple was not what Alan would have expected. 'Sean and Mairread are coming with us. Just prepare to leave. Mairread will help you. Mike, help Sean with their bags and to take their dinghy back to the Atlantic Lord.'

Mike looked oddly at Alan who shrugged and walked forward to the anchor windlass control in the bow. Mike and Sean rowed off and both returned in Wizard's dinghy. They hauled it aboard, made it fast and Mike started the yacht's diesel engine, before asking Mairread to take the helm and went forward to help Alan stow the anchor.

'What do you think about that?' whispered Mike.

'I don't know but it is odd. He doesn't usually ask us to get under way without being on deck. In fact I'm surprised that he invited them without discussing it with us. I know it is his boat but normally he would ask our opinion.'

The anchor rumbled slowly up and Mike peered over the side. 'By the way. Do you remember we thought it odd that they never asked us what we did for a living? Well, it just dawned on me that Mairread knows I own an hotel, and yet I didn't tell her.'

Alan's brows furrowed. 'Maybe Craig told her.'

'Well, if all this is just so he can get her aboard I don't think too much of it.'

'No. I don't think so. At least that wouldn't be like him. I wonder why he didn't come on deck?'

'He is probably tidying up below.'

At that moment the anchor broke the surface of the water and Alan shouted to Mairread, 'Anchor clear.' He glanced at his watch. It showed that this was one of their latest ever starts. The boat moved very slowly forward and as the anchor came above the surface Mike leaned forward to help bring it on deck. Wizard surged forward towards the mouth of the bay. 'Not too fast. We will be hoisting sails shortly.'

Mike and Alan leaned against the mast and shrouds and watched as the brightly coloured houses disappeared behind the ferry pier and the boat headed out of the bay. As they passed the lighthouse they moved back to the cockpit and Mike looked at Mairread. 'How did you know that I had an hotel?'

'Craig mentioned it when we were in the Mishnish. Why?'

'Oh nothing. I just knew I hadn't told you.'

Mike went to go below. It was just about time to break out the Gordons but he stopped when he looked down into the cabin. Craig was sitting behind the table with Sean opposite. Sean held a gun aimed at Craig's chest, and glanced up at Mike. 'No need for bother. No-one will be harmed. We just need to borrow your boat for a while. It appears that ours has become too well known. If you were about to pour a drink, that still seems a good idea. Just come down slowly and get on with it. I don't suppose you have a drop of Irish, do you? No. I thought not. A large Scotch will do just fine. Mairread would prefer a gin and tonic, I'm sure.'

Alan who had only heard snatches of the conversation turned to look at Mairread and found that she too had a gun aimed straight at him. She held it low enough to avoid it being seen from the shore but it was surely aimed at Alan's stomach. He wondered why Craig hadn't done anything when Sean and Mike left the boat. Now he knew.

The drinks were poured, if a little hesitantly, and they settled down with Craig now on the helm. Sean felt safer when he could see both of Craig's hands. 'Steer a course to clear the north end of Coll and then just south of Barra Head. There is no need to ask for other instructions. Share the steering between you, but don't be stupid. We will be watching.'

There was no recognisable emotion in the yellow eyes. They just stared straight through whom ever they were looking at.

Mike and Alan sat in the cockpit and with a mystified look peered at Craig as if they expected him to turn into Superman. Mairread produced coffee and Bovril at regular intervals and if it hadn't been for the confusing and unbelievable moments after leaving Tobermory it would have been a very pleasant day. The sun shone and it was a very special Western Isles day; it was warm even out on the sea. The mountains of Skye were clear and sharp forming a ragged edge as though a giant mouse had nibbled its way along them, as they lay framed between the curvaceous mountains of Rum and the wedge of Eigg rising to the sguirr at its east end. Coll lay like a half-submerged tree trunk in the calm sea, and the wind disappeared altogether. The sea of the Hebrides, often a turbulent and cold place, lay still, basking in the embrace of the high sun.

Mairread sat in the forward corner of the cockpit, half turned with the small automatic held low on her lap.

'Are you going to tell us what this is about?' asked Craig.

'Oh, it is just a spot of business, and under normal circumstances you wouldn't have known anything about it, but you were the insurance and we just happen to need your boat. Now that's all you are going to know.' Mairread seemed to have taken command. Sean nodded but sat still and watched them.

Sean turned to look directly at Craig. 'I don't know how much you value your wife, but you may as well know that she is with some colleagues of ours and if they don't hear from us regularly they may get nasty.'

Mairread leaned toward Sean as though she was about to interrupt but appeared to reconsider and sat back.

'For all I know that could be made up,' said Craig as he suddenly felt cold.

Mairread hesitated, then said, 'Tell him, Sean.'

Sean reeled off the children's names, where they were, and the SEC details, including a rundown of Patrick's meetings with Karen. He smirked at Craig.

'Sure, she is off for a dirty weekend in Liverpool, isn't she?'

Craig gripped the wheel more tightly. 'What the hell do you mean by that?'

'I just meant that from what we hear, being a hostage is likely to be quite a pleasant experience for her. Rumour has it that she has the hots for our man, and you know how kidnappers have to be kept happy and calm.'

Mairread leaned forward and put her fingers on Sean's lips. 'Shut up. That's enough. Just shut up.'

She turned to look up at Craig, the gun more firmly pointing in his direction.

'Convincing, isn't it?' smiled Mairread. 'We take precautions. We seldom need to action them, but this just happens to be one of the occasions.'

Craig's mind was in turmoil. *Their information seems to be accurate but how did they find out? What is their intention? Will they use the guns? Surely they wouldn't carry guns if they didn't intend to use them? Do they actually have the children as well as Karen? Do they really have Karen?*

His shoulders slumped and he leaned back against the helmsman's seat and despite the clear sky and bright sun he felt cold, damp and shivering.

As the day rolled on the warm sun traversing overhead made everyone sleepy and Sean who was sitting in the cockpit dozed, but Mairread who had moved up on to the deck continually switched her eyes from the trio to the horizon and back. Little conversation passed between the Irish couple as the yacht progressed steadily toward the distant Hebrides lying like eyeliner on the face of the ocean.

Apart from some light-hearted banter when they all had beers in mid-afternoon, only Mike tried to keep up a general chat but he got only cursory responses from Craig and Alan. It was obvious that their minds were on other matters.

Alan felt depressed. He could only imagine being shot and thrown over the side, or worse still, just being thrown over the side. Visions of sharks and being devoured by eels and other fish kept swimming through the turbulence of his mind.

Craig kept replaying Sean's remarks. It was frustrating to realise that he had become so remote from Karen that he wasn't sure whether or not there was even the remotest possibility of her having an affair. *Would I have smelled another man? Should I have noticed unusual telephone calls? She hasn't been going out more often, has she?*

And then he remembered the SEC meetings. They had been lasting longer. She was driving for that man who had the delivery business. He couldn't recall his name or that of the business. *Is that where she is having an affair? Is she meeting someone from the SEC?* All afternoon Craig's mind searched for answers, but lately his contact with Karen had been so superficial that there wasn't anything he could really get hold of.

Although Craig, Mike and Alan had taken spells at the wheel it was an abnormally subdued crew that took the yacht out towards the western horizon.

By early evening they were passing south of Barra Head and heading out into the Atlantic. Craig looked round for other boats but apart from a few fishing boats there was nothing, except that is, the fast grey craft coming toward them from the direction of Castlebay. Craig wondered if Mairread had seen it but just at that moment she said, 'Sean. Take Alan and Mike below and make sure they know how to behave.'

Alan and Sean went below and just as they reached the cabin sole, 'Alan'.

Alan turned and as he did Sean hit him viciously in the kidneys with the gun. 'Sit just there and don't move. That's just a little warning. When I say stand, you stand, look up through the hatch and smile. Keep your movements and words to a minimum but if you have to speak make it sound convincing. Do you understand, boyo? That goes for you too, Mike.' Alan winced and nodded.

The patrol craft came up and flew the yellow and black chequer 'heave to' signal, and a large inflatable, which had been hidden from them on the far side of the patrol craft came alongside. There were four Customs officers on board. 'Good evening. This is a routine Customs drugs patrol. Where have you come from?'

'Tobermory,' responded Craig.

'When did you last speak to the Coastguard?'

'This morning.'

'What is your destination?'

'Castlebay. We are just sailing out a bit further to see the sunset and then we will turn back.'

'Where is your home port?'

'Ardfern.'

'How many on board?'

'Five.'

'Thank you very much. Sorry for troubling you. Please take this card and if you see anything suspicious give us a call. Have a good trip.' After handing over the small yellow business card warning of the need for vigilance against drugs, the inflatable returned to the patrol craft, was swung back on deck, and the patrol boat turned away and headed in the direction of Coll.

'That wasn't very smart. They can check whether or not we go to Castlebay,' said Mairread.

'Where the bloody hell else could I say. There is damn all in this direction except America and it's obvious we aren't going there, isn't it?' sneered Craig.

Nothing further was said, and Sean, Mike and Alan came back on deck.

'Are you OK?' enquired Craig, noticing Alan's difficulty in climbing back to the cockpit.

'The Irish bastard belted me in the kidneys, but I'll be OK.'

'Nothing a good drink won't put right,' said Sean and disappeared below to return with several large Scotches, all of which were gratefully received.

The sun slowly settled into the Atlantic. Looking back, the normally steely green rock and sparse grass of the Outer Isles glowed red and in the distance the mountains of Skye were charcoal against the dark sky. The sun was as a furnace with flames which could be seen darting from its rim as the black sky overhead changed through royal and bluebell to yellows and Egyptian gold and finally with a flash the sun vanished. Within minutes, however, it again seemed like daylight as the eyes adjusted to the June sky. Craig had watched this many times and always felt that there should be a loud hiss with steam erupting from the horizon. He was always fascinated and couldn't stop staring until the scarlet orb had disappeared and only the afterglow remained.

Mairread and Sean took turns to sleep and it only made sense for Mike, Alan and Craig to try to do the same. Craig and Mike donned 'oilies' as midsummer nights at sea were still cool and the waterproofs were necessary to keep out the chill. They noticed that on the way from Tobermory Sean had screwed a substantial bolt to the outside of the aft cabin door. They had come aboard fully prepared. They must have known that the cabin door opened into the cabin and would require an additional lock.

CHAPTER VI

SEAN HAD ARRANGED that they could use the aft cabin to rest and allowed two at a time to go below carefully piling holdalls against the door to prevent any rapid exit. Now Mike was below sound asleep although Alan and Craig remained on deck, their minds too active to permit sleep.

At about 2 a.m. Mairread went up to the bow and Alan took the chance to whisper to Craig, 'How the hell do we get out of this? What are we going to do?'

'Not a lot just now unless we can get the guns and that seems bloody risky. I think we should just carry on as we are and don't provoke anything. On the other hand I can't see them just sailing back to Oban with us on board, but I don't have any other suggestion right now,' said Craig, trying hard not to give in to the temptation to burst out with, 'How the hell do I know? I'm not in the habit of being hijacked, you stupid bastard.'

The feeling of fear and concern for the future had been building all day and from time to time he felt cold as if he was suffering from flu and he was conscious that he had been to the toilet on about five occasions. *Stay quiet, be nice, offer to help, ask them to explain what they were doing and why, rush them, hit them with a spanner, a frying pan.* He had gone round and round the alternatives. Nothing seemed to be possible and when he was resting he remembered thinking that James Bond must have had some very stupid adversaries who always left themselves unguarded. *Where is Karen? Have they got Karen? Will they harm her? Do they know where the children are now?* Mairread and Sean had only to ensure that one of them was awake and it was difficult for the others to do anything against a gun.

'We could knacker the engine, and cut one of the hoses. They would think we were sinking,' muttered Alan.

'They know about boats. They aren't that stupid. Anyway why should they keep us here to tell the Coastguard when they arrive?' retorted Alan.

'Let's just keep things as they are just now. A better chance may come nearer to shore. I don't fancy the swim from here.'

Mairread walked slowly back to the cockpit and looked down at them. It was as though she had read their minds. 'It really would be stupid to try anything. We can manage this boat on our own if we have to. You are only useful if we are challenged and that isn't too much of a problem as we know your history inside out. I think we could be convincing enough.'

Alan got up. 'I'm going below. It's cooling down and I don't like the company.'

Mairread called Sean and he watched carefully as Alan made his way into the aft cabin.

Mairread stepped down into the cockpit and sat down beside Craig. 'When you are as involved as I am most decisions are clear cut. I think you should understand that even if I liked you, and I do, I would go through with this anyway and it would be as well if you impressed that on your friends. I am just a little afraid that Mike or Alan may try something very stupid. Do you understand? We believe in what we are doing and if you knew how important it was to us you would realise we have already sacrificed so much that we are prepared to do whatever is necessary to succeed.'

Craig looked at the attractive but intent features. 'I don't understand but I will try to prevent them doing anything dangerous.'

'That would be best.'

Mairread shivered. A light breeze had got up. 'Unfurl the headsail. We should cut down on fuel, and we don't have much further to go,' she said.

Craig did as he was asked and cut the engine. The peace on the beautiful evening was relaxing with a view of the Outer Hebrides in the clear moonlit distance. Craig was relaxing when Mairread said, 'Check our position.'

He thought about giving a false reading but couldn't think what it would achieve. Mairread changed course slightly south of west.

Craig turned up his collar and let his mind drift off from the present. He had sometimes dreamt about things like this happening, but in a dream he had always had the strength and immunity to be able to overcome the opposition. His life had been a bit like that. Work harder and you would succeed. That was his philosophy. At the end of a hard day there had usually been his capable, comforting and understanding secretary. He had become very close to Elspeth. She was married but the involvement and awareness she had developed meant that she had always sensed when he needed help. She could firmly remind the staff of the decisions that had been taken at the last meeting when they conveniently forgot. And she did it with the sort of smile that left them wondering if they should ask her out for a drink. They went off determined to impress.

More and more Craig had come to appreciate Elspeth's understanding. He knew that there was no need to spell out to her what to do. He resented going home and being asked about the business whilst Karen continued to do whatever it was she had been doing. He could see that she wasn't really listening or interested. Yes, he resented the waste of time making pointless explanations just because Karen had been brought up well and felt that she should show some interest in where her comfort came from. It was annoying at times how middle class she was. Just saying the right things at the right time was what mattered to her. If he questioned her about it she would respond with 'It's polite.' Fuck being polite.

Deep down he knew that was unfair. Karen had made a damned good job of the home and bringing up the children, but it was so undemanding, so boring. He needed the excitement of business and new experiences, but this had all the signs of being a bit too much. He sank back into the seat, pulling the high fleece-lined collar of his waterproofs up round his face. *Now this Irish woman seems to be a bit more exciting.*

Another hour had gone by when Craig became aware of Mairread standing and looking ahead through the binoculars. He stood and peered forward into the night sky and thought he glimpsed some small lights. They seemed to be very small or very far away, and stepped forward for a better look.

Mairread reacted immediately. 'Go below. Wake Sean.'

Craig went down but Sean was already awake. He rose and shouted. 'Get into the aft cabin. Now. And keep the lights off.'

The trio, now all settled in the owner's cabin, sat down and heard the door being jammed shut. It was dark as the dinghy was stowed over the hatch with the only light coming from the small side windows. They heard the sails being stowed and the engine started, and they had motored for about twenty minutes when the boat stopped.

'What do you think they are doing?, asked Alan.

'I don't think there is much doubt about it. They are picking up drugs or something like that,' muttered Craig. 'What's worrying me is where are we going next, and what will they do with us? I thought I saw some small lights just before she ordered me below. They must have been a pattern identifying the position of the floats. I have heard the islanders say that the drugs were being dropped into deep water with some sort of soluble fuse to delay the release of them and then they float to the surface. Only the collectors know when and where they will surface.'

There was constant movement on deck with what sounded like soft packages being dropped down into the cabin.

While the boat drifted they couldn't hear clearly as the idling engine muffled any speech, but just occasionally a berth locker lid could be heard being slammed shut.

Mike lay back on the large berth and thought about the hotel. He had saved for years as a pub tenant, and then as a drinks salesman for Scottish and Newcastle Breweries. Jenny seemed to have enjoyed the life. Always at licensed trade functions and always welcome at the bar, whether it was the local, a company inn, or the rugby club she had been the life and soul of the party. They had enjoyed holidays in Tenerife and Majorca, and as long as there had been a good, lively pub he hadn't made much of a fuss about where they went.

When he had suggested buying the hotel he had been completely taken aback when Jenny objected. 'I don't mind meeting with your business associates and drinking with them, but I don't want to live with the "trade",' she had said. 'Anyway, an hotel is no place to bring up a family.'

That was the first time he had been really aware that a family was even contemplated. Yes, there had been references, but always airily when they were with friends. They had never had a serious discussion about it. It seemed obvious now that spending five nights a week 'on the road' left little time for discussions about things like children, and he was keen to get out to see their friends at the weekend. The weekend usually meant parties, dinners, barbecues, and whilst he had occasionally strayed too far he was sure that Jenny had at times too. Or had she? Maybe he just wanted to believe that to justify his own behaviour.

When did Eric come on the scene? Perhaps if I had had an interest in sport, or a hobby things might have been different. I don't remember seeing him about the place. There had been quite a few nights when the telephone wasn't answered. *I wonder if they are happy.* A daughter, the security of a bank manager's job, nice house, holidays in the Algarve.

Mike's thoughts rambled on. *I'm still working seven days a week, except for this sail each year.* Sleeping with the occasional bar help wasn't much of a relationship. *Now this! What the hell is going to happen now? How in heavens name did this all happen? Christ, I don't even like sailing all that much. Are we going to get out of this alive? I can't just sit here and let it happen. This time I'm going to do something positive regardless of what Craig says.*

The engine note increased and the boat picked up speed. They all sat back, saying nothing, as the steady drum of the diesel beat out a soporific rhythm.

'Listen,' said Craig, 'Wind's getting up. I wonder which way we are going. It is difficult to tell but it looks as though we are going south. To Ireland maybe?'

'Come on. Let's break their bloody necks,' muttered Mike.

'How do you propose to do that. They jammed the door. By the time we cleared the door they would be standing waiting for us. No. Sit tight. There will be a better way. They can't miss with those guns in this space,' retorted Craig.

After his initial rashness that was a satisfactory answer for Mike.

Alan looked out through the small window. 'It does seem to be pretty dark for this time of year. There wasn't anything on the forecast about bad weather was there?'

'There was mention of a deepening Atlantic low in South Shannon. It may just have started to move east sooner and faster than expected and occasionally these things deepen quite quickly.'

Soon, all doubt was removed. Another thirty minutes and the wind was even stronger. The boat was rolling and pitching, and the engine revs had been increased.

Alan looked up. 'I've got it. If we stop the engine they will have to sail, and they may not be able to manage on their own if this wind keeps rising. Can we stop the engine without having to break out of here?'

Craig smiled, 'That sounds just possible. If all three of us can get on deck then we may catch them off guard. The exhaust travels under this berth. If we block it the engine will cut out, but we will be able to start it again whenever we need to. Lift those cushions off.'

It proved to be much harder than it looked to flatten the heavy duty rubber exhaust hose sufficiently for it to affect the engine, but slowly they got it flat enough to cause the engine to cough. After a few minutes of this Mairread shouted through the door. 'Are we running out of fuel? How much was there in the tank?'

'The tank was full at Ardfern, and there must still be plenty,' grinned Craig. Mairread returned to the cockpit.

Mike and Craig kept the engine running for a few minutes longer then flattened the hose completely. The engine stopped. The boat wallowed. Waves slapped against the stem, just under the berth. 'That's the damn noise you get when you try to sleep in this cabin when you're at anchor,' said Craig.

Alan looked just a little off colour. There was a vibration through the rigging. It sounded just like a heavy lorry on a road, except there wasn't a road anywhere near. The whipping of the burgee against the shrouds was increasing in frequency and force. The wind was rising and fairly quickly.

They heard noises as the engine-room covers were removed. Someone banged on the diesel tank. 'Come out slowly, Craig,' shouted Mairread, and whatever had been blocking the door was removed. Craig ducked his head and went through. The yacht layout made it easy for Sean and Mairread. There was only one access to the aft cabin, a passage with a low roof that necessitated bowing the head to pass by the single berth. Sean was able to stand well back into the main saloon and keep anyone in the passage covered whilst the other could only view ahead with peripheral vision.

'That's far enough. Now what the hell is wrong with the engine?' Sean looked distinctly unwell, and was shouting. The yellow eyes seemed to glow in the cabin light and he appeared to be on the verge of becoming totally irrational. His face was grey with a very high colour in the cheeks.

'How the hell do I know? That engine is barely used. It is as good as new, and is serviced every winter,' replied Craig.

'Well, look at it. See if you can get it started.'

'I don't know what to check. Did the overheat or charging alarm buzzer sound?'

'No there was no warning other than a slowing down of the engine before it eventually stopped.'

'I suppose it may be a fuel line blockage. Can I get the tool kit?'

Craig lifted the navigator's berth cushion and took out the kit, and set to uncoupling the fuel line. It didn't take too long to see that fuel was flowing, and he remade the union. 'Not lack of fuel then,' he said. 'In that case I don't know what it is.'

'Right. Back in there,' said Sean, and Craig joined the others.

Alan smiled at Craig. 'Well it certainly won't go now,' he hissed.

'That's right,' grinned Craig. 'I don't think they have remembered that it will have to have air released before it will start.'

'I would be more pleased if I didn't feel sick,' muttered Alan.

'What now?' asked Mike.

'We wait,' responded Craig.

As the time passed they heard occasional attempts to start the engine, but nothing else. Mike thought he heard someone in the saloon but couldn't be sure. By now the boat was rolling heavily, and was cork-screwing as she rode up the front and down the back of the steep seas. The wind strength was now so great that Wizard seemed to side-slip as she was lifted by the steep waves and it felt as if they were falling down the wave front from time to time. They were drifting nearly beam on. But where to?

The aft cabin door was opened and Mairread looked in. 'You will have to come on deck. I need a hand to sail her. We can't just wallow around any longer.'

'Alan can't make it,' said Craig. 'He's seasick.'

Alan was about to protest that he wasn't that sick, when he saw Craig's look. 'Alan will be best if he is left to lie down for a bit.'

'OK, OK. Come on. It is getting worse and visibility is decreasing too.'

As Craig got on deck he was surprised by just how rough it had become. The sea was a mass of white caps readily visible even in the little light that did exist. And the wind caught his breath. He had seen Sean lying on the port berth behind the table and he looked distinctly seedy. The bowl he was holding to his chest told the whole story, although the gun still remained firmly in his right hand. Despite it being June, it really felt very cold and the sky was shot with black and grey, veiling a ghostly creamy sky, the last efforts of the dying sun.

'Mairread. Take the helm and as we unfurl the headsail take her stern round to the wind,' shouted Craig.

Mike eased the furling line as Craig winched out just enough headsail to give steerage. Almost immediately there was a perceptible improvement. Slight, but the boat rolled less, and as she speeded up felt much safer. Craig and Mike then hoist a minimum of mainsail with the three furling pennants kept tight, and Wizard steadied, was no longer flotsam but a controlled boat again. As Mike turned he noticed that Mairread, despite her worry, and the effort to hold the helm was still pointing the gun in their general direction. She smiled at him but he did not feel much reassured. She looked good though. Her hair was blown, she looked cold and wet; she had not put on any waterproofs and he could not help noticing, even in these conditions, her firm breasts stood out against the wet shirt. She really did look good.

Mairread turned the wheel and Wizard came round and tried to come up to the wind. 'What the hell do you think you are doing. She won't go through the wind with this amount of sail. She'll just fall off again,' shouted Craig.

'Then we will have to jibe. Stand by to jibe.'

'I don't think that is a good idea,' retorted Craig. 'She won't sail against that wind very effectively anyway.'

'Then give me more sail,' yelled Mairread.

Craig, just for an instant, thought about trying to grab the gun, but changed his mind. *It will get even easier later*, he thought. 'Come on Mike. Let's get on with it.'

With more headsail they tacked and then let out a mainsail pennant. Wizard heeled until the lee was almost awash, and Mairread struggled to hold her as Wizard kept trying to come up to windward to ease the pressure on her hull. 'Take the helm, Mike,' ordered Mairread, and Mike obliged. Breaking waves showered over the bow and made the cockpit wet, and Mike kept dodging as the heavy spray flew at him, forcing him to duck or turn his head away. Looking forward the sea was white as long streaks of foam made the ocean into a giant mug of cappuccino. Craig looked down at the log, one knot. He tried to indicate to Mike with a nod to head even more into the wind and slow the boat yet further. He wasn't sure whether or not Mike had noticed.

'Where are you trying to go?' shouted Craig.

Mairread was screaming to be heard over the wind. 'Never mind. Just sheet that main in harder.'

'You aren't going anywhere at this speed, and if the wind gets any stronger we will be going sideways.'

'Sheet in hard.'

Craig tried to wind the handle of the self-tailing winch but made little impact. The pressure on the sail was too great. He sat down and held on. It was very wet and cold and Mairread now looked miserable.

The deepening darkness, made the weather seem much worse. Mike tried to peer for'ard to see the waves but it was difficult to pick them out from the sky which was tinged with ripples of light. The white horses, the spray, and the sky were indistinguishable. Only the acute angle of the bow, and the rare sight of breaking seas surging up the deck confirmed that these were big waves. Mike was cold. *Just don't let this get any worse. Please don't let the wind get any stronger.*

'I don't suppose someone could make a hot drink, could they?' he shouted.

'No. Keep her steady,' replied Mairread.

Wizard was going nowhere. She was now barely making way on her course, and even with a hardened mainsail, and very little headsail, she was luffing up so violently that she seemed like a speedboat turning. What frightened Mike more was that no sooner had she forced her way to the wind and come upright, than she sheered away again, accelerating across the wind with lee awash, until the log read 10 knots, only to turn violently to windward again forcing him to brace himself with one foot out at right angles on the cockpit seat, with the other leg bent to keep himself upright while both holding the wheel and trying to turn it. 'This is bloody well impossible. We can't keep going like this,' he yelled.

Craig ducked under the spray hood and looked at the wind speed. The needle flickered between 50 and 55 knots before dropping back to 40 knots. He looked round and found Mairread looking at him. There was a question in her eyes.

'We must run before. If we try to keep this up something will give; probably one of us,' he shouted.

Mairread nodded. 'OK. Let's go.'

Craig eased out a little more headsail. He grabbed the wheel from Mike and waited for a lull. Even trying to hold the yacht steady until she gained speed required a major effort and rapid adjustment of the wheel. As he felt the wind drop and sensed the pressure on the boat ease he put the helm hard over and Wizard surged round to bring her stern to the gale.

Despite the howl of the wind, the relief was fantastic. All of a sudden it seemed quieter, warmer and calmer. For a while everything seemed to be all right. Craig smiled at Mike and Mairread. They both smiled back.

After only a few minutes, however, Wizard was surging forward, burying her bow in the breaking sea, and still trying to hurl herself beam on to the wind. 'She is going too fast. Steering is too light. We must reduce speed,' yelled Craig. 'Drop the main completely. Mike you go up top. Mairread. When he gets up there, release the main halyard.'

Mike suddenly realised he had no life jacket or harness. Wizard had seemed a big boat until now. He thought about going for his waterproofs, but rejected the idea in favour of getting the job done as quickly as possible. Cold air seemed to be pouring through his summer-weight windcheater. He felt slightly sick, and he felt his hands shaking. As he stepped up onto the cockpit seat and coamings he was exposed to the full might of the wind. He grabbed the corner of the spray hood and it gave. He staggered forward, and luckily his shoulder hit the upper safety line. He reached forward, grabbed the teak deck rail and pulled himself forward until clear of the hood, and then holding on to the kicker that supported the boom he pulled himself up to the mast.

Holding on was just not possible if he was to pull on the sail, so he grabbed tight onto the luff with his right hand and tried to gather a fist full of sail in his left. 'Right. Let go the halyard.' He pulled but nothing moved. The pressure of the wind was too great even to allow the sail to slide down its track. 'Let go! Let go!' he screamed, and pulled again. The fear was slowly getting stronger, and spray was all over his face and running, chillingly, into the neck of his jacket. A violent plunge almost threw him off the deck and he grabbed frantically with both hands for the mast.

'Your foot. Move your foot,' screamed Mairread, and he looked down. Just where the halyard passed through the mast foot sheave he had his foot firmly wedged on the halyard. Quickly he shifted his weight. The sail collapsed, and he slipped, losing his grip on the halyard and mast, catching his hand on a sharp split pin, and staggering backwards. His back struck the shroud wire, and he was spun round, to fall forward. As he landed on the starboard deck he saw the mass of tumbling, crashing water sweep up the deck as Wizard again buried her bows in the sea.

Without much hope he grabbed at the spinnaker pole which was in its mount along the deck, and felt the lower guard line slide across his back as he fell through the lines and over the side. He grabbed at the toe rail but his body was forced out from the hull so violently that he could not hold on. His left arm was bent backwards over the toe rail and threatened to snap.

Jesus, I'm being pulled under.

One second his feet seemed to be being dragged forward, the next the boat accelerated and he was hurled back. Then he felt as if he was being sucked under. His head felt as though it was submerged for ever. He held his breath for what seemed a lifetime before his head cleared the wave, and he gulped in air but the salt made him gasp for more air and he swallowed yet more salt water. His gut wretched, bile surged into his throat and he choked.

It took quite a few seconds for him to realise that the pain in his left arm came from the wire rope of the spinnaker pole which had wound itself round his arm. His whole body was being pulled and pushed. Water was inside his boots and trousers, and washing over his head. His lower body felt heavy and beyond his control. Once more he grabbed with his other hand for the toe rail, trying to ease the pain in his left arm. *I can't hang on. Oh my God. My arm will break. Please help me.* He couldn't think clearly. It was like being hit time after time with a bag of sand around the ribs. *Oh God. Help me.*

Craig had watched as Mike, seemingly in slow motion, had pirouetted across the deck and fallen through the rail. He looked astern expecting to see him drift away, but when nothing appeared astern, he looked again along the deck and saw the arm supported by the spinnaker wire, and the other hand grabbing at the toe rail.

'Man Overboard!'

'Let go the jib sheet,' he shouted at Mairread, but she had already let it go. Craig scrambled forward, and braced himself against a guard rail stanchion. He reached down and grabbed Mike's shoulders, and pulled. He weighed a ton. Mike's jacket started to come up his back and felt as though any second it would rip. Craig felt his hands slipping and tried again to get his hands under Mike's armpits. He couldn't lift him. He could barely see Mike's face as the water rushed over it. Then Wizard slowed. She was beam on, but she had slowed. Mike's head and shoulders were now clear of the water but even more of his weight was now supported by the wire rope and his wrist. Strangely he felt even heavier to Craig.

Alan appeared from in front of Craig and reached down to grab Mike's arm. 'Take his arm. Just take one arm.' Craig didn't react at once. 'Come on. Come on,' shouted Alan, and Craig woke. He grabbed Mike's left arm and pulled. Slowly they inched him back through the wires. The cable that had held him safe now tried to prevent him coming back on board. The guard lines which were to prevent him going over suddenly did a good job of preventing him returning. The gap between the spinnaker pole and the bottom line seemed impossibly small. Every pocket, zip, stud and collar caught on every conceivable object, cleat, pole, line, toe rail. It seemed to take a lifetime but they got him back on board.

Mike was shaking, coughing and said nothing. Craig went first, and pulled whilst Alan pushed Mike back to the cockpit. The violently bucking and rolling deck made it deadly dangerous to try to manoeuvre a nearly inert body along the narrow deck. Time after time Craig's shoulders were through the guard rails. Struggling backwards past the spray hood he could not hold on as he heaved hard on Mike's legs, bracing himself from time to time against a stanchion before making the next heave. Something beneath Mike's body had snagged on his clothing and Mike would not pull further back. It was necessary to lift him but that could only be done by getting back into the cockpit in order to obtain the extra lift and purchase.

'Hold him. Hold him till I get into the cockpit,' Craig yelled above the screaming wind and crashing waves.

Alan braced himself and curled his fingers so tightly into Mike's clothing that he felt his nails breaking on the harsh nylon. Freezing water rushed up the deck and up the legs of his trousers and into his boots. He lay on top of Mike's body feeling the reassuring pressure of the lower guard rail along his side. *Hurry, hurry, for God's sake hurry.* Alan knew Craig would be going as fast as he could but it didn't stop the fear from twisting around in his mind.

'Now. Now push.'

Alan raised himself, lifted and pushed as Craig lifted Mike's legs over the coamings. Mike jammed against the winches but suddenly was free and slid over into the cockpit. With a sense of relief Alan quickly scrambled after him.

Alan was aware of Mairread standing at the helm looking pale. With as much care as they could they lowered Mike down through the hatch to Sean below. As Alan went below Craig sheeted in the jib again. Mairread was struggling to bring Wizard back round, stern to the wind. The wind was so strong now that even with minimal sail Wizard kept fighting up to the wind. However, as the wind eased momentarily the bows swung north-east, and Wizard again started to run before. Craig smiled briefly, and, he hoped, reassuringly at Mairread and went below to check on Mike.

Mike was as white as the spume. He laughed childishly and croaked that midnight swims were not for him.

'Let me see your arm,' said Craig, and Mike pulled up his sleeve. The wire of the spinnaker pole had taken a large area of skin off the arm and a deep groove spiralled around the muscle. It was bleeding slightly and the arm looked very painful. 'That's probably agony, but it saved your life,' muttered Craig, and lifted the first aid box from the port locker. A large mug of Bovril was pushed into Mike's hand and Craig looked up to see that Sean had hooked himself on to the cooker rail and despite looking like cold porridge had boiled a kettle and produced the hot drinks. Craig was satisfied that Mike was as comfortable as he could be under the circumstances and grabbing two mugs of steaming Bovril swung himself up into the cockpit.

As soon as he reached the deck he was aware that the noise had increased again as the badly stowed mainsail thrashed against the boom and the wind which was again in excess of 40 knots screamed through the back stay. The headsail was furled to a small triangle too far up the forestay and causing much greater heel than Craig would have liked but he did not feel like going for'ard to rig the storm jib. That should have been done ages ago.

'You must make sure that we run before. Don't let her broach,' he yelled at Mairread. She nodded but was obviously having difficulty with the wheel.

Alan had managed to wash Mike's arm with antiseptic wipes and applied a pad and bandage, but the effort of trying to work while the boat rolled violently was too much for his equilibrium and he eventually retired to the aft cabin to be sick into the toilet. Jammed into the small heads he actually felt better and improved even more when he remembered the gash on Sean's head where he had been thrown forward in his berth and struck the table leaf.

Mike had squeezed himself into the navigator's seat after forcing down the Bovril and a couple of aspirins. He kept telling himself he should be on deck but another voice insisted that he could do nothing useful anyway and he was better just recovering his strength. He suddenly became aware that he was shaking violently, and felt very cold.

On deck, the hot drink had helped and although the sea was still getting rougher the wind did not seem to be so strong and the wind instrument read 30-35 knots fairly consistently with only the odd gust reaching 40. Craig had often been out in these conditions and as he forgot the nature of his predicament and concentrated on sailing the boat he felt much better. Mairread looked very cold and frightened and he couldn't help putting his arm around her and taking hold of the wheel with his other hand to ease the strain. She looked up and a slight smile appeared before she again peered forward and concentrated on keeping Wizard in front of the wind. Craig screamed at Sean to hand up the waterproofs, and although it felt awful putting them on over already soaked clothing, the heavy nylon suits cut the wind and that was a true bonus.

A light flickered and Craig guessed it might be Barra Head lighthouse. 'I must go below and check the GPS position. Will you be OK?' He looked down at Mairread. She nodded. Hanging on as the boat heaved and rolled Craig dropped down into the cabin and grabbed at the grab rail on the cabin roof to pull himself over to the navigation table. Mike staggered forward from the navigator's seat, banged his head on the roof and cursed loudly, before pulling himself round to sit on the berth.

Craig slumped down awkwardly on the navigator's seat with one leg stretched out on the engine bulkhead to steady himself and pressed the position button on the Autohelm. He noted the co-ordinates and plotted them on the chart. That wasn't so easy as the rule wouldn't stay in place and the position lines he drew were slightly out. Staring at the constantly moving chart made him feel queasy but he managed to concentrate long enough to get a reasonable idea of where they were. He then entered a way point for a safe passage inside the islands and hoped that they would get some shelter there. He noted the course to steer and was glad to climb back on deck. The cold and wind helped clear away the sick feeling. He took the wheel. 'Sit down. Have a rest,' he shouted. Mairread curled up at the forward end of the cockpit, with her head pulled down into the high neck of her jacket. Craig wondered where the gun was.

A mental and physical numbness took over. The wind seemed less strong but Craig didn't really register the reading. The sea was not getting worse though the blown spray was unpleasant. There did not seem to be any prospect of major waves breaking over the stern but he could not resist the occasional look astern at the black mass with the white roaring mane that seemed to race up and threaten to pound the boat. At the last second the boat climbed into the sky and surged forward only to feel as though it was sliding backwards as the huge waves passed leaving the bow higher than the stern. He remembered to check the course and heading, asking Mairread to take the helm, and then he once again braced himself for the strain as Mairread shrank into the corner of the cockpit.

After what seemed to be an eternity the sky lightened and a break in the cloud allowed the pale light to spill through with arrows of light flighting across the sky. The near permanent daylight that was the norm at that time of year shone through and immediately Craig felt better. The feeling was not solely his. Mairread looked up and smiled, 'Is it getting better?' she queried.

'This storm wasn't forecast so it may well not last too long,' replied Craig, and at that moment a pale-faced Mike looked up through the companionway.

'I'm making soup. Fancy some?'

They both nodded.

Alan had also forced himself into action and the four of them sat huddled in the cockpit obtaining as much satisfaction from the warmth of the mug in their hands as from drinking the hot liquid. As the next hour passed the wind abated, and the sea state declined visibly although the swell continued to make seasickness the next obvious choice from the menu. As the islands came into view the morning sun shining off the wet rocks made them look like granite. Sean was also showing signs of life but he looked terrible with dried blood smeared about his face from the gash on his forehead.

Craig looked down at his hands and noted that they were white and wrinkled just as if they had been immersed in water for hours. There was a cut on the back of his right hand which must have occurred as he tried to pull Mike back under the safety lines. He felt that stomach-turning shiver that comes with intense emotion. He laughed inwardly. The last time he felt like that was when he was madly in love. Strange how danger produces the same reactions. He looked to the west. The outer isles were clearly visible with the buoy off the entrance to Castlebay like a black dot on a silver sea. They never stand out like that when you need them, he thought. He turned back to see Sean again holding the gun.

They sailed on and the swell was replaced by a residual chop in the Minch which was still not too pleasant but as they approached the small island of Eriskay, Mairread looked at Sean. 'Call home. Check what they want us to do,' she instructed, after which she sat down and produced the gun from her jacket pocket.

Sean went below to the radio, 'Skye Radio, Skye Radio, this is Wizard, Wizard, call sign Mike Golf Alpha Charlee Six. One link call please, over.' Craig tried to hear the conversation, but all he caught was the dialling code, 0151, although he couldn't recall where that was, and some general chat about the reasons for the diversion. He thought he heard '15500CC. Probably too tired,' but couldn't put it into context.

Sean hung up the handset. He looked enquiringly at Mairread. 'There is a major problem and it is too soon to go to any of the usual rendezvous. I think we should head for Eriskay. It's safe and there are very few people there.' Sean looked wan and tired but Craig felt he was still too alert to try anything.

For people who said they didn't cruise often, they seemed to know the ropes pretty well, thought Craig.

Mairread nodded slowly in agreement and turned to Craig. 'Let's make for Eriskay. At least it's a romantic spot.'

'Tricky entrance though,' smiled Craig.

'Not too tricky, if you know what's good for you,' laughed Mairread.

Craig thought how lovely she looked when she was happy.

The passage into the bay required care and with a wind from the west it would have been impossible under sail. However the south-south-west wind was backed and reduced by the land and it was a straight sail in.

The leading lights on the small headland were helpful and from time to time the local fishermen erected perches on the submerged rocks close to the shore to make the narrow passage just a bit easier.

The passage was uneventful and under different circumstances the achievement under sail might even have been enjoyable, although it entered Craig's head that he might have tried to put Wizard aground, but that doesn't come easily when your boat is the love of your life.

The long curve of the Minch between Skye and the Outer Isles was clear and the Cuillin Mountains mounted guard over the southern approaches to Skye. The bulk of Rum was less imposing than it can be in poor weather and the islands of Muck, Eigg and Canna were just visible in the heat haze.

It was now one in the afternoon, and once through the harbour entrance, Craig anchored in 4 metres of water with the bottom clearly visible. Mike served up mugs of soup and John West steak and kidney pies with mash and artichoke hearts so everyone was feeling much better, but desperately tired.

CHAPTER VII

W HEN SHE ARRIVED at the yard Patrick and another man whom she had seen around from time to time helping to load were both waiting. 'Good morning,' said Patrick. 'We have a slight problem. This load has to go to Liverpool and we both have to go too to negotiate a new contract. However, no-one will be travelling back with you. Could you even consider driving back by yourself? You could either drive overnight or if you wish I'll be happy to pay for you to stop at a hotel overnight.'

Karen's mind was spinning. *What will Craig say? Should I go at all?*

She did not have time to mull over all the factors and as she had done several trips already there did not seem to be a problem.

'Is that OK?' Patrick asked. She nodded.

'Oh but I don't have anything with me for an overnight.'

'That's no problem. You can pick up a bag from home on your way.'

'Sorry, I should have introduced you. Meet George. We all call him "Switch" because he used to run a business that never delivered what it advertised and eventually the Trade Descriptions Act caught up with him.'

'Hi' was all that Switch said, and the hand he held out was very large with thin fingers. He was a tall man, over 6 feet with a broad chest and no obvious signs of fat. Karen shook hands and thought that this man certainly didn't seem like a truck driver either. At least not the way she imagined them.

'Pleased to meet you,' she responded.

The telephone rang and Patrick went off to answer it. When he came back he announced that he would be driving down slightly later, but Switch would drive the van down. Karen could barely hide her disappointment but felt a little better when Patrick continued to say that he would be joining them in Liverpool in the evening. Patrick kissed her lightly on the cheek and they were off. She had some misgivings as the van rolled out of the yard and she waved to Patrick but she shrugged them off and settled down.

Although she tried to sit as far away as possible, being in the same van close up to Switch wasn't the most acceptable experience she had had. She felt very uncomfortable in his presence. His hand always seemed to be resting on the side of his knee next to her leg and there really wasn't anywhere to move. However, at least he was concentrating on the road and actually maintained a varied and interesting conversation about a wide range of topics.

She dozed. These early morning starts were unusual. Since the kids had become self-sufficient the start to the day had become more leisurely.

The van stopped and she banged her head against the side window. 'Sorry,' said Switch, 'I thought we could do with a bit of breakfast.'

Karen recognised Killington Lake Services on the M6. She had stopped there with Craig and the children when they used to go on caravanning holidays. Switch carried the tray to a window seat, and Karen felt much better after the bacon croissants and hot tea.

After they had eaten Karen made the excuse that she was tired and stretched out along the second row of seats. That was a relief but then she found she couldn't sleep so she pretended and looked into the back of the van. With a little surprise she saw several rolls of adhesive tape all printed with the SEC symbol and even the full name printed underneath Social Enterprise Committee – Charity Supply Service. She had never heard of that description. Even more odd were the piles of packages carrying the SEC logo. *I wonder who is sending so much?* She thought that the SEC markings on the packs at the photographic session had been prepared specially. She asked Switch if they carried much for the SEC, but his answer was not helpful. It varied a lot. Some weeks there was virtually nothing, but other weeks they had van loads.

'Who is the biggest user?' she enquired.

'Don't really know. I don't get involved with the customers.'

Karen looked at Switch. She had the impression that he really had avoided answering. He had fair, slightly wavy hair, broad shoulders with a slim waist and hips. His face was on the thin side, angular with grey eyes, nose tending to the Roman and thin lips. His dress, although casual, did not seem like the clothes a general driver-labourer would wear. The check shirt and Farah trousers were in good condition, and the black slip-on, thin-soled shoes were certainly not truck driver issue.

I don't like him, thought Karen. *I don't think Patrick can use him much. What possible use can Patrick have for a man like that?*

The breakfast and the heat in the van took effect and she must have dozed off as the next thing she remembered was the bump as the back of the van struck the loading dock at the Liverpool depot. Switch got out, with a 'It's OK. Just relax. We've got some loading to do.' However she felt that the fresh air would be welcome and would wake her up before driving back.

There weren't many people about, but it looked just like many of the old warehouses in Glasgow. The dirty stone building had obviously been a factory at some time and now with rusting pipes, green mossy growth over the fire escape and rubbish piled in the corners of the yard the look of total dereliction was complete. Karen got out of the van and wandered over to the warehouse and tried to look through a window. Although it was fairly grubby with the deposits of years of Liverpool air she could just make out empty flat cartons with the letters SEC on them. *Why in heavens name do all of these exist? What are they being used for?* She heard a scuff of feet and felt guilty; she had just stepped back from the window when she heard Switch say, 'Patrick has just phoned. He has had to go on into town, but he has asked me to take you for something to eat. Fancy anything in particular?'

The last thing she wanted was to eat with Switch but there was no other sensible suggestion in her mind so she nodded and said, 'Nothing too heavy. I don't want to fall asleep behind the wheel.' Karen was disturbed by Switch's odd laugh.

To her surprise they had eaten in a small 1920s-style restaurant, all shiny black and mirrors, where the food and the service was good and, to Karen's surprise, Switch had bought a bottle of 1970 Chateau Figeac which had left a lovely glow. Conversation was not too difficult. Karen didn't feel that she had anything in common with the man and despite his liking for and obvious interest in food and wine she could not believe he had anything else in common with her, although to her surprise his conversation ranged around politics, Domingo, Pavarotti and Carreras, and various parts of the world. She just had a strange feeling that not too many truck drivers spent as much as that on a bottle of wine or travelled quite so extensively. To her relief, just as they were about to leave, Patrick arrived.

'Hello. Have you had a good meal? This is a favourite spot of mine.' He didn't wait for an answer. 'I'm afraid there has been a delay with our load. It isn't going to be available until tomorrow morning. Can you manage that or would you like me to try to get you on a train or an early morning flight from Manchester?'

'Are you going to be able to get a driver?' asked Karen, while she added up the hours and tried to decide when she would be home.

'I would think so. I think I can probably hire a casual around here quite easily,' replied Patrick.

Karen struggled with the options, and was quiet for a few seconds. She was annoyed at the constant changes in the arrangements but did not like the feeling that she could be replaced so easily. Eventually she decided that having come all this way it would be ridiculous not to drive back. Anyway by the time she got to the station there was a good chance there would be no trains until the morning, and there certainly would not be any flights. Susan was at home so she would have to phone her and let her know about the delay. 'Oh, that'll be alright. I am quite happy to drive back tomorrow. I presume you will arrange somewhere for me to stay tonight?

'Oh I've taken care of that already.' Patrick's smile was reassuring.

'It does depend on my being able to phone Susan and her being OK about it.'

'Fine. You can phone from the car.'

She got into Patrick's BMW and called home.

Susan answered immediately, but was quite unconcerned at the delay in Karen's return home and joked, 'Too many attractions down there, are there? Is he tall, dark and handsome?'

Karen was glad that Susan couldn't see the huge blush which suffused her face. 'Chance would be a fine thing,' she responded. She told Susan that she would call again later when she knew where she was staying and give her the phone number. She still couldn't make up her mind what to do. *Should I just say that I have to get home? That will probably be the end of driving for the SEC. How will Patrick react? Will Craig understand that I feel committed to completing the job especially since it has now cost quite a lot and since it has after all for the SEC, really?* The easiest thing to do was nothing. Stay on and drive home tomorrow.

'I don't see too much of a problem as long as I can get home tomorrow,' said Karen.

'Well that's a great help. Thanks a lot.'

Patrick seemed relieved.

Patrick had booked them into the Hilton and Karen was pleased and relaxed to find that she had a large room with its own refrigerator/bar, and jacuzzi tub.

She phoned home again.

Susan answered. 'Dad called from the boat. He wasn't very pleased that you will be so late back. He did not seem to like the idea of you being away overnight. In fact he really sounded pissed off.'

Karen was furious. She suddenly found herself objecting to being treated as though she was Craig's property. She never queried his staying away on business, and not for the first time it crossed her mind that his nights in London may not have been spent alone. He certainly was tired when he came home. She shrugged off the thought as stupid and decided to try out the jacuzzi. Without thinking she poured in the small capsule of bubble bath and actually had the tub overflowing with bubbles. She thought they were going to run out of the bathroom door, but relaxed and consoled herself with a gin and tonic from the mini bar. By the time Patrick knocked on the door at nine-thirty she was feeling much better.

'Your room all right?' he asked.

'Yes. It really is comfortable.'

'We can't have you roughing it, can we? Some friends have asked us to join them for a buffet so that should help to pass the evening.' She was just mildly disappointed when they reached the taxi to find that Switch was joining them.

They didn't have too far to drive before they turned into a large house where there were about fifteen cars. The house, a large stone-fronted building, was similar in location to Patrick's house in that it stood well back, and invisible from the road in heavily treed grounds.

She was introduced to so many people that Karen found it difficult to remember many names, although she noted the predominance of London accents, but everyone was quite relaxed and easy to talk to, and although there was little sign of Patrick or Switch she found the occasional dance, chat, and the delightful miniature bread rolls with small noisettes of beef, veal, and chicken in delicate fennel, spice, and cream sauces, and the petit fours, irresistible. Champagne cocktails appeared whenever her glass was empty and all in all things weren't too bad.

Patrick appeared from time to time, and was friendly and interested and still apologising for not getting her home on time. They danced twice, his strange Irish humour was fun and his concern seemed genuine. Eventually the champagne decided that it wanted to go places and Karen set off upstairs as directed towards the Ladies.

As she walked along the hallway she heard laughing and shouts from several rooms, but approaching the end of the corridor a shout of 'Karen' drew her in. It was only when she was through the door did she realise that it was Switch who had called out and as she looked around in a slight panic for Patrick, she saw several very drunk men with a mixture of southern and Scottish accents, one of whom was lying on a bed with a totally undressed blonde girl; another was sitting on the floor with a girl trying to drink a fizzy drink out of a bottle and getting very wet in the process, while a third shouted, just as he disappeared through a door, 'The films are ready.'

Switch said, 'This is the lovely lady I told you about. This is Karen.'

The big man on the bed looked round, laughed and said, 'Well, you're in luck, it looks as if it's going to be fun as well as profitable.'

Karen forced a smile, and, trying to avoid anything that would delay her exit, didn't ask what he meant.

Switch's long hard fingers held her elbow and he pulled her into the adjoining room where the third man had gone. He was fiddling with a TV and video. 'It'll be on in a minute,' he said.

'Sit down,' said Switch, 'This is supposed to be good.'

'I'm on my way to the ladies' room,' said Karen, but Switch just said,'OK. OK. Just one drink and watch this. It isn't very long.'

She glanced over at the TV as the other man collapsed into a chair, and it didn't take many seconds to absorb the fact that close-ups of sexual intercourse and male and female genitals did not appear in BBC documentaries. She stood up and was on her way to the door when Switch laughed, grabbed her arm, gave her a push back onto the settee and thumped himself down beside her. He thrust a very full glass to her mouth. It was difficult to see what it was but he pushed so hard against her lips that she involuntarily opened her mouth and the first sip told her it was whisky; her throat burned.

Her eyes watered and as she tried to say something Switch leaned his full weight on her and kissed her. The taste and smell of whisky was foul, even after the champagne, and as he forced his tongue into her mouth she felt dizzy and sick. He was surprisingly strong. Instinct not to spill the drink delayed her reactions, until she felt the air on her shoulder as her dress was pulled down and a large hand forced its way into her bra. The strap was dragged off her shoulder and her breast was pulled free. She forced her head round away from the revolting smell and looked at the other man. There was just enough light to see that he was smiling and staring at them. She felt helpless.

'She looks fabulous,' she heard him say.

Then large powerful fingers squeezed hard on her nipple whilst his mouth worked around her neck and she pushed with both hands against his chest. Her legs were forced apart as a hand moved down her waist and she felt the fingers clawing at the waistband of her tights and pants.

Suddenly, the pressure was eased. She could breathe. She opened her eyes to see Patrick hit Switch straight on the end of his nose. Switch fell back with blood gushing over his mouth and chin. Patrick pulled her to her feet and shouted, 'Quick. Get out of here.'

Switch moved very quickly and grabbed Patrick's leg. Patrick tried to kick free, but he was pulled off balance. Before he could move Switch had heaved him over onto the floor, and had thrown his weight on top. The big man, whom Patrick told her later was Bernie, appeared and had hold of Patrick's hair with both hands. He banged Patrick's face against the floor and as Patrick tried to roll from side to side to get onto his back it just seemed to Karen that he increased the force with which his face hit the ground. For the second time within a few minutes she felt helpless and again there was sudden relief as two men from the other room rushed in.

'What the hell is going on? What's all the damn noise about? You'll have everyone in here soon.' They and a third man, who seemed to have sobered up all of a sudden, grabbed Switch and pulled him, struggling, to his feet. Bernie was still holding Patrick by the hair and Patrick looked bruised, bloody and confused.

'Stop it,' yelled one of the men, 'This is not the time to start a bloody riot.'

Switch had lost the excited look. His shoulders dropped back to normal, and Bernie let go of Patrick's hair, instead grabbing his shirt front.

'When we get this show on the road properly I'll remind you of this. Get her out of here and make sure things go right tomorrow,' growled Switch. Karen thought there was a moment when she saw fear in Patrick's eyes and wondered why he put up with being told what to do by an employee.

Patrick snapped to his senses. 'Come on,' he said, throwing his jacket around her. He took her hand and they went downstairs. 'We both need cleaning up. Use this washroom,' said Patrick, pushing her into a large bathroom. Patrick had buried his face in a basin of warm water, and Karen made an effort to tidy her hair and make-up. The reason why she had gone upstairs in the first place suddenly made itself known, and she hurriedly sat herself down on the toilet. Patrick, who was dabbing his swollen lips, eyes and nose with the towel, turned and grinned. They both burst out laughing, and Karen realised she was shivering.

For the third time Craig tried to call the Hilton hotel and for the third time the receptionist told him that there was no reply from Karen's room. 'OK. Thanks for trying. Good night.' Craig put down the handset, and returned to the others.

CHAPTER VIII

Patrick had ordered a taxi back to the hotel after they had cleaned up and had not stopped apologising for the trouble during the drive. When they got to their floor he had taken her hand and it had just seemed so natural to Karen to kiss him gently on his swollen lips. She was leaning hard against him as a noisy group of salesmen came out of the lift and stared at them, so she quickly stepped back from Patrick and said 'Good night.' It wasn't until they had parted and she was in her room that she realised that the kiss had been rather a long one, not just a good night peck, and she smiled to herself as she realised she had enjoyed it. She couldn't recall when last a kiss had brought these warm tingling feelings and a tension between her legs.

She made a hurried pretence of cleaning her teeth, smiled again at herself in the large bathroom mirror, almost jumped into bed and switched off the lights. She snuggled down into the full pillow, briefly recalling how she hated the tightly tied-in make-up of hotel beds and how she was always unable to pull the sheet and blanket over her head as she was so accustomed to doing. *I wish they had duvets.*

They met, as arranged, at 6 a.m. and had breakfast in the hotel dining room. Patrick had fresh fruit salad followed by a generous 'English' breakfast and coffee but Karen settled for a glass of orange juice and scrambled eggs. He appeared to have made a full recovery and was his usual buoyant self. They then set off for the yard where the van had been parked overnight. It didn't take long to get to the yard, but by the time they got there Switch and Bernie were standing by the van.

'All loaded and ready to go,' said Switch.

'Switch and Bernie will be taking a lift with you. They will be carrying on after you get off at Glasgow. They will unload and let you get home as quickly as possible since you have been delayed. OK?' said Patrick, and Karen nodded. 'Right. Off you go. And thanks again.' Patrick leaned forward and gave her a kiss on the cheek. Karen blushed and again was mystified by the constantly changing arrangements. It was as though they wanted her to be perplexed.

They climbed into the truck, and Karen moved off immediately with a wave to Patrick, and edged out onto the dockside road, looking for the first signs for the M6. Switch was sitting in front and Bernie was in the second row of seats which did not please Karen too much, but as she negotiated her way out of Liverpool they seemed engrossed in small-time chat and that was OK with her.

It didn't take too long before the van was roaring along at a steady 55 m.p.h. At least, that is, until it came to the hills when the grossly underpowered Ford slowed right down and in many cases required 3rd gear just to maintain 30 m.p.h. Everything seemed to pass them and Karen found the concentration more tiring than she had expected.

They were well on the way north when she became aware that no-one was talking. She looked round at Switch. He smiled. She looked away.

'I'm sorry about last night. Too much drink. I know we can get on much better.'

'Luckily we don't have to,' retorted Karen. However she was aware that Switch had edged just a bit closer on the bench seat and she felt distinctly uncomfortable; just like a visit to the doctors when the symptoms have just disappeared and the hacking cough you had when you left home seems to have gone completely.

Bernie leaned forward. 'How many others on the boat then?'

'Just two I think. They are moving it up there now.'

'What's it like?'

'It's a real pose, just like you'd expect from Mark. But it really is cool.' Karen's stomach took a heave, with that 'someone is walking over your grave feeling', and couldn't help wondering what a boat had to do with things, but she didn't feel like asking. She did not have to wait long.

'Do you like boats? Powerboats I mean.' Switch was obviously directing the question at her.

'I don't really know. I've never been on one. In fact I'm not too keen on the sea at all. My husband has a —'

'Yeah, yeah, I know, a sail boat. Can't stand those. Don't like the way they lie over,' responded Switch.

Once again Karen wondered how he knew about their sailing boat, and once again she chose to keep her mind on her driving.

They were well past Killington Lake Service Station and Karen

70

estimated that she may still be home fairly early. Her gaze drifted over to where she knew the small lake lay and envisaged the small sailing dinghies all lined along the shore. That was when she felt Switch's hand on her leg. She was wearing blue polyester trousers and his hand came to rest midway along her thigh.

'Get your hand off my leg. I had more than enough of you last night,' she said, and attempted to lift his hand away. The hand was firmly clamped to her leg and the effort to move it caused the van to swerve slightly in its lane.

'Careful, lady. We don't want to have an accident just because I happen to like you a lot,' said Switch.

'If you like me you'll remove that hand now,' she shouted, with her voice rising in pitch and fear creating a tight chill in her chest. 'I'll stop. I'll stop right now if you don't take that hand off me,' she shouted.

'I wouldn't do that if I were you,' muttered Bernie into her ear, and she saw the dark barrel of the gun right alongside her left eye.

'Oh no. Oh no,' was all she could say.

Switch kept his hand roaming around Karen's leg for the next thirty miles and at one stage Bernie leaned over and ran the palm of his hand over her breasts. 'Lovely, I'm looking forward to these,' he said.

Just north of Gretna, Switch told Bernie to drive and with a warning not to be stupid, he made Karen climb into the second row of seats with him. As the van got under way Switch slowly pulled her shirt out from the waist band of her trousers and slipped his arm around her pulling her towards him. He pulled the shirt up at the back until he could unhook her bra, and then, pulling her hard against him he put his arms around her and fondled her breasts and nipples. Apart from the drive through Glasgow when he kept her pulled hard against him he nuzzled and kissed her face and neck until they were well north of the city. He seemed content and Karen sat as still as possible as every movement seemed to encourage him farther. The smell of stale whisky on his breath nearly made her sick, and she considered that as a way of discouraging his attentions. However, as soon as she had thought of it the nauseous feeling disappeared.

Bernie looked in the mirror. 'Some folk have all the luck. What's she like then?'

'You may get some later. Just keep driving,' muttered Switch.

Karen pulled away. 'No. Patrick won't stand for this. You know what he did to you last night.'

'I don't think he is going to reach us in time to do anything. Anyway, you've got the position wrong. Patrick does what I tell him. He won't make last night's mistake again if he knows what is good for him, and he does.'

Just to emphasise the point he reached down and pulled the zip of her trousers down, pushed his left hand into her pants, and wriggled his fingers down over her stomach. Karen gasped and forced her knees together but he pressed harder until he was able to move his fingers up and down between her legs. Still not satisfied he pushed her roughly back along the seat, then reached down and pulled her trousers and pants to below her knees. 'Just for security you know. I wouldn't want you to think about jumping out. Lovely little bush here, Bernie,' he laughed. His fingers now easily reached their target and his other hand returned to squeeze her right breast.

'Good girl,' he said and kissed her. Karen was cold with terror.

For the next few miles Switch's hands explored all of her, at one stage forcing her face down along the seat, but slowly he settled back into a doze. Karen sat rigid, afraid to move in case she roused him again, but every so often Bernie would turn and look at her with a leer that made her feel very afraid.

Karen realised that they were heading up Loch Lomond side and asked, 'Where are we going? I was supposed to be going home.'

Bernie laughed, 'Maybe you should tell her what it's about. Maybe she would shut up then and co-operate.'

'Tell me what?'

Switch had been dozing for the last few miles and Karen immediately regretted saying anything as he sat up. She hoped that the hands that had been stationary for the past half hour or so wouldn't start wandering again. To her relief Switch removed his hands from under her clothes and looking straight at her said, 'Lady, your hubby and his mates are helping us with a small cargo we were having difficulty in picking up. You are here just to make sure that they don't have second thoughts about it all.'

Karen felt cold. She actually shivered. It needed quite an effort not to be sick and the bumping of the van as it climbed over the twisting road to Arrochar suddenly felt much worse. She closed her eyes and tried to lean away from Switch and to her relief he did not prevent her from resting against the side of the van. She found some bare metal and the cold against her head helped as she wriggled into her trousers and tried to think of the options she had, and what possibly lay ahead.

It was strange to look out at a road she had driven many times and for the first time she thought that the hills looked cold, lonely and dangerous places, the river looked grey and gloomy, not shimmering as it often did and the sky was an overall steely shade. At least she was able to take the opportunity to tidy herself up.

Switch and Bernie talked incessantly and the van progressed through Inverary and Lochgilphead before turning north-west towards Crinan. Karen hoped that when they got wherever they were headed Craig and Wizard would be waiting. She hoped but not with great conviction. She felt empty; the way it feels when experiencing a severe disappointment; when realising that a love affair is over; a feeling of helplessness; nothing is worthwhile.

The van crawled past the Crinan Hotel and along into the car park at the canal basin and stopped. Switch reached over the seat and pulled up two holdalls. 'Bring your bag,' he said, and Karen lifted her small case and got out.

Bernie made sure she saw the gun, and said, 'It really would be silly to try anything.'

They walked slowly over the lock gates and down to the outer harbour pier. There were a few tourists about but surprisingly few boats. As they approached the pier the outline of the superstructure of a powerboat was visible. When they got close someone with a very English voice called out, 'Hello, George?' and to Karen's surprise Switch shouted back 'Yes, and you should see what we've brought.'

They climbed down the ladder onto the deck of a large motor cruiser. Karen could see that it was very well equipped and she could just make out the name 'Fast Lady.' The voice materialised from the doorway and slapped Switch on the shoulder. 'How was the journey, and who is this?' he asked. Karen looked at the tall man with the sophisticated appearance. Rohan safari shirt, Rohan trousers, and Sebago dockside deck shoes. Her depression lifted slightly.

'This is the security. I thought it would be best if she stayed with us just in case of problems. Anyway, she will help to pass the time.' He laughed.

'Very smart,' smiled the other man.

They passed into a saloon, and a younger man in his twenties stepped forward. He had a scar on his forehead and he appeared to have a limp. 'Jimmy. We have company. Put the lady into the forward cabin,' ordered the man. Karen had time to notice that the youngest man was dressed in a smart blue wool shirt with navy trousers with an anchor motif on the pocket, and blue deck shoes, all of which were very good quality. It looked just like a modern uniform.

'That's right, just you have a tidy up and look your best,' smiled Switch.

Karen quickly looked away as the young man grabbed her by the shoulder and pushed along to the forward cabin. He pushed her inside and shut the door.

The cabin was well equipped and had its own heads. It was pleasant to have a wash. Karen felt very tired and hungry. She hadn't had anything but a sandwich which Bernie had bought when they filled up with diesel, and that was hours ago. She washed quickly, tidied her hair, and but for the hunger, felt much better. She felt safer with more men around, and at least the older man looked fairly wealthy and more importantly, respectable. She wasn't sure what to think about the young one. She lay back on the double berth and thought about Craig and the others. She was sure that the door was not locked but didn't feel up to trying anything. She could hear music and murmured conversations, but no detail.

In the saloon the group of George, Bernie and the Londoner whose name was Mark were sitting with large whiskies, and Jimmy was working in the for'ard companionway at the galley. Mark said, 'We had something ready for you. It won't take Jimmy more than a minute or two to increase it slightly for our guest.'

'Isn't she something special?' said Switch, and Bernie laughed and replied, 'It's OK for George. He's been feeling her all the way here.'

'You can tell me about that later. After I bring you up to date,' replied Mark.

Jimmy served bowls of lobster bisque with croutons and fresh cream, and nothing much was said as they sipped the Chablis and consumed the soup. It wasn't until the beef stroganoff with rice and broccoli was on the table that Mark spoke again.

'The position is this. We received a tip that the Lord is known. Sean and Mairread have got control of the other yacht and as far as I know everything is going as planned. Wizard, that's the boat, is a regular around here, well known to Coastguard and Customs, and there is no reason to believe that anything is suspected. All going well we will slip out from here through Dorus Mhor and meet up with them in the bay, Bagh Gleann nam Muc, on the south-west of Corryvreckan, the north-west corner of Jura.

'It is a pity that they have to sail so far but I don't want to risk taking this boat too far out to make the transfer. It may be spotted and could look suspicious. In shore we are just another cruising yacht. Fairly anonymous. After the transfer we will head south and the guests will be left on Jura. By the time they are found we will be well away.'

Switch smiled. 'They will have a good description of us though.'

'Only the lady on board here, but I am toying with the idea of taking her with us, at least for a while,' laughed Mark.

'I thought you might.'

As Mark opened another bottle of the wine he told Jimmy to bring Karen through for some food. Jimmy departed and a minute or two later arrived back with Karen. He pointed to a seat at the end of the table and Karen sat down. She was conscious of all of the men watching her closely but she was so hungry that she was able to ignore them as she ate first the soup and then the stroganoff. Jimmy had also poured a glass of wine for her and despite her underlying fear she actually enjoyed the meal. The cropped head and hard face was somewhat countered by his obvious attentiveness.

As she ate the others were talking and as they seemed to be making no effort to prevent her overhearing it wasn't difficult to work out that they were planning to sail soon and intended to rendezvous with Craig and the Wizard somewhere off the west coast of Jura. Thoughts of what might happen then flashed into her mind but she concentrated on what was being said to avoid thinking the worst. It also occurred to her that Patrick must have known she was being brought to the boat. She felt so stupid to have been so easily misled, especially when she had had constant misgivings about the Liverpool journey, even quite early on.

She was just finishing when Jimmy poured her another glass of wine and without realising the absurdity of the situation she looked up at him, smiled, and said, 'That was a lovely meal. Did you cook it?'

Jimmy blushed and nodded. There was a belly laugh from Bernie, who shouted, 'Look at Jimmy. He really fancies her. He's gone all pink.

Who would have thought that about a hard bastard like him.' The others laughed, and Jimmy went scarlet and turned away to take the plates to the galley. 'Tough luck, Jimmy. She's already spoken for. If there's any left you might get a taste,' teased Bernie.

'I'm sorry, Jimmy,' smiled Karen, 'I really think that was lovely. You should be proud of your cooking. It's almost certainly more than any of these animals could do.'

'Well said, lady,' laughed Mark. 'George's cooking is so expert that he can manage to burn potatoes and boiled eggs.'

There was general laughter, but all Karen noticed was the scowl on Switch's face. She had made an enemy. Probably not the brightest thing to do.

At that moment Mark said, 'George. I'm going to buy you a drink up at the hotel. Bernie. See that our guest doesn't try to leave. We should not be very long.'

'Sure thing, Guv. Seamus an' me. We'll look after things all right.'

Mark and George then left for the Crinan Hotel and Karen wondered if she dare rise and go back to the forward cabin. She had noticed that there were no locks on the door but she hoped that she could block it with something.

She stood up. 'That's good timing. I was just going to ask you to entertain us,' said Bernie. Karen stood still. She was sure her heart had stopped. Bernie put a disc in the CD player.

'Come here, Jimmy. Here's a real show for you.'

Jimmy ambled back from the galley and looked at Bernie.

'Karen is going to do a strip for us. Aren't you, love?'

'No. I am not,' forced out Karen.

'Get me a piece of rope,' smiled Bernie, and Jimmy disappeared to re-emerge with a length of 12mm rope. The thought of being tied up terrified Karen, but before she could say anything Bernie had grabbed her and forced her down over the end of the saloon table. The stinging pain as the rope bit into the back of her thighs made her scream, and half a dozen more lashes in rapid succession left her gasping for breath. The pressure on her back eased and she stood up. 'Now strip.'

Time seemed important. Karen started to dance, and reached behind to unbutton her blouse as slowly as she possibly could.

Bernie watched intently until he realised that this was going to be a long-drawn-out affair. 'Stop. I've a better idea. Have you ever been this close to a lovely lady like this before, Jimmy?' asked Switch.

'Nuh,' responded Jimmy.

'Well, here's a real chance for you. You take off her clothes when I tell you. Right?' Jimmy looked unsure. 'The Guv won't like you damaging the goods.'

'I'm not damaging her. She's made to be looked at, among other things.'

'That's what I mean. Other things.'

'Shut up and do as I say, or you'll be out after this trip.'

Jimmy had a flash of the flat in Moss Side where he had lived, glanced at the luxury of the boat, and shrugged his shoulders.

Karen stood still while Jimmy was instructed to remove all of her clothing item by item. Bernie sat still and watched, occasionally encouraging Jimmy to touch Karen as he removed something until she was left only in her pants. 'Come here,' said Bernie, and Jimmy pushed her to him. The large hands mauled her breasts and then dropped to her waist and hauled down her pants. He pulled her face down onto the settee, and pulled the small pants completely off. 'Isn't she lovely?' He panted as he held her down with his knee and forced her legs apart with his hands. 'Look. Is that not just what you fancy?' he shouted at Jimmy, pulling her buttocks apart.

Jimmy actually looked embarrassed.

'God. I thought you were a hard little bugger. No, not really. I always knew you northerners were all mouth and back alleys.'

'Come on,' said Bernie and dragged Karen along the companion-way to the forward cabin. He forced her onto the bed, and started to undress. Karen had never even seen a naked man other than Craig, and the sight of Bernie aroused made her feel helpless.

Bernie did not react to the noise on deck. He did not hear the banging of doors until Switch burst into the room. 'Come on, you bastard. The Guv is in a good mood. Get through there before he realises what you are doing. I think he fancies it himself. If he saw you now he'd cut it off. Now move yourself.'

Momentarily Bernie looked afraid, and grabbed his clothes and left.

There was a knock at the door and Jimmy came in with Karen's clothes. He held them out and examined her carefully as she walked over to collect them. He smiled and watched closely as she dressed and then made her lie on her side whilst he carefully roped her feet, wrists and neck so that any movement of her arms or legs pulled on her neck. He then disappeared back to the saloon and despite her discomfort Karen felt relieved.

She tried to sleep and did manage to drift into a half sleep where she was aware of background talk and noises around the boat, but was wakened fully when she heard someone coming aboard. She strained trying to hear the tones of the newcomer's voice, and shortly afterwards the boat vibrated as the large engines started up. Karen eased herself onto her elbow and looked out of the window to see that they were slowly moving away from the harbour and the hotel.

It had not been until Monday evening that Patrick had set off north, and he was feeling relaxed. The arrangements for future deliveries had been resolved. Since Customs appeared to have identified the yachts being used for the 'pick-ups' it was agreed that the faster power launch would be used while new cover was being arranged. The latest, and largest, consignment should be well on its way. He smiled as he imagined Switch's expression when the yacht did not arrive at the bay in Corryvreckan. The reputation of the Gulf restricted the number of possibly curious eyes whilst being remarkably convenient for deliveries onto the mainland.

The only misgivings he had featured Karen. Switch was normally very self-controlled when business was involved but he obviously fancied Karen and that escapade at the party hadn't been too clever. That was the first time he had crossed Switch and if he had told the London boys about it there just may be trouble. The motorway didn't take long to reach and without realising it his foot pressed harder on the accelerator as the BMW eased up to 100 m.p.h.

Patrick lived well from the income from the business. Others at home had been forced into a clandestine existence whereas he had made many contacts and friends. He had served for a time in the Army and even had a spell in Ulster with Army Intelligence. The Army had been good for him. Until he had joined he had had no real view about his life, and by assisting him through university the Army had made the most of his scholastic achievements. However, he had finally decided that he wanted to start his own business, and as soon as his commission was over he resigned and started up a haulage business in the Liverpool area. The need to improve cash flow was a constant problem but he had made many contacts when in Belfast and his first regular service had been established between the UK and Ireland.

His outspoken views had been well known to many parties in the North and South, and then to his dismay he discovered that he had become a popular individual; popular with Special Branch and Military Intelligence, and the IRA, to such an extent that after a couple of years trading and with unusually generous financial support, ostensibly from the Department of Trade, he was encouraged to open a depot in Glasgow, and advised to relocate his home to Scotland.

Women took to his firm, open approach. He came over as a broadly experienced and knowledgeable man who listened well and always sounded helpful. The regular affairs he had never left him with anything other than a temporary regret when they ended, but after meeting Karen he often found that his concentration wandered when he was working alone. A disconcerting coldness affected his stomach; the days until their next meeting were disrupted by fleeting visions of her; he found himself imagining holding her, the warmth of her. Away from her he felt nauseous, but wasn't sick, just overcome with a lethargy that made him walk from room to room aimlessly until he shook himself and found something to do. He found himself staring at television programmes he hated but couldn't remember anyway. He analysed and re-analysed their meetings wishing he had said some things and regretted saying others. It was almost as if he perpetually wanted to sigh deeply, to fill the void that absorbed his chest. Thoughts of her stirred him just enough to be disconcerting. With all his experience he was now having juvenile doubts. *Will I be able to do it right; to make it last; to please her? Stop it. Stop driving yourself crazy. The more you think about it the worse it will get. Where is she? Is she thinking about me? Does it matter to her where I am? Why in heavens name have I involved her? Am I in love with her? I am in love with her.*

The kiss at the hotel had been wonderful. He couldn't stop thinking about how to get close to her; how to say something that had nothing to do with the business so that they could start talking about each other. *Does she want to be with me again? Is she safe?*

The closeness of the back of the truck in front as its brake lights screamed at him forced him into the world and as a quick glance in the mirror showed the outside lane to be clear he swung out and overtook the truck. The speedometer showed 135 m.p.h. Patrick lifted off and dropped back to about 90 m.p.h. as he became aware of the discomfort in his groin. *Bloody Hell, I am behaving like a love-sick teenager.* He stared hard at the road, but it wasn't long before thoughts of Karen again intruded and pictures of her flooded into his mind.

He pressed on through Glasgow and was halfway to Tarbert on Loch Lomond side, albeit without much awareness of the passing countryside, when he remembered to switch on the car phone. The bleep coming almost immediately insisted on an answer. The call from Liverpool was short and to the point. 'Our target has been diverted due to the storm. They are now making for Eriskay. They will need help, and the others must be delayed. John is now heading after them.'

Patrick responded, 'The others have a thirty-mile start but shouldn't suspect anything yet. I will join them but I don't know how I can delay them.' He didn't replace the phone but dialled another number, gave a coded response and asked, 'Did you get that?'

The reply came back instantly, 'Totally.'

Thoughts of Karen had gone. Now there really was trouble. The BMW was driven hard through the bends and the gearbox worked overtime as Patrick dragged maximum acceleration from the powerful car. He cursed that he was not more familiar with the road as he was finding it difficult to remember just where the straight sections were. A white van going the other way flashed its lights and the car he had just overtaken blew loudly on the horn as he pulled in fiercely and accelerated hard round the left-hand bend at the top of Loch Fyne. As he pulled out and accelerated violently past the Volvo 3 series in Lochgilphead he attracted the attention of the two police in the white and orange patrol car.

'Jesus. He's going some. Let's go,' said the driver, and the police car shot forward to the road junction, stopped briefly to let a pick-up truck past and then accelerated hard away from the town centre after Patrick.

Patrick was lucky. There was no-one about and he crossed straight across the town centre junction without any other traffic and was on the Crinan to Oban road in a few seconds more. With only a glance in the mirror at the clear road behind the BMW whispered up to read 120 m.p.h. before slowing for the Cairnbaan turn-off and the bridge over the canal. It was the early hours when he reached Crinan, and after parking the car in the car park, he stopped only to grab his holdall, remove a small package, unwrap a small black object which he applied to the middle of a large piece of sticking plaster which he placed firmly onto the skin immediately between his anus and scrotum. *Could they have thought of a more uncomfortable place?* he wondered, as he left the car and ran across the lock gates and over to the quay. There was the sound of talking and glasses as he climbed down the ladder onto the deck.

The police car screamed past the Cairnbaan turn-off, heading for Oban and it was not until several miles on when they could see the road was clear along the straights past Kilmartin that they realised the BMW had turned off.

Mark was standing at the bar telling a joke to Switch, Bernie and Jimmy when Patrick entered the saloon. Switch gave him a strange look but said nothing. Mark turned, smiled and said, 'Hi Pat, glad you've arrived. Now. Let's get going. If we slip out of here now no-one will see us go and we should get into the Corryvreckan without attracting attention. Check that we can be there at slack water. I don't much fancy heading into it after these gales unless the tide is slack.'

Jimmy disappeared only to pop back in a couple of minutes. 'It's just right. If we take it slowly we will arrive at the time you want.'

A few minutes later the big powerboat slipped her moorings and headed down Loch Crinan, out through the Dorus Mhor and over to Jura. Just as it was really getting light they anchored in the pool on the north-west corner of the island and settled down to wait for Wizard.

The police car arrived in the car park at Crinan Harbour just as the stern light of Fast Lady disappeared around the headland. 'That's the BMW. Do you want to have a look around?'

'No,' said the passenger. 'He's probably on that boat.'

'I suppose so. It's been around here for a few days. Registered in London and real class.'

'Let's just run a check on the BMW.'

After a few minutes they were advised that the big car was clean.

'Come on. Back on patrol before they are screaming for us.'

The patrol car reversed away from the quay and drove back up the hill towards Cairnbaan.

CHAPTER IX

They sat looking at the silver grey rock of the Hebrides, interspersed with sparse grass on which grazed even sparser sheep. 'It must always have been a hard living here. But it is the only island that was not affected by the Clearances. The English didn't think it was worth it,' mused Alan.

'Isn't this where Charles Edward Stuart landed from France?' queried Sean.

'Yes,' replied Alan, 'The beach is just over the hill on the other side of the island.'

Mairread looked up. 'I would like to see that.'

Sean stood up, 'I'm going to find out what is wrong with the engine. I've found the handbook.' With that he went below, opened up the engine-room hatch and his head and shoulders disappeared as he started checking through the different items.

Mairread ordered Mike and Alan below and secured them in the aft cabin, but told Craig to stay in the cockpit. 'As soon as Sean is finished I am going ashore, and you will row,' she said. Craig noticed that the gun was tucked into the waistband of her trousers beneath a light sweater.

'Why go ashore? There's no pub here. The pub is about a mile and a half away.'

'It will pass the time. We shouldn't have to wait long. I am sorry if you are bored, but you can tell me some more of the island's history. Maybe we will find one of the bottles of the famous whisky.'

'Whatever else you may do, you certainly don't bore me,' responded Craig, and blushed.

Mairread smiled. 'That's nice to hear.'

A yell from Sean made them lean forward and peer down the hatch. Craig was aware of the softness of Mairread's sweater as they pressed against each other.

'There was air in the system,' shouted Sean, 'I'll release it at the filter, the pump and the injectors. I sure bet she goes then.'

As Mairread turned her lips brushed Craig's cheek and he saw the gleam in her eyes.

'Once it starts keep it running at about 1500 rpm. The batteries could do with charging up.'

After he had said it Craig thought how stupid it had been to give any sensible advice, but Mairread was having an effect on him.

'Launch the dinghy but let me make it fast first,' ordered Mairread, as Craig pushed the dinghy over the stern.

The row ashore did not take long and Craig and Mairread seemed to spend the time looking straight at each other, until the rasp of the hull fabric on the rock next to the pier caused Craig to catch a crab and shower Mairread with sea water. 'Hey. Watch out. Don't you think I've had enough soaking recently?' They both laughed as Craig pulled the dinghy up beyond the highwater mark and made it fast to a large rock, then clambered up on to the concrete steps alongside the pier.

'I don't know who designed these steps but he didn't have anything to do with the sea,' laughed Craig.

'Why'll that be?'

'Well until a few years ago there were no steps alongside this pier and it could be a nightmare getting back to the water if the tide went out while you were ashore. Especially at spring tides. I remember four of us coming back from the pub at about one in the morning only to find the dinghy hanging by its painter down this rocky slope. The other chap who was with us had to more or less abseil down the painter until he could reach the dinghy and then climb into it while the rest of us lowered him into the water.'

'That must have been fun, and no doubt you were pissed.'

'Yes, but that wasn't all. The fishing boats had returned and the fishermen were sorting and gutting fish, and as he rowed round he had to pass through a barrage of fish guts to get round to the ladder down the pier.'

'I bet he stank.'

'Then a year or so later we arrived to find that steps and a small landing stage had been constructed at the side of the pier. It seemed very thoughtful until we found out that it had been planned to reach the sea at high water but at low water and particularly low water spring tides the small platform was too high to reach even when standing up in a dinghy. The work was practically useless. But then that is local authority work for you.'

'Oh well, it isn't going to bother us. We won't be ashore for the tide to be a nuisance.'

'That's a shame. I thought we were eloping.'

'Mairread looked up at Craig. A teasing smile flitted across her lips and her eyes sparkled. 'Is that what you would like?'

'It certainly beats being locked into the aft cabin.'

They made fast the tender and wandered up the slope from the pier to the small single track island road.

Climbing up the hill on the only road to Haun, they walked on, in the afternoon sun, passing the unsightly new houses, until they came to an old derelict property overlooking the beautiful white sand of the Prince's beach, skirting a bay with rocky islets around. The blue sky and white powdery clouds stretched out into a distant heat haze.

'Out there in that haze is the Statue of Liberty. Next stop America.' Craig stared wistfully out over the shimmering sea.

'You like it here don't you?'

'Yes. I think it is my favourite view. At least it is in this weather. It can look so different on a wild day.

'Legend has it that this is the house where Charles Edward Stuart, Bonnie Prince Charlie, stayed when he landed here from France. It surprises me just a bit that a French captain had adequate charts to find a location like this, but that's how the story goes.'

'It's sure a lovely story anyway. He had to have landed somewhere around here and it's good for the imagination to have a spot identified. I love to let my mind explore when I come to such gorgeous places,' responded Mairread.

From the high vantage point the Atlantic was bright green and the wavelets on the sea as white as the sand as the high sun reflected off the rippled surface. The wind had almost died and Craig found it hard to visualise what it must have looked like the previous night.

'Come on, I have something to show you.'

They turned off the road, across the course grass and scrambled down to the beautiful beach below. Craig often reached back and up to give his hand to Mairread as she followed him, until she jumped down beside him and their feet sank into the crisp dry sand. As she fell gently against him Craig allowed his lips to kiss her cheek and he squeezed her against him before stepping back and turning towards the sea.

They strolled along the sand looking into the distance, observing the gulls and gannets making their way from one fishing ground to the next and seeing the white houses on South Uist stretching away westwards to the Atlantic coast of the larger island.

A short distance along the beach Craig scrambled back up the bank and stopped beside a small monument. 'Oh what a shame. This was built by the local schoolchildren to mark the position of Charlie's landing but I'm afraid it has suffered from the winter gales.'

Mairread's fair hair drifted gently in the warm breeze and as she ran her hand through the escaping strands Craig was roused by the outline of her body against the blue green of the sea.

'Is it always as quiet as this?'

Craig smiled. 'Yes. Normally. Just occasionally you will find another couple on this beach but that is unusual. Sometimes a local with a dog comes along but normally it is very quiet.'

Craig again gazed out to sea, over to Barra. It was unbelievable that he had been kidnapped. As he stood contemplating the inspiring view Mairread gently squeezed his hand.

'How lovely. How really, really lovely.'

They walked on and turned right up the hill, scrambling and walking alternately over the warm grey rock, and the springy but sparse grass. In the distance on a small knoll seven Eriskay ponies grazed, paying scant attention to the two intruders in their domain.

Craig climbed the hill behind Mairread and was embarrassed to realise that he was staring at the taut blue trousers that rippled over her small, firm, round bottom. He looked at the strong thighs and calf muscles as she stretched to step up onto a large flat boulder. He felt an urge to touch her and only just resisted the temptation. They recrossed the road and continued upwards through hollows and over mounds which presented ever-changing views of Barra and its close neighbouring islands, until they crossed the ridge of the island and looked east from Eriskay.

Mairread had brought the boat's binoculars and as they reached the last hill overlooking the Sea of the Hebrides she swept the horizon to the east, whilst Craig sat down on the springy turf and felt remarkably relaxed. Mairread turned and caught him gazing at the outline of her breasts as she held the binoculars to her eyes.

She smiled, 'Lovely view, isn't it?'

The Minch sparkled grey and silver as though a shoal of mackerel were playing just below the surface in the mellowing breeze.

Mairread sat down beside him.

'Isn't this a magical place? The steel blue mountains, silver sea, warm air and a beautiful woman. What more could anyone ask for?' murmured Craig.

'A bottle of champagne would be nice, with maybe a lobster grilled in butter, fresh asparagus, and a lightly dressed salad,' laughed Mairread. 'But I might settle for a kiss.'

Craig turned towards her. The sparkle was there in her eyes again. The pale blue sweater and navy trousers seemed to emphasise every beautiful soft curve of her body.

He leaned forward. 'I can't manage the champagne here, but the kiss I can just about handle.'

Mairread lay back on the grass and Craig's lips found a warm welcome. Craig had become used to Karen's quiet acceptance of his way of lovemaking and Mairread's responses as his hands eased over her breasts surprised and excited him. Her kisses became more hurried and there was no resistance as he slipped his right hand under the soft sweater and caressed her breast while his fingers teased the nipple. Mairread turned towards him and he felt her thigh pressing hard against him. It had been a long time since a fully dressed woman had produced this sensation and he was embarrassed at the confusion as he tried to remove her sweater whilst Mairread pulled his shirt from him. 'Slowly,' she whispered, as he fumbled with the waistband of her trousers. Mairread took his hands and moved them to her breasts, and moaned slightly as he allowed her nipples to thrust through between his fingers. Craig felt his trousers and pants slipping down and the heat as Mairread's hand cupped his balls, before her fingers tightened around him, stroking and squeezing hard at the root of his manhood.

Without realising fully how, Craig removed Mairread's trousers and pants and ran his fingers through the hair around her secret opening, felt the heat surging through his body as Mairread whimpered and cried out when he found entrance. His fingers eased in and out and the base of his hand rubbed against her sensitive skin, whilst his tongue rolled the firm nipples of her breasts. Mairread's fingers were pulling hard on his buttocks and Craig slid his legs over and between her inviting thighs. As he kissed her eyes and face Craig felt Mairread reach down between them and felt himself thrust in, and in. He pressed harder. He wanted to fill her whole body, and the force of her legs around him urged him on until he felt himself drive forward and a great power surged up through him. He groaned, shuddered, and felt the release. He kept thrusting and shaking as if he couldn't stop.

'Oh God, I love you,' he gasped, embarrassed at the speed with which his pleasure had been achieved. 'I'm sorry but . . . '

Before he could finish she whispered, 'It's lovely to feel a man out of control. Don't worry. That's probably the most natural response I've had in years.' Craig looked down to see that smile again on Mairread's lips as she reached up to kiss him.

They lay on their backs holding hands for some time until Craig rolled over and enquired, 'What are we going to do?'

Mairread smiled and looked slightly quizzical. 'I don't think there is anything we must do right now. Just enjoy knowing each other.' Her hand reached down, gripped him firmly and stroked him gently until she got the response she was waiting for when she pulled him towards her and they made love again; this time more slowly, watching each other's eyes, responding to the movements of the other, touching, and looking at each other's body, until again they came to a fiery plunging conclusion.

Craig shivered. The passion subsiding had left his naked body aware of the breeze, light but which was still present, and he suddenly thought about the gun. He slowly eased himself on to his elbows and looked for Mairread's trousers. They were lying where he had thrown them when he removed them. Mairread's eyes were closed, and he reached down to pull the trousers towards him.

'Thank you. I really should put them on again. I hope after that "I love you" bit, you weren't looking for this.' Craig looked round and, glancing down from Mairread's smiling eyes he saw the gun in her hand.

'Oh to hell. Surely you aren't going to go on with this?' he muttered.

They dressed, and walked a little way towards the shore.

'I've been involved for a long time. I was convinced years ago that Irish history was not like the complexities of the Middle East or Europe. The problems in Ireland are relatively modern. The background to them is easily understood by anyone who wants to be fair. The English, yes, and the Scots, could put right the position if they really wanted to.' Mairread looked quite passionate.

Craig felt confused. 'What the hell has Ireland got to do with what I've been through?'

'Sorry. I shouldn't have said anything but I am sure that you have worked out that what we picked up was drugs. However, this trip the drugs aren't going to the people who arranged the delivery. We are taking them to support our cause. At least that way some good will come out of all this.'

'Some good. Some good. Don't make me sick. It doesn't make much difference to people whether they are killed by drugs or bullets. The end result seems pretty much the same. I haven't seen any evidence of any ground swell of public opinion in Ireland for killing, or for independence for the North for that matter,' shouted Craig.

'Don't be ridiculous. People generally are quite passive about what they believe in. It takes the committed activist to stimulate their responses. After all half a dozen Scot Nats seem to want to make a stink about Scottish independence and in proportion they have got far less support. In reality there are many groups who have prior claim to parts of Scotland from long before the Irish arrived.'

'That just confirms what I've said. Most of the Scot Nats leaders are simply industrial, social, or political misfits. Their sole interest in Nationalism is personally motivated. And, the truth is that the Scots people aren't interested. I believe that the Nationalists are just one more group that wants history to start at the point in time that suits them. We have the same situation with certain professors of weird subjects like the "Scot's Tongue", bastard dialect that it is. At least we have some evidence of that. You lot wouldn't want to know the real opinions of the Irish people,' Craig bitterly spat out.

'There wouldn't be any point in an Eire referendum as you would just say that the decision must be up to the people of the North, and their views are coloured by the errors of history and an inbuilt bias. Ask the true Irish what they think and you will get the real answer, but that won't happen. The British Government must be made to think again. No other way will work. Eventually you will recognise the truth. It won't be too long before the Nationalists have a majority in the North, and it will be interesting to see how keen you are on democratic decisions then.'

'You are right about one thing. At the rate you Catholics are breeding you will soon be in the majority,' Craig laughed, 'but surely now that we have a ceasefire there is no need for you to go on with this?'

'You really don't understand. The need for resources is even greater now. We have the South to influence as well, and we have to be sure that the Americans will help Eire. The South could not afford to simply absorb the enormous costs of the North when we are united and we will need help. Now our actions are designed to ensure that help is forthcoming.'

The beat of an aircraft made them look around but there was nothing to be seen to the east of the island. The noise became a roar and a light helicopter soared up out of the bay behind them and passed by so close that the faces peering down could be clearly seen.

'Noisy bastard. That's becoming a bloody nuisance. More and more people seem to be able to afford one of these beasts. There are times when I wish the damned thing would fall into the sea,' growled Craig.

'Wizard tender. Wizard tender. Wizard tender,' crackled the hand-held VHF, and broke into the intimacy of the moment. Mairread pulled the radio from her belt and responded. Craig heard Sean's voice 'We have a problem. They came in very close and were definitely looking for us. You had better come back right now.'

Mairread nodded to Craig. 'Let's go.' They turned and moved purposefully over the short wiry grass, back to the pier. They held hands as they strode out over the hill and down to the bay but the spell was broken.

As they rounded the last bend before the pier they came upon Alan and Sean. Alan was getting to his feet with a pipe in his hands and about to charge at Sean who had a gun aimed at him. Craig started forward but Mairread restrained him, and he noticed she had pulled the gun from her pocket and was walking slowly forward without saying anything or attempting to intervene in the affray in front of them.

CHAPTER X

ON WIZARD, Mike and Alan had listened to the departure of Craig and Mairread and the noises as Sean scrambled in and out of the engine-room hatches as he set about bleeding the air from the fuel system. A lethargic helplessness had taken over and they rested with their backs to the bulkhead, legs stretched out before them, almost asleep in the comforting warmth, when Alan jerked upright.

He tapped Mike on the shoulder and pointed upwards. He whispered, 'I've got it. The dinghy is gone and they have forgotten that now we can open the hatch. I am going to try to get out without him knowing. With the dinghy gone he won't expect anything.'

'Where will you go?'

'Well I have two choices. I can swim to the south side of the bay and try to phone from one of the houses there, or the north side. I think I prefer the north side as it will probably take some time for help to arrive. I don't think there are police on the island. They will have to come from Lochboisdale. At least on the north side, after I make the phone call, I can make my way towards the ferry. Maybe I will intercept the police.'

Mike looked dubious. 'What about me? What if he hears you? He could just shoot you.'

'Think about it. He isn't going to risk firing here. He could be seen, but more importantly, he isn't going to risk that when his partner is ashore and probably going to take some time to get back here.'

Mike was not convinced. They discussed alternatives, and went round and round in circles with ideas which became more and more unrealistic. An hour, then an hour and a half went by until there was the beat of a helicopter passing close overhead and they heard Sean calling Mairread ashore.

'That's it then. Plan A it has to be,' whispered Alan.

Mike still did not look convinced. 'OK then. What about me? What will I do?'

'Nothing unless you think he is about to go on deck. Then make a noise but don't let him in here to find out what is happening. The longer you can keep him down below the better.'

Alan, suddenly, was quite caught up in his own enthusiasm, but the chill of reality returned when Mike nodded his head. 'OK. Let's get on with it.'

They waited until they heard Sean back working at the engine compartment then Alan clapped Mike on the back, knelt on the berth cushions and took a firm grip on the hatch handles. He tensed and waited until Sean was making a noise and then swung the two latches to the open position. He stopped, waiting to see if Sean had heard the thump of the handles swinging open. He pushed and the hatch slowly swung upwards.

'Good Luck,' whispered Mike as Alan prepared to pull himself through the hatch.

Alan couldn't believe how much noise he was making wriggling up through the opening but he was free. He made his way stealthily to the stem, intending to slide slowly and quietly off the bathing platform into the sea, when he heard the banging and shouting from below. He stopped and swithered and stared at the entrance to the saloon. *Should I go back? Will Mike be alright? Will Sean come on deck and shoot me?*

He turned and climbed down the boarding ladder which stopped short of the water, let go, and began swimming for all he was worth.

Mike sat on the berth, tense, straining to hear Sean and Alan. The sound of Alan's clothes rubbing against the hatch surround had been like a waterfall. He was sure that Sean must have heard, but there was silence. Mike caught the slightest sound of a scuff as Alan straightened up on deck. There was still no sound from Sean, and Mike panicked. Visions of Sean standing watching Alan extract himself from the hatch flashed into Mike's mind. He was just waiting to shoot Alan.

Mike yelled out, 'Sean. Sean.' He banged on the cabin wall and heard Sean crashing to the door. He heard the bolt being slid back. Mike leaned all his weight against the door and braced his feet against the step in the cabin sole. Sean called out, 'What is it? What the fuck is it?'

'Hurry. Hurry,' screamed Mike as loud as he could. *Get away. Get away. Quickly.* Mike willed Alan on his way.

Mike suddenly felt the door crash against him. His foot slipped, his legs buckled and the door slammed inwards. Sean had thrown his weight against the door.

Sean stepped into the cabin, looked at Mike and up again in time to hear the splash as Alan jumped into the water. Instantly the gun was in his hand. 'Lie down. Lie down. Face down. Put your hands behind your back.'

Mike felt the cable tie tightening around his wrists and Sean was gone.

Alan swam like he had never swam before. He was a good swimmer; had been a very good diver, but had never worked as he worked now. His arms came over and his legs kicked out. Salt water filled his mouth as he breathed irregularly. Sharp bile shot into his throat and he coughed, but he swam. *Oh God. Any second now he will shoot. Why did Mike scream? Don't let me drown. Must keep going.*

It wasn't a great distance to the shore but it took for ever until his hands and knees simultaneously struck the seaweed-covered rock. He looked up. He had come ashore at a fairly steep section of the shore but there were enough rocks to grab and he pulled himself up slipping all the time on the seaweed. *Is he coming? How far behind is he? Can I make it to the house?*

He struggled to the top of the bank and his hand and footholds improved, first on a large mooring rope that fishermen had strung along the rocks, and again as he reached the coarse grass. He dragged himself onto the flat area at the top of the rocks, stood upright and looked back. He was coming. Sean was swimming steadily towards him. He was obviously not a fast swimmer and was doing the breaststroke but he looked more than strong enough to reach the shore. Alan took off towards the stone-built house ahead of him.

Alan remembered that the house was occupied by an old fisherman. Once, when they were on their way to the pub, the old man's family who had been visiting him stopped and gave them a lift. *I hope this isn't going to cause him any trouble.*

He gasped for breath as he tried to run across the rough ground, stumbling over the uneven surface. His hands landed against the cool stone as he reached the building. A quick look back confirmed that Sean had not yet reached the shore, and he staggered round to the front of the house. *The door.* He crashed into the porch door and tried to open it. Locked! He knocked loudly and again. *No reply. He must be out.*

Alan looked through the window next to the porch. Devastation.

Broken chairs, and a table lying drunkenly with a leg missing. Old papers and handleless saucepans lay on the floor. *Abandoned. The house is abandoned.*

Alan took off as fast as his shortage of breath would allow, along the short rubble drive towards the road. As he reached the junction with the road from the pier he stopped for breath and looked back. Sean appeared around the far corner of the old house, and peered in the window.

Which way? Which way now? If I carry on along the road to the village he will see me easily, and there are bleak isolated spots where he could shoot me. Back down the pier road. Hide by the shed or the diesel tank. Alan ran.

Sean looked around as he realised that the house was empty, just in time to see Alan start down the road to the left. Sean ran.

Alan passed the large waste container by the car park and on towards the pier. He remembered that the dinghy would be tied alongside the pier somewhere but realised that by the time he had launched it Sean would have reached him.

The diesel tank! Alan carried on down the small slope to the jetty until he had reached the big oil tank which sat up on a brick foundation. It was the main source of supply for the fishing boats, although it was also used to fill 25-litre containers for the small boats and they sat on a low platform actually on the pier itself. He stopped, slipped in beside the tank and scrambled up onto the top of the tank itself. By supporting himself over the back of the tank he was hidden from anyone on the pier.

The noise of his breathing roared in his head. His gasping intake of air must be heard by Sean. With several deep and sustained breaths Alan tried to calm himself Every muscle in his body was taut. No longer did he believe that Sean wouldn't shoot. He lay still and listened. The strain on his arms was becoming noticeable when he heard the sound of running and he was sure that it was Sean.

The footsteps went past the tank and changed as the runner reached the wooden deck of the pier. Alan heard them continue across the pier and stop. *He's checking the dinghy.*

Alan looked for a weapon. There was nothing on the tank but as he looked down he saw several lengths of pipe which had been abandoned behind the tank when some modification had been made. There was a short length of about half a metre which would be just right. He twisted himself slowly and, holding more tightly with one hand reached down with his other hand to grasp the pipe. It was just out of reach. He could touch it with his fingers but not actually grasp it.

He heard the footsteps returning across the jetty and he lay still, barely breathing. Fear thrust every possible scenario through his mind in micro seconds. It was all he could do to restrain himself from jumping out and throwing himself at Sean.

The footsteps reached the gravel and carried on up the slope, and then silence.

There was a large shed used by the fishermen just off the road and it was surrounded by grass. *He is going round the shed.*

Alan lowered himself slowly until his feet were firmly planted on the mound and reached down and picked up the pipe. Slowly inching himself back up towards the top of the oil tank Alan was able to peer over the top. As he looked towards the green shed he saw Sean reappear and, with a perplexed look on his face, once again walked down towards the jetty. Alan lowered himself until he was not visible and listened to the footsteps on the gravel as Sean approached.

Should I attack him? Should I stay hidden? No I can't stay hidden. He will just go on looking until he finds me.

The footsteps slowed as Alan heard the change from gravel to timber and he thrust upwards onto the top of the tank. It is doubtful if Sean would have heard anything if the piece of pipe hadn't struck the tank as Alan launched himself downwards. As Alan crashed down on Sean's back he saw the amazement in Sean's eyes as he looked over his shoulder. They both collapsed onto the pier and as they rolled apart Alan lashed out at Sean striking him on the collarbone, and it was then, as Sean's hand shot up to the source of the pain, that Alan saw the gun in Sean's hand.

Now. You must get him now. The thought that he must strike again before Sean could recover from the surprise and pain and use the gun screamed into his mind, and half scrambling Alan again launched himself at the Irishman.

Lashing out with the pipe Alan tried to aim at Sean's head but Sean's gun arm came up to ward off the blow and the pipe struck his wrist, knocking the gun clear. Before he could hit out again Sean kicked upwards at Alan and gained time as his foot connected with Alan's groin, sending him rolling off to the side holding the damaged parts.

Through a haze Alan knew he just had to keep trying and raised himself in agony as shooting pains ripped through his stomach and hips. He was about to rush Sean again when he saw that Sean had recovered the gun and was on one knee and raising it. Everything seemed to stop. It was as though it was all happening in slow motion. For what seemed an eternity Alan tried to focus on Sean's hand and then something snapped.

Try. Try. If you don't try he will kill you anyway. Now. Hit him again.

Alan started forward, and saw the smirk on Sean's face as he fired, and fired again.

Nothing. Nothing has happened. Why? Have I been hit? There was no sound.

Alan's impetus carried him on and in a frenzy he struck out, again and again. The gun flew out of Sean's hand as he struck out at Alan's head and body until Alan felt the sudden shock through his arm as the pipe smashed into Sean's head. Sean collapsed to the ground.

Alan struggled upright, pain shooting through his body and knelt over Sean. 'You bastard. I'm going to kill you for what you are doing.'

Sean lay, almost motionless, one hand covering his forehead, but as he saw the hatred in Alan's eyes he tried to roll onto his front to crawl away and felt the thud of the pipe land between his shoulders, knocking him flat on the ground and all his breath from him. Alan stood and then dropped with his knees in the small of Sean's back, leaned forward and slipped the pipe under the fallen man's throat. Holding it with both hands he braced himself with his knees firmly in the small of Sean's back and leaned back.

Sean's hand gabbed at the restriction but the blow to his head had weakened him too much, and his neck was slowly forced back.

Alan's vision was blurred and his mind confused. He just knew he had to win, but the cold muzzle of the gun against his temple was unmistakable.

'OK. That'll be enough. Drop the pipe, and get off his back.'

The red haze cleared.

Alan let go the weapon and rolled aside and looked up to see Mairread standing with her gun pointing at his chest. All resistance ebbed and all he could feel was pain and frustration. He could feel the salt of tears in his eyes and then was aware of Craig's arms lifting him to his feet. 'Good try, son. Great try.'

CHAPTER XI

CRAIG ROWED BACK to Wizard, and as they climbed aboard he heard Sean make a radio call. He overheard, 'I've checked. The Rascal has been delayed. We are to get out of here as Fast Lady must be on her way. We continue to use the agreed codes for our location.'

Alan had cleaned himself up and changed his clothes. His face was ashen and he moved awkwardly, just as an exhausted and dispirited man would move.

He explained briefly to Mike what had arisen but there was a coldness in his attitude towards Craig.

Very shortly afterwards Mairread called them on deck.

It didn't take very long to get under way and in the light breeze Wizard surged toward the mouth of the bay and the Sea of the Hebrides. Sean had asked Craig to take the helm, and again, for a moment, Craig thought of running her aground, but a glance at Sean drew a thin smile and a shake of the head. Sean had guessed what he was thinking. As they cleared the rocks at the entrance Sean said, 'Make for Lochboisdale. And make sure you stay outside the rocks ahead.'

Craig examined the strange chisel-like islet of Hartamul and marvelled that in such an exposed position there was plant life, not seaweed or just purely lichens but green grassy growth, towards its higher points.

Mike reset the sails to compensate for the wind from the quarter, and 6 knots came up on the log as Wizard responded to the added power.

Sean, who seemed to have recovered from his ordeal and did not even appear to be annoyed, looked over to the Cuillin Mountains and murmured, 'Sure is a lovely part of the world. Wish I could spend more time here.'

'Where do you come from?' asked Craig.

'Ireland,' replied Sean sharply.

Craig tried again. 'Don't you wish for a peaceful life with loved ones?'

'They're dead,' came the response, and Craig decided that trying to establish a close relationship with your captors wasn't as easy as journalists made it seem when they reported on hostage situations.

Alan complied with Mairread's command to get on deck when he returned to the saloon after checking the chain stowage, and on clambering into the cockpit observed Craig at the helm, Mike standing at the stern holding the backstay and the rail, and Sean seated in the forward corner of the cockpit on the starboard side with his gun hand resting on top of the mainsail halyard winch. He pulled himself onto the side of the cockpit and sat with his feet on the cockpit seat. Mairread positioned herself alongside Craig.

Mike stared at Mairread. He knew there was something between Mairread and Craig. He was sure something had happened when they were ashore, and yet. When she smiled at him it was more than just a friendly smile; more than a casual acknowledgement. Double-dealing bitch, he thought, but a twist of the lemon of jealousy added a sour piquancy to what he was planning to do. He watched as she stretched and leaned back on her outstretched arms. She joked with Craig, never taking her eyes off him. The gun was in the waistband of her trousers and her hands were nowhere near it.

Sean's eyes were closed. He appeared to be dozing. The blow on the head had certainly slowed him down. He had cleaned up now and there was little outward sign of the fight.

Now! Mike jumped forward and cupped his left hand under Mairread's chin and pulled her backwards. The sudden surprise left her falling backwards onto the aft cabin roof, and Mike's right hand reached for the gun. His fingers closed around the gun butt and he pulled. As Mike swung the gun up towards Mairread's head, Sean saw the muzzle turn in his direction. His belief that Mike was about to shoot at him was understandable and he fired. Alan dived forward from the other side of the cockpit and landed on Sean just as he fired another shot. The gun spun out of Sean's hand to land on the side deck just at the toe rail. As Alan and Sean struggled in the cockpit trying to reach over to the deck, Craig turned to grab Mairread who was struggling back to try to retrieve the gun which had dropped as Mike tried to grasp it. Craig hung on to her leg and saw Mike kneeling with blood running down his face and soaking through his sweater. The gun had fallen on the aft cabin hatch and Mairread was stretching for it. Craig's freedom was restricted by being jammed behind the wheel and he heaved hard in an attempt to pull Mairread away from the gun. Mike, who could only see the gun through a haze, grabbed for it, just snatching it away as Mairread's fingers scrabbled for it. Mike laughed and staggered as he stood up with the gun. 'What does it feel like to make love to a black widow spider?' he sneered at Craig, who was lying across Mairread's legs and looking up at him. 'There, I've —'

Wizard had been luffing up into the wind after Craig released the helm, and just as Mike sensed his triumph the boom hurtled round and hit his head with a dull thud. The force of the blow threw him across the deck and cartwheeled him over the rail. Craig watched mesmerised. It seemed like a slow-motion replay, as Mike's body spun around and splashed into the sea.

'Oh my God! He's over.' Craig turned to grab the wheel without taking his eyes off Mike's body where it floated in the swell. 'Christ. He's not moving. Come on. Get the lifeline.' Nothing happened. Mairread was sitting with her back to the rail pointing the gun at him.

Craig could not believe that she had taken time to recover the fallen gun whilst a man was going over the side. *Surely any normal person would have grabbed at the man?*

'Just get back on course.'

'We can't leave him.'

'He's dead. No-one could take that blow to the head and survive.'

'You don't know that. You don't know that.'

'I do. Now steer.'

Craig turned away from Mairread and turned the yacht for Lochboisdale, coming back on course just as he was violently sick.

Alan had struggled with Sean, but after the previous exertions he was no match for the hardened professional. A knee to the groin, a forearm across his throat, and several violent blows to the stomach and head left him lying on the cockpit sole in agony. Sean stood up. Mairread looked at him, nodded and turning to Craig, said, 'Turn back. Let's see if we can find him.'

They looked aimlessly. Without a precise fix on the position where Mike had gone overboard it was pointless, but they looked. The stilling sea remained rough enough for the head of a man to be impossible to spot if it was as much as 50 yards away. For an hour they sailed up and down as Craig tried to remember something about search patterns. Eventually Mairread said, 'Let's go. I'm sorry, but it's no use.'

Repeatedly Craig had asked her to put out a Mayday, but she simply stated, 'No signals.'

They turned back to their original heading and continued on their way.

Shortly before they started up the channel to Lochboisdale, Alan heard Mairread send a radio telephone message. He could only catch bits of it but got, 'New position achieved. 2731WI.' He made a note to ask Craig about it. Shortly afterwards they had picked up a mooring off the ferry pier.

They overheard Sean and Mairread discussing the situation but the scraps they could pick up were not very helpful. Eventually Mairread came to the cabin and announced that she wanted two ashore and indicated that it was to be Alan and Sean. Alan's aches made him reluctant to go anywhere but his will was not great enough to give rise to a protest and they duly went ashore to the pub after Mairread callously reminded him that Karen was a hostage and that any further stupidity on his part would result in Karen's death.

Alan rowed whilst Sean sat watching him closely, with somewhat more respect than before.

The pub and hotel for that matter appeared to have changed little over the previous fifty years. The high-quality food and accommodation and the extensive angling opportunities still attracted a regular and fairly well-heeled clientele but the less prominent areas of external paintwork needed attention.

Despite his early misgivings Alan found that the break was welcome and his headache eased with the second large Scotch. He was aware that separating him and Craig while they were in harbour was probably deliberate to ensure that they were unsure of what was happening to each other. There were only two other men in the bar and they were engrossed in conversation at the other end of the room.

They sat quietly, not speaking, and Sean smiled only slightly when Alan observed, as Sean paid for another round, that at least the drinks were free. The time passed slowly but Alan was feeling much better and again began to consider his options.

Mairread and Craig had returned to the deck and spent the time relaxing and chatting about Mairread's childhood. The inability of her father to get a job in Protestant-owned mills and shipyards, and the rigidity of doctrine, but nevertheless ineffectual influence of the Church had been a simple catalyst to becoming involved in the IRA. The family had always been short of money and the IRA appeared to offer a means of doing something positive to change things. Mairread felt courts without juries were just another way of thwarting the will of the people.

Craig sensed a tiredness.

She continued. It was proving hard to keep up the momentum for change when the day-to-day activities of the IRA were apparently subdued.

Craig became more confident that the warmth she had shown when they were alone could be channelled into less violent involvement. 'Surely you realise that the drugs you have stolen will still end up destroying the lives of others? Probably your own Irish children.'

'That won't happen. The drugs will not be used by us, only sold to finance our political actions. We are totally opposed to a drug culture. We punish anyone dealing in drugs.'

'That is naive. Any increase in drug traffic and use simply spreads the availability. Ireland will not be immune. Worse still, you are creating chaos by taking the law into your own hands. You will survive only until someone stronger and even more violent takes over.'

'Someone more violent has already taken over. The British Government. When you are unable to support yourself any other way it is necessary to take some risks.'

'That's an easy philosophy when it's other people's lives you are playing with. You don't seem to be taking much of a risk with your own.'

'If the situation arises I will do what is necessary.'

They lapsed into silence and had been sitting for a long time when Mairread noticed a small motor fishing boat stopping just off the end of the ro-ro pier head. A man in dark sweater and trousers was looking at them through binoculars. She automatically turned her head away, and said, 'Get below, quickly.'

'What's wrong?'

'I'm not sure anything is wrong, but we are being examined through binoculars and I don't like it.'

Mairread went to the radio. 'Wizard tender. Wizard tender.'

Sean's voice crackled back. 'Wizard Wizard. Go ahead, over.'

'Return immediately. We are getting under way. Over.'

'Understood. Out.'

Shortly afterwards Sean and Alan came aboard and hauled the dinghy after them.

CHAPTER XII

MIKE FLOATED, looking over his shoulder at the disappearing yacht, and tried to paddle himself around to face it. As the initial shock of falling into the sea receded he spat out the salt water in his mouth. *Bastards, Bastards, Bastards.* 'Come back. Come back here,' he screamed.

Within seconds the yacht was out of his range of vision and he was alone. He coughed and gasped as waves broke on his head and filled his nostrils. Wiping his face he became aware of the water penetrating his clothes and realised that it wasn't too cold although the salt made the shallow bullet wound on the side of his head sting madly. He tried twisting to look around but even with the calming sea the waves were too high to see anything and he always seemed to be at the bottom of the trough.

Remembering a little of his survival course he tried to pull his legs up and curl into a ball, but the bulk of his jacket made it too difficult to sustain and he relaxed again.

How long can I last? They will come back. Won't they? He became aware of the throbbing in his head. It was slowly turning into the grand-daddy of all headaches. *Please save me. I shouldn't have gone sailing. I don't even like sailing very much.*

A stinging sensation in his arm when the salt water penetrated the bandages and reached the grazes and cuts from the guard rail woke him up sharply.

Now he was on top of the waves. He could see the land clearly. *Eriskay, that's Eriskay.* He looked up at the sun, rolled over onto his front, and started to swim. It was nearly impossible. The life jacket lifted him too far out of the water to get any real power. His arms were too widely spread out by the jacket.

Mike allowed the jacket to roll him over onto his back again, glanced briefly to determine the direction of the sun, and slowly paddled towards the land.

They were wrong. Craig laughed when he bought the new waterproofs with the built-in harness and life jacket. Too expensive, they said. A waste of money they said. Not now. I am afloat. I am still afloat. But does it really matter? Will I be found?

It isn't cold. It's quite pleasant. Should I shout? Would anyone hear me? Can I swim to the shore? Bloody hell. In the sea twice in two days. That's enough for a lifetime.

It was easier to keep swimming slowly than to lie and do nothing.

The near silence was surprising. Only the bursting of the bubbles in the foam ripples on the small wave crests made any sound. And the occasional gull. Mike glanced around to find a small fat puffin staring at him from about an arm's length away. The strange little bird seemed to be puzzled by this odd orange object. As they alternately bobbed up and down they kept peering at each other. *What beautiful colours and such a funny face. I bet he thinks the same about me. But he should be here. I shouldn't.*

And then it was gone. Just as it had appeared with the waves so it disappeared. One second sitting close by, the next gone.

'Help. Help. Help me.' It seemed so stupid to shout but at the same time he had to do it. As he gathered his breath for a loud shout a small wave broke over head. The mouthful of salt water burned the back of his throat as he gasped and choked. The more he gasped and coughed the more he choked.

At last he got it under control, but his eyes watered so much he could hardly see. Mike resumed the gentle paddling.

The whistle. Where is the whistle? His hands scrabbled at the chest of his jacket and a finger caught in the cord. The whistle pulled free. *Yes, yes. Now I can be heard.*

Putting the whistle to his lips he blew. He kept the whistle between his lips and paddled, each outgoing breath blowing the whistle. The sun was drying the salt on his face and it felt hot, and the sea now felt cool, not yet cold, but distinctly cool.

With an effort Mike paddled himself around, trying again to spot the land. Nothing but wave tops. He looked at his watch. It was still going. *So it is waterproof.* This minor revelation pleased him and he smiled to himself. He continued to propel himself, feet first, in the general direction of land.

Land. Yes it is land. Definitely closer. Still a long way off though.

There was an increased sound of waves breaking. Where? He kept looking from side to side. He had learned that instead of being in the troughs eventually he would rise up on the wave and if he was lucky would be held there by several waves and would see around.

Yes. Over there. Very close. Well quite close. Mike recognised the rock. *The north-going current has carried me with it. Towards the rock. I forgot about the currents.*

Mike adjusted his direction, turned again to paddle backwards which was easier, and again started to blow the whistle.

The sea state was easing all the time and he could see around him more often. The rock was much nearer. *Two hours. I will reach it. I will. I will. Will I be able to get on to it? I might just be smashed against it by the swell. No choice. I have no choice.*

Mike kept on paddling in the general direction of the rock. Suddenly his mind screamed. *Tide. Which way is the current flowing? At what time does it turn? Oh! Please no! If it turns south before I reach the rock I will never make it. I will be swept away.*

He swam a little more quickly trying to keep panic from taking over. He whistled less frequently. He didn't want to look again. He couldn't bear the thought of drifting away from the rock. The rock had assumed the position of saviour. *The sound of waves breaking is closer, clearer, isn't it? Just keep trying.*

His shoulders ached. He kept telling himself not to waste energy, but he was so close. He stopped using his arms and let his hands trail and just kicked with his legs.

The whistle had dropped from his lips. He picked it up, whistled twice and kept going.

Tiredness was winning and taking over. He gave in and looked. The rock was no nearer. In fact it was probably further away. He stopped, and pulled his legs up. *Just rest. Just a little rest. No more effort. Mars bar. I have a Mars bar.*

With great difficulty he reached under his jacket which was stiff with the life jacket and found the Mars bar. He fished it out. Being so tightly pressed in his pocket it was dry and the wrapper intact. He tore it open and bit. *Heaven. It tastes unimaginably good.*

It was then he saw the jellyfish. Normally he would have rushed away from the Portuguese man o' war, but this time he watched it. Somehow it was reassuring. Then he noticed the long tentacles streaming out with the current. He was going the wrong way now.

Don't fall asleep. He forced his mind into action.

His thoughts drifted to his ex-wife. *Is it so unreasonable to expect her to enjoy the same things I want? Surely the constant changes and excitement of the hotel business is enough. Other people bring up children in hotels. Don't they?* He searched and searched the recesses of his mind but he was unable to recall anyone he knew who was in the trade and had children.

Think! Who are these people – Mairread and Sean? Have they been watching us for a long time? Why do they hate me enough to leave me here?

It was too tiring to swim. He held his hands up and saw the white wrinkled skin. He forced his hands into his pockets and lay still. He was beginning to be cold and could hardly feel his lower legs and feet. The sun had moved into the west and the daylight displayed an orange hue. Mike closed his eyes to ease the stinging of the salt, and gave a long blast on the whistle.

His thoughts again drifted off to the hotel. *It isn't all hard work. Craig, Karen and others come up for weekends in the off season when business is slack. She always enjoys that. I'm not demanding sexually, and she doesn't often make an approach. We both got enough, didn't we?*

Pictures, clearer than he could ever before recall floated in and out of his mind's vision. Images that he hadn't thought of for years. Clear scenes of his mother and father which he couldn't remember ever seeing in photographs. Holidays with parents and Craig. On the beach. A vivid picture of a railway carriage. Craig was there and his father always produced a small notebook with sketches of all the places the train passed through and little stories to go with them. They huddled together at the carriage window, each trying to be first to spot the next place in the notebook, and yells, he could almost hear them, as one or other saw the place mentioned.

Mike opened his eyes and looked around. The sea was calm, almost ripple free with only the slightest of swell. Beside him was a plastic bag. He manoeuvred himself over to it, and grabbed it by the handle. There was a newspaper and rubbish in it and he pulled out the newspaper. The bag filled with water, gurgled and sank out of sight.

He peered at the paper. It was only the front and back sheets of the *Herald*. His eyes stung from the salt but he peered closely at the page. The words Starr, Lewinski, Clinton, jumped off the page at him and he let forth a loud raucous laugh. *Here am I drowning, and reading a newspaper.*

As he was about to crush the paper he noted a small section on the inner front page.

'Major Initiative to Curb Drug Smuggling on the West Coast.'

Out loud he said, 'I wish they were a bit nearer to catching them. I wouldn't be in this goddamn mess.'

He tried to read more but his stinging eyes were defeated by the failing light. He screwed the paper into a ball and laid it on the surface of the sea. He watched it drift alongside him. A gentle push and the ball bobbled away only to slowly return to his side. Each time he pushed it a little further and it returned until a whisper of breeze enfolded the paper ball and sailed it off out of sight.

It was as though he had said 'goodbye' to a friend and he felt alone as the gentle darkness that was June crept over from the islands and the sea took on a black and silver sheen. Looking landward he could make out what he was sure were the lights of cottages in the harbour at Eriskay. *Too far to swim.* Tiredness made his neck ache, but he remembered the whistle and he blew until the desperately distorting sound died away on the night air.

He lay back. It was cold. He couldn't feel his feet and he felt sick. He closed his eyes and it felt warmer.

The two fishermen in the small powerful lobster boat from Eriskay were laying another string of pots. 'That's a whistle. I'm sure I heard a whistle earlier too.'

The taller of the two looked over his shoulder and laughed, 'After last night you've probably got a permanent whistle in your head.'

'I'm serious.'

'Who the hell would have a whistle out here? Go on. Tell me that.'

'I don't know, but before we go in I think we should have a listen again with the engine off.'

The soft island lilt did not easily convey a serious urgency but enough of the concern came through for the tall man to say, 'OK. I'm knackered but just a few minutes then we head home.' He stepped into the small wheelhouse and stopped the powerful diesel engine.

The two men stood with their backs to the wheelhouse and smoked in silence, and stared at the wonderful panorama of stars overhead. Neither would admit to it but despite the hard life and the poor returns especially in the wild winter it was at times like this they knew why they were still on the island.

The smaller man turned towards the cabin. 'I wish we could eat thon stars. Let's go.'

'Och, just look at that.'

He turned to see his mate pointing out to seaward. 'What is it?'

'Look there. That's not one of our buoys. The orange one. Now who the fuck is dropping them right off here. Let's go and see.'

The engine roared into life spitting a stream of warm water and steam from its exhaust and swung in a tight arc towards the buoy to pull alongside only seconds later.

As the smaller man came out from the wheelhouse he started to see his partner begin to pull the body of a man over the side.

'It's OK mate. You are going to be OK. You are safe now.'

Mike woke to hear the words and looked up only to see the stars. He turned his head towards the sound and could only see darkness. A large black shape cut out all the light. 'Oh God,' he cried out.

'No no, lad, just call me Jamie. My mate here is Charlie.'

Mike focused his sore eyes and saw the bearded, smiling face and the large strong hands reaching for him, hands that went under his shoulders and pulled. He was aware of a second man grabbing his legs and dragging him over the gunwale. He collapsed into a seated position and looked up.

The reassuring lilt of Jamie's voice penetrated the tired brain, 'Welcome aboard. Funny time of day to be going for a swim.'

The smaller man appeared with a mug of hot soup, a foil blanket and heavy quilted jacket. The surge of power nearly tipped the soup from the cup but Mike tried to smile and cupped his hands around the mug. 'Thank you. Thank you. Thank you,' whispered from his swollen lips.

The bearded man tried to get a few answers from Mike but quickly realised there was something peculiar about the situation. 'I'm off to call some help for you.'

He entered the wheelhouse and picked up the handset of the VHF telephone. 'Funny there's been no Mayday, isn't it? These damn yachties are usually never off the radio.'

'How do you know he's off a yacht?'

'Who else would have gear like that, and anyway I think that's what he was trying to tell me.'

'Stornoway Coastguard, Stornoway Coastguard, this is Eriskay Mary, Eriskay Mary. I have a casualty and require immediate assistance. Over.'

Shortly after Mike was able to sit and watch as the boat surged up

Lochboisdale to pull into the small harbour behind the ro-ro terminal where a military ambulance with blue flashing light was waiting. Two soldiers quickly descended to the boat and helped Mike up to the quayside and into the ambulance. A young man with short cropped hair and wearing a leather jacket looked down at the two fishermen. 'You did a great job. We will be in touch.'

The big man started. 'And who are you,' but his words were wasted as the young man turned away and jumped into the ambulance which rapidly disappeared westwards along the road to Daliburgh and Benbecula.

'Oh well, Charlie this must be worth a pint or two. Let's get home now.'

With that the small fishing boat swung away from the harbour and headed back to sea and only the wake was left shimmering in the night light.

Mike sat on the ambulance seat whilst a doctor checked his pulse and blood pressure. The young man opposite smiled at him. 'From here on you can enjoy this. I have quite a lot to tell you.'

CHAPTER XIII

THE DIESEL ENGINE fired first spin and as Alan hauled the anchor clear of the water, Mairread engaged the drive and Wizard eased her way back down the channel.

'Down below. You for'ard, and you aft,' said Sean pointing the gun at Alan and Craig alternately. They obliged.

It was just before midnight. Craig listened for indications of what was happening and wondered how Alan was feeling. He kept having thoughts about Mike. *What if he is still floating out there.* Every time he would shake off thoughts of Mike, fear for Karen took over. *If they are as casual about death as they have been with Mike what will they do to her?*

Mairread can't really be as cruel. I think I know her. She is soft, warm, loving. She really must have thought Mike was dead. Or did she wait until Sean had overcome Alan before turning back? Was one man less just that much less trouble? He went into the heads and was sick, then lay down on the bed.

Mairread entered the cabin with a bowl of hot soup and bread. 'Eat this. I thought I heard you being sick. You can't go on like this.'

Craig sat up and supped the soup. Mairread had cleaned up. She was wearing one of his shirts and looked lovely. 'Why didn't you send a Mayday?'

'The others would have got to us first. They couldn't be far away. If they had reached us we would all be dead. If they could make contact with us they would be able to use your wife to try to influence you. They wouldn't care whether or not you could do anything to help. They would use her anyway. Just think what effect that would have on you, but more importantly think of the effect on her.'

Craig was tired and although he couldn't see why they would want to influence him it seemed an acceptable answer. Mairread removed the bowl, but returned immediately. She lay down beside him and pulled him to her. 'You don't think I could let your friend just die out there, do you? We really had no alternative, and I

109

really believe he was killed outright by that blow to the head.' As her lips kissed him Craig felt very tired and he fell asleep almost instantly.

He awoke about an hour later, just as Sean unblocked the cabin door and said, 'You can come on deck now if you like.' He had not been aware of Mairread leaving the cabin.

Along with Alan he climbed on deck and looked around, trying to work out where they were and in which direction they were sailing. A traditional West Coast drizzle was falling, the atmosphere was heavy and visibility was very poor. He could see no sign of land on either side even though the June night was really almost over. 'Where are we going now?' he enquired, turning to Mairread who was almost hidden by the high collar of her waterproofs.

'You'll just have to guess for a while,' she laughed, and to his surprise she leaned forward and kissed him on the cheek.

They were all wearing warm jackets in the damp night air, and Craig sat at the stern with his back against the life raft. Alan had made cups of Bovril and had returned below with Sean. Craig's mind drifted to Karen and the pictures of her as she dressed to go to the SEC meetings were sharp. She had brightened considerably over the last few months and there had been moments when he had wondered about another man. She had never shown any deep interest in other men although she fitted into male company very well, and he shrugged off these fleeting thoughts.

The lovemaking which had always been so important when it had been hurriedly enjoyed while the children were occupied had become much less frequent although more time had been available with the children grown up and away from home. More importantly though, he was conscious that just touching had become something of a rarity, and although they still talked about the same things, previously intimate chats were less frequent and less protracted. The long discussions they had had were ended and were now little more than an exchange of comments.

Karen, in the silken white nightdresses she loved, still walked slowly before him, but the desire to be part of her had disappeared. He still loved her but the all-consuming interest that they had experienced and which saw them through the bad patches when he had been regularly away from home, when the baby cried all night, and one of the children had been ill, had gone. She was still lovely,

110

but it was different. He couldn't quite decide what had changed, but it surely was different.

Memories of the days when they were newly-weds came to the fore. He saw them walk hand in hand on the shore, and remembered drives to the West Coast to the boat, which was much smaller and intimate than Wizard. The pictures all jumped about creating shifting images of warmth, laughter, tears and excitement.

He recalled one evening he had returned late from London when Karen, in a way most unlike her, undressed and lay on the bed in a provocative pose, hands behind her head thrusting her small breasts up and with her legs apart. He shuddered as he remembered saying, 'I'm just going to shower. I'll be back in a minute.' *How could I have been so cruel, so selfish?*

When he had returned to the bedroom Karen had put on her nightdress and was facing away from him. They had both gone to sleep.

Craig shuddered again. He was feeling very chilled. He looked up to see Mairread smiling at him. 'I thought you had gone to sleep,' she said.

'No. Just thinking.'

'I think we need a hot drink.'

Craig went below, put on the kettle and soon reappeared with two cups of coffee. As he handed the cup to her he leaned forward and kissed her lips so gently but as she didn't pull away the kiss increased in passion until Mairread jumped back. 'Ouch. That coffee is hot.'

They both laughed as Craig looked down to see the coffee swilling gently over the edge of his cup in sweet accord with the swell of the sea.

Craig perched on the coach roof alongside Mairread. He couldn't stop himself running his hand up and down her back. 'How will this end?' he mused.

'How do you want it to end?'

'I don't know. I'm confused. I can't remember feeling like this before. I suppose I hope it will end with us being together but that doesn't seem possible.'

'I don't think it is possible. At best we may be able to meet sometimes but that may be too dangerous. Let's just enjoy each other now. The future is far too difficult to see at the moment.'

Craig felt an intense sense of loss. A desperation was killing the joy of being with her. He fought hard to bring the happiness to the surface but a tightness in his chest and the thought of never seeing her again kept sinking him down again and he sighed loudly.

Mairread sensed his trouble, switched on the Autohelm and put her arms around him. 'There is no point in sitting there feeling like that.'

She kissed him but he couldn't respond. He felt as though life was ending. She kissed him again and there were tears in his eyes.

'Wait a minute,' she whispered, and peering down below shouted, 'Sean, Alan. Take over here.'

After a couple of minutes two bleary-eyed individuals arrived on deck. 'Everything OK?' said Sean.

'Yes. Carry on as we agreed.'

Mairread tugged at Craig's jacket and they went below. It just seemed right to go to the aft cabin and without removing any clothes they lay on the large berth, holding each other as tightly as possible, kissing gently but saying nothing.

Slowly the caressing became more adventurous and Craig was just aware of Mairread unfastening his trousers. His mind crashed into wakefulness as his emotions thrashed their way between horror and embarrassment as he realised that there was no response.

'Oh God. Oh God. I'm sorry,' he mumbled.

'Hey, take it easy. It's been a tough spell.'

They lay close, still kissing gently and slowly he became only aware of how much he loved her, until without realising how it happened he felt himself enter her and everything seemed perfect.

On deck, Alan sat in the corner of the cockpit, unable from that position to see the compass, and Sean stood by the wheel. The Autohelm was still working and there was little to do except keep lookout.

Alan struggled to make up his mind where they were and which direction they were going in. He was sure they had turned north immediately after leaving Lochboisdale but it was difficult from down below to be absolutely sure of the turns of the boat. There were good reasons why they could have gone either way but his instinct favoured north up the Minch, as, if Mairread was right and they were being chased, there were many more opportunities to hide than if they were forced into the open sea further south.

Thoughts of Mike made him furious and he failed to understand the coupling that instinctively he knew was taking place below deck when he thought of Karen being held by unknown people. He suddenly realised that he was scowling at Sean, who, in turn, was peering quizzically at him. He remembered vividly the pain Sean had inflicted when they had tangled on the deck and vowed to pay him back just as soon as the opportunity presented itself. The memory of the steel pipe thudding onto Sean's head and shoulders did provide some recompense. The time just had to be right. Alan's lack of physical exercise had not left him especially active and he did not relish the thought of another tussle.

Also, the bulge of the gun projecting from Sean's jacket was a fairly convincing argument at the moment. Sean had to be more occupied before he would try again.

Alan smiled at Sean who smiled back, a little mystified but saying nothing. Alan subsided into the corner. The wind had all but died and Sean started the diesel and the throb of the engine had a soporific effect compounded by the effect of several large whiskies.

As he dozed Alan recalled the excitement he had felt when his appointment as Buying Director had been followed by a 20 per cent uplift in sales as his new ranges hit the departments. He recalled the congratulations from his colleagues for the successes, and the memory of his worried anticipation at the board meeting when he was being pressed for a justification of a sales slump well out of his control.

Sylvia's response was predictable. 'Just think about it, darling. You will come up with an answer.'

Jesus. How stupid. I had thought and thought for bloody hours. How could she make such an inane remark when our very life depended on it.

He found himself again contemplating launching himself at Sean but yet again thought better of it.

Alan consoled himself by watching the Uist, Benbecula, Harris and Skye coasts slowly appearing and tried to spot the landing places of Bonnie Prince Charlie. He had read the history of the uprising and was well through Eric Linklater's *A Prince in the Heather.* It was hard to appreciate the problems encountered rowing a boat around the Minch and even harder to understand why the English frigates had failed to find them. The Minch seemed quite wide even on a good day and a long slow row. Visions of roughly garbed highlanders nursing Culloden injuries and the fear and mistrust felt by the Pretender was not hard to envisage under present circumstances.

Below deck Mairread and Craig lay kissing and talking. The noise from the engine compartment had killed off the remaining passion.

'Why did you abandon Mike? You seem a very sensitive woman.'

'I told you. The bang on the head must have finished him, and the danger to us and your wife is immense. It would have been too dangerous for too many of us to have hung around there any longer than we did.'

How do you know that? Craig wasn't wholly satisfied with the repeated answer which did not meet all the doubts in his mind but the strength of his feeling for Mairread drove the unresolved questions into the mire of the mind where questions he would rather not ask lay buried.

Mairread sat up tidying her clothes. 'We must go on deck. I want to check the approach to our next anchorage.'

'Where is it?'

'Wait and see. It won't be long now.'

They went on deck after Mairread had read the GPS. Craig was unable to see the reading but did notice that they were still using a Minch chart. Once on deck they encountered a less misty situation and as the sun brightened the sky and burned off the thin cloud Craig was convinced that he could now clearly make out land on both hands. *Yes,* he thought, *we're still travelling north up the Minch.*

He wandered forward and was joined by Alan. 'Where are we going?'

Craig shook his head. 'I don't know. I don't know,' he muttered irritably.

Alan's crop of fair hair was unusually dishevelled and his boyish features were drawn and grey.

'By the way. I forgot to mention it before but when you were ashore on Eriskay Sean gave the aft cabin a good going over under the pretext of his restarting the engine. I don't know why.'

'Mm. He may suspect we had something to do with the engine failure. If he was thorough he probably noticed the kink in the exhaust hose.'

Shortly afterwards they changed course and Craig recognised the islands and the land form with the high lighthouse of Uisnish. 'Loch Skiport. That's where we are going.'

They both returned to the cockpit.

As they dropped sail and motored in, Mairread lifted the VHF handset and called, 'Stornoway Radio, Stornoway Radio, this is Wizard, Wizard. One link call please. Over.' She had switched off the speaker and the responses were inaudible. 'Our position is 3042WI. No trouble, but we need a rest and this se_ms a suitable spot with no obvious housing.' There was a silence while she listened. 'I see. Mmm. Understood. Out.'

They sailed on into the bay and past the fish farm, turning sharply to port and into the Wizard Pool.

'I named the boat after this pool,' smiled Craig. 'It is such a magical place and I love to come here. You've chosen a good spot as there are two ways in and out.'

'Just put it down to Irish luck,' laughed Mairread.

Craig felt sure that it had not been luck at all. He was absolutely certain she had known precisely where they were going and what conditions existed there. However, the sun was now warming the air and he felt very tired.

'Craig. You and Alan go and rest in the aft cabin. Sean you have a break. I will take the first watch.'

No-one argued. They just went below and fell asleep almost instantly.

Craig awoke to find Alan looking out of the window.

'You know we are not far from the shore. If one of us distracted them the other would almost certainly make it to the shore, and what with the rocks and bracken it should be possible to escape.'

'Never,' retorted Craig, 'They would shoot you long before you could reach cover.'

'Not with the pea-shooters they've got,' scorned Alan. 'Anyway Sean didn't shoot me on Eriskay.' He was careful not to mention the jammed gun, as he tried to needle Craig. It annoyed him that Craig had made no obvious effort to escape.

'Christ! You are such a bloody expert. You just know fucking everything. Don't you? There is no way we could distract two people with guns long enough for one of us to swim far enough away from the boat to avoid being shot.'

'I'm not sure you want to get away. You are infatuated with that Irish bitch, and we'll end up being killed to please your cock.'

Craig swung his fist at Alan but Alan, who had been resting his head in his hand, let his head fall out of the way so that Craig's fist smashed into the cabin bulkhead and he yelped.

They both burst out laughing.

'You are right. You are right. We must make an attempt to get away, but seriously, I don't think it is here or now.'

'Probably,' mused Alan, 'But we must stay alert.'

'Agreed.'

At that moment the door opened. 'What are you two finding so bloody funny,' scowled Sean.

'This,' said Craig, holding up his grazed fist.

Sean just scowled more deeply and shook his head in puzzlement. 'There's something to eat out here. Come and get it.'

Craig and Alan entered the saloon to be met by the smell of a rich stew.

'Help yourself.'

Sean hoisted himself up to sit at the top of the companionway steps so that he could see the bay and his charges at the same time.

Craig helped Alan and then himself to a large plateful of stew, noticed the two cans of beer left for them, said 'Thanks,' and wondered why Mairread had gone to sleep forward without saying anything to him.

The sky was darkening slowly but at that time it often barely got really dark, and sometimes it stayed light enough to read all night.

When they had eaten Craig and Alan sat drinking their beers until Sean looked down at them, and with a sideways nod of his head said, 'Back into the cabin. And keep quiet. I don't like the noise you make.'

Despite the afternoon sleep, exhaustion took over and Craig and Alan again fell asleep quickly but just before he drifted off Craig was sure he heard noises in the boat which he assumed was Mairread and Sean changing over, but she did not come for him.

CHAPTER XIV

It WAS WELL INTO Tuesday afternoon when the radio message came in. Wizard had been spotted anchored in Acairseid Mhor on Eriskay.

'Patrick, Patrick,' shouted Mark. 'We must get going now. You navigate. This is your home country.'

Patrick went slowly to the wheelhouse and pored over the charts and the tide tables. He struggled to think of a way of delaying the pursuit as he hoped that Irish Rascal was now either alongside Wizard or very close to Eriskay.

Eventually, when he felt further delay would arouse suspicion he gave the orders to raise the anchor and Fast Lady motored out of the pool into a violently choppy sea. Patrick throttled back to avoid the bow burying itself in the steep sea as water broke over the wheel house. Corryvreckan wasn't going to let them go without teaching them a little of why it had its fearsome reputation.

Bernie immediately started clearing up the debris of drinks and food in the saloon while the others went on deck and to the wheelhouse. They had been drinking for some time but Patrick noticed that they were all still carrying guns.

Mark turned to Switch. 'Make sure the lady can't cause any trouble while we are at sea.' Switch lurched aft.

All day Patrick's thoughts had turned to Karen. He was desperate to ask how she was, but didn't want to show too much interest. However, he noted that she was sent food and drink. He didn't like the idea of Switch going to the aft cabin with it but as there was no sound he settled down to wait for a real opportunity.

His first preoccupation had been to delay Fast Lady as long as possible and to formulate his reaction when they realised that the yacht wasn't coming. They would almost certainly have to go and look for it and he knew that the cargo was so big they would do everything possible to locate it.

Patrick knew that Jimmy normally helmed Fast Lady but he did not know the West Coast of Scotland, and under these circumstances they were bound to ask him to navigate. With a heavy sea running he

117

would go along the south coast of Mull, via the Torran Rocks and the Sound of Iona, and for safety that area would have to be negotiated slowly. With a bit of luck the sea state would be sufficiently rough to slow them down. If they went north via the Sound of Mull it would be relatively calm and they could motor at full speed.

Fast Lady wasn't a fast boat and he felt he could delay her long enough for Irish Rascal which could do up to 30 knots to be well clear. As they came out from the eerie stillness of Corryvreckan he handed the wheel back to Jimmy. 'Keep her on that heading and wake me when we are about half a mile from the Torran Rocks. You can read the GPS, can't you?' looking pointedly at Jimmy, and Jimmy with a look that could have killed just nodded.

'I could do with some sleep. Where can I lie down?'

'Port side forward cabin,' said Mark.

'Careful you don't turn the wrong way,' jeered Switch. 'You might wake up sleeping beauty.'

Patrick ignored the comment and went below.

The port cabin was a narrow affair with twin bunks and a small wardrobe. Patrick looked in and then opened the door to the other cabin. He quietly stepped inside and walked round to look down at Karen whose eyes were closed. He felt the tightening of his chest and a speeding up of his heart. She was trussed up with her hands behind her back and tied to her feet. Another rope ran from her feet through the rope around her hands and round her neck. He turned and moved quietly back to the door.

'Patrick.' He turned. 'I think I am glad to see you. Can you get me out of this?' she asked.

'I hope so, but you will just have to wait until I tell you what to do. Did they hurt you?'

'Not really. I am afraid they will though, if they get the chance,' she whispered.

'Get some rest now if you can. I don't think anything will happen just now.' Patrick, pursed his lips in a kiss. He opened the door and went to his cabin, reassured.

Karen felt relieved and smiled to herself at the memory of the blown kiss. She snuggled down and despite her discomfort and bewilderment, tried to sleep.

A telephone caller, quoting a recognised code, to the Coastguard at

Oban enquired if they knew the whereabouts of a pleasure boat called Fast Lady. The Coastguard said that they hadn't heard any radio traffic but would report anything heard.

Patrick was wakened by a knock on the door. Bernie stood there. 'Jimmy says he needs you.'

'Right. I'll be up in a moment.'

In the wheelhouse Jimmy stood alone. 'We are close to the rocks now,' he said. There was a thick haze which made distances difficult to estimate. Patrick took the reading from the GPS and plotted it on the chart.

'Damn you. We're in the rocks, never mind near them.'

Fortunately Jimmy had maintained a fairly accurate course, and Patrick was able to make a sharp turn to starboard and take the big boat through the rocks past the concrete pillar on one of the few clear passages so it wasn't long before they were entering the Sound of Iona.

Mark appeared in the saloon. 'Show me where we are.'

Jimmy pointed to the position on the chart.

'What the hell are we doing here? Surely we should be in the Sound of Mull.'

Patrick had been waiting for this moment. 'The Sound of Mull is far too busy. We are much less likely to be seen coming this way. And there is nothing in it as far as distance goes.' He was surprised how controlled and confident he sounded.

'That takes some believing, but I'll take your word for it.'

They had encountered a large swell with an unpleasant chop on top of it all the way out from Crinan, and the speed had been well down, but Patrick felt he had no option but to open up the engines and start motoring. He hoped that the others had made good time from South Jura. They motored on past Staffa and out towards Coll with Switch and Bernie feeling distinctly unwell as the boat corkscrewed down the waves which increased dramatically as they cleared the sound.

Progress was very uncomfortable as they motored across the south-westerly swell, past Staffa and the Dutchman's Cap, and on to the Sound of Gunna. Patrick stared across at Fingal's cave and noted the huge white spray that threatened the cliffs as the waves broke on the rocks. Landing to visit the cave would not be possible today.

Patrick smiled inwardly as every so often Bernie and Switch passed through the wheelhouse to stand outside taking deep breaths, before returning inside with an over-emphasised casualness. The secret, however, was leaked by the colourless faces and the grey blue bags under their eyes.

'Nothing quite like a good chop to make sailing interesting, is there?'

The forced smiles on their faces as they nodded their agreement was very satisfying.

Mark asked Patrick to put in a VHF call to Wizard as they cleared the Sound of Gunna but there was no response. After several tries Patrick declared. 'They must be shielded by the island.'

The Coastguard on watch at Oban remembered the previous enquiry for Fast Lady, noted the call, and then remembered a report from a Customs vessel checking that a yacht named Wizard had been in touch the day before. Apparently the yacht had intended to return to Castlebay but must have been caught up in the storm. *Is there any relationship between the two vessels and the two enquiries? Why are the security services interested?* He turned to consult the watch leader.

The rest of the passage was extremely unpleasant as they motored across the lumpy unpredictable Sea of the Hebrides, and there was a feeling of tension. Patrick noted that they were all carrying guns and felt the reassuring bulge under his sweater. Somehow only Bernie was actually seasick but Switch obviously didn't enjoy the passage too much.

The Outer Isles remained shrouded in haze right up to dusk and it wasn't until they were close inshore, with the leading lights of Eriskay clearly visible, that it became possible to discern the heights of South Uist to the north-west and similar hills on Barra to the south-west.

Approaching slowly and with care, Patrick, who was on the helm with Mark alongside him, toyed with the idea of putting the boat on the rocks at the entrance to the harbour. They weren't too obvious and he felt he could do it without it appearing to be intentional although he was surprised to find that perches had been erected on most of the more dangerous rocks. *Karen might be hurt. None of us might get ashore.* He rejected the idea and headed close to the south-west headland and into the bay. Wizard was not there. Three fishing boats were alongside the pier discharging their catches.

'Where the hell are they? There are no yachts here.'

'I think they must have been here and left again. But why? They should have reported. I suppose they may have been picked up, but Bernie would have logged the radio traffic. OK. Just anchor in a bit while I try to find out what has happened.'

Patrick motored the big powerboat into the anchorage and Switch dropped the anchor.

As soon as they were secure, Mark disappeared to his cabin muttering about making phone calls to find out what the hell was happening. The others settled down in the saloon.

The chat became quite amiable, then Jimmy piped up, 'Hey, Switch, can I go check that bitch now. Just to see she's all right and remind her we're watching. I'm due her one.'

'No. Forget it. I'll go and check her.' Switch ambled off.

He opened the cabin door and laughed at the sight of Karen's predicament. 'Please. I'm choking,' croaked Karen.

'Well, we can't have that. We all seem to want to have some fun with you before this trip is done. You should really end up getting your share all right.' He eased the main rope slightly and Karen breathed more easily. His hands strayed to the elastic waistband of her trousers, pulled them and her pants down to expose her small bottom and then gave it an almighty smack. Karen gave out a howl that was heard in the saloon. Patrick jumped up and stormed aft, getting only a glimpse of Karen's predicament before Switch closed the door. 'Only a friendly pat, mate,' he smirked, pushing Patrick back to the saloon. 'Got a soft spot, or maybe a hard spot, for the little lady has Patrick, lads.'

Mark had returned to the saloon, 'So I've noticed,' he said. 'Don't get too attached to her Pat. She's my version of the ship's mistress. Bernie, I want you to keep a listening watch. Let me know if you pick up any transmissions from our friends.'

Patrick laughed and sat down but felt sick and cold. Fortunately no-one appeared to notice as they all went on drinking. Mark had again gone to contact the London associates.

'What's the position then, Guv?' enquired Switch as Mark re-entered the saloon.

'London doesn't know. They are trying their contacts, but they are suspicious. We just sit tight and wait.'

They had been drinking only for a short time when Bernie came in.

'I picked up this message. I don't understand it but it sounds like the yacht's position. 2731WI.'

'It doesn't mean anything to me,' said Mark. 'What about you, Patrick?'

'It certainly isn't chart co-ordinates around here. It must be a prearranged code. I'll think about it.'

At around three in the morning the gathering broke up with Bernie and Jimmy told to share the watch until morning. As Switch left the saloon he spoke to Mark. 'I think we should keep the lady on this boat. It will give us just a little extra edge. Pat is behaving strangely. I'm certain we could have made better time from Crinan.'

'I intended to anyway. I've rather grown to like her.'

Switch scowled and went on his way.

Patrick lay on his berth and listened for any movement. The boat had quietened down very quickly, but he could hear nothing. He slipped quietly out of his cabin, listened but heard only snoring, and stepped into the starboard cabin, and immediately untied Karen. 'Do you think you can swim ashore?' he queried.

'My hands are numb,' replied Karen.

'Here, massage them and your arms like this.' Patrick then stood on the bed and unscrewed the catches on the roof hatch which had not been locked. He inched it open and looked around but there was no-one on the after deck. He dropped back down. 'How are you now?' he inquired.

'Better. I think I should be OK.' Karen suddenly realised that rather a lot was visible and grabbed for her clothes, pulling them up.

Despite the circumstances Patrick chuckled, and said, 'With reactions like that you'll be just fine.'

Karen blushed and then smiled at him.

'Come on. Let's get on with it,' whispered Patrick. He helped her through the hatch then crossed to the stern, down the boarding ladder and into the water.

The short swim was accomplished without difficulty, illuminated by the light spilling from the powerful floodlights on the pier, and once ashore they left the narrow road and set off up the hill. Despite the clear June evening they stumbled and fell regularly, but the outlines of the hills were visible as shades of grey. Remaining close to the shore they came across a grass track that led to a dilapidated cottage being used as a farm shed. Patrick could see that Karen was struggling. He would have liked to have gone further but it was out of the question.

'This will do. It's unlikely they will look for us for long as they are bound to be worried that we may have found help. Hopefully they will clear out without trying too hard to find us.' Patrick hoped he sounded more convincing than he felt. He forced the lock as carefully as he could and they almost fell inside.

Karen just dropped into the corner and Patrick sat down beside her. 'I'm sorry I got you into this mess, but I will get you out of it.'

Karen was shaking and he put his arm around her. 'You do at least seem to be trying,' Karen smiled, gave him a kiss on the cheek, and lay down.

Patrick put his arm over her, pulled her towards him and they both fell asleep.

At Crinan a large, fast powerboat was misfiring and blowing clouds of smoke as the crew worked to change filters and drain the diesel tanks. Irish Rascal was still trying to clear her pipes of the filthy diesel that had filled her tanks.

CHAPTER XV

PATRICK WOKE, glanced at his watch, noon, they had slept for nine hours. He raised himself on one elbow and looked at Karen. He saw the small laughter lines at the side of her eyes, the slightly curved nose, and her lovely mouth. He leaned forward and kissed her lightly. He felt again that desire to melt into her, to be so close that they were just one person. The knowledge that he had to return to Fast Lady annoyed him, but first he would get Karen to safety.

Karen opened her eyes to see the blue smiling eyes of Patrick, the soft wavy brown hair falling over his forehead, and reached up for him. She pulled him down against her and they kissed gently, their tongues playing games with each other. Patrick kissed her nose and then her eyes before running his lips along her forehead and down to her ear. He heard her moan and he whispered, 'I love you.' She felt Patrick gently caress her breasts, then lower his mouth to kiss them through the sweater. She felt that same hot feeling again, but did not resist as he pulled the sweater over her head, reached around her and undid her bra and allowed his lips and tongue to tease her nipples until they stood proud of her breasts. She trembled as her small firm breast was swallowed into Patrick's mouth, and he pulled her hard against him. Patrick pulled his shirt off and they held each other so tightly she could hardly breathe. They crushed against each other as though their bodies could merge, as though they could generate sufficient power to create a mighty human fusion.

Patrick had never wanted to please someone so much and yet for the first time he needed help. He didn't want to rush her but at the same time he wanted to know all of her, and wanted to feel her hold him tight. He moved his hands down her ribs into the hollow of her waist and down over her thighs. His right hand slipped up between her legs and over her stomach up to her breasts and there was no resistance. His lips and teeth teased her eyes, nose, ears and neck before tugging gently at her nipples. The elastic waistband of her trousers slid evenly as she lifted herself to allow him to pull down the restricting clothes.

Patrick was annoyed with himself as the bundle of pants and trousers stuck and he had to pull hard to slip them over her feet. He was sure he had broken the spell, but she smiled and kissed him lightly. His fingers roamed through the soft hair and found the warm moist softness of her sheath. He pulled her close, cupping his hand around the small firm buttocks, his fingers teasing that small sensitive spot between her thighs.

Karen gasped and allowed the shaking and clutching to increase. She wanted him further into her and shuddered as one finger thrust hard while the others probed and caressed all the sensitive spots around the secret openings.

Karen wanted to be closer and closer to him. Her hands found the hook and zip on his trousers and undid them. She pushed them down, quickly followed by his shorts and reached between his legs. It seemed so right to hold him. She had never touched or looked at anyone other than Craig, and the flush which covered her when she stroked him, gripped him tightly, and feeling him stiffen was like nothing she had experienced before.

'My darling, it's yours, only yours.'

'Yes. Yes. I love you.' Words that away from the passion would sound so superficial; words she had never thought she could say to any other man flowed out. 'Now please. Please love me.'

Patrick was surprised she was so ready. He lowered himself between her legs and her hand which had never left him gripped him tightly and thrust him into her body. She gasped and wrapped her arms and slim legs around him and he responded with a desperation to please her.

Karen could not maintain her normal calm and her cries became louder and more intense as she tried to get him deeper and deeper into her body. She thrust upwards against him until she shook violently with a frantic release of tension and crushed him to herself.

Patrick eased his weight from her and kissed her face gently. 'God, I love you. I need nothing but you,' he said.

Karen looked up, straight into his blue eyes, and saw the love shining there. 'That was wonderful. I love you too.' Patrick moved slowly and gently, his weight off Karen until she closed her eyes and moved with him. Steadily she responded until he stiffened and an urgency took over and again she pulled him hard into her. 'Now, please, now,' she cried out and gasped as she felt him drive hard into her body, feeling the surge of semen as he collapsed onto her. They lay tightly bound together, saying nothing but Karen felt the slow withdrawal and was confused by the mixture of happiness and sadness, pleasure and exhaustion.

The warmth of the sun broke through parts of the roof. 'You know, I love Craig. He has done everything for me. I can't understand how I can love two men so differently. I don't think I could ever leave him, but I can't even think about losing you. Is that selfish?'

Patrick was quiet. He looked closely at her. 'I can't help you. I love you too much to give you an objective answer. I think you may be confusing habit with love and living. I suspect that you were looking for new interests and that I may be just part of that. It isn't simple. I just know that I want to be part of your life.'

Karen looked down at Patrick's legs. They were brown and strong, and the hairs were golden in the sun. She reached out and curled her fingers around his penis, slowly but firmly slipping her hand up and down it. She had never watched the change before. The change from soft and gentle to powerful and demanding amazed her. As she felt Patrick's fingers in her hair she leaned forward and slowly kissed his chest, moving slowly down until she was able to look at the swollen organ. The large blue red head seemed to be about to burst and small bubbles of shiny liquid oozed from the small opening. Her tongue enveloped his manhood. She took him slowly at first then more urgently as she felt his response. Sucking, raking her teeth along him she held the precious vessel on her tongue until she felt him shudder, tense and then release himself. Karen could not believe that she had never before wanted to do this but the obvious pleasure Patrick was getting felt wonderful. Patrick shuddered and lay back. They gazed into each other's eyes seeing nothing but wonder until the cool air slowly revived them.

They kissed and dressed and Patrick said, 'Wait here. I must go and see if they are close by. Then I will find help for you.' He looked out of the shed, glanced around then set off back up to the crest of the hill.

Karen lay back and smiled to herself, and then became sombre as she wondered where Patrick was, and what was happening to him. *It sounds as though he intends to leave me here. How could I? I hope I'm not pregnant. God, that was stupid.*

Patrick had been gone some time when Karen decided to look outside. There was no one visible and she walked out in the sun. The

126

island looked lovely and she wanted to see the sea. It must be sparkling in the light. After a few more steps she stopped, turned back to the hut and went inside.

'Hello again.' Her eyes adjusted slowly to the dark inside the hut. Switch was standing pointing a gun at her. 'I hope you enjoyed your walk. Now you are coming back with me.' He stepped forward and grabbed her face in one large hand and kissed her.

'Get away. Get away,' she screamed. Switch just laughed. 'Now get going.'

At the top of the hill Patrick had been lying still watching Fast Lady. They were waiting and the tender was missing. *Had Irish Rascal already rendezvoused with the yacht?* He tried to see who was on board. He had definitely seen Mark and Jimmy, but nobody else had been on deck.

Just at that moment he heard Karen's scream. He jumped up and ran down the hill to the hut, slowing as he approached and dropping into the ferns just short of the entrance. Karen appeared followed by Switch who held a gun. Patrick waited until they were just ahead of him with Switch's back towards him, then stood up and spat out, 'Stop. Don't move an inch or your dead. I hate your guts. Any excuse will do. Drop the gun behind you.'

'I don't think you need to do that, Switch,' came Bernie's voice, and Patrick felt the muzzle of the gun on the back of his head.

A fool, a complete fool. After all the training I rushed straight into the very situation I should have been able to avoid. The anger surging through his head tempted him to lash out and only a flash of insight slowed him enough to march on in silence.

They walked in line back to the harbour and climbed into the dinghy. Switch sat in the bow, Bernie rowed and Patrick and Karen sat in the stern. As they approached Fast Lady, Mark and Jimmy came on deck and watched their progress.

They climbed aboard and whilst Bernie raised the dinghy in the davits the others went below. Nothing was said. Mark looked out of the window for what seemed like an eternity, then turned and looked at Patrick. 'Because I can't think of any other reason I am going to assume that your crazy behaviour is solely as a result of your infatuation with this woman. This had better be the last of these stupid escapades.'

Patrick nodded. 'I was just trying to see her safe.'

Mark had a cynical look. 'That's not your concern. She will be quite safe with us on board.'

Bernie sniggered.

Patrick felt Karen tense. Mark turned to Karen. 'Come with me.' Patrick felt cold. His heart almost stopped, then raced. He had a real fear of Mark, but couldn't think of anything to say. Karen rose and left the saloon in front of Mark.

Switch looked furious. 'I hope the bastard isn't going to keep her to himself. It isn't every day a little lady like that is around. I suppose you got yours when you were ashore?' Patrick's fist connected with Switch's mouth and Switch rolled backwards off the seat: Bernie and Jimmy laughed as Patrick's knees landed in Switch's stomach. Switch gasped and spluttered, 'OK. OK. Forget it. I was only joking.'

Patrick stopped just as he was about to smash his fist down into Switch's face, and the hesitation was enough. Switch's knee came up hard into Patrick's groin and he doubled up. As his head jerked forward Switch's forehead smashed into his nose and Patrick could neither see nor fight as his hands instinctively covered his face. Switch rolled on top of Patrick and launched a vicious barrage of punches into Patrick's stomach. When he realised Patrick wasn't fighting back he drove two fierce blows into Patrick's groin. 'Well, if you didn't get it, you sure won't be wanting it now.'

Switch pulled himself up onto the settee and Jimmy handed him a can of Schlitz. 'Good thinking, Jimmy. I need that. Push that bastard out of the road.'

Jimmy dragged Patrick into the corner of the saloon and they ignored him.

Meanwhile, Mark was showing Karen the delights of his quarters. The cabin was luxurious, with matching carpet, wall coverings, and bed linen. There was a full-size circular bed with an enormous duvet, and around the bed were two wardrobes and several chests of drawers with a dressing table immediately in front of the bed. All the furnishings were in a beautiful polished mahogany, and a TV, CD player and drinks cabinet were neatly housed adjacent to a small bar unit in front of which were four armchairs and a table. He opened a door to the radio room and proudly demonstrated the different radios, weather fax, depth, radar, and Global Positioning System.

'We can record all radio messages transmitted in our vicinity.'

They returned to the cabin and with his arm around her waist he showed her the en suite shower room lavishly fitted out in mahogany and a combination of marble and matching veneers. Mark explained that marble throughout would have been too heavy but it had been used where it had the most effect.

Karen was impressed but afraid, although there was no sign of any underhand intentions from Mark. They heard the noises from the main saloon, but Mark laughed and said, 'The lads seem to be having an altercation. Don't concern yourself. They will soon sort it out.'

He signalled to Karen to sit down, and took a bottle of Lanson champagne from the refrigerator in the bar. He poured two drinks and handed one to Karen. He stood looking out of the window. 'It is a pity that you are involved. I like you. This situation is almost unheard of and most people never know how close they have been to being used like you. Don't worry though. I am sure we will get in contact with the yacht and collect our goods, and then you will again meet your husband. I can't think why they were not here to meet us. Why would they say they were going to be here, and then move? Why are they sending signals to someone else? Has Patrick told you anything?'

He turned from the window and looked straight at Karen.

'No. I was just pleased that he helped me to escape, but he hasn't told me anything.'

Can I believe you, I wonder? 'Patrick fought with George in Liverpool. He brought us out here by a very devious route. At least not by the route which was obvious. Then he helps you to escape. I have no doubt that was him fighting again next door. He has been quite out of character recently.'

Karen said nothing. Mark walked slowly up and down carrying the champagne and occasionally topped up her glass.

Mark looked at the clock and went through to the adjoining radio room and closed the door. Karen heard him speaking but couldn't make out what was being said. She heard the other door to the radio room slam shut and the sound of people rushing on deck.

Mark had burst into the saloon, and given only a glance at Patrick who was sitting hunched in the corner.

'Get a move on. They were seen in Lochboisdale last night. We may be able to catch them if we get this boat going.'

Karen had been forgotten, so she sat down and sipped the champagne.

It was noon and within fifteen minutes the anchor was stowed and

Fast Lady motored out of Big Bay on her way up the Outer Hebrides. A short distance out a helicopter flew overhead and a Coastguard vessel and lifeboat passed them, heading for the mainland. Mark watched anxiously as they passed within half a mile of the Coastguard vessel, but he visibly relaxed when they had moved apart. He wondered what had happened but couldn't see that it could have any bearing on his plans.

They were fast approaching South Uist when Bernie came on deck with another message. 'They were certainly seen in Lochboisdale but must have been aware of that as they left almost immediately, Guv. London want us to go up the islands and keep a lookout for them.'

'Mmm. We will have to locate them before dark or find somewhere to anchor. It would be futile just charging around in the dark.'

'But they wouldn't have to stop. They could just keep going.'

'I know that full well. But what's the alternative?'

The weather which had been misty was improving and Mark took the big boat close inshore without dropping speed.

There are dozens of places they could hide, but they must be trying to reach someone. Who? Why? What the hell has happened? They were supposed to be meeting us. Now they seem to be trying to avoid us. Someone is trying to pick up our cargo. I wonder who? Mark stared hard at the shore. Unless they got more information about the possible position of the yacht they could search forever. They were still making a good 10 knots but Mark felt frustrated.

He stood up. 'Take the wheel, Bernie. George, come with me. I think Pat must know something.'

They went below and Mark pulled Patrick onto a chair by the table. 'Well Patrick, we have been working together for some time now, but this time things seem to be going horribly wrong, and you are behaving very strangely. I don't suppose the two things could be linked. Could they? This is the big one. You wouldn't double cross your friends, would you?'

Patrick was feeling slightly sick, but he managed to smile. 'The way I feel must be much worse than what is happening. I certainly wouldn't want to be blamed for that too.' He tried to laugh but was aware that neither Mark nor Switch were laughing.

'Perhaps you'd like to ask Patrick a few questions.' Mark addressed the statement to Switch, and turned to sit on a settee and look out of the window.

Switch stood in front of Patrick with his fists clenched one on top of the other. Patrick had seen him do it before when he was determined about something, and felt unsure.

'Just so you're not tempted to lie, you should know that we have a record of all of your calls from you car on Monday. Why did you call a Belfast number?' Mark turned only slightly as he spoke.

Patrick wondered if they had dialled the number and decided that it was best to assume that they had. 'A friend at the Glenvalla Bar.'

'That's an IRA haunt.'

'How the hell would you know?' retorted Patrick.

Mark looked round. 'We know,' he said quietly.

'Anyway, I've many friends whose politics I don't know. It isn't always wise to ask questions.'

'It usually is in this business,' retorted Switch.

'OK. What about the call to London?' asked Mark.

'Same thing. But I'll pay for personal calls if you are feeling hard up.'

'Don't be fucking stupid. The London number is special. They just hang up if you don't give the right response. Whose number is it? If it's a friend I'm sure you won't mind telling us. Just so we can check it out.'

'I wouldn't tell you about my enemies, never mind my friends. I don't mix my friends up with my business colleagues. I wouldn't enquire too closely about that number. Just remember the rules of this game. We all have a contact. You just don't know who your guv is.

Switch looked mystified, and turned to Mark, but Mark just walked quietly from the cabin. The silence was only broken by the noise of the boat. Switch stared at Patrick. Patrick stared back but felt very queasy deep down.

After an expectant silence, Mark re-entered the cabin and shook his head in Switch's direction. Patrick looked up in time to take the full force of Switch's fist on the cheek, and before he could recover a second blow hit him just above his left eye. As the haze cleared Patrick saw Switch looking at his slit knuckles, and heard Mark say, 'Don't make a mess here. Get him on deck.'

Jimmy stepped forward and with Switch they dragged Patrick out onto the aft deck. Jimmy tied Patrick's hands behind his back and his ankles together, lowered a davit hook and clamped it around the ankle rope.

They hauled him up and pushed him over the stern rail and suspended him there. 'Lower away,' shouted Switch.

'Wait just a minute,' muttered Mark and vanished below, only to reappear almost immediately with Karen. He held her firmly by her arm in what looked to be a friendly way but there was no doubting the strength of his grip. He positioned them where they could get a clear view of the stern. 'OK. Go ahead.'

Jimmy laughed and he lowered Patrick until his head was just in the surging wash from the stern of the boat.

The blows to the head had left Patrick feeling very dizzy and swinging upside down he retched and thought he was choking. The spray revived him just in time to be engulfed in the surge. The force swung him out and clear of the stern only for him to fall back and hit his back against the bathing platform. As he again sunk below the surface his neck and shoulder muscles screamed as his head was twisted and his body was spun round and round. His lungs were burning and he was about to gulp in water when he came clear and was hauled back on deck. The bile and stomach fluids scorched his throat.

All through the short time that Patrick had been suspended over the stern Karen had been screaming at them to stop. Her voice nearly disappeared as it shrieked and then cracked. She slumped against Mark and cried.

Patrick was dumped on the deck and Jimmy kicked him in the stomach for luck.

'Well Karen. What do you know about your friend's activities? Who does he work for?' Mark looked at her expectantly.

'I don't know. I thought he owned the van business. If I knew I'd tell you now.' The tears were coursing down Karen's cheeks as she watched Patrick lying on the deck. He was just moving.

'Somehow I just about believe you. Oh well, I suppose we have to get Pat here to tell us. Give him another swing.'

Jimmy gleefully operated the davits, hoist Patrick over the stern once more and lowered away until again his head was just in the wake. They left him for what seemed an eternity and Patrick found himself swallowing large mouthfuls of sea water as he tried to gasp for breath. He choked and the sound of the rush of the water faded.

'Bring him up.'

Patrick was dumped on the deck, barely conscious.

132

'Take him below.'

This time Patrick was sat in a chair and his feet were tied to the cross member; the rope from his hands was looped around his neck and down the back of the chair to his feet. Mark stepped forward and gave Patrick a drink of water. Patrick gulped it down, glad to be rid of the salty taste of the sea and his own blood and vomit.

'Come on now, Pat. We have had a good relationship for a long time. Tell me what your connection to the IRA is and maybe I can help you,' smiled Mark.

'I don't know anything about the IRA these days. They don't operate the way they did during the troubles when I was in the Army.'

'Hey, Guv,' interposed Switch, 'The two on the Wizard. They are Irish, aren't they?'

'Thank you, George. I am aware of that,' sneered Mark. 'For the last time. Tell me what has happened to our goods. You must know how important they are.'

'I wish I knew what had happened. I make money from this deal too, you know.'

'Think again. Think harder.'

Patrick said nothing. The appeal was so childish. Mark knew that he was aware that any admission that he was double dealing was the end. Neither really expected any answer, yet Patrick felt he should say something else but nothing sensible came to mind.

Mark walked over to the saloon window again. He stared out. There seemed to be such a long silence. 'It seems such a waste. Such a great waste.' He paused.

'Bring the lady to my cabin. She may know something. I doubt it, but it may encourage Patrick to be more talkative. Silence Pat before you bring her.'

Mark turned and walked out of the saloon and into his private cabin. Patrick heard the sound of Handel's Water Music.

'Now your little lady is going to find out that it doesn't pay to mix with traitors. Jimmy tape up his mouth,' smirked Switch.

Switch knocked on Mark's cabin door and entered. 'This way, lady.' Karen walked into Mark's cabin, her mind in turmoil. She was frightened for herself, and frightened of what was happening to Patrick.

Mark turned from the drinks cabinet where he had poured himself a Scotch. 'Persevere with Pat. I will let you know when to start taking him to pieces but you can let him know that his lady friend is enjoying herself here.' Then he spoke to Karen.

'I know you wouldn't want to put undue pressure on Pat so I suggest you do everything I ask quietly.' He looked long and intently at her. 'I believe that you don't know anything important but I have to use every means to find out why my business is being thwarted. I am sure you will understand.'

He walked over to the bed and sat down, leaning against the headboard and swinging his legs up onto the white silk coverlet. 'Take my shoes off.'

Karen was shaking but trying not to show it. Her weakness would just make it easier for them to hurt Patrick. She stepped forward and reached down and pulled off Mark's deck shoes.

'Well done. If you go on like that you will do fine. Would you like a drink? If you would then just pour yourself one.'

'No thank you.'

The sound of dull thuds permeated the cabin and she tried not to let her mind run wild imagining what was going on.

'I don't believe you are a man who needs to descend to this. You are too well educated to want to force me to do this. Please leave me alone. What can you possibly gain by humiliating me?'

'I have desires like most other men. Only I am able to admit to them and to satisfy them.' Karen's hands strayed to the hem of her sweater and she started to pull it up and then stopped. There was no reason why she should make it easy for him.

'You can't go on beating him like that. You must stop.'

'Karen, you are a beautiful woman. I don't expect you to like me immediately but I am sure you are sensible enough to realise how much I can do for you; how much enjoyment we could have together. I don't often have the chance to meet women like you and I like the feelings it gives me. I know you are not involved in the little problem we have and your best approach is to stay close by me and avoid getting involved at this late stage. I am fairly sure that Patrick is double dealing and you shouldn't have sympathy for him. It is just sympathy, isn't it?'

Karen could still hear the thuds and tears started to trickle down her cheeks. 'Please stop. It's uncivilised. You can't treat a man like that.'

'My dear, we are dealing with a nasty character. He is almost certainly a senior member of the IRA and I am sure you know the sort of things they can get up to. The best thing you can do is to look out for yourself. I wouldn't risk my own safety if I were in your situation. Especially for a man like that.'

'I don't care. I just don't want you to go on like that. They'll kill him.'

'They aren't anywhere near that yet. However, if he doesn't speak soon they will start cutting things off. A finger, an ear, a nipple. If that isn't enough they'll nail his balls to the chair then cut off his penis. Do you understand?'

'Yes. Yes. I understand. You are just a monster.'

'Not at all. You have no concept of what a monster is. They are the monsters. I am just a businessman protecting my interests.'

A hot and cold flush engulfed her and she gagged as the scalding nauseous fluids surged into her throat.

'All right. All right. It wouldn't be very pleasant to have him screaming while we are enjoying ourselves, would it. Here. Let me pour you a drink. You look as if you could do with one.'

Mark poured out a glass of champagne and offered it to her. Karen turned her head away.

'Come on now. Drink that and I will tell them to leave him alone just now.'

Karen still refused to accept the glass. He laid it on the bedside table and walked over to the door. 'OK lads. We are busy just now. Leave Pat to have a rest.'

The relief suddenly made her feel much better and she smiled involuntarily, sat down on the bed and picked up the champagne. She hadn't realised how dry her mouth had been, and the drink slipped down so easily that Mark had filled her glass for the third time before she realised that he was talking about his life in London. The clean, but slightly craggy looks and soft sophisticated voice was so different to the coarseness she had just experienced. It was easy just to let her mind relax and allow her tortured brain to try to eliminate the recent memories. She felt warmth instead of the freezing fear of just a few minutes before.

The gentleness now did not come as too much of a surprise even after the brutality she had previously witnessed but her own calmness amazed her. Karen felt as though she was standing back from what was happening and the turmoil of her mind seemed to have resolved itself into the simplistic feeling that as long as things were like this they wouldn't be hurting Patrick.

She relaxed, and as if from a distance, she listened to him telling about his two labradors; how his housekeeper looked after them most of the time but how he loved to walk with them in the hills whenever he had the chance. How his home was filled with paintings by Scottish artists, and of the grey, blue, green and purple mountains and valleys of the West of Scotland. How he spent his quiet evenings listening to the great tenors. The horrors of her earlier thoughts drifted away behind a screen of mental fog.

Mark sat down at her right-hand side and slipped his left arm round her. She was about to pull away when she decided to avoid any action that might change the present situation.

'This is a really messy business. I don't know how I got involved, you know; I had a textile importing business when I was offered a huge amount of money to bring some packages back from the Far East. I won't bother you with all the details but basically the fabric was woven in Korea, and shipped to Israel for duty avoidance, before being transferred to France as Israeli cloth under a special agreement between them and the French. It was printed in France before being shipped to me. Of course I was in good company. At least one household name retailer used this route for its "Made in Britain" labelled goods. So it was easy to insert a few packages en route. It was quite painless but the quantities that could come that way were only limited by the volume of imports of my own materials.

'I am sure you can see that by the time it came from France to the UK it was a European product. Checks were minimal and the packages came in very easily.

'Well, once I had done it a couple of times it became easy and the people at the London end started to depend on me. I just got stronger. To increase the volume I also improved the systems here on the West Coast. Before I started up here others used to send yachts out over the horizon to meet up with ships from North Africa and South America, but they were far too easy to track. Now I have the goods dumped over the side of the ships with a hydrostatic fuse attached.

'I am sure you know the sort of thing. You have one on your boat attached to your life raft so that the life raft can spring free if the boat sinks. I have been just a little more clever in so far as when the goods sink they return to the surface after a known period, say a week or two and only I know when. That way any vessel cruising quietly along can collect the packages.

'The other advantage is that we no longer have to drop the stuff off out at sea. We can vary the place regularly, even coming fairly close inshore.

'From time to time I wish I could reverse out but I am locked in. No-one ever gets out, and I have become very used to all this comfort.'

'You could stop, you know,' responded Karen. 'You could. Surely anything would be better than hurting people like this and all the people who buy the nasty stuff.'

'No-one is compelled to buy. Only the weak will become hooked and they are not much use to society. Anyway you really don't know the type of associates I have. They would kill me if they found out that I was even thinking of such a thing. In any case I don't distribute drugs, I only arrange the transport for them to people who use them to finance other things. Items needed by some very important people; even governments.'

'You could contact the drugs squad or something.'

'They don't care either. In fact, they would welcome someone trying to eliminate me. It would just do part of their job for them. As soon as I tried to contact them they would be on me or, what is much more likely, they would leak it to others who would be more efficient.'

'I could speak to them for you. I know I could help if you will just get us safely out of here.'

'Us. Don't even think of us. That cannot be. I couldn't do anything that would risk your life.'

Karen realised he had thought she meant himself not Patrick and her. She felt it was best left uncorrected but Mark was obviously encouraged. He allowed his hand to drop down the back of her sweater and slide up again underneath to rest on the curve of her breast. He laid his drink down on the table, pulled her round to face him and kissed her very gently. As they kissed Mark's right hand slid up under the back of Karen's sweater until he found the bra cup and he eased her breast free. His fingers caressed her while his tongue thrust into her mouth.

Karen jerked back involuntarily, and only slightly, hoping he had not noticed. She had tried so hard not to react badly but his probing tongue was more upsetting than his hands on her body.

Mark stood up and smiled. 'If you were trying to help Pat, you should really have tried harder not to show how much you dislike me.'

'I don't dislike you. I can tell that you are a clever man. I don't dislike you. I'm just not used to men. I've only ever slept with my husband.' Karen didn't feel the situation demanded absolute truthfulness.

'Our information suggested that you didn't have too close a relationship with your husband. Indeed, Pat told us that he felt he could lay you any time the situation required it.' Karen felt a cold surge of disappointment, and it showed.

'Oh,' was all she could muster.

'I had hoped that if you were really looking for a new interest I could have persuaded you that I was a much better bet than Pat. But, he appears to have, eh, shall we say, got to you. You are quite fond of him, aren't you?'

Karen was confused. She didn't know what her response should be. Mark seemed normal and balanced but how could any normal person be in his business?

'Yes, I have come to know him quite well at the Association meetings and I probably encouraged him more than I should have done.'

'That's all right. You don't have to bare your soul to me. Pat kept us well informed about you. You see, that's the problem with a liaison with the oily rag. You would have been much wiser to throw in your lot with the engineer. I could give you the life you need and can take care of you. I have the power to make sure you are never in this situation again. Don't you agree?'

'I didn't have a liaison, as you say, and I could not choose a man on the basis of his wealth. I would have to like him for the way he lives his life, and I certainly don't like the way you live yours.'

Mark's lips formed a smile but his eyes glistened with ill-disguised anger. 'Well that counts out Pat then, doesn't it?'

'Yes. I suppose it does. You are an attractive man but your methods would make me sick. I can only despise someone whose income arises from the misery of others and I could never have any happiness with a man who is making my family pay such a horrible price.'

'Once again that seems to count out Pat. You are on your own then. A pity. I think we could have got along well and you would have been so helpful to Pat, but I don't have the time to persuade you. Your attractions will just have to be left to Switch, Bernie and Jimmy who seem to get their satisfaction in such basic ways. They don't appreciate the pleasure of a woman who gives. They just take what they want. I think you have made a mistake.'

Mark walked to the door and called out, 'Jimmy. Put Karen in the forepeak and make sure she stays put. I don't think she appreciates the nicer things in life so she doesn't need a cabin.'

Jimmy appeared immediately and taking Karen by the elbow propelled her to the bow. He pushed her into the bow locker and made her lie down on a coil of rope which lay on the cabin sole. Once again Karen's hands and feet were taped but she was sure she sensed signs of sympathy in Jimmy's eyes, and the tape was not as tight as it had been previously.

'Jimmy, I don't think you are like these men,' she appealed. 'I think you are gentle and I saw you didn't start any of the trouble. I think I could like you. Please help me.'

Karen knew she was playing with fire, but she realised that if she was to get help Jimmy was the likeliest bet.

Jimmy looked straight at her.

'I just take orders. I get well paid. The only pay I've ever had. Where I lived you got what your mates allowed you. Either that or you stole or starved. You should tell them what they want to know. Otherwise they will hurt you. Make something up if you have to. I can't help you.'

'I don't know anything. Really. Patrick didn't tell me anything. But I do need a friend.'

'Maybe,' murmured Jimmy as he closed the door.

Karen thought that was the most encouraging word she had heard for a long time.

CHAPTER XVI

CRAIG HAD BEEN awake for some time when Sean entered. 'If the two of you want something to eat before we get going you had better be getting through here now.'

Alan looked at the galley as they entered the saloon and didn't see any sign of breakfast.

Sean turned as he climbed to the cockpit. 'Alan. I quite fancy some sausage, bacon and egg, but for yourself just make whatever you fancy.'

'Looks like you're the chef today,' laughed Craig.

Mairread looked up from the chart table and smiled. Craig noticed that she had a list of waypoints which she was keying into the Autohelm plotter. She called out to Sean, 'Let's get the show on the road.'

'Raise the anchor.'

Craig turned and scowled at Sean, with an obvious distaste for his lack of manners.

Sean smirked and snarled, 'Get a bloody move on. You'll not be waiting for me to say please, will you?'

Craig shrugged his shoulders and went to the bow. Despite the good holding, the lack of wind during the night meant that the anchor was not too heavily embedded and the windlass effortlessly raised the chain and anchor aboard.

The boat had swung through 180° and was heading out from the pool while Craig stood holding on to the forestay, absorbing the quiet ambience of the lonely islands. The austere sweep of Hecla astern was clear in the morning sun with its barren boulders throwing sharp shadows. There was some activity on the fish farm and to the north the low bleak hills of Harris were clearly visible. Ahead Skye was sharply defined with the cliffs of Dunvegan Head, McLeod's Tables and the Waternish Peninsula all prominent.

It is warm, thought Craig. *No. It is hot, or it will be very shortly.* Days like these were to be savoured in the Outer Isles. He had experienced many a sunny day 'midst the Outer Hebrides, but truly hot days were still remarkable.

The bow hissed into the slight swell from the Minch as they neared the mouth of the Loch and Craig's shoulders lifted, his back straightened and he almost floated as the warm light breeze toyed with his tousled hair. For those few glorious moments he completely forgot about the predicament he was in.

The boat swung round hard to starboard. They hoist the main and unfurled the genoa and Wizard heeled hard over as she drove out once again into the Minch with the southerly breeze urging her forward into the short sea that rolled across the mouth of the inlet to Loch Skiport. The hiss and spray from the driving yacht was exhilarating. The curve of the Outer Hebrides was clearly visible and the lightening shape of Skye loomed to the east. Spray and breaking waves leapt into the air off the starboard bow before sweeping over the foredeck, swirling into the headsail, and sweeping from the foot of the sail back to the sea from whence they came. Craig noted that it was an unusual sea as Wizard rarely shipped a heavy spray into the cockpit but the flying spume certainly made him duck and weave.

The sun's rays dashed through the doorways in the remaining clouds, creating golden creases in the blue grey swathe. Small blue patches flirted with each other, teasing the sun to watch them couple, and when at last they merged into one, the flash of sunlight bursting through was more powerful than any human union.

They seemed to be racing across the Minch and soon the island of Fladda Chuam off the north-west point of Skye was visible. Craig revelled in the performance of the boat. The Corsair wasn't a pretty boat and those who had no knowledge of them failed to appreciate the speed that could be maintained. The feeling of affinity with his boat was great. It was a love affair of a special type.

Craig and Alan ate breakfast slowly, each finding it difficult to believe that they were in such a predicament.

Craig was aware of constantly positioning himself close to Mairread and felt hurt if she moved away from him to do something. He kept telling himself that he was being stupid, juvenile, and jealous but he couldn't shake off the disappointment when she wasn't close.

'Look. Puffins,' shouted Mairread, pointing to the sea close by, and they all peered at the strange little birds with the peculiar beaks, some of which were sitting on the water with their beaks full of small fish or eels whilst others paddled around apparently completely oblivious to the passing tourists.

Craig recognised the Skye coastline and the islands that were appearing dead ahead. The course seemed faulty, and he went below. Hoping that he wasn't observed he read the GPS waypoint, and quickly used the Breton rule to plot their position and heading on the chart. Mairread had erred. The waypoint she had entered was going to take them onto Eilean Trodday. They were going to get a truly close-up view of the puffins. Craig noticed that she had misinterpreted her own writing. She had written a seven but had keyed it as a one. Craig smiled. He always wrote a seven with the continental-style slash to avoid just such a mistake which was only too easy to make, especially when there was a touch of mal de mer. He went on deck.

The southerly wind at the north end of Skye off Ruibha Huinish was broken by the high headlands and although probably a near-perfect Force 4 in the open sea it was gusting strongly in the passage. Wizard was surging towards the islands and Craig prayed that Mairread would join Sean below until he could run the boat aground. 'You must have been awake most of the night. You must be tired,' he said. 'Why don't you have a rest? I'll keep watch. Nothing very much can happen here.'

To his surprise she agreed, giving him a slightly quizzical look. Craig felt sure that as long as he steered the expected course, even if Mairread checked the instruments below, she wouldn't realise anything was wrong unless she looked closely at the plotter.

The frustration of watching the islands seemingly creep towards them was intense. The yacht had been going so quickly before. He glanced at the log; it indicated 7 knots. If anything Wizard was going slightly faster. Only his perception had changed. He willed the boat to speed up.

As the islands approached Craig's mind was full of questions and doubts. *Will I have the courage to beach the boat?* His whole instinct was to keep the boat away from danger. *Can I get the flares from the cockpit locker? Will we get ashore safely? Can I let Alan know what I intend? Where is Karen? How long will we have to wait for help? Will we be alive when help arrives? Where is that other boat?*

The islands were much clearer. He could see the small flowers crowning the rocks at the high-water area of the shore quite clearly. He would have loved to look at the charts to find a course to close with the island avoiding the offshore rocks. He maintained the course and hoped.

His heart leapt with fright as Mairread's head appeared in the hatch. 'I've been watching. I thought you would change course. What a good lad you are. I'm just going to catch forty winks. See you soon.'

Craig realised that the wind was shifting as they crossed across the north of Skye. It was coming round onto the bow. Despite his annoyance he couldn't help but marvel at the wonderful panorama of the Scottish mainland stretching away north to the headland of Loch Ewe, and East to the mountains of Torridon. At any other time this would have been perfection.

He looked again at the island. He could see the birds, the rocky mounds, and the tufts of grass very clearly. He imagined that he could see changes in colour of the sea. Were they rocks? Wizard was slowing. The wind had come right round to the north-east and was blowing almost directly onto the boat's nose. *Shit. Shit. Shit. Can I reach the shore?* In desperation he threw the wheel over and tried to point straight in to the shore. The boat shuddered. The headsail thrashed and the mainsail collapsed and refilled with a bang. *I can't do it. I can't get her close enough.* He turned the helm back and Wizard had just enough way on her to lurch to starboard forcing the headsail to crackle as it filled with wind and with a thrust that shook the hull. Through the wind as she rolled on to her beam Wizard headed off towards the north-east coast of Skye. As she gathered speed he looked at the island. He had probably failed to ground her by about twenty yards.

At that Sean came on deck with a gun in his hand. 'What the hell are you doing? Are you trying to run us aground?'

'Don't be so bloody stupid. Ask Mairread if I'm on course. And what's more if I'd tried to run us aground you'd be bollock deep in sea water by now, you idiot. The course must have been wrong. If I'd stayed on that course we would all have been swimming by now. But who ever heard of a stupid Mick who could read?'

Craig was cold, shaking and on the point of hysteria.

Sean's face was scarlet. 'You may be screwing my woman,' he screamed, 'but don't you call me a Mick and an idiot.'

'In that case you're an even bigger idiot than I thought. A thick, squat, Irish idiot.'

Sean lashed out and the gun grazed Craig's temple, knocking him back onto the cockpit seat; he kicked out at Sean catching him in the stomach. Wizard sheered off violently and Sean stumbled to his hands and knees on the cockpit sole. Craig dropped with both knees onto

Sean's back and he crashed forward, smashing Sean's chin against the steering pedestal. Sliding to the floor he punched out wildly and fortunately connected with the side of Sean's head. Sean grunted and threw his arm out sideways, his fingers catching Craig on the eye. Tears flooded into Craig's eye and coursed down his cheek. As he rocked backwards he kicked out and his foot found a mark between Sean's legs. Another kick directed at the same place landed more forcefully and Sean involuntarily stopped defending himself and grabbed at his genitals.

Elated Craig forced himself erect and swung round to find the gun which had dropped onto the cockpit sole. Mairread was standing calmly in the hatchway aiming her gun at Alan. 'OK. I know you enjoyed that. I'm not sure it was a clever thing to do, but do you want to lose another friend so soon?' She saw his shoulders slump and continued. 'Get this boat under control now.'

Craig turned away. Sean was struggling to his feet as Craig tried to get back to the wheel. Craig kicked Sean's hand away from him and Sean again hit his head, this time against the cockpit seat. He snarled and grabbed for his gun.

'That's enough. You are as bad as he is,' shouted Mairread. 'Get down here.' Sean went below and Mairread came on deck. Craig thought he could discern the trace of a smile but she turned away and stared at the cliffs of Skye, and Wizard picked up speed as though the brakes had been taken off.

'I could use a hot drink,' said Craig. Mairread nodded. 'Alan. You steer.'

Alan came on deck followed by Sean who scowled at Craig but said nothing. Craig went to the galley feeling satisfied with the large gash along Sean's top lip and the bruise on his cheek. While the kettle boiled he wondered where they were going to stop. If it was Portree there could be some opportunity to escape.

When he returned on deck with the four mugs of Bovril they all seemed grateful and even Sean had mellowed. Alan was more cheerful and there was a slight smile when he took the drink.

They all cupped their hands around the mugs and were grateful as much for the hand-warming effect as for the nourishing drink. The peace was disturbed only by the gulls and the beat of a helicopter which circled overhead, apparently on its way into the naval communications base on the island of Rona.

The wind had steadied in the east at a gentle 12 knots; the sun was out and with the warmth everything seemed much better. Craig sat on the foredeck looking at the waterfalls and Alan joined him. 'That was bad luck,' he whispered. 'You nearly brought that off, but I think we should be careful now. They will be more cautious. And, what is more, I would like to come out of this alive.'

Craig looked at him and smiled. 'It really wasn't as clever as you think. I tried to run us aground. The fight was an accident. Mairread had keyed the wrong waypoint and I thought it would be possible to put her aground without anyone below noticing, but I hadn't planned for the wind shifts.'

Alan grinned. 'Some tale. No-one will believe you couldn't even find the shore.'

'I seem to remember that wasn't one of your problems,' laughed Craig, remembering a previous occasion when Alan had done much the same thing as Mairread.

Craig shrugged and continued, 'There isn't much we can do now until we stop somewhere. We may as well enjoy this. We would have loved it if this had been our cruise. We have actually been sailing quite well and the winds have been mostly co-operative.'

'I suppose you are right,' Alan responded, and they both sat admiring the rugged scenery. Craig looked to the stern. Mairread smiled. Sean was on the helm. They had been long days with limited rest and all were feeling tired and in need of sleep.

'This is a bit more than you bargained for this year, isn't it?'

'Yes. I sit in London dreaming about this week. There is normally just enough excitement and sometimes I have wished for more but I could do without this situation,' mused Alan.

'How have things been?' enquired Craig.

'I keep hoping they will decide to let me go but at present there are so many possible changes that it seems unlikely. In fact it would cost so much to get rid of me I just can't see them doing it. Sales have been very variable and I think the Board are waiting for me to come up with yet another miracle. The problem as I see it is that stores like M&S have run into trouble. For a long time they were able to obtain quality goods from the manufacturers at good prices and that meant that we could offer both branded goods and our own label and get the best of both worlds. Now, however, with business volumes falling M&S seem to have gone abroad for many of their products at very sharp prices and the customer has not twigged that they aren't getting what they used to expect. You know. The ninety per cent made in Britain bit.

'We have had to cut so much to match them that I now feel we should abandon our own label and return to offering a range of branded merchandise in pleasant and comfortable surroundings and with some genuinely trained and informed staff. In fact just what department stores should never have gone away from. Leave Marks to go on cutting staff numbers, quality and putting up prices.

'Some of the manufacturers have smiled when I have discussed it with them. To be fair it is much the sort of thing the branded line manufacturers have always said. I now believe they were right, and the volumes and margins on things like Timberland and Ralph Lauren rather prove the point. The Board are nearly convinced but I am pretty tired and our back-up teams are not all they might be.'

'How are the family?' queried Craig.

'Fine. They have all got pretty good jobs. The kids seem happy enough. They have got their cars and holidays abroad. No trouble really. It's Sylvia who is fed up. We leave home about six-thirty of a morning and rarely meet up again until around eight-thirty at night. To have time together or eat out means a late night. I don't notice usually but at times it gets me down. We seem to be managing though. I've got so used to the money.'

Craig considered Alan's remarks and responded. 'I know the problem. I have found it difficult to rely on the managers as much as I should. I just can't let go either. I always remember the difficult times and worry if I don't meet the architects, engineers and contractors personally we just won't get the business. I'm rarely home until late and quite often I am away entertaining. As you say, it's not right but I don't see any short-term alternative.'

'You are lucky with Karen. Most men would give their right arm for a woman like her.'

'Yes. You are probably right there too, but she has developed other interests and was away driving a charity truck last weekend. I don't mind her doing it during the week but I do object to her using up scarce weekends.'

'Come on now, be reasonable. You were up here last weekend anyway.'

'But look at the trouble she is in.'

'And we aren't?'

Craig shrugged and allowed his gaze to wander over the magnificent cliffs of east Skye. They both lapsed into silence.

It seemed to take quite a long time before Wizard turned the headland into Portree Bay and immediately after they had handed the sails, a period when Craig and Alan were alert for an opportunity to overcome their captors, Sean ordered Alan and Craig into the aft cabin, handcuffed them with cable ties and secured the door. Mairread anchored the yacht well out from the harbour area and away from the visitors moorings. She was trying to minimise any possible opportunity for her two captives to escape or make contact with others. She looked around for a sign of Irish Rascal but it was not there.

'Let them know we have arrived,' Mairread called out, and Sean made a call which Craig and Alan could barely hear but were able to ascertain that the yacht's position had been passed on.

Sean turned away from the radio. 'They don't want us to stay here. Firstly because they assume that Fast Lady is still chasing and may well be intercepting our signals, as well as having a network of contacts around the coast, and secondly, there is a lot of Admiralty activity around here and we may just be stopped for a routine check.'

Mairread looked worried. 'We must get water here, and some diesel would be useful.'

Sean stood up. 'OK. I'll go ashore with containers. We can't risk taking her alongside, but I'll have to hurry. Everything will be closing.'

Craig and Alan heard the dinghy being launched, but could not make out what was going on.

Alan stared hard at Craig. 'You have fallen for that woman. Do you realise that she is very likely to kill us both? What about Karen? Have you forgotten about her totally?'

Craig sat with his head bowed. 'I don't know what I feel. Karen has been a good wife in many ways but we haven't had a lot in common for a long time. I suppose part of that is the business, at least she says that is the trouble, but as I tried to make more time she was getting involved more deeply in her own interests. It just seemed that we didn't matter too much to each other except as companions.

'It came home to me very clearly when she came in one day and said that she had seen some elderly couples coming out of Sainsburys and she thought we would be like that. I know she didn't mean to suggest that we were getting old but it felt as though there was nothing left to do except vegetate.

'She knows that I've had the odd affair but they didn't matter as she was sure that they were just casual relationships and she was confident that I would always be there. I don't think she cared too much for sex anyway. My mind goes round and round in a muddle of feeling that I owe her loyalty and at the same time wondering what the future holds for me.'

Alan stared hard at Craig. 'I know something of how you feel. Sylvia and I had a pretty turbulent time about five years ago. Both of us had brief affairs but we have a much happier relationship now. The sex can't be good for ever, you know. There has to be more. You must develop other interests.'

Craig thought for some time, and then responded, 'We don't have any common interests. The kids are self-sufficient. Karen doesn't like sailing. I am at home on my own, or she is, pretty regularly. And I don't think that the sexual part of relationships should end. I know they do, but they shouldn't.

'As for Mairread. I am not sure either and under these circumstances it is probably best to remain as friendly as possible. At least that's what I've read about captives and captors.'

Craig knew he was not being honest. He couldn't wait to hold Mairread again.

Alan laughed. 'I don't think that when they said the captive should attempt to establish a relationship with his captors they actually meant fucking them.'

Craig grinned. 'Well it's my way.'

Not much else was said as tiredness overtook them and they both fell asleep.

After what only seemed like a few minutes Sean re-entered the cabin, removed the handcuffs and said, 'Up you get.'

Alan and Craig went on deck a bit bleary eyed, to be greeted by a smiling Mairread. 'You pair look like a real load of sleepy heads. Let's have dinner. Craig. You are the chef.'

'OK. What have you got?'

'Sean has managed to get some fresh scallops, and no doubt you know what to do with them.'

'Yes, I think I can handle that.'

Craig went below, peeled some sweet potatoes and put them on to boil. The butter, lemon juice, garlic and parsley were all fished out from the chill locker as he started to prepare the sauce for the scallops, when he became aware that the others were occupied on deck. He wanted to be sure that he had time to look around. Looking up through the companionway he laughed, 'Can I interest anyone in a glass of Sancerre while you are waiting?'

Vigorous head nodding accompanied the response from Mairread of, 'That seems a good idea.'

Craig moved over to the centre of the cabin and lifted off the top of the drinks locker which was part of the table, before taking out the bottle of wine and the glasses. He glanced up. They were all talking animatedly and Alan had interposed himself between the others and the cabin hatch. Mairread's holdall was lying on the settee berth on the starboard side so he thrust his hand into the bag and groped around hurriedly. He felt the chill of fear engulf him, and as panic swept in, his hand closed on a small object which he quickly removed. He glanced down as he turned back to pour the wine and saw the small automatic. His lips were dry and he tried to say something light-hearted but the words died in his throat. As he turned with two glasses in his hand Sean had pushed past Alan and was leaning on the coach roof just preparing to come below.

'Good. You can pass these up,' Craig croaked and hoped the smile covered up the fear he felt.

Craig was about to pass up the other two glasses when Mairread came below.

'It's OK. I'll pass them up.' She handed Alan's glass up to him and sat down on the settee berth next to her bag. Craig prayed that she would not notice that the items were rumpled.

'How is our chef getting on?' she asked.

'Just fine. Won't be long now,' said Craig, as he put the sweet potatoes into the oven to roast, and started to prepare the sauce for the scallops.

They ate well on lobster bisque with cream followed by the scallops and a second bottle of Sancerre left them all feeling drowsy and sated.

'I think we just have to take the risk of a short sleep,' said Mairread. 'Sean. You take the first three hours and I'll take the next three.'

'I don't mind taking my turn,' interposed Alan, laughingly.

'I don't suppose you would,' smiled Mairread, 'But I think we will leave your tasks till later. You beauties need your sleep.'

'Oh, by the way. I know about the exhaust trick. Don't be tempted to try that twice,' growled Sean, as Craig and Alan ducked their heads and turned to the aft cabin.

'Just a minute, Craig. I'd like to have a word with you on deck.'

Craig felt a thrill sweep over him as he turned to smile at Mairread. She nodded to the steps up and he climbed into the cockpit seating himself as far away from the hatch as possible. Mairread sat close to him with her back to the hatch and Craig glimpsed Sean trying to see what was happening.

'I'm sure I don't need this but then why would you need one?'

Craig felt the dig in his ribs and looked down to see the gun probing his waist. Mairread had leaned forward and although her lips still smiled her eyes were lacking any warmth.

'Put it into my left hand now before Sean realises you have it. It wouldn't be any use to you anyway, it's unloaded.' she hissed.

Craig's buoyant mood subsided like a cold souffle, and he slipped the small automatic into Mairread's hand.

'How did you know?'

'I was sitting on the side deck watching you through the cabin window and admiring you at work when I saw you rifling my holdall. What did you plan to do with it?'

'I don't really know. I just don't know, but I don't trust Sean, I suppose.'

'Well, he doesn't much like you either and if you want me to stay in charge of this situation you better pray he doesn't catch you doing anything as stupid again.'

She leaned forward still further, feathered a kiss across his lips and said more loudly, 'Time we turned in. See you in the morning.'

She indicated that Craig should go below and he felt so deflated he climbed down into the saloon missing the strange look Sean gave him.

He entered the aft cabin and heard the door jammed and locked behind him.

When they had clambered into their sleeping bags, Alan looked at Craig and asked, 'I need to know where you stand. Are you still going to try to beat this pair of murderers, or have you just fallen under her spell?'

'Shut up. I don't need any lectures from you. It should be bloody obvious from what happened today that I want to get out of here. We will get out of this.'

'Maybe. But are we going to try to escape or have you become a lap dog?' niggled Alan.

He jumped back banging his head against the shelf as Craig grabbed him by the throat. 'Listen to this.'

Craig told Alan what had happened with the gun and as he released his grip and settled back on the berth he snarled, 'Does that answer your fucking question?' He turned away.

CHAPTER XVII

Patrick used the break to recover his senses. He tried to get enough air into his lungs to ease the blinding pain in his forehead but not so much that he strained his tortured lungs. At the same time his mind buzzed with thoughts of escape, London, Karen, and anticipation of what was coming next.

Jimmy returned to the saloon, and Mark followed slowly, apparently deep in thought 'Now, Patrick. Who are you working for?'

Mark sat on the large window settee and looked at Patrick, directly. His eyes were darkened without any gleam just as though they were endless unlit caves.

'I don't believe that beating you again will help us but unless you come to your senses I will just have to let George get on with it. Just for my own protection, you see. They would think it odd if I hadn't used every possible method to get information from you. Of course I could hand your lady friend over to George and Bernie. I gather that they would rather enjoy educating a middle-class lady.'

Patrick looked straight at him. 'That would be a waste of time. She doesn't know anything.'

'You are so right. I have had a chat with her and I am sure you are right, but you do know more than you have told us, and as I have just explained I am obliged to try every method I can to find those goods. I think you might just be influenced by the lady's situation. What about it, George? Do you think you could get the lady to make enough noise to influence Pat?'

Switch laughed. 'I've already had enough to know that I could have a great time, and I guarantee Pat will hear her above the 1812 overture.'

'An interesting thought,' mused Mark and he did seem to be genuinely considering the possibility.

'OK. I don't see why I should give that bastard that pleasure. The IRA,' said Patrick.

'I shan't ask you why. I presume something went on when you were fighting there. That's your business, but what is going on now?'

'The yacht was supposed to meet up with an Irish boat. For some reason that did not happen and they appear to simply be trying to stay away from you.'

'So, where will they go?'

'I don't know. I really don't.'

'What is the name of the pick-up boat?'

Patrick hesitated briefly. 'Irish Rascal.'

'Fine,' murmured Mark.

'Now. We have picked up two messages from Wizard, quoting two different numbers of four or five digits followed by WI. What can that mean?'

'That is strange. It is not any code that I have heard,' replied Patrick.

Mark walked to the companionway 'Oh come, come. I can't keep on offering George his pleasure and then withdrawing the offer. He will become frustrated, and you know that's not good for him.'

Patrick paused for a moment or two, then seemed to come to a conclusion. 'It's simple. The WI just stands for Western Isles, the name of the Martin Lawrence Pilot for the area. There should be up to three digits for the page and two for the line number of their destination.'

'Thank you. That will do just now. Put him in the cabin with the woman. It should keep him mellow and occupied.'

Switch nodded to Jimmy and Patrick was marched off to the forepeak.

Mark stood by Bernie on the bridge. 'Lochmaddy. Get this machine going.'

Bernie pushed the throttle levers forward and the throb of the engines increased as the boat thrust its way up the Minch.

Down below Patrick tried to comfort Karen. He was so angry that he gagged slightly as he tried to say the right things; to keep his voice calm; to be reassuring. He noted how she looked distressed every time he let himself show anger, and slowly he settled down, and as their pain subsided they fell asleep hard against each other.

An uneventful afternoon was disturbed as Switch came into the forepeak with sandwiches and tea. 'Lucky for you the guvnor is a gentleman. I wouldn't have bothered with you after what you done to us.' He released their hands, turned and left the cabin. They heard the bolt slide closed.

153

Moving was agony for both Patrick and Karen, but as they moved slowly and the aches eased the tea was drunk and the sandwiches were eaten without a word being said.

'Are we going to get out of this alive?'

'Of course. I have some friends who will free us.' Patrick stopped, realising that to say more just put Karen in even greater danger. 'I can't say more. Just believe we will escape.' He tried to give her a kiss but bruised lips only managed to brush her cheek.

Patrick heard the engines throttling back, and tried to look out of the window. Although it was still light he couldn't make out where they were but he was fairly sure that it was Lochmaddy. He heard the dinghy being launched and the outboard start up, and a short while later the cabin door opened and Mark entered with Bernie standing behind him. 'Both of you come this way. I presume you would like a drink. I can see no reason to continue with this brutality. Just co-operate and I will see that our friends don't do any more damage.'

Patrick shivered.

'Bernie. Bring Pat's bag. He could really use some dry clothes.'

They proceeded into the saloon where the smell of coffee made Karen feel slightly better.

'Help yourself,' gestured Mark.

Bernie returned with Patrick's bag and Patrick stood in the corner of the saloon and changed into clean dry clothes.

Patrick poured Karen a coffee and helped himself to an outsize Glenfiddich. He noted that Bernie had positioned himself at the door to the deck and wheelhouse. There was no sign of Switch or Jimmy.

'I still feel that you must have had an unfortunate experience when you were in Ireland, Patrick,' smiled Mark. 'Why don't you tell me about it? Perhaps we can find an answer to our problem together. You know that the value of the missing consignment is such that your help will be well rewarded. Will you reconsider your situation?'

Patrick's first instinct was to tell Mark to piss off, but he was in no condition to take another beating. 'You may be right. I may have been conned into supporting something I didn't really believe in. Let me think about it.'

'Yes, well not too long. We may need your help at any time and it had better be given wholeheartedly.'

Mark sounded pleasant enough but Karen saw a strange look in his eyes and as he turned towards the window Karen was sure his pupils actually disappeared up behind his eyelids.

Patrick poured a small drop of whisky into Karen's cup and topped it up with more hot coffee. He smiled at her as reassuringly as he could manage and was pleased that she managed to smile back. Her colour was returning and she looked healthier.

Mark turned on the TV and they all sat quiet until about ten-thirty when they heard the dinghy returning, and shortly afterwards Switch and Jimmy came on board, and into the saloon. Mark nodded to Jimmy and they disappeared into the master cabin. Jimmy sat down opposite Karen, smiled and said, 'I hope you are feeling better. I'm sorry if they hurt you.'

'We are getting the "nice guy" treatment now, are we? Well don't worry, dumbo. Whichever side I end up on you are going to regret it,' said Patrick.

Karen almost imperceptibly shook her head and tried to catch Patrick's eye. She did not want Jimmy upset now that she had made some progress. She wasn't sure whether or not Patrick had seen her and she couldn't risk being any more obvious.

'That's easy to say. Time will tell if you have the bottle to do anything about it,' retorted Jimmy.

Just then Mark and Switch re-entered the cabin. 'Well Patrick. It seems your pals didn't actually come here. For some reason or other they were stopped on the way and we don't have another destination. Where do you think they will go now?'

'I don't know. They should be trying to rendezvous with the powerboat but for some reason they aren't doing that. I can't guess why.'

'The reason, Pat, is that the boat is stuck at Crinan. Does that help?'

'No. If that is the situation then they could go almost anywhere. It is not a scenario that I have ever heard discussed.'

Mark looked mildly annoyed but quickly mellowed. 'Then we will all get some sleep. I am sure we will hear shortly where they are. Jimmy. Put Pat and Karen in the forepeak again.'

In the bow Karen snuggled up to Patrick. It wasn't the most comfortable place to be but the warm weather made it tolerable. They were both so very tired and Karen soon dropped off, but

Patrick was interested in small engraved plaques that lay around. He picked them up and examined them. 'Reddingvest', 'Ankerlier', 'Hoofmotor', 'Gegiste Positie', 'Radio Zonder'. The boat had obviously been foreign. Perhaps it still was foreign. The language seemed familiar but he couldn't decide finally whether it was German or Dutch.

Karen woke to see brilliant sunshine pouring through the portholes. It was already stuffy in the confined cabin. Patrick was still asleep and she tried not too waken him but she was too uncomfortable to lie still and just trying to read her watch roused him.

'Hi. What time is it?'

'Ten-thirty. There's not a lot of movement about.'

'That's probably good news. Are you OK?'

'Yes, more or less. Leaning against these piles of rope makes me wish that I had just a bit more padding. A little middle-aged spread,' she joked.

'You are just perfect as you are,' Patrick smiled.

Karen smiled and looked thoughtfully at Patrick. 'An explanation of how I happen to be here would be helpful.'

'I really think that it would be best if you didn't know too much, but I suppose it may help you if I even confirmed the obvious.'

Just at that the forecabin door opened and George looked in. 'How charming. Come on, Patrick. We need your advice.'

Patrick struggled awake. Every time he moved he ached and his lungs were still very painful if he breathed deeply. He climbed to his feet and left with Switch.

When he entered the saloon Mark was sitting on the edge of the table with the pilot book and a piece of paper in his hand.

'I would like you to confirm this for me.'

Mark handed Patrick the Western Isles Pilot. 'The reference is 09433WI.'

Patrick turned to the appropriate page and said, 'Oh. That's odd. It doesn't really make any sense. The reference page is an aerial photograph of Loch Mariveg in south-east Lewis, but that is very unlikely as it is not the safest place to enter.' He hesitated and looked puzzled. 'That doesn't actually ring true to me. Are you sure you got the correct code? I find it difficult to believe that they would be sent in there.'

Mark looked straight at him.

'That's why I wanted your opinion.'

'Well, you have it. I definitely don't think they would go to Loch Mariveg.'

Switch looked at Mark and shrugged. 'That's the number they gave me, Guv.'

Mark swithered for a few seconds. 'OK. Let's go and have a look.'

'Thank you, Patrick. Cast off and let's get going. Sorry Pat. Back to the cabin just now. I want more time to think before you can consider yourself rehabilitated.'

Jimmy set off for the wheelhouse as Bernie ushered Patrick forward, and locked the door.

The big boat motored out of Lochmaddy and skirted the shallow waters of the Sound of Harris. They crept past the South Channel until the water became too shallow, sidled up to many of the small islands and then crossed the main channels to Rodel and then on up the coast.

'We can't enter there, Guv. Too shallow,' announced Jimmy as they approached the entrance to the rocky mouth of the loch.

'Drop the tender and have a look, George.'

George and Bernie went aft and Patrick and Karen heard the dinghy motor off.

After about fifteen minutes they heard the return of the tender and shortly afterwards Jimmy opened the door. 'This way.'

He pointed the gun in the direction of the saloon and Patrick did as indicated.

Patrick entered the saloon and sat down.

'Well Patrick. It seems as though your doubts were justified. We have seen no sign of them. Unless, of course, they have gone right in.'

'I don't think they will have done that. The tides were wrong if they were trying this morning.'

Patrick turned to Switch. 'Get me the Skye and north-west Scotland pilot book'

'Who the hell do you think you are talking to?'

'I don't know. No animal I know smells as bad as that.'

Switch started across the saloon with his fists clenched and rising.

Mark stepped forward and stuck out a foot tripping Switch onto the settee.

'Bernie. Go and get the pilot, and George, stop behaving like an idiot. If you can.'

Bernie strode off and returned with Martin Lawrence's *Yachtsman's Pilot* for the area.

Patrick opened it up, counted down the page and said, 'That's more like it. Portree. That's where they will be heading. Portree. The reference should have been 09433SNS.'

Mark smiled. 'Thank you.'

He stared hard at Bernie. 'If you got that message wrong I'll have you castrated. Now get this ship moving.'

Bernie swung round and disappeared into the wheelhouse.

'George. See our friend back to the bow.'

Later, Mark and Switch stood in the large wheelhouse and peered out into the dusk.

'That was a good idea, Mark. He genuinely had to think about that. He could have tried to take us into the loch.'

Mark smiled. 'Well, it was a simple test, but I am not sure we can rely too much on it.'

'Maybe you are right not to trust him, Guv. He has certainly given as little help as possible. Just enough to save his neck.'

'Maybe. However, there is still the question of the telephone calls to London. He didn't answer us about that. If I get a convincing and verifiable reply to that I may think again. That will have to be the next thing we check. In the meantime we will keep a close eye on him. Separate him and the lady. Put them back in separate cabins, and lock them. In fact, put Pat in the twin-bunk cabin. The hatch in there is too small for any funny business.'

'OK, Guv.'

As Switch turned away he looked over his shoulder at Jimmy. 'I hope you can find the north of Skye at night, Jimmy. Just as well it doesn't really get dark at this time of year. Shall I bring Patrick to help you?' laughed Switch.

'Fuck off,' shouted Jimmy. 'Give me half a chance and the only thing you'll find will be the bottom,' he yelled.

'Calm down you two. Just steer, Jimmy, and get us there as fast as you can.'

Once again the cruiser resounded to the drumming sound of the big diesels as it turned its head toward the north of Skye.

In the late afternoon there were few puffins around to hear the rhythmic throb of the helicopter rotors as the small machine came south from the direction of Stornoway, overflew the powerboat and disappeared in the direction of Waternish.

Mark looked skywards in the direction of the aircraft. 'Sometimes I feel that we are being watched. At other times I know we are being watched. And this is the latter.'

'But who could it be, Guv?' enquired Switch.

'I don't know, but it could be one of several possibilities and I don't like any of them.'

With that Mark turned away, and went below, leaving Switch, Bernie and Jimmy looking puzzled.

In his suite Mark pondered over the London telephone calls. For some time he had been unsure about his relationship with some of his associates. He had always skimmed a little off the top. No-one had ever said anything but he had some misgivings over the amount he had removed from the last few larger consignments. These calls could be Patrick reporting independently on him and the operation. After all Pat knew how much was actually collected and shipped south. If he was reporting that back there could be trouble.

The problem with multiple masters is that it is difficult to be sure who is doing the checking up.

Or was it the IRA as Pat said? They could have helicopter surveillance and a London phone number would be necessary in order to avoid suspicion.

Perhaps even the Customs have already discovered that they have changed the route and the vessels. They have only just changed in time previously, but how could they possibly have found out again so soon?

The misgivings continued to run through his head as dusk fell, and still he could not make up his mind about the role of Patrick. *It's probably best to give the impression of trusting him but to keep a close watch on everything he does. If I keep the woman confined I should have some guarantee of Pat's behaviour. Indeed, who was Pat reporting to? He could be connected to any of a number of possibilities. Or even several of them. A grass or triple agent.*

At last sleep overtook him and to the deep rumble of the engines and the gentle roll of the Minch's beam swell the problems faded away.

CHAPTER XVIII

It was five a.m. when Sean's head appeared round the cabin door. 'Get up and hurry about it.' He wagged a gun in their general direction just to make the point more emphatically, then left.

'We are in for a bit of a blow with heavy rain but it is supposed to clear for the afternoon so let's have the mainsail up before we get going. We have an appointment to keep,' said Mairread as Craig and Alan arrived on deck a few minutes later.

Sean leaned against the back stay and watched as Craig and Alan went through a routine they had completed so many times until the big main was crackling lightly in the wind. As soon as it was made off Alan went up to the bow and raised the anchor, Craig sheeted in and the yacht eased forward and turned towards the harbour mouth. The headsail rolled out and Wizard shuddered, heeled gently and the slicing of the bow through the water was the only sound to be heard on an overcast and blowy summer morning. Craig looked back at the town and harbour. Portree was not the nicest place to be but it always looked attractive as you sailed in or out. He noted the high Cirrus and the black mass of cloud behind it, and thought that it might just get shitty later on. It was a fresh south-westerly and as they rounded the point to enter the Sound of Raasay the yacht heeled still further but picked up speed; Craig couldn't help a smile. He loved the way Wizard settled into a beat. The power and the high centre cockpit gave him a great feeling of elation.

They had just rounded the southern point of the bay and surged into the Sound of Raasay when Sean, who had been staring astern, turned and hurried below, to return seconds later with a pair of binoculars. 'That looks hellishly like Fast Lady,' he said, pointing north, and handing the glasses to Mairread.

Mairread ranged the binoculars and concentrated.

'I'm not sure, but let's keep an eye on them. There aren't too many boats about at this time of day so we should be careful. Let's wait and see if they go into Portree.'

Wizard continued to pick up speed, and as they entered the Raasay

160

narrows the log was reading a steady 7 knots. Alan pointed at the white horses surging across the channel from Loch Sligachan. 'Should we reef now?' he asked.

'Yes,' responded Craig and stepped forward to the mainsheet and reefing pennant winches.

Sean stepped across in front of him. 'Let's just keep our speed up.'

'Don't continue to show how thick you are,' snarled Craig, 'We will go just as fast, and probably faster, if we don't let her sink too much beam in the water.'

'Not yet,' screamed Sean, and pushed Craig, who fell against the winch handle.

Craig just stopped himself as his hand shot towards the winch handle. How he resisted the impulse to grab the handle and smash it into Sean's head would always surprise him. He pulled himself upright, laughed, and said, 'OK. You're the yachtmaster, I presume.'

'No. But I have the gun,' retorted Sean.

Mairread was looking intently astern. 'I'm beginning to think you are right about that being Fast Lady. It just remains to see whether or not they have seen us.'

Wizard was just nosing into the white horses, and the noise of the wind was now becoming oppressive. The occasional spray broke over the bow as it cut into a wave and the wind played with the spume.

Craig looked back. *Is Karen on that boat? Is she all right? What will the children have done? Will they have realised that when Karen did not go home that something was wrong? How can all this be going on without the police knowing about it? Should I just take a chance now and try to overcome both Sean and Mairread? If the police come will they just give in? Can I save Alan and Karen and still escape with Mairread? Does she even want me?*

The radio crackled into life. 'Wizard, Wizard, Wizard. This is Irish Rascal, Irish Rascal, Irish Rascal.'

Sean went below and they heard him pass channel 69 as the working channel. The link was re-established on channel 69 and Sean asked for their position.

Mairread jumped forward and leaned through the hatch. 'Don't tell them where we are but try to find out where they are.'

Sean tried several times but got no reply.

Mairread smiled, 'I think that tells us who is astern. Just keep going.'

Craig looked ahead. The excess sail was increasing the leeway so much that it was doubtful if they would round the south-west corner of Raasay. They were being pushed far too close to the shore of Raasay. He was tempted to say something but thought that as there was so little danger off the shore any grounding could be their best chance of getting ashore and away. Wizard had slowed significantly as she heeled hard over and she was pointing so high that the wind was steadily increasing their leeway, and they were now rapidly slowing down.

It was getting really dark and starting to rain with big spots of water splattering the windscreen and spray hood. Alan had gone below and appeared on deck with the 'oilies' and they all put them on. Craig found himself standing close to Mairread at the stern, holding on to the back stay. Sean was on the helm and Alan gripped the edge of the spray hood with both hands and peered ahead. Craig swung round to look astern, then dropped his face to kiss Mairread on the lips. The kiss lingered and as he pulled away he said, 'I've fallen in love with you. Can we get out of this alive?'

'Of course we can. If we work together. Will you help me?'

He nodded, and she smiled.

Craig looked at Mairread with drips of water now cascading from the hood of her waterproofs onto her nose and chin and thought what a lovely woman she was, but as he turned away the thought flashed through his mind that the smile on her face did not seem to be reflected in her eyes. There was a hardness, and perhaps even a flash of dislike that Craig could not understand. He looked back but she had turned to watch the fast approaching headland and shore.

'One reef in the main then reef the headsail. Take in about half,' she shouted, and instinctively Alan jumped over to the winch and prepared to take in the pennant. 'Craig,' called out Mairread, 'ease the sheet.'

Craig delayed as long as he could but slowly did as asked and Wizard steadied and when he looked forward he could see that even allowing for the leeway they were going to round the headland and they would then pick up speed. Surely as the yacht rounded the point she came further upright and the noise dropped. A quick glance at the log showed 8 knots. Fast Lady, if it was her, wasn't going to catch them very quickly. 'Take the wheel, Sean,' ordered Mairread, and Sean obliged.

Wizard surged through the narrows of Caol Mhor and out to cross towards the rainbow-shaped arc of the new bridge between Skye and Kyle of Lochaish. Craig sat down beside Alan, and felt just a bit disappointed that again he had been unable to find a way out of the mess. He turned to Alan. 'I don't think we really want to be caught by that other lot. I just feel that it could prove to be more dangerous than being here.'

'Probably,' muttered Alan, 'but I don't know what we are going to do. Maybe we can attract attention as we pass through the Kyles.'

He was cut short as Mairread sat down opposite. 'Don't let me interrupt. I am sure you were discussing something interesting.'

'You are so wrong,' said Alan. 'The only thing that could possibly interest me just now is to see you fall overboard.'

Mairread laughed. 'Sure that's not so friendly, but then again you English always were an unfriendly lot.'

Although Wizard was almost flying along past the islands of Scalpay and Longay, there was no doubt that Fast Lady was slowly closing the gap. The different shades of the hull were slowly becoming more discernible and it was only a matter of time until the big powerboat caught up with them. The bridge at Kyle of Lochalsh approached and Mairread ordered Alan below. 'You are just irrational enough to do something very stupid. I think you will be much safer down there.'

The weather had closed in very quickly and the wind was slowly dropping as the black sky and rain enveloped the slopes of Sgurr na Coinnich at the mouth of the narrows of Glenelg. Looking back Craig could barely see Fast Lady through the rain even though she was now much closer. With the falling wind the large raindrops beat the waves into submission. Mairread saw him looking and observed, 'We will get a lift from the current through the narrows. It should be in full ebb when we get there.'

'That's so, but there is absolutely nowhere to go at the other end. Any possible anchorage is easily inspected by them when they arrive and we can't outrun them much further unless we take a chance and go up one of the lochs. That's certainly possible but it would also become a trap.'

'We don't have much choice.' muttered Mairread. 'I hope you come out of this OK. I really would like you to get away. I don't want you to come to any harm.'

Craig didn't feel too confident.

'What about Alan? Will he get away too?

Mairread looked at Craig. The smile was just visible in her eyes. 'That depends on whether or not you can keep him under control.'

'I will try,' responded Craig.

'Do that. Just do that,' said Mairread sharply as they once again turned to look astern.

Fast Lady could not be seen. In fact the beautiful arcing span of the bridge was lost in the torrential Scottish rain.

Craig turned and looked ahead once more. He started. 'I've got it. I know what to do. Listen. We won't turn south into Kyle Rhea. We will go straight on. We can hide behind Glas Eilean in Loch Duich. They will expect us to make a run for it with the tide. Even if they realise their mistake quickly, and that is unlikely, we will have slipped back through the Kyle of Lochalsh, and once through there they won't know where we have gone. They could spend days looking for us south of Kyle Rhea and then again west of Kyle of Lochalsh when they eventually come back through.'

'That sounds good but doesn't the tide run against us going back through the bridge?' queried Sean, who was standing below deck at the galley.

'Yes, but not so fast that we can't motor against it if we turn back as soon as we think they are past,' replied Craig.

'OK. I'm in favour. What do you think, Sean?' asked Mairread.

'I agree that's our best bet,' smiled Sean.

'So you can think then,' sneered Craig.

For the first time Craig felt that Sean had relaxed only a little, but he felt significantly more comfortable.

They kept the yacht on a heading into Loch Duich and hoped that the weather would not lift too soon. They had no need to worry. The fine Scottish rain and mist continued until they were out of sight, had dropped anchor behind Glas Eilean and brewed a hot cup of tea.

Mairread and Sean sat in the cockpit under the cover of the canopy, and their conversation was pitched so low that neither Craig nor Alan could make it out.

Craig looked intensely at Alan. 'I think we have a slight chance if we can get well away from that powerboat. This pair would probably relax a bit if they thought they were well clear and we could use that to escape.'

Alan's face portrayed the doubts that Craig felt but hid. 'That seems highly unlikely. We would never get the dinghy launched and any swim is likely to be too far. For me at least.'

They both subsided into opposite corners of the settee berth.

Craig thought back to Karen and the SEC. *She must have been naive to get mixed up with these people.* As his mind wandered over their discussions he realised that it wasn't very often that they talked these days, and when they did the SEC always had figured prominently. As he tried to remember individual nights the awareness returned of meetings going on longer than when Karen had first joined. Or was it that the get-together at the pub was lasting longer? Certainly Karen seemed either to be on a high when she got home, or did not appear to want to talk about anything. He remembered one evening when she was unwilling to talk at all and had dashed upstairs for a shower, embarrassed he had thought at the time. He had rejected that as stupid, but it did not seem so stupid now.

Craig sat up and looked out at the grey sky. The lower slopes of the surrounding hills were just visible. Water flowed along the boom until it reached a fitting or ropes end and then changed into a small waterfall, coursed down onto the steering wheel and compass binnacle before flooding along the cockpit floor and out through the drains. He shuddered and watched the water as it determinedly raced back to the sea. *That is it. Karen is having an affair. But who with?* He ran through as many of the members of the SEC as he could recall and rejected most of them as stupid old farts or wimps and not Karen's type.

There had been one guy she had mentioned regularly. Lived quite close by. Had a haulage business or something like that.

Craig was able to connect a few of their less satisfactory moments with mention of this . . . *What was his name? And does he have anything to do with all this?* He dozed.

'OK. Let's get the show on the road.'

Mairread's lilt broke the silence.

'I think we should get out of here, don't you think?'

She looked at Craig.

Craig glanced at his watch. It was noon. 'Yes. We should be able to go now without any fear of them spotting us. And in any case they will be at the fastest area of current so they can't come straight back now.'

They all went on deck. There was a general urgency about getting underway. Even Alan sensed that mixing it with the crew of the powerboat would probably be worse than living with the present uncertainty. Within ten minutes they were once again heading for the Skye bridge.

The interminable grey was interspersed with black clouds which were scurrying away and the bridge was clearing against the backdrop of Raasay and Skye.

'I don't know what the fuss was about. I think it looks rather attractive. The curve is pleasant,' murmured Craig.

'I just think that the view was better before they built it,' retorted Alan.

'Oh come on now. The only thing the Skye English are complaining about is the toll charge. They have wanted a bridge for years.

'And as for the beauty thing. At least if future generations don't want it they can take it away and in a few years it will be as though it had never existed. That's a damned sight more than you can say about the Sligachan quarry just around the corner, or the Glensanda excavations on the mountain sides of Loch Linnhe. Once you have removed the mountain you can't put it back again. Some people just choose issues from which they will personally get some recognition, albeit locally. They are from the same egg as the other "do gooders". They won't admit it but the vast majority are simply doing it because it is an easy life. Very few are in it because of firmly held beliefs. They are generally the modern generation of professional thugs. A slightly more delicate "rent a mob", but much much more insidious. Most of their protests are fallacious and self-seeking. Even their so-called hunger strikes are a fix. They try to get their way by outrageous acts to obtain media coverage whilst the majority view is ignored as it is not newsworthy. These high-profile action groups are the same. Minority interests at the expense of the majority.'

'I'm inclined to agree with you,' interrupted Alan. He was not usually so ready to agree with Craig's more vitriolic outbursts but he felt that if they could stir up the Irish pair something to help them to gain control might occur, just a small opportunity to overpower them could arise.

'In fact,' Alan continued, 'It's the same in Africa. These damned agencies keep stirring us up to feed the thousands of hungry refugees, but all that happens is that we defeat the normal effects of nature and they breed even harder. The whole operation is a total waste of resources unless the money is literally ploughed into real land management to produce food and jobs. But that can't be done because the countries are run by sleazy dictators who don't see any benefit in giving up anything as long as a few dinners for the directors of Help the African or some other charity or agency will ensure that they go on getting the rest of the world to foot the bill. What is more the agencies have the same motivation. It keeps them in business too. The whole "green" thing is a major con. You know, drive the refugees in one direction one month then back again the next; Rwanda and Zaire. Keeps the rest of us on our toes and brings in huge funds. Only trouble was the refugees were given the wrong timetable and went back before the major governments could blow even more money on troops and aid.'

Craig, nodded his head violently in agreement and jumped in. He was red in the face and spitting out the words. 'All the same. Absolutely all the same. Sheer bloody-minded selfishness and that goes for you Irish bastards too. North or South. You know damn well that if the North became part of the South the first thing you would do would be to appeal to us for money to help you to integrate everyone as without it the Eire economy would sink without trace. You would rapidly return to the potato-eating loonies you were a century ago. And the North only wants to stay British because they wouldn't get so many free handouts in Eire.'

He stopped. He looked straight at Sean. 'In fact the best thing we could do is tow the fucking lot of you across the Atlantic and dump you on the Americans' doorstep. Although it would be even better if the whole bloody island sank on the way.' He sat down in the corner of the cockpit.

Sean had leaned forward, chin thrust out and his fists clenched. His whole demeanour was aggressive but he was restrained by Mairread's hand.

'My, my, aren't we feeling shitty today. Where is the, "Try to make contact with your captors" philosophy you are supposed to adopt. Well, at least we don't have to feel too sorry for you, since you don't seem to relish us very much,' said Mairread, a bemused smile hovering about her lips.

167

Wizard was motor sailing under the bridge and the only other vessels on the sea were a small prawn boat over towards Pabay and two range patrol boats heading up the inner sound, off for a day of listening to submarines.

Craig had relaxed and going forward sat on the coach roof, soon followed by Alan who sat down beside him.

They both gazed at the landscape they had both come to know so well over many years.

The early morning grey on grey tones, featured in Colin Baxter photographs, that delineated the many toothed ridges and ranges had blossomed into the bracken greens and steely rock shades which were so much the uniform of the north-west Highlands. Trees where they existed were bent to the wind like the people who lived and loved in their shade. The rarity of trees simply emphasised the harshness of the living conditions and the hardiness of the occupants of the landscape.

The wind was backing all the time and a fine force 4 from the south chased them to the north. The light lower cloud danced across the steel grey of the sky. Mairread had stopped the engine as Wizard was logging 6 knots continuously.

'I'm not too sure about this weather. It still doesn't have the settled feel we normally get at this time,' mused Craig.

Alan looked around at the sky. 'It's a pleasant enough day but it could go either way.'

His eyes strayed to the slowly disappearing mountains of Torridon. 'How do we get out of this? Do you really think we will get out alive? Are you going to take a chance on that woman liking you enough to let you go? She has probably killed before and she isn't going to let a little problem like you, or me, stop her.'

Craig turned from examining the rock formations of Skye. 'You may be right. I'll think about it.'

Alan noticed a lack of the usual sparkle in Craig's eyes. He seemed to be only partially aware of what he was saying.

'She is just what I've always needed.'

'Oh come on. Karen has everything: looks, style, wit, intelligence.'

'No sex.'

Alan looked slightly embarrassed.

'She has always seemed sexy enough to me.'

'Yes, I know you fancied her, but simply wanting to sleep with her once or twice is OK, but when you know her you realise there's no substance; nothing to keep the excitement going.'

'You are playing with fire. And in this case that much-used phrase is literally correct. You will end up losing so much you value.'

'You have no idea what I value. Anyway, you would soon end up comforting her if she hasn't already found someone to do just that.'

Alan blushed faintly, but responded. 'Yes, I do like her and I don't think she has been unfaithful. On the contrary, she seems to have tried hard to find useful interests to fill in the time when you are away.'

'Well, you would probably know. You can't keep your hands off her whenever she is near you.'

'Don't be so bloody ridiculous.'

Alan's placid nature was stirred. He could cheerfully have punched Craig, but instead took a deep breath and stared again at the rugged beauty of the cliffs. His mind wandered over the differences between his life and Craig's. Craig was constantly trying to stay ahead of the pack. It was obvious that Craig had to combine the need for routine cash flow projections, balance sheets and business plans, with the fact that so many of the contractual decisions affecting the business were of a political nature. The contracts did not always go to the best contractor. Karen was a vital part of that situation. Mairread spelt death to the organisation and control of a businessman. He shuddered as the reality of that thought flashed through his mind.

Business was a pig. What a difference here to the steady round of dinner parties, club meetings, barbecues, company functions, theatre outings and general social whirl of the South which precluded all of the life he truly wanted. He had more income than he needed but although it had never been said he knew his wife would not welcome a retirement to the country scene.

The wind was picking up slowly but consistently and Wizard was singing along, heeled moderately and clocking up a steady 6 knots. The sea was still quite flat and the bow made the sound of a knife blade cutting cloth as it creased the silk surface of the inner sound and once more headed for the northern reaches of Scotland's most famous island.

Mairread appeared in the cockpit. 'Come back here.' Craig and Alan obliged.

She looked straight at Alan. 'Go below.'

Alan turned away and complied and Sean went after him.

Mairread smiled at Craig. 'Have you got over your bad temper of this morning then?'

'I suppose so. I just don't know how to take you. I don't know what you want.'

'I think you do. I'm so bad at hiding my feelings Sean is sure I will just turn everything over to the police, and yet he has known me for a very long time.'

She smiled at Craig a full smile and said, 'Here take the wheel. I feel that you love the boat when she goes like this.'

Craig stepped behind the wheel and Mairread perched on the coamings alongside him with her hand on his shoulder, steadying herself.

'Where are you going now?' queried Craig.

'Back south, just as fast as we can. It will be much safer if we can get nearer to the people we have to hand this stuff over to.'

'Well if you are planning to round the north end of Skye again we could cut through Caol Rona between Rona and Raasay. It would be a little quicker.'

'Sean. Have a look at Caol Rona. OK to go through?'

There was a short silence. Craig thought, *Doesn't trust me too much, obviously.* Sean's voice came up from below. 'Yes. Just keep clear of all islands. Pretty straightforward.'

The wind which had now further backed easterly made the course change easy and the yacht powered its way through the narrow channel towards Skye.

As the boat sprang free from the channel Craig pointed over to the island of Rona. 'There is a beautiful anchorage just in there. It is totally sheltered, with a lovely walk ashore. Showers too at the keeper's cottage. I'd love to take you there if you come back.'

'That would be nice.' She squeezed his hand.

Just as Craig bent to kiss her Mairread looked away as the roar of two jet fighter planes crashed onto the hills and bounced back. She looked around in time to see the two planes bank steeply and turn rapidly around Applecross and disappear up Loch Carron.

'A lovely village up there. Plockton,' commented Craig.

'Yes. I recall watching a series which had been filmed there. Hamish —' she broke off as the two fighter-bombers once again screamed overhead.

They watched the two aircraft fly north and then turn inland in the direction of Suilven, to vanish into the dusk. They did not see the small helicopter sitting on the hillside at the northern tip of Raasay. Nor therefore did they notice the man lying on a large flat rock observing them through field glasses.

The evening sky was slowly enveloping them as Sean handed two plates of stew and potatoes up through the hatch.

'That smells good. Thanks,' said Craig as Mairread took the plates and passed one to him.

Sean looked surprised. 'Och, it's no trouble. It is nothing at all. There is a mug of cocoa to follow when you're ready.'

'Sean. When you have finished eating get your head down. I want to press on through the night.'

'Sure thing.'

As Wizard rounded Rubha-na-h-Aiseig once again they stared straight into a shaft of sunlight in the June evening and a clearance of cloud over the far-off Outer Hebrides produced a startling panorama of colour radiating from the bright glow of the retiring sun. From the orange red of the orb emanated gold, silver, blue, navy, and lilac ribbons of sky flirting with the disappearing clouds.

'Fabulous, just bloody magnificent,' exclaimed Craig. No matter how many times he sailed the Scottish waters at least once on every holiday something quite indescribable burst in on the senses to leave a mark that could never be erased. Something so outstanding that neither art nor science could ever surpass.

Looking up at Craig's face Mairread smiled. 'You are just like a little boy with a new toy and I love you for it.'

She stretched up and kissed him gently but longingly.

As they pulled slowly apart Craig felt a warmth which spilled into the worries of his mind and washed them away.

'We are fortunate that we are again with the tide,' he observed. It can be pretty horrid here with wind over tide.'

'I am sure we would have made it. I think we can manage whatever we set our minds to,' whispered Mairread.

'I hope so. I really hope so,'responded Craig.

The yacht rushed onwards out into the Minch before changing course to the south.

CHAPTER XIX

IT WAS ABOUT SIX in the morning when there was a knock on his cabin door and Switch entered. 'Mark. Wake up. We think we have them in sight.'

Mark sat up and swung his legs over the side of the bed and onto the floor. He stood up so quickly that he staggered and nearly fell as his brain attempted to get all his faculties working at once. He slipped into his clothes, donned a waterproof jacket to combat the early morning chill and went to the wheelhouse.

On entering he observed Bernie at the helm and Jimmy was peering through binoculars into the grey of the morning. Certainly he was able to identify the sails of a yacht a mile or two ahead. He looked around. 'Where are we?' he enquired.

'Just coming up to Portree,' responded Switch.

'Jimmy has the best eyesight. I thought he could identify the Wizard,' shouted Switch.

Mark laughed. 'Yes, but can Bernie drive? Let me have a look.'

Jimmy passed the binoculars. 'It's about the right size but it's too far away to be sure.'

'Turn up the wick,' ordered Mark.

Jimmy had taken over the helm again and he pushed the throttle levers fully forward. The speed crept up and the whole boat vibrated as it punched forward.

'Bernie. Our two guests will probably be needing a pee. See to it and then let Patrick come up here. Make sure the lady is locked in the small cabin.'

Shortly after Patrick appeared followed by Bernie.

'Good morning, Pat. I hope you have recovered from yesterday's exertion.'

'Yes, Mark. I am feeling a lot better.'

Mark passed the binoculars to Patrick. 'If you look ahead you will see our friends with the cargo. I hope to catch them before too long.'

Patrick looked hard at the vessel ahead of them and noted how well it was coping with the wind. As he watched he saw the sails being reduced and found himself looking at the length of the yacht as it turned to pass south of Raasay. 'If you are going to catch them you had better hurry. The weather is closing in and they are going fast,' he observed. Mark turned to Jimmy. 'Can you get any more out of her?'

'No. We are flat out. This is a long-range boat not a speed boat. We are catching them though.'

Patrick grinned. 'Bloody slowly. At walking pace to be truthful. It will take us all day if we ever see them again. And if it is them.'

Mark picked the VHF handset from its rest. 'Wizard, Wizard, Wizard. This is Irish Rascal, Irish Rascal, Irish Rascal. Over.'

After a short time the radio shouted forth. 'Irish Rascal, Irish Rascal. This is Wizard, Wizard. Channel six nine. Over.'

Mark adjusted the transmission channel. 'Wizard. This is Irish Rascal. We are in your area. Pass your position. Over.'

There was a noticeable delay before the reply came.

'This is Sean. What is your position?'

Mark smiled and replaced the handset on its hook.

'They have rumbled us. Just keep after them.'

They heard Wizard repeat the request for a fix three times before silence again reigned.

The rain increased dramatically and even with the windscreen wipers going at full speed visibility was so poor that Jimmy was compelled to throttle back and reduce speed to 7 knots, and even at that it was none too easy to see the navigational features. Wizard slowly but surely disappeared from view. Mark's face showed a cocktail of emotions ranging from frustration through anger.

'Get some information about Irish Rascal,' snapped Mark to Switch who disappeared below to the communications centre.

Oban Coastguard noted a signal from Irish Rascal on their Skye aerials and puzzled as they were aware that a vessel of that name was being worked on at the boatyard at Ardfern, and was awaiting a new fuel pump. However, they passed the information on via the contact number they had been given.

Switch returned. 'Irish Rascal left Crinan smoking like an oil fire and hasn't been seen since.'

'We must assume that they are heading this way. We must catch up as soon as we can.'

'It will be after Kylerhea,' mused Jimmy.

'As long as it is at the north end of the Sound of Sleat, as further down we are likely to have to tangle with the Rascal. Keep that speed as high as you dare,' stated Mark.

Patrick had moved over to the screen of the radar. He changed the screen mode from 'position' to 'plot'. 'There are some nasty rocks just out from the sound,' he observed.

As he had expected Jimmy bristled. 'I don't need you to tell me how to navigate.' However, he turned and glanced at the chart. The cursor showed that they were clearing the rocks on the current heading. He turned back to the wheel.

Patrick knew that if they hit the rocks at the current speed the damage would be considerable. Certainly enough to disable the vessel although probably not enough to cause it to sink. At least he hoped that. He braced himself for the impact, ready to dash below to release Karen.

As the next few minutes went by he tried not to appear to be concerned. The heavy rain had made the radar picture a forest of lines. The signal from the rocks was never good and was unreadable in that weather.

Suddenly the rain stopped and about 50 yards away, and dead ahead, was the cage beacon on the rocks of Sgeir Thraid.

Jimmy threw the throttles astern and steered violently to port. They were all thrown about the wheelhouse but he had reacted just in time and slipped the boat past the extreme end of the deadly patch.

'Bastard! You incompetent, stupid, bastard,' yelled Switch. 'Pat warned you but you are so determined to show off you bloody well nearly killed us. I'd kick your fuckin' brains out if you had any,' he screamed.

'Shut up.' The cold, detached command came from Mark. Keep going, and get that speed up.'

'Patrick. Take over the navigation.'

'Switch. Check what he does.'

'Jimmy. Keep your eyes wide open and the speed up.'

'Bernie. Stand there and make sure none of them does anything stupid. If you have any doubts, shoot them.'

Mark went below and went to Karen's cabin. When he opened the door Karen was sitting on the edge of the berth.

'What happened? I thought we had hit something,' blurted Karen.

'We very nearly did. I think we could all do with something hot to eat and drink. Can I trust you to prepare breakfast for us all? I will be very grateful.'

'Yes. I would like to do something useful.'

'Good. Come along then. I will show you the business end of the galley. Oh and I will have Jimmy count the knives afterwards,' smiled Mark.

Karen could see that the smile did not reach his eyes and knew that he meant what he said, but she was pleased to be out of the small cabin, and set to to prepare a meal. She suddenly felt very hungry herself.

The radar was picking out the position of several boats between Scalpay and the Kyle.

'I'd be a little careful if I were you. The range patrol boats come in and out of Kyle of Lochalsh regularly and some of them are quite quick,' offered Patrick.

Jimmy grimaced but nodded and throttled back to a steady 7 knots.

Patrick stared ahead and was sure they were overhauling two boats on course for the bridge. It was unlikely that Mark would try anything so close to the Kyles but he certainly would attempt to overtake the yacht at the first isolated place, probably the start of the Sound of Sleat.

Patrick's mind wandered to the last time he had been in the Glenelg area. He had been quite young and his parents had taken him to see the cottage where Gavin Maxwell lived just shortly after he had read *Ring of Bright Water*. It was a lovely place. It was now likely to become known for a gun battle and almost certainly death.

Karen arrived with orange juice, bacon and egg rolls, toast, marmalade and coffee. She appeared much brighter and smiled as she laid the tray down.

Mark looked at her. 'Thank you so much. That really does look just perfect. We will all benefit from that, especially those with short tempers.'

'How are you?' enquired Patrick.

'Much better now that I'm not having to lie on those ropes.' She tried to make it sound frivolous and the others except Switch did smile.

'Please eat yours below. Bernie, you too.' Mark nodded at Karen and she turned and went below to the saloon.

The bridge and the approach roads were clearly visible and the now dwarfed lighthouse looked rather inadequate in the context of the kilowatts of light that would emanate directly from the bridge.

The yacht ahead was certainly identifiable as Wizard and they would be up with her before they finally passed out of Kyle Rhea. The very strong current through the channel would prevent any attack being made actually in the narrows but the opportunity would arise just a short way south of Glenelg and before they came in view of Duisdale and Oronsay. The end was near.

Patrick's mind flailed around with one option after another as to the best way of interfering with the progress of Fast Lady but nothing he thought of would be effective and simultaneously assist Karen's escape. Unconsciously Patrick's hand slipped between his legs and touched the adhesive patch.

They were concentrating on the yacht ahead. Switch fiddled with his gun. Mark unlocked a cupboard and drew out a sporting rifle. He looked down into the saloon. 'Bernie. Take the lady back to her cabin and come here. Things are about to happen.'

It was like a waterfall. In ten seconds the clearing sky was blackened. It was as though a giant chimney had just belched forth a swathe of thick soot. The light went out and the rain washed everything more than 100 metres away from view.

Jimmy instinctively throttled the boat speed down to around 3 knots, and glanced apprehensively at the radar.

Patrick laughed, 'Shit. At least there are no ferries to worry about now.'

Mark looked worried for the first time in hours. 'Can you find the passage?'

'Of course I can. There really isn't a problem with that and they will still be close when we get through this. Speed up a bit, Jimmy.'

Mark seemed relieved to hear Patrick's confident assessment, and visibly relaxed.

'It will be interesting to see how fast we go through here. Tides run at seven or eight knots and with our speed on top we could be like a speedboat.'

'Do you think Jimmy is capable of steering at fifteen miles per hour?' sneered Bernie.

Jimmy, peering into the rain, snarled, 'Straight into your mouth.'

'My God. You two are completely mental. You take it from me that one of you will not be working with me again. So shut up or I will deal with you now.' Mark looked menacingly from Bernie to Jimmy and back again.

They were turning into the narrows and the rain was easing. Visibility was still less than about quarter of a mile.

'That's better. We should be alongside them by the time we get through here. I can step up the speed now.' Jimmy increased speed again.

Mark leaned casually against the bulkhead. 'I don't want to be alongside. Just behind them. So when you see them just hold about one hundred yards astern until I give you the word.'

'OK, Guv.'

The current picked them up and they were travelling at 16 knots as they negotiated the bend and rushed across the stern of the Glenelg ferry. Fast Lady surged out of the narrows and into the Sound of Sleat just as the rain stopped.

There was no sign of Wizard.

Mark looked exhausted. 'Where are they? Where the hell are they? They must have doubled back in the rain. Where the hell have they gone now?'

'Turn back. Get us back to the Kyle of Lochalsh.'

Patrick shook his head. 'You are wasting your time. We can't get through the narrows again until the current decreases substantially. We would just sit there and look stupid. You may as well drop anchor and wait.'

With a look of disgust, Mark nodded his agreement and the powerboat was turned around and the anchor dropped in a small bay at the south end of the gulf just out of the current to await the change of tide.

A grey launch flying a Customs ensign stopped at the north end of Kyle Rhea. On the bridge an officer looked at the flashing cursor. 'Strange. They have gone different ways.'

One of three men in casual clothes stepped forward. He was holding a small instrument that showed a flashing dot, a compass heading and a GPS position. 'Yes. You're correct. The yacht has given them the slip in the rain. Go back to Kyle. We will wait and see what happens next.'

The grey launch turned and headed back to the harbour to be lost amidst the BUTEC range boats sitting there.

CHAPTER XX

SEVERAL HOURS LATER Fast Lady nosed her way up to the refuelling berth nominated by the harbour master. There she filled up with diesel.

Patrick was back in the forepeak and Karen was in the small cabin. Both were thoroughly taped by Jimmy but he was gentle with Karen and smiled back when she smiled at him.

'Please look after me, Jimmy. Please don't let them hurt me.'

'I can't talk now. I do like you. But a woman like you wouldn't be interested in someone like me.'

'Yes I am. I think you cook so well and you try hard to please everybody.'

Jimmy shrugged. 'They would kick my balls off if I didn't.'

'I know you can stand up to them and be your own man.'

Jimmy looked puzzled, but looked her over longingly as he smiled and closed the door.

Switch was trying to find out if 'head office' had any news of Wizard. It was late in the afternoon when he knocked on Mark's cabin door and entered without waiting. Mark looked up from the chair where he was sitting.

'London ain't pleased. Wizard is heading back around Skye, and there is still no sign of Irish Rascal.'

Mark looked irritated. 'Has Bernie finished with the fuel and water?'

'Just tidying up now. We can be underway when you settle up with the harbour master.'

Mark went ashore to the harbour master's office, exchanged a few pleasantries about cruising the isles, and the weather, but was conscious of three men standing in an inner office who watched him closely all the time he was in there. He was certain they were more than harbour employees but comforted himself with the thought that there were several foreign boats including Saudi patrol craft moored in the area, all involved with underwater testing on the inner sound range.

As he left to return to the boat the men looked at several photographs. Two of them nodded as they replied to a question asked of them by the third man, a big man with a scar running from his left ear to the middle of his forehead. They left the office soon after Mark.

When Mark arrived back at Fast Lady, the engines were running, most of the dock lines were away and Bernie and Switch were standing by the remaining warps ready to cast off. Jimmy was watching from the bridge.

Mark stepped aboard. 'Let's go hunting.'

The ropes were cast off at about 6 p.m. and the big boat motored out under the Skye bridge and into the inner sound.

Mark spent a considerable time in his cabin alone, talking occasionally to his contacts. Information that Irish Rascal had still not left Loch Craignish confirmed his belief that Wizard would not remain in the inner sound but would try to return south to make eventual contact easier.

When Mark arrived on deck both Switch and Bernie looked expectantly at him, conscious they may just be hunting the proverbial needle in the haystack.

'Right lads. Back around Skye. They will have a good start but we must get to them before our cargo goes missing for good.'

With the lessened wind and the brightening sky Fast Lady made good time, rounded Rona and headed through the passage between En Trodday and Skye. It had been dark for some time and the remaining cloud made for poorer visibility than normal at the time of year. Mark looked around. They were all visibly tired and he still had the feeling that the finish of this business was likely to be unpleasant.

'I think it would do us all some good if we had a shower and some rest. George, you can use the shower in my cabin and Jimmy, you use the other. Grab some sleep and I will wake you in four hours. Oh, and send the lady through here. She can make something to eat. Bernie, you steer. I will join you soon.'

Just as Karen arrived in the saloon Jimmy wandered naked through to the shower.

'Jimmy, you are embarrassing our guest,' laughed Mark. 'You should have wrapped that monster in a towel.'

Jimmy turned and shook his hips. 'I don't think she should be done out of a view of this. It's the biggest one she will have seen.'

Karen turned to Mark. 'What did you want?'

'Well, as you know, quite a few things but just now I would like something to eat and drink.'

'I cooked a meal just a few hours ago.'

'You don't get a free passage on this boat so just get on with it again. If you are lucky you may manage a few hours before you have to cook for the others.'

'It would be less of a chore if I could have a shower too.'

'Oh for God's sake. I know why I've never married. Right. After George is finished you can use the shower in my cabin.'

'Patrick too?'

'Yes, Yes. Yes. Let me know when you are finished and I will get him.'

Karen walked over to the galley and started examining the contents of the refrigerator. Satisfied she set about preparing some loin of lamb.

Mark walked over to her. 'This should help.' He smiled and handed her a glass of wine. 'You really should reconsider my offer. I have contacts all around the world. Europe, Asia, South America, the Far East. We could travel and dine with the wealthiest men in the world. I am very generous to those whom I trust, and who support me. You would have a comfortable and exciting life.'

'Until I was shot by your enemies who must be numerous, no doubt.'

'No, that won't happen. I have too many at high level indebted to me. I am totally protected.'

'What about the people we are chasing? They would surely try to kill you?'

'Oh, they are an inconvenience. They will be dealt with in due course.'

'Why are you here? Why haven't you left all this to the others? If you are so powerful why aren't you sitting at the opera or relaxing in the sun? Why are you doing this dirty work? It doesn't seem to be the job for the man you are purporting to be.'

'This delivery is rather special. And I felt it presented some unusual problems. I wanted to keep control myself.'

'What kind of problems?'

The question went unanswered as Switch and Jimmy passed through the saloon. Karen saw the hatred in Jimmy's eyes. It was not the look of a loyal lieutenant.

Mark did not look round at them. 'Goodnight,' was all he said.

'Goodnight, Guv.'

Mark pulled himself upright. 'Off you go and have that shower. We have plenty of water now. I'll look after the cooker.'

Karen couldn't help it. 'Thanks,' she said and went off to the shower in the master cabin.

The warm water was wonderful. To wash her hair felt like heaven. She reached out, grabbed for a towel. Damn! She had left it on the bed. She stepped out of the shower into the cabin and standing facing her holding out the towel was Mark. She gasped and then her composure reasserted itself and she smiled. 'Thank you. I had quite forgotten about that.'

'It's no trouble. I have been rewarded with the sight of one of the most beautiful women I have ever seen. You really have the most wonderful legs and breasts.'

'Thank you. You can be so charming. Perhaps at another time, in a different place, who knows?'

Karen was surprised at how easily she had responded. For once she had not blushed furiously and blustered.

'Yes. Who knows. I could almost give it all up for you. But that would be the sort of weakness I can not afford. Get dressed and I'll see you next door. There's no hurry. Everything is under control.'

Mark turned and left the cabin.

Karen relished the luxury of clean clothes for the first time in absolutely ages.

When she returned to the saloon the lamb steaks were ready for serving and she dished them up with the mashed potatoes and pepper sauce and handed a plate up to Bernie in the wheelhouse.

'This is great, Guv. We should have a woman around on all our trips.'

'I am trying, Bernie old son. I am trying.'

Mark smiled at her as he said it. 'You see. You really are appreciated.'

'Thanks. It is better than lying in that forepeak.'

'Oh yes. I will get our friend.'

Despite the failure to locate the yacht the atmosphere had relaxed considerably, but Mark still drew his gun when he went forward. Karen heard him tell Patrick to collect his clothes and then ushered him into the shower compartment, but not the luxurious en-suite one. 'Shout when you are ready. Don't come out until I tell you.'

Mark returned, poured another two glasses of Chablis, sat down alongside Karen and they ate in silence.

In about five minutes there was a call from Patrick and Mark walked to the end of the passage. 'Now, Pat, come out slowly and walk to the saloon. Slowly. In fact, just do everything very slowly. I feel nervous, and you know how dangerous a nervous man with a gun can be.'

Patrick exited the shower compartment. 'You don't have enough humanity to be nervous.'

'Come, come now, Pat. Here am I entertaining your lady with the best wine that France can produce and you are so ungrateful.'

'If you are being nice to anyone it is for what you think it may bring you.'

'Well, so be it. I am a businessman, you know.'

'I didn't know that being a businessman could sound like such a dirty trade.'

They had entered the saloon and Mark signalled Patrick to sit opposite Karen and himself. Karen rose and served a portion of the lamb to Patrick. Mark leaned forward and poured a glass of wine. 'Oh, and don't worry. It is not poisoned,' Mark laughed.

When they had finished and Karen was clearing away the remnants of the meal, Mark suddenly looked serious. 'Why are you mixed up with the IRA? Why are you maintaining secret contacts with London? Why haven't you been satisfied with the rewards I have made available to you? You puzzle me. We are doing very well. You know I have the contacts to do much more. I have ministers dining with me. The world could be ours. You are the smartest fellow in this organisation. You can run a legitimate business and be comfortable with people at all levels of government. For God's sake tell me why you have gone off the rails.' Mark leaned back on the settee and looked hard at Patrick.

There was a long deep silence. Karen tried not to clink the dishes. She found herself straining to catch the slightest sound above the throb of the diesels.

'It was tough in Ireland. You can only live as a double for so long. It's not so bad if you are a "sleeper", but when you are reporting continuously there is always a feeling that you will be found out.'

Patrick sat with his chin cupped in his hands. It was clear that he intended to continue but was struggling to find the right words. Mark watched impassively. Karen placed cups of coffee in front of them. Patrick did not look at her although she longed just to look into his eyes. To know what he was thinking and planning.

Patrick was fighting to clear his mind. Too many facts were circulating in his brain at the same time. He struggled to try to get priorities into perspective. So many briefings. So many debriefings. So many indoctrinations. Sometimes it was hard to sort out who was right and who was wrong.

'I heard and saw so much that I suppose I let them get to me. I formed a lot of friends in the Nationalist community. Not terrorists but just the average people. I felt for them. I realised that, being part Irish myself, I did want to help. Not just put terrorists behind bars but really help.'

Patrick stopped and took a large mouthful of wine which he swilled around the dryness of his mouth.

'Go on. I am interested,' encouraged Mark.

'I think I could have gone a long way in Military Intelligence, but it became clear to me that I could not go on much longer in Ireland. The conflict between liking the people, watching the political hypocrisy and hating the gunmen was becoming so intense that I was bound to do something stupid. In fact the so-called peace process just made matters worse. It was even less tenable to listen to the hypocrisy of the different groups while sensing the urgent need, the feeling of urgency, in the ordinary people for relief, whilst I knew that behind it all was just the usual fight for power. I got out.'

Mark stared straight at him. 'You know that it was a prominent Joint Intelligence Committee member who recommended you to me. They thought very highly of you.'

Patrick had always wondered how Mark had known enough about him to get in touch. How much did he really know? The confusion in Patrick's mind just increased. He had suspected that there had been leaks from Military Intelligence but it was worrying to think that members of the JIC, controllers of all of Britain's security services, and the minders of prime ministers, were actively selling the services of ex-intelligence personnel to illegal groups – *or is it an illegal organisation?* He had read of the almost unbelievable influence of the senior civil service on government ministers and opposition politicians. Indeed he had been shown documents almost certainly linking senior ministers to illegal oil sales, arms shipments and drug handling, but he had not realised that the distorted belief that what they were doing was for the country's good had been twisted to the extent that the identities of agents and spies were being openly traded with organisations such as Mark's.

'I was quite content operating with you. But when the IRA cease-fire was called they contacted me. The "nice guys" pointed out that to operate democratically they would need even greater resources than bombers. They asked for my help. I was still in that confused state and felt that they were probably right, so I agreed. Wrongly, as we now can all see. But nevertheless through a misplaced nationalism. I don't suppose there is much point in saying I regret it now, but I do.'

Patrick sighed and sat back.

Mark actually smiled. 'I would like to believe you. In fact I really need to believe you, but in this business any doubt about someone can be destructive. As soon as you start worrying that a "friend" might be doubtful it becomes almost impossible to keep your mind on the job.

'I would like to tell you a lot more about this business but I cannot under these circumstances. I would like you to believe that I am not in this for drug money. Yes. I do take it. But I am helping this country in more ways than you can imagine, but I don't suppose you care.'

Patrick grunted and stared back. 'If you are trying to tell me that you are really a good guy you are wasting your breath.'

Mark shrugged his shoulders. 'Fair enough. We all have our reasons for our actions. I almost believe that you would rather help me than your Irish friends but I just can't take the chance. Now I must ask you to return to the cabin.'

Whether intentionally or by lack of concern Mark said nothing when both Patrick and Karen went into the passage cabin. He locked the door, climbed to the wheelhouse, sat in the navigator's swivel chair and stared out over the night sea.

Bernie sensed that no conversation was required. Only the flashing of the lighthouses and the navigation lights of a few other vessels interrupted the summer darkness.

The big boat throbbed on.

Patrick sat beside Karen and put his arm around her. 'I don't think it will be too long before this nightmare is over. There are bound to be developments soon.'

'I don't want it to be over if it means I don't see you again but I am not sure I can stand much more of the strain of all of this. I can't help wondering about the children. Do you think they have harmed them?'

'I honestly don't think so. This situation was never envisaged and you should have been sufficient security.'

Karen was silent for a few seconds then asked, 'You know more about this than you have told me, don't you?'

'Yes, but it is still not wise for you to have that information. Let me just say that as long as Mark and his mates are kept sweet we are probably in a lot less danger than you think.'

'Well, I suppose that is reassuring. Mark can actually seem quite nice at times.'

'Don't be fooled. That man is phenomenally wealthy and, as far as I know, is mixed up in almost everything nasty all round the world. He is here only because this deal will give him an introduction to one of the most corrupt regimes ever known and I am not referring to the British Government,' he smiled. He continued. 'This boat was converted to carry drugs or arms, both of which are currency with the small countries who act as fronts for the big arms deals that the real troublemakers of the world need. Countries like Iraq, Iran, Libya, Chile. When did you ever see a private yacht with a radio installation like this one, where all the doors have locks? Never in my experience. I am not sure who ultimately pulls the strings, but I am fairly sure it isn't Mark.'

Karen sighed and pulled herself close to Patrick. He lifted her chin and kissed her gently and they slowly sank back onto the berth.

As their kisses grew more sensuous Karen allowed her hand to slip down onto Patrick's trousers, undoing the zip and slipping inside to cradle his penis in her hand. She was amazed at herself. Never before would she have dreamt of doing such a thing but the feel of the soft penis in her hand was reassuring and comforting.

Patrick moaned quietly and caressed her.

Karen smiled to herself as she felt the stiffening, the twitching and straightening. It was wonderful to feel him respond just to her touch. She just wanted to please him, to relax and comfort him. She started to move her hand up and down the length of the member when Patrick's hand shot down between his legs, and he sat bolt upright, banging his head on the overhead berth. 'My God! Hell!'

Patrick rarely swore and Karen thought she must have hurt him. 'I'm so sorry. What did I do?'

'Nothing. It's not your fault. I have just realised that I have lost a small radio transmitter. It must have come off when I was washing or drying myself in the shower.'

'What does that mean?'

'I am not sure. We have to assume that they must have found it by now. If they have I dread to think what conclusions they will come to but it has almost certainly been destroyed. Shit. Oh well there is nothing I can do now. Let's try to get some rest.'

Despite being cramped into the single berth they were both so tired that not even the latest development kept them awake for more than few seconds.

The dawn was just starting to flicker into life over Skye when Jimmy and Switch arrived in the wheelhouse. 'Hi, Guv. Everything OK?'

'Yes. Fairly uneventful. I think we may have even passed them, but in any event they won't be far away. This time we must not lose them. Listen to all calls. They must transmit soon. Do not miss their call and wake me immediately. There is food on the cooker. Just heat it up. Our lady guest made it. So remember to say thank you.'

Bernie laughed. 'Oh, I won't forget that. Goodnight.'

Mark had just come out of his shower when Bernie knocked and entered the cabin. 'What do you think this is boss?'

Bernie was holding out his hand and lying in the palm was an adhesive pad with a small black device attached.

'Where did you get that?'

'Lying on the floor of the shower.'

'I'm not sure, but it could be a transmitter. If it is I know where it came from.'

Mark held the unit into the door frame and forced the door shut. There was a crack and a crunch. 'I just hope we have eliminated this thing in time. Anyway, get some rest. We will deal with it tomorrow.' The safe house telephone number and the transmitter were starting to make sense to Mark. He smiled to himself. *Perhaps he is not as great a danger as I feared.* With that comforting thought he slept.

It seemed as if he had only recently fallen asleep when Mark heard Switch's dulcet tones calling him awake. He struggled to orientate himself. At first he could not fully grasp where he was, but then the news broke through the haze.

'We got two new co-ordinates. I have checked. The first is Canna, and we are almost there. The second is a small island I haven't heard of called Gometra.'

'I'm not surprised. You hadn't heard of Mull, one of the largest islands around Britain. Geography is not your strong point.'

'Well. They have been told to stay at Canna today and to go to Gometra tonight. We can probably get them on Canna.'

Mark shrugged and pulled on his clothes. He was still cold from lack of sleep and he donned a heavy fleece top. 'Show me the position of Gometra.'

They went to the wheelhouse.

'Good news, Guv, int it,' bubbled Jimmy.

'Yes, Jimmy,' agreed Mark, 'We have a few more hours of work to do and then we all can go home. You have a break. Come below. I have something right up your street.'

Mark was by this time peering at the charts and gauging the relative positions of Canna and Gometra.

'Did you hear who they were speaking to?'

'Not really. It was a link call.'

'The total failure of mobile phones up here has been a bonus. They wouldn't have used the VHF if they could have used telephones,' mused Mark. 'OK. This is what we do.'

They listened whilst Mark detailed the action they were to take to collect the goods.

After they had been through it three times, Mark stood up. 'I think we should have another talk with Pat. I may just know a little more about our mystery telephone number. Bring him here.'

Minutes later Patrick came into the saloon accompanied by Jimmy. The gun held by Switch and pointed at his stomach was the first thing he saw, seconds before he was struck on the back of the neck. He fell forward onto his knees and just stopped himself from pitching right forward onto his face.

'Hands behind your back,' screamed Jimmy in an hysterical high-pitched voice. He then bent and taped Patrick's wrists tightly together.

'I am so sorry, Patrick. I really had hoped that you were still working with me.' Mark looked at Patrick with an obviously false look of disappointment.

'Where did you get this, and who is picking up the signals?'

Mark held out his hand showing the small smashed transmitter and the adhesive pad.

Patrick tried to appear more comfortable than he felt. 'Some of your associates are very unhappy with you and asked me to keep tabs on you. If I hadn't used the bug they would have been suspicious. I didn't feel it mattered as long as we were doing what they expected. They sure as hell will be worried now.'

'That sounds very feasible, but I would have expected you to tell me if anything like this happened. After all you work for me. I pay you. But of course, others may also pay you. How do you communicate with these "associates"?'

Patrick hesitated and received a kick in the small of the back. 'I use the London number. They gave me the number.'

'How do you know who they are? How do you know they are contacts of mine. They could be police, couldn't they?'

'No. They had too much detail of you for them to be cops.'

'OK. Let's confirm it. I'll phone them now. You can give me the password.'

Again Patrick hesitated, with the same result. He gasped with pain. It felt as though his ribs had caved in.

'All right. When they ask which service, just say "Tell Tale". They will respond with "Are you travelling?" You reply "Collection and Delivery".'

Mark looked less concerned. He knew that the 'no service' indication on his phone was typical of the north-west Highlands. He couldn't make the call even if he wanted to.

'Put Pat away and make sure he gives us no trouble. I don't like even the thought that he was prepared to talk to some third party.'

Jimmy and Switch dragged Patrick to his feet and pushed him to the forepeak.

Once they were inside the small confined space they both set about punching and kicking him until he wretched and was sick. Switch was about to tape his ankles and hands together when Jimmy pushed him away. 'I've got something else to attend to.'

With eyes staring as though seeing nothing Jimmy balanced himself and stamped repeatedly on Patrick's groin until there was no sound or voluntary movement. 'He won't be giving us or her much trouble now.'

They taped the ankles and hands together behind Patrick's back and left. Patrick groaned but did not move.

In the middle of a gloriously sunny afternoon the big cruiser turned sharply north past the reefs and eased its way into Gometra harbour on the south coast of the island, a beautifully sheltered haven lying between the islands of Gometra to the west and Ulva to the east. As usual the sheltered bay was deserted and despite it being so early in the year the warmth trapped in the bay was tangible. Fast Lady eased over to the west side of the bay and stopped. The anchor ran out and Bernie and Switch busied themselves launching an inflatable dinghy, as Mark lowered the boat's main tender.

They rowed the inflatable over to the small stone jetty and then carried it up the slope to the old ferrymen's cottages where they hid it in the long grass and ferns. Switch looked about. He was sweating in the warm sunshine. 'Look at that,' he shouted, pointing to the ridge to the north. Upon the promontory a regal stag looked down on them, unmoving. As they watched other deer slowly rounded the hillside just below the stag and disappeared over the shoulder, looking jet black against the azure sky. The stag turned his head from side to side then swung round and dropped down beyond the crest.

'Fantastic place.' Bernie was beaming. 'I've never seen real deer like that before. I'm going to come back here.'

'I don't know when, and there aren't too many pubs,' laughed Switch.

'Mmm. Well maybe just for a day sometime.'

'C'mon. Let's get back.'

They walked back down the hill to where Mark was waiting in the tender. Because of the weed and rock he hadn't been able to get close in and Switch and Bernie were forced to remove their shoes and socks and wade out.

'Jesus, that's cold. I think I was just about ten when I last went wading.'

'Judging by the colour of your feet, I'd say that was the last time you washed them,' joked Switch.

'Belt up. I had a shower last night just like you.'

They had reached the tender, climbed in and returned to the boat. As soon as they were aboard Jimmy carefully took the powerboat out of the lagoon, staring at the reef to the east with a concerned look as if the reef could be kept at bay by threat. As soon as they were clear of the headland they turned to the west, where the flat-topped Treshnish Isles stood beckoning, inviting exploration, and, to the south, floating craggily in the shimmering sea Staffa promised the inspiration of Mendlesohn.

Mark stared out at the view stretching away to the distant isles of Tiree and Coll, then turned slowly to look south at Iona with the cathedral visible against the sky. He walked to the windows facing the stern, picked up the binoculars and drifted his vision over the high cliffs and the might of Ben More, then down seaward again to the island of Little Colonsay.

Lowering the glasses he returned to his seat. 'I could live here if only it didn't get so cold in the winter.'

Switch smiled, 'Well you could always sail to the Med for the winter.'

The dark blue vessel changed course as it rounded the Maisgeir reef and headed north.

CHAPTER XXI

AT ABOUT TWO A.M. Sean reappeared and looked up at Craig. 'OK, down you come.'

Craig looked at Mairread and she smiled, nodded her head slowly and said, 'Go on. Get some rest. I'll see you later.'

Craig fought hard to hide his disappointment. He no sooner had reassured himself that Mairread cared for him deeply than something happened which totally destroyed that feeling. He went below and Sean handcuffed him with a cable tie; as he entered the aft cabin he noticed Alan's hands had been similarly secured. He heard the bolt slide home and something heavy being laid against the cabin door. The door opened inwards but he guessed that sail bags or holdalls had been positioned against the door to prevent any rapid exit. So much for trust.

He lay down, and heard the radio being used. 'We are well on our way' he overheard and then nothing until '15446CC. Goodnight.' He started to think again about these codes but the West Highland air and tiredness soon overcame him and with visions of Mairread and Eriskay drifting through his mind, he fell asleep.

Craig woke regularly and looked from the cabin windows. He saw the gleam of lights which he guessed were Waternish, and Uisgnish. By the time he recognised Neist Point it was getting quite light and the sun was brightening the sky with streaks of gold which kissed the low clouds and graded the sky from pale blue to deepest black where the messengers of morning had yet to penetrate.

Alan was awake but they said little until the sound of the heavy weight being moved was a precursor to the cabin door opening.

'Good morning.'

Sean entered holding a knife and cut the wrist ties.

'Craig. On deck. Alan. Cook up some breakfast.'

As Craig rubbed his wrists he smiled at Sean. 'You don't look too well. Lack of sleep?'

'Enough. I've had enough. Now hurry.'

'Why? Where are we going?'

'Shut up and just get on with it.'

Craig climbed into the cockpit where Mairread sat looking over to the east.

She peered at the cliffs. 'These are interesting rocks. Do you know them?'

Craig looked at the mouth of Loch Bracadale and the rock stacks at the north-west corner of the entrance.

'Yes. That's McLeod's maidens.'

'Nasty looking maidens,' smiled Mairread.

Rum was still shrouded in mist and the highest peaks were lost in the clouds. Canna was a dark strip in the distance, and the sun's rays were just lighting up the long low cloud marking the position of the Outer Isles. The course of the boat was straight at Canna and Craig felt confident that it was the next port of call.

The unmistakable smell of bacon wafted up and shortly afterwards the plates of bacon, mushrooms and eggs arrived accompanied by a slice of fried bread.

'Well done, Alan. Just what I needed,' laughed Craig.

'I thought the cholesterol should be ignored under the present circumstances,' responded Alan, and soon they were all speechless as they demolished the breakfast spread.

Craig and Alan strained their hearing as they caught snatches of a radio conversation. Sean was speaking to what became evident was the rendezvous vessel.

'At last . . . Not before bloody time . . . No sign of the opposition . . . Oh that's not so good . . . 15446CC . . . 09967CC. Fine. Out.'

Sean came up bringing with him the binoculars and as he scanned the sea astern Craig hoped fervently that there was no sign of the pursuers. He believed that if everything now went smoothly there was a much improved chance of getting away alive. He hated the thought but he was still unable to decide what Mairread and Sean would do with them, and he was confused.

Sean returned to the cockpit from the stern. 'No sign of them this time. Everything should be OK for tomorrow. We stay where we planned today and move again tonight.'

He sat down at the forward end of the cockpit next to the hatch with his hand in his pocket, obviously holding the gun. It seemed to be his favourite place.

Mairread looked relieved. 'That's good. What's the news of Fast Lady?'

'Last seen leaving Kyle of Lochalsh. I think we have to assume we have been spotted and they are following.'

'In that case they won't be too far astern. This could all prove to be very tricky,' muttered Mairread.

A large helicopter marked 'RESCUE' flew overhead in the direction of the Uists, followed a short time later by a small Cessna which flew parallel with them for a few minutes and then buzzed off in the direction of Skye or the mainland.

'The engines of these things always sound as though they are about to cut out,' observed Alan.

By the time large mugs of hot coffee had been consumed there was a warmth in the sun and the island of Canna was approaching rapidly.

Craig glanced at his watch. It was 10 a.m. Another day well under way. He looked skyward to see the vapour trails of the big jets on their way to Boston, New York, Los Angeles and Seattle and despite his fear he was just glad he wasn't sitting all cooped up in that sticky, unpleasant cabin trying to read, stretching his legs and hoping for sleep all at the same time. He really hated long-distance flying.

At this time of day the cruising yachts of the late risers were just leaving the beautiful anchorage. They passed by with a wave as they eased out into the swell of the Minch and headed for the Outer Hebrides, or for the less adventurous a return to the safety of the inshore waters.

They anchored Wizard well to the west of the bay and even then it needed three attempts to get the anchor to hold in the heavy kelp growth that had appeared in recent years.

'This used to be a great anchorage, but the weed now is terrible. We dragged here last year even after driving the hook in with the engine,' commented Craig as he returned to the cockpit. 'How long will we be staying?'

'Don't know,' was the sharp response from Mairread.

Mairread turned to Craig. 'We will go ashore. Get the dinghy organised.'

Mairread turned to Sean. 'I'm just going to the telephone box. I would like to confirm a few things and I would rather not have it on the VHF.'

Craig's heart rate increased noticeably as he lowered the tender into the bay. Mairread passed the oars down then joined him in the boat.

The Mariner outboard started first pull and they set off for the shore immediately below the track to the pier.

Together they lifted the dinghy over the shingle and made off the painter to a large boulder before heading off along the track towards the village, such as it was.

The sun was warm and the wind was dying rapidly. They passed the big house and the small post office to reach the telephone box. They had not spoken, and Craig allowed his eyes to rove over the hillside to the rowan and hazel and numerous other varieties of tree which had been introduced to the island over many years, and on to the craggy basaltic columns forming the lava backbone of Rabbit Island.

'Wait where I can see you. Don't speak to anyone.'

Craig looked around. It wasn't Sauchiehall Street on a Saturday. Speaking to someone would prove difficult. He could just make out a tractor on the far side of the bay behind some derelict cottages but there wasn't anyone else to talk to. He contemplated making a run for it but that he rejected as he was uncertain about locating any help, and, anyway, what would happen to Alan? The island had been donated to the National Trust for Scotland although the owner still lived in the big house. He contemplated running up to the house but rejected it again for the same reasons.

He could see that Mairread wasn't actually doing much talking but she was holding the handset to her ear and listening intently. He shifted his attention to Wizard and caught the glimpse of sun reflecting off binoculars. The boat looked good out there.

Mairread came out of the booth. 'We have a bit of time to waste. Let's take a walk up to the church. This one back here with the odd-looking round steeple.'

'I didn't think you would want to go there. That's the Scot's church, the Protestant Church. The Catholic Church used to be the more impressive one over there on Sanday but that is now abandoned and derelict. Now there is a small cottage church just a bit further along this track.'

'No, it's all right. Let's head for your Scottish Church. It looks unusual.'

They walked back along the track and up to the small church, had a look inside at the odd bell ringing arrangement inside the Celtic-style tower, and then passed around the outside to the rear.

'Come on, let's go a bit further.'

Mairread smiled at him.

She led the way from the church to another path which ran in the direction of the large hill. The ground was covered in a coarse grass which grew in tufts interspersed with moss green where the poor drainage resulted in water lying when the rain was heavy.

Craig noticed that she was careful to keep the church between them and the yacht. Obviously those on Wizard were not intended to see where they were bound.

'Come on then, tell me. What else do you know about this island?'

'Oh I've been coming here for so long that I have forgotten most of the stories. I believe Canna means rabbit island and there are certainly too many rabbits here. The whole place is riddled with them and unless some action is taken I think they will eventually destroy the island. In fact it is the only place where I have seen old rabbits. There don't seem to be any natural predators.

'The island belonged, way back, to the Benedictines when they were on Iona but changed hands many times including occupation by the Norse and now it's owned by the National Trust.'

They were holding hands and Craig's enthusiasm was growing.

'On the north shore, almost halfway along the island, is a Viking ship grave. It is actually more obvious when you sail past the north coast than it is when you are on land. They have found Norse graves on both Canna and Sanday but they had all been robbed so not too much was learned.

'There was a convent on the south shore and the only way down to it is on a rope. Saint Columba must have been pretty energetic when he and his monks came to visit.'

Pointing up at a pillar of rock ahead of them, he said, 'That, up there, An Coroghon was a medieval prison where a chief, I think a Clanranald chief put his unfaithful wife to keep her away from her lover. Sir Walter Scott wrote about it. They used to take these things seriously.

'And that big lump on the left is Compass Hill. The story goes that the magnetic effect of the hill badly affects compasses, but I have climbed it and walked around it on numerous occasions and like so many of these old stories they were probably told the first time by an inebriated Viking as I could find no effect whatsoever.'

'You obviously love this area to remember the stories.'

'I have just skimmed over them. I could tell you a lot more about the island including its modern history, and how fertile it was and so on.'

'Next time. Now I want a kiss.' Mairread put her arms around his neck and pulled his face towards her. They walked behind the BT communications dish and up into a sheltered hollow on the hill. The sun beat down from a cloudless sky and with no breeze it was very warm. They kissed and looked out to the Cuillin ranges of Skye where the last light clouds were just clinging on to the jagged tops as the wind tried to drag them off to play on the mountains of Loch Nevis.

'I can see why you like it here so much. I understand why you would want to come back again and again.'

They lay close together, Craig gently running his hands over the shapely form of her body. He plucked open her check shirt, eased away the soft bra and allowed his lips to caress the full firm breast.

His hand slid down over her stomach and undid the button waistband of the trousers. The zip slid down of its own accord as his fingers sought the inside of her pants and pressed down through the light hair until they rested on the small bud he remembered so well from Eriskay.

As his fingers caressed her intimacy Mairread kissed him more feverishly and worked at the belt of his trousers, pulling hard on the belt to disengage the tongue from the buckle. She pushed the zip down and taking the waistband of his trousers and pants together pushed them down until her hand grabbed the hardness and she squeezed.

'Now. Now. Don't wait.'

Craig felt his body burning hot. Even in the open he was sweating. She raised her hips to allow him to push the clothing down and raised one leg so that he could slip the pants over her foot.

As soon as they were clear he rolled on top of her and before he could do any more Mairread had pressed him into herself.

He immediately thrust violently and faster. It was so different to making love with Karen. Mairread shouted,'Yes. Now, Yes.'

He crashed into her over and over again until suddenly drained of all energy he could hold back no longer. He gasped a long sigh and collapsed on top of her.

They lay still for some minutes whilst she kissed gently at his ear until the coolness of the air reached the hot exposed parts of their bodies. 'Oh, that is cold,' she laughed and they rolled apart feeling self-conscious as they pulled their pants and trousers on and pushed shirt tails inside waistbands, until Craig leaned on one elbow and looked straight into her sparkling eyes.

'What happens now? Will we be together again?'

'Of course we will. Tomorrow this will all be over. We will have passed on the goods and we will be free to do whatever we like.'

'How can that be? What about Alan? He knows and would spoil everything.'

'Can you persuade him not to say anything?'

'Never. He is bound to report Mike's death.'

'You must persuade him to keep quiet. Threaten him if necessary. Otherwise we may have to persuade him.'

All of a sudden Craig felt afraid. *She suddenly was so cold and unaffected by the thought of Alan. Surely that means only one thing.* Craig wondered where that left himself. *Does she really want me or is sex a convenient weapon to keep me quiet? No. She loves me. Surely she couldn't react so spontaneously if she didn't care. Could she?*

'Come on. We had better get back to the boat.'

They walked back down the track with their arms around each other until they could see the masts of the yacht when Mairread disengaged and walked on about a metre apart. They said nothing until they reached the shore and only then did they speak with just sufficient words to enable them to launch the dinghy, and row back to the yacht.

'Raise the dinghy into the davits.'

Alan went to the stern to help, whilst Mairread stood at the forward end of the cockpit whispering to Sean.

'Have a good walk?' enquired Alan. 'You must have gone a long way. You've been away for hours. I thought poor old Sean was going to have a heart attack, and I am not sure my first aid is up to that.'

'Yes. It really is warm and pleasant over the hill.'

'Where do we go from here?'

'I am not sure but we must be extra careful. I think we are nearing the end of this affair. Be careful.'

Alan smirked. 'I am careful, but I am not so sure about you. I hope you used a condom. You stink of sex.'

Craig finished making off the davit ropes and turned back to the cockpit. He ignored the last comments and sat down in the sun. His thoughts were confused. Certainly tonight and tomorrow could be very dangerous. He decided that he would try to secure Alan's release before finally deciding what to do himself. If, of course he was given any options. He shivered slightly despite the warmth in the air.

Fresh food stocks were almost exhausted. Mairread cooked for the first time and produced pasta with a sauce of tinned salmon, anchovies with red peppers and spicy sausage, in cream. Washed down with two bottles of Macon Uchizy it was a highly acceptable meal and Craig said so. 'Under different circumstances I would have said that was the best makeshift meal I have ever had.'

Mairread laughed. 'Under different circumstances I would have said that was a complement.'

Sean, who looked slightly embarrassed by the mutual admiration, muttered, 'Under different circumstances I would have said that was a very ordinary wine.'

Craig smiled. He sensed Sean's discomfort. 'Yes. But Chateau Lafitte doesn't travel too well or appreciate being bounced about in stormy weather. Just like you.' Looking directly at Mairread he announced, 'When we get ashore I will treat you to the Lafitte.'

'I look forward to that.'

Alan, for the first time, felt an empathy with Sean. 'Can we do something before I am sick?'

Sean rose from his seat. 'Good idea. Let's be going.'

It was close to four o'clock in the afternoon when Wizard motored from Canna, turned east and then south into the channel between Canna and Rum.

There was little or no wind and the yacht was running under engine. Craig sat in the bow with Alan whilst Sean and Mairread conversed in the cockpit.

'I suppose they are working out the best time, place and method for killing us,' mused Alan.

'I don't think it will come to that.'

'Why? What the hell are they going to do with us? We know them. We can recognise them anywhere. They would be useless in this area again once we give out their descriptions.'

Craig leaned back against the guard rail, trying to look and sound more confident than he felt. 'You may be correct but they would ruin the whole of this area for drug collection if they murder us. Remember, by now Mike's body has been found. That may just pass as an accident for a while, but two more, probably shot. No, they would not risk that.'

'For the sort of money we are probably carrying I think they would risk almost anything. To hold on to this stuff for as long as this probably means it is worth millions. Otherwise they would have thrown it overboard and escaped. I am not optimistic.'

'OK. We just keep alert. Next chance we get we will risk it.'

'As long as the transfer isn't made at sea. I am not jumping over the side.'

'We will have to wait and see.' Craig closed his eyes and dozed.

Alan lay back on the deck and stared high into the sky and watched the thin cloud racing across. Would Craig act with him or was he so besotted with Mairread that he would actually do nothing? Was he right? Would they simply be freed after the transfer or would they be got rid off? On balance Alan felt that they would be shot, as they knew the death of Mike would be investigated. There was no alternative unless they were intending to vanish completely. More so if there was any trouble with the transfer. Especially if they became a burden.

He decided that he would take any opportunity to try to escape at the first sign of trouble. He wasn't going to sit around to be shot. What if he was shot jumping over the side? He didn't fancy the thought of drowning. He felt the surge of nausea flood over him. He had to concentrate to avoid being sick with fear.

Sean stood on the cockpit seats, leaned on the spray hood and shouted, 'Right you two. Back below and into the aft cabin.'

As they went below Craig looked enquiringly at Mairread.

She smiled, but Craig did not feel too reassured.

Once into the cabin, they heard the door being locked and jammed.

Craig inspected the hatch. Sean had been busy. The pins holding the handles had been removed. It could no longer be opened.

CHAPTER XXII

Fast Lady nosed her way into the Acairseid Mhor, the almost enclosed natural harbour of the north bay of Gometra and anchored under the cliff. The area, with depth suitable for a big boat like Fast Lady, was very restricted and Jimmy was careful to make sure they had enough swinging room. They could see a small shed and an old pier evidently used by fishermen, and a small fishing boat hauled up onto a stone slipway.

Mark, Switch and Bernie changed into black trousers and sweaters, and each stuffed a black balaclava into his pocket. Mark handed out guns, and hand lamps from the engine-room lockers.

'Jimmy. Row us ashore. Bring the boat when I call. Are you happy you can get her out of here and back to the south bay on your own and in the dark?'

'Yes, boss. There won't be any problem. I would rather be coming with you though.'

'I know, but you are the best man with the boat. You can keep Pat's lady company. That should help you pass the time.'

Jimmy laughed. 'I'll show her things she has only dreamed of.'

They all climbed down into the tender and rowed ashore. Jimmy stood on the old pier and watched the others climb the hill track, then turn south out of view before rowing back to the big motor cruiser. Once back on board he checked the anchor was fast and the depth of water, thumbed through the Almanac until he found the tide tables, and scribbled a few notes. Satisfied they were not going to go aground he made his way forward.

At the sound of the door opening Patrick twisted his aching frame round to look up.

Jimmy stood there with a strange grin on his face. 'I'm going to entertain your lady. If you hear her you shouldn't worry. She will just be enjoying herself. I'll look after her for you.'

Patrick jerked at the bindings but only succeeded in sending a violent pain through his groin as bruised nerves objected. Jimmy closed the door and laughed loudly as he turned away.

Patrick lay still and listened. Straining his hearing he caught snatches of Karen's voice, and was aware of footsteps, followed by the closing of what he took to be the saloon door.

When they entered the saloon Karen's hopes fell when she realised that there was no-one else present.

Jimmy turned to face her. 'This is what we have been waiting for, isn't it? You said you liked me. Now we are alone together.'

There was a strange staring look in Jimmy's eyes. Karen shuddered slightly at the way he stared without blinking. 'Yes, I did, but I don't like what you have done to Patrick. I can't respect someone who behaves like that.'

'That wasn't really me. I only take orders. They have been good to me. I just try to repay them. I won't let them hurt you. You are the only person who has actually ever said they like me. You do. Don't you?'

Karen said nothing but felt she should nod and the small movement she made seemed to satisfy him.

They sat on the long settee and Jimmy cut the tapes from Karen's wrists. He raised her hands to his mouth and kissed the red marks where the edges of the tape had bitten into the skin. Karen was desperate to keep Jimmy talking and gentle.

'Surely your mother and father were good to you?'

'I didn't have a mother and father.'

'You must have had a mother and father.'

She stopped abruptly. He seemed to have gone into a trance.

'Shut up. Are you calling me a liar? You don't know anything about me. Why must I have had a mother and father? I hate my mother. She was either out or was in the bedroom with a man.'

He was nearly screaming so high pitched was his voice. 'I never had a father. Can you hear me? Are you calling me a liar? I'll teach you to respect me.'

Karen was cold with fear. Shivers enveloped her body. She felt nauseous. 'No,' she whispered. 'I am not calling you a liar. I just don't understand. Tell me.'

Jimmy's eyes were focussed beyond her as if he could see through her head but he relaxed visibly.

'I lived most with my aunt. I hate her too. She beat me with a poker if I forgot anything, even when I couldn't help it. Even when other boys had stolen from the shopping bags. My teacher said I was important but she only wanted me to get crack for her. She said she liked me. She said she would let me fuck her if I got what she wanted but she kept making excuses. She isn't making excuses now.'

Karen shuddered, but thought it best not to ask what he meant.

Jimmy grabbed hold of her wrists. 'I think you might be just like the other women. Like my teacher. Are you changing your mind now?'

'What do you mean?'

'You said you liked me. You said I wasn't like the others. Now we are together you are changing your mind, aren't you?'

A cold clamminess started to creep up from Karen's waist until she shivered. She had to reduce the tension. 'No. I do like you, but I need to know you better.' Her mind flailed around for words that would make sense; for words that would calm him down; for words that could reach the recesses of his mind; that would stimulate the pleasant experiences.

'Surely we can have a drink together?' She had to say something and it sounded so insincere.

Jimmy did not seem to notice, but snapped out of the trance-like state. 'Yes. Yes. I'll get something.' He stood, walked to the drinks cabinet and picked up a bottle of whisky.

'I can't drink whisky, Jimmy. Can you find some wine?'

'I'll get you the best.'

Jimmy left the saloon and entered Mark's cabin.

Karen looked around frantically for a weapon. 'Could she escape? Could she just jump overboard and swim for it? What would happen to Patrick?'

Jimmy reappeared carrying a bottle of Bollinger. 'Will this do?'

'Yes. That is perfect. You really do have such good taste.'

Jimmy bloomed with pride and his attitude noticeably softened.

Jimmy found a wine glass and poured a glass for Karen, but poured a very large whisky for himself and sat close beside her.

She sipped the champagne. 'Some nuts would be nice.'

The bubbles and bittersweet taste relaxed her.

A fleeting look of doubt crossed Jimmy's face, but he pivoted on his heel and went to the galley, returning with a pack of cashew nuts.

'Where have the others gone?'

'I don't know. Does it matter?'

'I thought you and I could escape. Get away before they return. We could take Patrick and the three of us should have a good chance of finding help.'

'Why do you want Patrick? The two of us would be enough. He would just be in the way.'

'I was just trying to help someone who has been hurt. Wouldn't you like to do that?'

Jimmy stood again. His brows furrowed, and his eyes closed slightly. 'They were right. They said you were his. They said you were doing it with him when you were ashore. You are just making a fool of me. Just like all women.'

Suddenly he stepped towards her. His fingers drove deeply into her cheek between her teeth, forcing her mouth open. Her hands flew to her face spilling the wine from the glass as it fell to the floor.

'Have more. Have more.'

Jimmy grabbed the whisky bottle, forced it into her mouth and tilted it to pour the fiery liquid down her throat.

She swallowed as fast as she could but the alcohol grabbed at her throat, choking her. She retched and he withdrew the bottle. She coughed and breathed deeply, and tried to compose herself. Her throat was stinging and she wanted to scream at him but she resisted the temptation although the tears stung her cheeks.

Jimmy poured another glass of champagne and handed it to her. Sipping it slowly eased her throat.

'Please let me recover. My throat is sore.'

'Drink.'

She sipped and gradually she felt better. Jimmy was drinking yet another enormous whisky, and topped up her glass at every mouthful.

She tried again. 'Why try to hurt me? I haven't done anything to harm you. I understand that you feel, well, let down by people you trusted but unless you are prepared to give others a chance you will never have any friends.'

He sat beside her. 'I've heard all that sort of shit before. You sound like a social worker.' His eyes probed deep into hers trying to see her mind. Then he let his gaze wander down over her breasts, across her stomach to her legs. He reached out and placed his hand on her thigh.

She sensed danger. 'Try again to make me understand. I like listening to you.'

Jimmy's eyes returned to her face. She breathed an inward sigh of relief.

'You can't understand unless you've been there. When the only way to survive is to be stronger than anyone else you just have to be part of a gang. If you can't be the strongest, you must be with the strongest. You do what you can, no matter what that is.'

'Couldn't you get out?'

Jimmy sneered, 'Out, this is out? Where to? How? When you are broke where do you go? You can't get anywhere to live. Only way you can get help with housing is to stay where you are. Move out and you start again with nothing, bottom of the list. It's easier to stay where you are.'

'There must have been some people in your area who weren't stealing or selling drugs.'

He grunted. 'Yes. There were. And they had nothing. It wasn't even worth their while getting anything. As soon as they made their house nice it was broken into. First time they went out the door was kicked in. You know the best job in my area? Replacing doors and windows. It's a full-time job for some joiners!'

'So what did you do all day?' Karen kept sipping.

'Same as I did at night. The pubs give credit. You pay off most of it when the dole comes through and start again. If you can't pay it off you get it some other way.'

'How did you get to know Mark and the others?'

'A few of us had some money and we went to London. I met Bernie in a pub. He was having some trouble with a couple of guys and I gave him a hand. He introduced me to Switch. It all followed from there. I got a flat in Bayswater. I don't go near Manchester any more. Too many people there want to see me.'

Karen realised she had finished the champagne and moved her hand to cup the glass and hide the fact that it was nearly empty. Too late. Jimmy topped up the glass with whisky after finishing off his own and pouring himself another.

'I don't drink whisky,' she smiled, trying to sound calm. She realised she was slurring her words slightly and was conscious of having drunk almost a bottle of wine.

'You do now. Go on, drink it.'

They stared at each other. Karen tried not to show her fear, but the glass trembled in her hand. Jimmy could not miss it.

He reached forward and started to unbutton her shirt from the neck. His hands were removed as Karen lifted the glass to her lips, and tilted it just enough to let the liquid now against her lips. The eyes stared at her mouth. She drank, just a little, but it burned her throat. The glass dropped away from her lips and Jimmy filled it until it spilled over. He took a mouthful from his own glass and slowly undid another two buttons. Again she drank. By now it was virtually neat whisky. She coughed and her eyes watered.

'Please stop. Please don't make me drink any more.'

'You can stop when you finish that.'

He continued to stare as he reached the waistband of her trousers. He tugged the shirt free, and Karen drank again. The shirt was falling free from her shoulders and Jimmy pulled it open. His eyes rested on the brassiere and the small breasts swelling from the lace.

'You are just wasting time. Now finish it.' He clenched a fist and made a gesture of hitting her in the face.

She swallowed as quickly as she could, and finished the glass.

The whisky bottle was all but empty. She was thankful that she had only drunk a small fraction of the contents. It was sufficient, however, mixed with most of the champagne, to make her head spin.

Jimmy moved suddenly. Rising, almost jumping to his feet he grabbed Karen's hair and dragged her off the seat. With both hands holding his wrists to stop her hair being ripped out she staggered behind him, crashing off the table and the door jams; bouncing from the companionway sides she was hauled into the large guest cabin. When they were inside Jimmy threw her onto the bed and turned and slid the bolt.

She sat up on the edge of the bed and looked around in panic. Two windows, too small to get through, a doorway to the heads, a dressing table and two chairs.

Jimmy had thrown off his fleece jacket, his shoulder holster and gun and was in the process of unbuttoning his shirt. 'Now you can convince me that an upper-class, snobbish bitch like you really does like me. I've met women like you in London. You always expect things to be the way you want them. Well, now you're going to learn different. Get your clothes off.'

Karen sat still. She was petrified. Slowly she pulled her shirt back around her. She just watched in disbelief. This could not be happening. She did not know why but she prayed for the others to return. His shirt was thrown on the floor and he was unzipping his trousers, pushing them down. He stepped out of them and then pulled his pants down and staggered as he stood on one leg. The sight of the huge, swollen, purple organ erect in front of the small man looked funny even through her fear. She uttered a low hysterical laugh. It was a mistake. It had been an involuntary laugh and she regretted it instantly. She saw the faraway look in Jimmy's eyes again as he approached.

'Don't worry. You don't have to take them off. I'd rather do it for you.'

Jackknifing her legs she tried to thrust herself backwards across the bed but he moved too quickly, curling his fingers over the cups of her bra and jerking her forward against him. One arm encircled her whilst the other sensed the form of her breast through the silk. His mouth found hers and despite the whisky she had swallowed his breath was strong and sickening. She turned her head away; so far that her neck ached, but his mouth roamed over her cheek and neck whilst his hand roved over her breasts and down over her belly.

'No. Please no,' she gasped. 'You know what it is like to be hurt. Please don't hurt me.'

Jimmy let go and stood upright. There was no longer any sign of a smile; no kindness even flickered in his eyes. He stopped and stared at her. 'Take your clothes off. I want to see all of you.'

'No. I won't do that.' Her mind flailed around looking for a seed of an idea. 'You know Mark wants me. He won't like it if you take me first.'

'Mark can have any woman he really wants. He isn't bothered about you any more. You're too middle class and uninteresting for someone like him. In fact, it was him who told me to enjoy myself with you and I'm going to do just that. So you see that's why I work with them. They look after me. Now take your clothes off.'

Karen frantically looked around the cabin for some way of defending herself but could see nothing of use. She turned and dived across the bed and stood at the far side facing him.

'I can see you need to be taught to do as you are told. Women never seem to be able to do things the easy way.' He slowly withdrew the heavy leather belt from his trousers then started round the bed. 'You will do exactly what I say. One way or another. It's up to you.'

Karen had never seen anything like him. A mass of black hair covered his chest and back to his neck. Hair grew over his stomach and formed a forest around the large almost vertical purple member that stood out from his thighs. Hair grew down his legs and his knees protruded from the black mass. Only his shoulders were free of hair. She was mesmerised and when he lunged at her she was just a fraction of a second slow in again throwing herself back across the top of the bed. She felt her ankle being grabbed and felt herself being drawn towards the foot of the bed. She clung tightly to the bedclothes but he was too strong and the kicking of her other leg only seemed to help him.

Terror turned her cold. She had never known physical pain. Her father had never smacked her and 'the belt' was unknown for girls at school although she knew some boys in her class who had been belted. She felt dizzy.

Her head and neck jerked back as his hands grabbed the collar of her shirt. Her legs were trapped between his and her arms were jerked backwards as he wrenched the shirt clear. A hand grabbed her neck; the fingers choking her as she struggled. She was unaware of the catch of her bra being undone. The room spun round; she could only see the lamp at the bed head. It seemed to be growing larger but hazier.

Both of his hands reached the waistband of her trousers and pulled. With one hand she tried to claw her way up the bed and with the other to hold onto her clothing. She heard, rather than felt the zip of her trousers give and the trousers were dragged from her legs. She was free and scrambled to the bed head, where she curled herself into a ball covering her breasts.

'Beautiful. I like it when they fight back. Now your pants.'

Karen was unable to move as his hand reached for her ankle. Slowly she was dragged back down the bed. A sharp pain roared up into her head as strong fingers curled round her neck crushing her windpipe. Desperately her hands clawed at the tourniquet around her throat.

Jimmy reached the waistband of the small white pants and drew them slowly down the slim thighs. He stopped as they covered her knees and slid his fingers through the fair bush of hair between her legs, probed with his fingers and then swiftly removed the last of her clothing.

'Stand up. I want to look at you.'

She did not move, conscious only of this black apparition towering above her.

'You heard me. Stand up and put your hands behind your head.'

The inevitable grab at her resulted in her being pulled towards him by the hair until he was able to trap her head between his legs. He forced her further down until her arms and shoulders were thrust between his legs and his thighs closed tightly around her.

She tried to twist round but her arms could barely reach the floor and could not reach behind her at all.

She heard the crack fractions of a second before the pain reached her brain. By the time she screamed another blow from the black leather belt had struck her buttocks.

Jimmy for once felt power. Here was a human being helpless in his grasp. He felt the surge and a stiffening. The sweat started to bead on his body as he watched the small white body jerking, writhing and squirming with each blow. He watched the redness grow, the white weals criss-crossing the small reddening globes. He thrashed on and saw the small blood blisters forming. He thrashed the helpless form until his arms ached. He heard nothing.

Karen lost all sense of time. The pain was unending. Her scream deafened her as it became continuous.

Suddenly Jimmy stepped back, releasing her. Sweat poured from him, matting the hair on his chest and forearms. 'Now will you do what I say?'

She could hardly see him. Her vision was blurred with tears and alcohol, but she knew he had to stop.

'Yes. Yes. I can't fight you.'

'Now stand up like I told you. Hands behind your head.'

Karen struggled to her feet, doing as she had been ordered.

'God, you are lovely. You are the loveliest woman I've ever seen.'

'Then please don't hurt me any more.'

'You are mine. I'll look after you. No-one else will have you. Come here.'

She stepped forward.

She stood still as he kissed her, probing with his tongue deep into her mouth. He grasped the small breasts, crushing her nipples between his fingers, all the time looking like a child. He ran his hand though her hair and over her shoulders.

She stood motionless. Anything to avoid being touched by that hair.

Jimmy stopped and listened. There was a loud banging from the forepeak.

'Sounds like your friend is upset. Let's go talk to him.'

He grabbed Karen by the hand and set off along the passage. As he opened the door he pushed Karen ahead of him. It was obvious that Patrick had been trying to kick the door. He was sweating profusely.

Karen gasped at the sight of him.

'It doesn't seem as though he's learned his lesson. The noise you made enjoying yourself has obviously upset him.'

Jimmy picked up a boat-hook and prodded Patrick in an already bloody groin. Patrick groaned and tried to turn away, as Jimmy stepped nearer to thrust again.

Karen grabbed his raised arm. 'Don't waste time. We have other things to do.' She couldn't believe the sound of her own voice. She couldn't be saying this. She just wanted to get out of that cabin.

Jimmy looked astonished but the evil grin soon replaced surprise. He looked down at Patrick. 'You see, she can't wait to be alone with me. Keep listening, buddy,' He turned away, pushing Karen before him, pausing only to latch the door.

As they re-entered the guest cabin Karen could see the gun in its holster tying on the chair by the door, but she had no opportunity to reach it.

Jimmy immediately pulled her against him, his hands caressing and probing, touching and rubbing over her private places and onto her legs. 'Perfect, just perfect,' he muttered.

Karen moved as little as the searching fingers would allow. *Remain calm. Don't do anything to anger him. Don't encourage him. Stay calm. Stay alert.* Anything to stop that torso pressing down on her, but his breathing was faster. He was gripping her more tightly. His tongue was all over her face, neck and breasts. He bent, picked her up and laid her on the bed. Like a rag doll he turned her face down and ran his hands over her back and buttocks, spreading, opening, looking . . . then it stopped.

She twisted round to see what he was doing in time to see a look of pure lust suffuse his features. With horror she realised why the others had joked about him. It was now obvious. She had never imagined anything about a human being could look so obnoxious, so frightening. More like a purple cosh than a part of love-making. He stepped forward and parted her legs. 'Kneel. Kneel. No, not like that. With your head on the bed and your arse up.'

She tried. She must not anger him.

She felt the pressure. She tried to stay closed. His hands gripped tightly around her small waist, and he dug his fingers in to her side. She gasped and relaxed and felt him thrust forward. The other hand traversed her buttocks and his fingers opened her. His member slid between the small globes, through the juices of her vagina, then higher.

'No. No. Please not there.'

She felt him straighten and withdraw from her.

'A virgin. You're a fucking virgin. You've never had it like this, have you?'

Karen knew. She didn't want to know but she knew. It was hopeless to go on trying not to annoy him. He was going to do just whatever he wanted. She tried to scramble up the bed, grabbing frantically at the duvet and cover until she felt the blow on her head. Everything swam. The room swirled up and down and her vision was misty. She was aware of his left arm encircling her waist and then his fingers penetrated the small tight opening. She gasped and cried out, and heard someone far off laughing.

Relief; he stopped, and then a different pressure. This time he pulled her back towards him and she could feel herself spring open. The sharp pain screamed through her. The fire inside her filled her stomach. Blood rushed from her head and she passed out.

Jimmy sweated and thrust and grunted, unaware that he had neither co-operation nor resistance. He drove on and on until he collapsed on the still body. He withdrew and looking down at the blood-smeared buttocks he mumbled, 'Great. You won't forget me. More later.' The whisky and exertions had the inevitable effect. He rolled on to his side and drifted off into oblivion.

CHAPTER XXIII

IT WAS DARK, or at least as dark as it gets in the west of Scotland on a warm June evening, as Wizard nosed her way into south harbour, Gometra. Sean knelt in the bow readying the anchor and peering forward, trying to gauge the distance from the slowly enveloping shores. Mairread too concentrated on trying to identify their precise position as they edged forward. It was just on low water and she was concerned more with maintaining clear swinging room than the depth. She called out, 'Five metres. Let go.'

The watchers on the shore, now accustomed to the darkness, saw and heard the splash of the anchor and the chain running free. They watched silently as the yacht stopped and then went astern as the occupants bedded the anchor. Every word spoken on the yacht skipped undistorted across the water, undiminished in volume and tone and was received by the observers as crystal clear as when it was uttered.

Mark, Switch and Bernie sat in the blackness of the large rocky bank at the old landing area. The black trousers, balaclava, sweaters, cagoule, trainers and gloves they wore, left only their eyes visible. Torches were slung around their necks. Immediately behind them lay the inflatable dinghy. Not a word passed between them.

Sean's voice almost bellowed across the bay, 'That is fine. That chain is taut, boyo. The pick is in solid sure enough.'

Mairread switched off the engine, had a last look around the anchorage and went below, followed by Sean.

The watchers waited. The clink of glasses, and the whistle of a kettle told them all they needed to know of the activities of the yacht crew.

They remained still and quiet until after a short time all the yacht's lights went out. Mark glanced at his watch. Midnight.

After about half an hour he whispered the one command, 'Now.'

Bernie and Switch lifted the dinghy to the water and waded out until it floated clear. Mark stepped into the bow. Switch sat on the inflatable thwart with the paddles and Bernie continued to push the

212

dinghy clear of the weeds and small rocks before heaving himself over the stern.

Switch rowed slowly and carefully with only the gentle plop of the paddles entering and clearing the water.

Mark again checked the gun in his pocket and held the other against his chest, keeping his left hand free. Bernie held an automatic and Switch had one in a shoulder holster and another in his pocket.

Switch stopped rowing short of Wizard and allowed the dinghy to drift gently up to the stern of the yacht until it kissed the boarding ladder. Mark leaned over, grasped the ladder, and steadily eased himself up onto the deck. Bernie followed, as did Switch after gently making the painter fast to the ladder. All three stood in the cockpit. The main saloon hatch was open in the warm summer air.

Sean, who had been asleep in the main cabin, was wakened by the pressure of the gun muzzle on his head.

'Move very slowly. Roll on to your front and put your hands behind your back.'

Sean hesitated, briefly, and felt the thrust of the gun increase. He rolled over, unable to identify anything but a black shape, but felt the band tighten around his wrists. He curled his fingers as tightly as he could to expand his wrists and leave the ties as loose as he could.

'Now then, Paddy. Stand up.'

As he rose to his feet he was aware of three black figures, all with handguns: one for'ard covering Mairread; the one who had spoken, now standing at the far side of the saloon table; and another tall figure at the foot of the companionway steps. The tall man climbed back into the cockpit, and gestured with his gun hand.

'Up here,' he said. The voice was cold and precise.

Without the use of his hands Sean was able to ascend only with the benefit of a push as he tried to climb the ladder but made it into the cockpit. A second man descended to the dinghy and was followed by Mairread. Sean was man-handled down. The tall man watched closely as the third man climbed down and settled himself in the rowing position.

'Get back here as soon as you can.'

Mark removed the stifling balaclava and went below.

Bernie rowed and the dinghy merged with the darkness as it made its way back to the shore.

As the tender went on its way Mark hauled the cushions from the seats and berths in the forepeak, saloon and navigator's berths. He smiled with satisfaction as he saw the watertight bags all packed tightly into every bit of space. He stepped past the galley and pulled away the toolboxes and holdalls from the aft cabin door, slid the catch, opened it and stepped inside.

'Well, well. Who are you?

Craig and Alan had heard the few commands and assumed that they had been boarded by police or coastguard. The gun seemed to indicate that they had been wrong.

Through thin lips whitened by pressure, Craig responded, 'I could ask you the same question. This is my boat and we have been hijacked.'

Mark smiled. 'Then I am sorry to have to tell you that you are a very unlucky man because the bad news is that it has just happened again. However, don't worry. You will be joining your Irish friends shortly and the good news is that we will not be taking your boat.'

Glancing at the taped wrists Mark observed, 'I see that you are already prepared. If you would just follow me I will assist you into the cockpit.'

He backed slowly out of the cabin and into the saloon.

With some heaving and twisting Craig and Alan managed to scramble their way into the cockpit just as the dinghy returned.

'Two more for the skylark.'

Without anything else being said Bernie climbed on deck and repeated the manoeuvre of forcing the two captives into the dinghy.

As he started to row, Mark stood leaning on the pulpit rail watching the departure. 'Cheer up, lads. Everything here is shipshape and Bristol fashion.'

Bernie uttered an 'Uh,' and continued to row.

Mark again returned below and seated himself at the navigation table, selected the handset of the VHF radio, switched to channel 69 and called, 'Fast Lady, Fast Lady, Fast Lady, this is Wizard, Wizard, over.'

He relaxed against the seat back and waited for Jimmy's tender tones to issue from the speaker. His demeanour was unchanged when the first call went unanswered, but he sat upright again after his third call brought no response. 'Damn,' he muttered under his breath, and once again climbed to the stern of the yacht.

It was some time until the dinghy reappeared and he was fretting considerably by the time Bernie climbed aboard.

'Stay there, George. There is no response from Jimmy. I don't know whether he has fallen asleep or whether something more serious has happened, but you had better go and find out. If there is a major problem when you get there come straight back and we will move out on this boat. Now get going.'

Switch swung the dinghy around and yet again made his way ashore, muttering something about midnight hill-walking being just what he had always wanted to do.

CHAPTER XXIV

KAREN CAME TO, slowly. There was only the sound of the breeze, slight and gentle, and a low elongated hissing whistle of breathing. The pain made her gasp, but cleared her mind instantly. She moved her head very slowly to look left. A hairy back, backside and thighs was all she could see. She listened intently. Nothing and then, suddenly a thick snore, and another. She froze. Motionless. It stopped, returning to low, long, throaty breathing.

She turned her head the other way, not daring to move any other part of her body. *Yes. It's there. The gun. Still on the chair by the door.* She lay, checking for other sounds. *Is there anyone else on board? Dare I shift off the bed and get the gun? Could I use it if I had to?* She hadn't the faintest idea of how to fire a gun. No choice. Her mind was now screaming at her. *You have no choice. Eventually he will kill you, but you will die ten times before then. You must get the gun.*

She shifted as slowly as she could. Thank God for the duvet. It transmitted little of any movement. Inch by inch she slid her legs to the bed side. Over, they were over the edge. She rotated herself very slowly. Her face came around to inches from Jimmy's back. She smelt the sweat, and musk, and her head started to swim. She pushed backwards and he moved. *No. No. No. Please. No.* She lay still.

After an eternity she moved again and felt her toes touch the carpet. One more small push backwards and she was able to stand. And she stood. Stock still. Staring at the object on the bed. For the first time in her life she hated. Hated the horrible, foul being who had invaded her. Hated the foul being who had so cruelly treated Patrick. Hated the animal who should have known; who should have learned better from the treatment he had had himself.

She turned slowly and stepped to the chair, lifted back the shirt front that partially covered the gun; the noise of the fabric wrinkling burst through her brain like crashing waves. She lifted the pistol out of its holster. She almost released a sigh but caught herself in time. She turned towards the cabin door and stopped. The latch. It would make too much noise. *How can I open it without waking Jimmy?*

She stared at the catch but her mind didn't this time scream. *Go on. Go on.* Caution took command. *Think. Think.*

She stared and suddenly she remembered. The heads had another entrance from the companionway. She had to walk past the end of the bed, but it was the only way. She looked again to confirm that Jimmy was sound asleep. She saw clearly the stains on the bedding at his midriff and realised it was her own blood, and she hated. Emotions she had never before experienced crashed over her. Kill him! Kill him! She steadied herself. *Slowly! Stop!*

She moved slowly, positively, without hesitation until she had passed the sleeping body and was at the door into the toilet compartment. She gently rotated the handle of the door. Her hands were damp with sweat and she was sure that they were slipping, but it swung open easily. Almost too easily. It swung back and she just caught it in time to prevent it striking the bulkhead.

The temptation to run was almost overwhelming. The outer door rubbed slightly on the surround and it sounded like a saw mill in her tense mind, but it opened and she stepped through. She eased the cabin door to, just sufficiently to cut down on sound without taking the risk of clicking it fully closed.

The boat was quiet. The hiss of her own escaping breath stopped her in her tracks and her heartbeat drummed in her head. Every movement seemed to reverberate around the boat, but she walked on and opened the forepeak door.

Patrick looked up apprehensively. Her finger went to her lips, and she shook her head. The tapes around his wrists would not tear and she felt the first surge of panic, and then she knelt and bit a piece out of the edge of the tape. Patrick forced his wrists apart, and she bit again and he was free. He quickly released his feet, and seeing the dazed and haunted look in Karen's eyes he leaned towards her and kissed her on the nose. 'I love you.'

'I hope so. I do hope so,' she whispered, and smiled.

'Where is he?'

'I'll show you.' Without thinking she held out the gun and felt a surge of relief as Patrick took it from her.

Patrick started out of the door, turned and whispered, 'Bring that tape.'

They made their way to the guest cabin and entered through the heads without ceremony.

The look of bewilderment on Jimmy's face as he woke and turned to see Patrick and Karen standing there made Karen relax for the first time. Jimmy's eyes travelled from Patrick's face to Karen, and then descended to hover on the automatic in Patrick's hand.

'Nice lady you've got there, Pat. You'll enjoy her. You take it from me,' he sneered.

Karen blushed, suddenly aware that she was still naked. Mad at herself she felt so stupid at being so middle class that she was embarrassed by the man who raped her. 'Shoot him. Shoot him,' she whispered.

'No, lady. You're not that type,' grinned Jimmy.

Patrick almost shouted as he snarled back, 'Shut up. The only thing I'll take from you are your guts, you horrible little creep. Now tie him up.'

Karen started, then diffidently approached Jimmy's back even though Patrick had turned him onto his face.

'Tight. Really tight. If we're lucky the circulation will stop and his hands will fall off.'

Karen taped the wrists and ankles before Patrick taped the hands to the ankles and then around Jimmy's neck.

'See how you manage with that,' said Patrick as he wrapped tape across Jimmy's mouth. 'I'm tempted to cover your nose as well.'

'OK. Let's get ourselves cleaned up.'

Karen collected her clothes and they left the cabin and made their way to Mark's owner's suite.

'You go first. I'm going to dig out some clean clothes and other bits and pieces.'

Karen stepped into the shower and turned on the spray. It felt so good to be clean. She washed herself again and again until she was sure there was not the slightest trace of Jimmy. She shuddered occasionally as a picture of him flashed into her mind. She heard movement in the cabin and guessed that Patrick had returned. She stepped out and picked up a towel.

'You look wonderful.' Patrick bent and kissed her lightly.

'Not here,' whispered Karen as she twisted to show him the bruises.

'Bastard. But they will go away. And they don't stop you from looking beautiful.' Patrick pulled off his bloodied pants and stepped into the shower. Karen heard him gasp as the water sprayed over him, but soon she heard him humming and for the first time for as long as she could remember a genuine smile flashed across her lips. It just felt so good to be clean and have fresh clothes. She felt alive again, brushed her hair and looked at herself in the mirror.

'You don't need to look there. You are just perfect as you are.'

Karen spun round to see Patrick drop the towel from his waist and start to pull on clean clothes. 'So are you. I probably should be angry with you but I am so pleased to be with you again that I can't be angry.'

Patrick had finished dressing. He turned and went to the door. 'Wait a sec. I must send a message.'

He was back within a couple of minutes. 'OK. Let's get off this prison ship.'

As they went on deck, Karen noted that Patrick was carrying two guns and two torches. The tender was still in the water moored to the stern of the large craft.

'Down you go. I'll be there in a tick.'

He turned and went below.

Jimmy twisted round as he heard the cabin door open. There was disappointment in his eyes as he saw Patrick. He reacted too slowly, however, as Patrick's fist crashed into his face, crushing his nose and splitting an eyebrow.

'That's a little of what I've got lined up for you when I get back. Then I'll repay you for what you did to a very lovely lady.' He turned and left and Jimmy coughed trying to clear the blood from his mouth. He tried to shout but the tape muffled his efforts and he uttered what sounded like a sob.

Patrick went to the bridge and checked the instruments and chart before climbing into the tender.

They left the tender alongside the old jetty and climbed the track up the hill on a night so clear that the islands were as blue black blots on a sea of royal blue ink. The shimmering of the moonlight on the sea broken by a slight swell created flashes as if a giant shoal of herring were breaching the surface. Small white clouds rested to await the dawn before scurrying off about their business.

'I checked the GPS before we came ashore. We are on Gometra. Does that mean anything to you?'

'Oh yes,' exclaimed Karen. 'It's a lovely spot. The island has wild and farmed deer, eagles, a pet goat, highland cattle, all sorts of unusual ducks and about every other sort of animal and bird you would expect to find in Scotland. It's owned by a family from London, an unusual name. Yes, I remember. The owner is Roc Sandford. I think he is in publishing or property. He has put up notices all round the island welcoming people. It's so nice to be allowed to wander.'

'That's becoming increasingly rare these days. I hope people respect the place.'

'I think so. Anyone I've met has been delighted with the island.'

'I had a quick look at the chart and I presume this track takes us over to the other bay. Jimmy's navigational notes all referred to that.'

'It does. To Gometra harbour. It's a lovely walk during the day. We may even get some views tonight. It's not really very dark.'

'We must keep quiet from now on. They are bound to try to contact Jimmy and when they fail, they will send someone to check. We must be careful not to run into whoever comes back.'

'Sorry. I was rabbiting on a bit.'

'That's all right. But speak quietly, and only in short phrases. Then listen.'

They had reached the plateau and stopped to look out to sea where the dark shapes of the Treshnish Isles and Staffa were clearly visible. The track was well defined and they followed it without difficulty until on cresting a rise the dark shape of the gable of a large house was visible.

'Gometra House. It isn't often occupied.'

'How far is it to the harbour from here?' enquired Patrick.

'It's still a good walk but it's not difficult.'

'Let's press on, but be more careful. The nearer we get the more likely we are to bump into one of them.'

They passed by the newer bunkhouse-style building and started down the slope past the old teacher's house when Patrick stopped suddenly. They had been walking on the grass verge and when they stopped the sound of feet crunching the gravel of the track was clear.

Patrick took Karen by the hand and pulled her off the track about twenty metres into the field and they both lay flat on the ground. They lay motionless as the sound of gravel slipping closed in. The glow of a cigarette appeared as the walker reached the top of the hill. His face was lit up as he stopped to draw on the cigarette. It was Switch. He hesitated only for a few seconds then set off again at a brisk pace in the direction of Fast Lady.

They lay only until he had vanished into the darkness and the shadows of the trees around the house, when Patrick rose and they marched briskly on down the hill.

'We should be fine now. I can't see them sending anyone else yet and that's one less to deal with.'

They hurried on, trying to stay on the grass verge to deaden their stride. Down into the curve by the bay and past the rocky outcrop.

'I always called that Pulpit Rock. I had visions of the minister calling fire and brimstone down on the heads of the farming and fisher folk as they stood around the rock.'

'Yes. I can imagine that,' laughed Patrick.

Climbing the next hill took longer than she had imagined but when they rounded the cornice and looked down towards the bay she stopped, grabbing Patrick's elbow. 'Quietly now. There are some old ferrymen's cottages down here and although the new owner was improving them they were only used as stores when I was last here but there may be someone living there now.'

'Or they may be used for an ambush,' murmured Patrick. 'I need a moment anyway. I've got aches and pains all over but as far as I can tell I still seem to be in working order.'

Karen grinned, and kissed him lightly on the cheek.

'Well, I'm glad about that. I'd hate to think I've gone through all this to find that you were broken down.'

Patrick hugged her.

'I'm not too sure, but we can check later. Meantime I'm going to have to examine these cottages. Stay here. I won't be long.'

With that he stepped into the night.

Karen could just see a shadow move silently from rock to rock until he disappeared against the background of the cottages. She turned to peer over at the old graveyard trying to remember the story about the place, but a spasm of pain made her gasp and she sat down by the roadside.

Patrick made his way warily to the first cottage which was close by the road, and cautiously peered in the windows. He could see nothing. Even in the grey light of the Scottish June he could only vaguely make out shapes inside the building. Cautiously he made his way around the cottage to the doorway, pushed it open and stood back. Only a muffled thumping sound came forth, and he stepped inside, gun at the ready, and switched on the flashlight.

Quickly glancing around the single room his vision alighted on Alan who was banging his heels against the floor. Slowly swinging the lamp beam he found two other men and a woman all sitting on the floor with their feet taped together and their hands taped behind their backs. Their backs were to the wall. He pointed the gun at the head of the man who had been banging his feet and looking straight into his eyes he muttered through clenched teeth, 'I'm going to take the gag off. Don't say anything until I say so.'

With that he pulled the tape from Alan's mouth. He kept the muzzle pressing against Alan's head as he manoeuvred himself so that he could see all of the room's occupants.

'Your name.'

'Alan. I . . . ' he tailed off.

'Shut up. Just answer. Why are you here?'

Nodding in the direction of Sean and Mairread, Alan blurted out, 'They took over our yacht. They killed one of the crew. Then we were all captured by another bunch and they dumped us here. Does that make sense?'

Patrick nodded.

'I can only tell you that I mean you no harm and I could use your help. Are you game?'

Having no doubts that any change must be for the better, Alan nodded vigorously. Patrick undid the tapes on Alan's wrists and stepped back.

Alan nodded in Craig's direction. 'Can I free him? It is his yacht.'

'So this is Craig?'

Alan nodded and stooped to free Craig. 'Can you walk?'

Both men nodded, staggered slightly but made their way out of the cottage.

Patrick prodded them up the hill towards Karen who rose to her feet as they approached.

'Karen, you stay with Craig.'

Patrick hesitated, but only momentarily. 'Wait over there in the cemetery and stay out of sight. Take this, but don't use it unless you have to.' He passed the small VHF set to Craig.

He swivelled on his heel and set off down the hill, beckoning to Alan. 'Come on. Come on.'

They made their way down to the shingle beach and didn't take long to locate the dinghy left by Switch. Between them they carried it to the darkness of the cliff and made themselves comfortable on the overturned boat.

'This will do nicely,' whispered Patrick as he eased his shoulders against the cliff face.

Nothing was said for what seemed an eternity until Alan, who was finding it difficult to relax, enquired, 'What are we waiting for?'

'There will be another boat here shortly. We will have to wait until then before we can make the next move.'

Alan's mind was in turmoil. He was free and yet here he was with the feeling that he was jeopardising that freedom by remaining with this man; a man he did not know, did not understand, but whom Karen seemed to trust.

'Who are you?' he blurted out. He just had to speak.

Patrick hesitated and then whispered, 'I am a,' he hesitated again, 'a civil servant. I am part of a team that specialises in the trapping of importers of illegal goods and subversive groups. I just need your help for a while. It may be a little dangerous but I will try to keep you out of the firing line.'

'You mean you are a spy.'

'More of a spy catcher, I think,' smiled Patrick. 'This makes you one too.'

'I suppose it does. I suppose it does,' repeated Alan with just a small degree of satisfaction.

'Of course, you will never be able to tell anyone about this,' said Patrick with a note of mock seriousness in his voice.

Alan did not notice. He was far away, imagining all sorts of feats of bravado. Patrick relaxed again, content with the silence.

CHAPTER XXV

CRAIG AND KAREN had scrambled down through the tall grass and thick bracken, stumbling over rocks only occasionally, to the old cemetery, and had sat down, leaning against the tombstones. It was remarkable how easy it was to negotiate the uneven ground once eyes were accustomed to the moonlight shadows. Neither spoke for some time, until Craig coughed quietly, clearing his throat before asking very quietly, 'Are you all right?'

'Just about OK, but I'll recover. It hasn't been very pleasant.'

'Did they hurt you? Did . . . ' his voice tailed off.

'Oh, for God's sake. You mean did they rape me, don't you? Why don't you ever say what you mean? You never talk to me like a real person.'

Craig sniffed. 'I didn't want to embarrass you.'

'You could hardly do that after the last few days, and yes, they raped me.'

'Oh God. I'm so sorry.'

'Sorry! Sorry! Why are you sorry? Did you have something to do with it?'

She did not mean to snap but she couldn't help it although she realised that she was very short. The self-control of the past few hours was snapping.

'No I didn't, but I should never have let you get into that delivery nonsense. That's the cause of all this.'

Karen suddenly felt the fear, horror and tension lift to be replaced with a blazing anger. She had great difficulty keeping her voice down but the fury resonated in her words. 'You have got a damn nerve. You shouldn't have let me! Who the hell do you think you are to have to let me do anything? You are just like a Victorian middle-class husband whose wife is for the home and the children while he has his fun playing away from home. Don't tell me what you should or should not have let me do. You were storming around like a foot-loose Lothario and you want to tell me what I can or cannot do. Of all the bloody nerve.'

Karen breathed deeply. Her mind was confused but her instincts screamed out, *There is something worse than risking your life. Being a slave.*

She stared at the moon. 'My God, for the first time in my life I have lived my own life. I haven't enjoyed it much but I am damned well going to if I get out of here. And I am not at all sure you feature in it. I've learned a lot about myself in the past days. I certainly know I can survive more than I ever dreamt of.'

Craig was glad of the dark. His face was afire with embarrassment. Although he felt sure it was impossible it seemed that she knew of Mairread. 'I was only trying to express my concern; to take some of the blame.'

Craig was conscious that it all sounded woefully inadequate, and sat back in silence.

Karen continued, not really speaking to Craig, more just talking herself through the problems that were flooding her mind. 'You can't apportion blame when this sort of thing happens. No-one could ever foresee this sort of thing happening, so how can you blame anyone, even yourself? Of course, you may know differently. From what you've told me that Ardfern place seems to be the escape pod for all sorts of weirdos and dropouts and people who have been involved in a mass of government malpractices. Maybe you are deeply involved in all this.'

They lapsed into silence.

Karen became aware of the fact that they hadn't touched. In the past when there was a problem he would have taken her hand, or put an arm around her. She would have thrown her arms around him and kissed him. She realised she hadn't even asked him how he was, and guilt flooded over her.

'What about you? How are you?'

'Yes. I'm fine, but we lost Mike. He went overboard. We couldn't find him.'

'Oh no! What about the Coastguard and the Lifeboat? Surely they found him?'

'They wouldn't call the Coastguard. They said it was too dangerous.'

'And you let them get away with that. Why didn't you force them to do something?'

'That's easy to say. They had guns. Anyway, we did try but they just wouldn't listen. I've just kept hoping he was picked up. But I doubt it, or if he was he must have been dead or they would have known what happened and would have found us sooner.'

Silence again enveloped them. Karen could hear the grazing cattle nearby. There didn't seem anything to say but thoughts flitted in and out of her mind. *Craig ought to have tried to do something. Mike can't just be allowed to vanish.*

Craig closed his eyes and the picture of Mike cartwheeling over the guard rail flashed into his consciousness, only to be replaced microseconds later by Mairread and Sean. He pushed aside the pictures of horror. He forced himself to recall the lovemaking in the sun and the warmth as she held him; the softness of her against him; the firmness as she pulled him on top of her. He had to do something now, or it would all be gone.

Craig stood up. 'Stay here. I'll be back soon.'

'Where are you going?'

'I'm going to check on the others.'

'Why? There's no need to do that. You are just taking unnecessary risks. They could have killed you. Why are you going to them?'

'I just have to, that's all. Keep quiet. Stay out of sight. I will be back very quickly.'

With that he rounded the tombstone and set off down the slope.

Karen was confused. *Why is he leaving me to go back to the cottage? Where is Patrick? Is he all right?*

She strained to hear but the only sound discernible was of the irregular rustle of the ferns as the nearby highland cattle grazed. She stared upwards again at the moon. How bright it was and yet the sky around it was not black but a deep blue as the sun chased the moon so closely that night could not overwhelm the sky. Two heroes fighting off the blackness of the night.

A slight unusual sound disturbed her reverie. She rose on one knee and peered around the gravestone. There was movement. People were climbing from the cottage towards the track and were already halfway up the slope. There were three people. She almost shouted out when it was clear that one of them was Craig. He was going with them voluntarily. He was not being abducted. As they crested the rise and the sound of their feet faded she sat down again. *Why?*

Craig had made his way back to the cottage and pushed open the door. His vision, now adjusted to the night light picked out Mairread and Sean trusted and lying on the floor, backs against the wall. He quickly removed the tapes.

'Boyo, you aren't so bad after all,' came the lilt from Sean.

Mairread gripped his hand and squeezed hard. She leaned forward and kissed him gently on the lips. 'Thank you. Thank you so much. I just know we will meet again.'

'No. I'm coming with you,' blurted out Craig.

'You can't. It just isn't possible. You will probably be shot. Stay here. Don't risk it. I will get in touch with you.'

Craig felt the cold of fear surge through him. Lose her now and he would never find her again, and Karen must guess why he had left.

'No. I must come. You must see that Alan will tell everything about us and how I helped you. I am in real trouble anyway.'

Sean grabbed them both by the shoulders. 'For Christ sake. C'mon. We haven't got time to argue.'

After only a moment of hesitancy Mairread agreed and they set off towards the track. Craig stopped momentarily. 'Why are we going this way? The best way off the island is the other way. We could probably steal a boat at Ulva Ferry and get to the mainland.'

Sean grabbed his collar, 'Shut up, Craig. If you want to stay with us, just follow. We know what we are doing.'

They pressed on in silence until they reached the inlet. They stopped by the dilapidated hut and Sean reached out his hand for the VHF. Craig handed it to him without question.

Sean walked towards the shore, raising the radio antenna, and Craig just caught the call sign, 'Irish Rascal, Irish Rascal.'

Craig turned and put his arms around Mairread. 'Will we be safe?'

'Yes, I think so, as long as we can get well away from here before any more trouble arrives.'

They stood in silence as Sean turned back from the shore. When he spoke he seemed lifted and it was obvious that his call had been answered. 'They will be here in half an hour.'

Mairread looked around. 'Then we should get away from the track and down towards the water's edge.'

They walked slowly towards the beach which glistened white in the moonlight and, midst the shadows of the boulders and turf they lay down just short of it. The gentle surf lightened to a greenish hue as it caressed the beach and left small bubbles of foam to dissipate themselves stranded on the shore. Despite the warm night Craig suddenly felt cold and as the last week reprised itself in his mind he shivered with uncertainty, all the time expecting to hear the sounds of approaching footsteps.

After what seemed like a long time the throb of engines was just audible, but just as they caught the sound it stopped to be replaced with the higher pitch of a large outboard engine, and within seconds the white crest of the bow wave of the rigid-hulled inflatable could be seen approaching the bay. The craft slowed down as it approached the shallow water, and Mairread stood. 'Follow me,' she whispered.

Craig followed Mairread with Sean bringing up the rear. He could see the black shapes of two persons in dark clothes just visible in the boat which had stopped close to the shore but without actually grounding.

Mairread turned to him 'Come on. We will have to wade out a bit,' and she waded cautiously into the sea.

The blow to the head did not bring immediate unconsciousness, perhaps because the wooden block Sean wielded had been picked up from the shore and it was partially rotted. Craig stumbled and half turned with his arm rising in protection, as Sean brought the batten down again. The blow numbed Craig's arm which dropped. Sean struck him again and pain screamed through his skull and neck, while his gut wretched as it contracted violently. Arms outstretched to block his fall. Craig heard his disembodied voice scream out 'No. No. I love you,' and then he fell into the abyss. The small craft with four now on board spun around and the scream from the engines built up as it raced from the bay to the dark shape of the mother ship beyond the headland.

Sean and Mairread sat with an arm around each other.

'Thank you. Thank you for not killing him.'

'I should have. I have probably taken an unforgivable risk, but I knew you liked him.'

'I did, so thank you anyway.'

They pulled closer together and disappeared into the night.

Shortly afterwards an observer would have heard the throb of powerful engines and seen the faint fluorescence of the wake as the large powerboat accelerated away from the island.

CHAPTER XXVI

ALAN HAD WAITED impatiently as Patrick had remained silent and, Alan believed, asleep, when the bulk of Fast Lady entered the harbour. Alan had failed to hear the sounds from the engines, shielded as he was from the open sea by the cliff face. However, he noted that Patrick had stirred slightly and he now had a feeling of excitement, of danger, but still Patrick remained almost motionless.

After some manoeuvres Fast Lady tied up alongside the yacht and shortly after the two shapes from Wizard had boarded the powerboat, they all reappeared on deck and could be made out manhandling packages from the yacht. The packs then vanished into the depths of the power cruiser.

Half an hour went by and the activity ceased. All of the bodies left the deck and passed through the doorway into Fast Lady. Alan felt distinctly uncomfortable as Patrick waited. Another long half hour went by.

'Let's go. Stay right behind me. Don't be tempted to do anything until I tell you, and don't get between me and them.'

They eased the dinghy into the water.

'You row, and keep it quiet. Head for the boarding ladder.'

Alan heard the regular beat of a small diesel generator break the silence and his worry about the noise of the paddles vanished.

Alongside, Patrick quietly made fast the dinghy, glanced up at the deck and stealthily made his way aboard. Apart from the hum of the generator all was quiet with only a few small lights on. Fortunately the warm weather had encouraged them to leave the doors open and entry was simple.

Alan remained about a metre behind, and found that he was shaking, his stomach cold and tense, expecting the lights to flash on and guns to open fire all round.

Patrick first entered the aft cabin. Jimmy lay snoring, mouth wide open, as his obviously broken nose restricted his breathing. A grin of satisfaction momentarily flitted across Patrick's face as he noted the bloodstains still marking Jimmy's cheeks.

Stooping, he thrust the gun barrel into Jimmy's mouth, and pressed his knee gently onto the sleeping man's chest. Jimmy's eyes suddenly sprang open and terror flashed in them.

Patrick hissed, 'Not a sound. Not a murmur. Not a movement. Not one inch, or you're head comes off.'

Jimmy tried to nod but his teeth rattled against the cold steel. His eyes darted and fro, Patrick to Alan and back. He clearly could not work out who Alan was but the fear was unmistakable.

Alan quickly lifted a face cloth from the wash basin and stuffed it into Jimmy's mouth, whilst the muzzle of the pistol hovered close to Jimmy's eyes. Patrick wound a trouser belt tightly around the prisoner's wrists. He then removed the pillowcase and lowered it over Jimmy's head.

Patrick bent low by Jimmy's ear. 'Not a sound. Don't even move. I just need an opportunity to finish you, but I'd rather save you for later.'

They moved silently and quickly to the other stern cabin, opened the door and shone the torch. A sleepy looking Bernie was sitting on the edge of the bunk with nothing but underpants on.

'Going for a pee, are we? Good. Come this way and keep quiet.' They made their way to the saloon.

'Sit there.'

Bernie seated himself on the edge of the saloon seat, and the flash of hatred was starting to drive the sleep from his eyes.

Patrick's foot shot up and kicked him on the shin. 'Sit back. Right back so hard I can see you disappear into the cushion.'

Bernie grunted but complied.

Alan stood, gun in hand, watching the proceedings. The shivering had stopped. It was as though he was only a spectator.

'Alan. Just open and close that door quietly. Just enough noise to be annoying.'

Alan smiled despite himself, remembering the annoyance of a door left ajar on a boat when even the slightest ripples on the water made the latch rattle infuriatingly. He recalled eventually slipping out of a sleeping bag after trying to ignore the noise and going to close the door. The same feeling as waking in the night and needing to go to the toilet. Ignoring it just doesn't work.

After only a few minutes a bleary-eyed Mark entered, pants on but without his shirt, obviously trying to determine the source of the annoying knock. Instantly he straightened and recovered his poise. 'Ah! Good evening, Pat. Did you bring your lady friend with you? We could have had a party. Jimmy says she really enters into the spirit of things. And who is your friend? Pat. Please introduce me, Pat.'

Too late Patrick sensed the oft-repeated 'Pat' was for Switch's benefit as he burst into the saloon, his gun hand coming to the horizontal.

Before he had completed the move there was a loud explosion, Switch sinking to the floor with a cry and dropping the gun. Both his hands grabbed at his thigh.

Patrick laughed. He couldn't restrain himself. 'Shot yourself in the foot again, Switch?'

His eyes flashed to Alan who was now sitting looking at the gun and with the smell of the shot making his eyes water. 'Well done. That was good timing.'

Bernie made a dive for the fallen weapon but screamed and pulled back as Patrick's foot stamped down on his fingers.

Mark shrugged his shoulders. 'I don't think this is getting us anywhere. Before you break everything we should talk privately.'

Mark's statement was clearly directed at Patrick.

Patrick snorted. 'I don't think we have anything to talk about. In fact the only thing I am going to do before I finish with you is blow your balls off.'

Mark drew himself up straight. 'You and your Irish friends won't get away with this, you know. There are too many parties interested in this transaction and they all have more muscle than you.'

'I don't need to get away with anything as you will shortly find out. Now sit down.'

Mark walked to the end of the saloon and sat in an armchair.

'Pat. I think you are into something much bigger than you appreciate. I believe you are making a mistake. I even think I can help you. Come with me. Let me put a shirt on and I will tell you who I am working for. I think you will be surprised.'

Mark's attitude, his confidence, made Patrick sense that perhaps he did not have the whole story. Mark could be persuasive. 'OK. Move slowly. Alan, keep an eye on this pair. If you are the slightest bit worried just shoot them. They will be no loss to society.'

Patrick motioned to Switch, who was trying to stem a steadily flowing stream of blood from his leg, to sit on the settee beside Bernie.

'Just keep some pressure on it, Switch. You probably won't bleed to death.'

Patrick pushed his gun into Mark's back. 'Hands on your head. Move steadily. I am just waiting for the right time to finish you.'

They swung into the luxury cabin and Patrick positioned himself so that he could see the whole cabin and the doors to the radio room and the companionway. 'Now dress and talk.'

Mark pulled on trousers, sweater and socks and shoes.

He looked up. 'I am just guessing,' he began, 'but I think it is a good guess. I believe you are an agent, maybe even a double or triple agent, and at least one of your masters is the same or related to mine.'

He stopped and looked at Patrick.

'Go on. I am interested.'

'There is a possibility that you are disloyal to everyone, but I think that unlikely. The safe house telephone number has me puzzled but I think you may yet be working for the British Security Services. Of course, that doesn't mean you are working for the government, at least not the British Government, but it does put us close together.'

'Nothing. Not even the same womb could put us close together.'

'We will see. I think we are more or less on the same side, providing a service for or to Her Majesty's Government, or the Joint Intelligence Committee, which is to all intents and purposes much the same thing. You would be wise to consider your position now. It is not too late to rectify your mistakes, and anyway I quite admire you.'

Patrick stared hard at Mark. There was something convincing about Mark's demeanour although he really had said nothing to identify who he was referring to.

'If Her Majesty's Government is availing themselves of your services it is even more corrupt than I had imagined. Illegal arms transactions backed by aid agreements with the funds going to prominent members of the government is bad enough but I don't think even the government could use drugs.'

'But who are the government? You and I know that real power rests elsewhere. Especially now that there is no surplus wealth for the socialists to fund their crazy welfare schemes. All politicians stoop to the same level and the sources of these funds are controlled by the J —' and he stopped dead. 'I think I have said enough. Are you with me?'

Patrick signalled to Mark to stand. 'It doesn't matter whether or not you are right. I just hope you are wrong, but I dislike you enough to ignore what you are saying. I have a raw pain between my legs that is motivating enough. Now back to the saloon.'

Mark did as he was bidden, turning only to murmur. 'You will regret ignoring my offer.'

In the saloon Mark returned to the armchair. Nothing else had changed. Alan was standing again at the corner of the saloon blocking the way to the exit to the deck. He looked tired.

'Keep an eye on them for just a few minutes more. I have some messages to send.'

Patrick again left the saloon and this time went to the radio room. He concentrated for a few minutes on speaking to several different stations until he heard a noise in Mark's cabin. Instantly he left the seat and pressed himself against the bulkhead by the door leading into the main cabin. A bullet smashed into the woodwork beside his head, and he cursed quietly as he realised he had been observed via the mirror in the cabin. Another shot crashed into the door.

His mind was a tangle of thoughts. *What has happened in the saloon? How many are trying to get to me? Where is that gunman now?*

'Patrick. There's no way you can escape now. Give yourself up and save your friend.'

Patrick recognised Bernie's voice. His spirits sank and he took a step towards the door. *If Alan is alive they would have made him call for help. In fact why isn't Mark doing the talking? Mark would know that I would respond to him better than Bernie. Bernie is alone!*

As his thought clarified he realised he may be wrong but he didn't feel he had a choice. He banked on the fact that Bernie probably couldn't move very quickly because of the furnishings and he had to watch both exits from the radio cabin so he must be at the door of the master cabin.

Patrick ran to the door from the radio room to the passage and slammed it, then spun round, stepped back across the room and threw himself through the doorway into the master cabin, twisting as he went to face the entrance door. As he landed he saw Bernie turn back from peering down the passage, and he fired twice at the slowly turning man. One shot hit Bernie in the middle of the chest, and he crashed back into the passage and slumped to the floor. He sat staring up at Patrick with a confused expression until his head fell forward onto his chest and his gun dropped to his side.

Picking up the gun Patrick cautiously entered the saloon. It was empty!

Alan had arranged himself between the others and their exit route. He suddenly felt tired. He hadn't realised a gun could be so heavy. They didn't seem like that in films. His shoulders were sore. He was hungry. Perhaps they could make something to eat. His mind drifted off to home, to the garden, to dinner at the club, to a warm bed. He felt the ordeal was just about over until the hand covered his mouth, and the muzzle of a gun rested against the back of his head. He didn't move. It just wasn't worth trying any more. He vaguely heard someone say, 'I'll stay and deal with Pat.'

Alan was more angry than afraid. He had allowed his eyes to close and now he waited to hear the shots on the boat. Shots he knew would come.

He was aware of being pushed up onto the deck and down into the dinghy. All four were crushed together and Switch rowed, grunting with pain each time he thrust with his legs and the wound opened.

The explosions of the two shots was unmuffled on that still night and reverberated around the bay.

Alan looked back at the two boats and saw Patrick appear at the rail. Jimmy yelled 'Bastard,' and fired in the general direction of Patrick.

Alan's relief at the sight of Patrick was immediately replaced by fear for himself. *What will happen now?*

'Why are we going, boss? Why don't we just shoot him and take the gear?'

'First, because he is armed and I have no wish to be shot, and second, because there is no need as I have organised some assistance. We don't need to do anything except stay out of the way for a bit.'

Switch looked puzzled, but he had accepted Mark's instructions for so long that he didn't think to question any further.

When Patrick reached the deck he had just been in time to see the dinghy halfway to the shore, and heard Jimmy shout, 'Stay where you are or he gets it,' as he fired in the general direction of the boats.

In the gentle light of dawn the tender reached the shore and as the four occupants climbed from the boat, Patrick watched Jimmy turn and strike Alan on the head with the gun. Alan toppled backwards into the dinghy whilst the others passed from view past the 'Welcome' sign and up the hill.

Patrick scrambled across to Wizard, launched the yacht's own dinghy and paddled frantically ashore.

The sky was lightening all the time and shortly both sun and moon would soon be vying for pride of place in the firmament.

The tender struck the bottom alongside Alan, who, with a gash on his forehead and blood running down the bridge of his nose, was pulling himself upright.

'Sorry. I am sorry. I didn't hear him creep up on me. I guess I am not cut out for this sort of stuff.'

'My fault,' proffered Patrick. 'I should have made a better job of tying the little bastard up, and I should have made sure there were no guns in the aft cabins. Let me have a look at your head.'

Patrick eased the hair back from Alan's forehead. 'You aren't dying yet. C'mon.'

They made their way up the slope to the cottages, and glanced inside.

'Obviously your friend released the Irish, so I want you to find his wife. She should be over there in the cemetery. You can look after her, or her you as appropriate.'

'I didn't think he would do that,' Alan gasped. 'He had fallen for the woman, but I thought when he was back with his wife things would be OK. Where are you going?'

'I wish I had known that before. Off you go, but be careful. I must get after them. I think they may just have another exit route but I don't think they will go too far. The cargo is precious. They won't abandon it and they'll be pretty confident I will follow. Keep out of sight.'

Alan took a small handgun Patrick had brought from the boat, whilst Patrick kept the automatic pistol he had removed from Bernie.

Patrick smiled at Alan. 'Just don't use that unless you have no alternative.'

Patrick set off up the track and Alan made his way over to where he could just make out Karen standing in the half light.

The burgeoning dawn was improving visibility by the minute, and Patrick broke into a trot, staying low and switching to whichever side of the track had the most accessible cover. He kept the gun in his hand. Cresting the hill he slowed and examined the going ahead. He was certain that Mark wouldn't be too far from the road. *He won't take to the hills. He won't want to be too far away from boats. He will want to disable me, though, before he goes back for the goods.*

Patrick was fairly sure that Mark sensed that he was not IRA but obviously had not been prepared to wait on the boat to find out. It probably meant that he was expecting other visitors. A gentle smile flirted with his lips. *Well, don't we all?*

Patrick leaned hard against the bank to regain his breath and considered the small building standing close by the track and in the bottom of a dip. The only movement came from a few highland cattle grazing on either side of the road.

The ground ahead opened out and flattened as the road reached the building. On the left the tussock grass sloped gently down to the bay and about 50 metres behind the building the land rose steeply upward to terminate in a shallow cliff face. He would be exposed. He remained motionless for a few moments longer and had just decided to proceed when a cow was attracted by something in the hut. It stopped half in and half out and then took a small jump backwards, before backing completely out and moving away to graze again by the roadside.

The hillside behind the hut was also fairly open, offering little cover, but if he went higher up someone in the hut would have to expose themselves to get a good shot at him. Patrick climbed. There was a pile of old timber stacked against the back of the hut covering the only window. That was a bonus. Now whoever was there would have to leave the building if they suspected anything. Patrick was sure someone was there. He moved cautiously glancing at his footing but retaining the hut well within his peripheral vision. Nothing happened. He stopped from time to time to examine the track and surrounding hillside, and once when a stone rolled down from above, he threw himself flat and looked up to see a small herd of deer making their way along the face of the hill. His heartbeat slowed again and his attention returned to his own progress.

Well past the hut now he slowly descended as he went, intending to regain the track as it turned upwards again. The light was now almost perfect and the glow over the cliffs from the rising sun was brilliant yellow. It was going to be another gorgeous morning.

He sensed rather than heard the movement of the cows and turned to see Switch peering around the end of the shed. Patrick dropped immediately. The hillocky turf made Patrick a difficult target and he lay flat, legs spread wide, feet splayed, and with his arms outstretched, both hands steadying the gun as it followed Switch's stumbling zig-zag as he approached at a limping trot across the intervening space.

He was crouching low and from the way he was looking around he obviously could not spot Patrick but sensed that someone was there. Patrick aimed at Switch's ample chest and squeezed the trigger gently when the large reddish brown bulk of the cow ambled across in front of his target. When the cow moved on Switch was invisible. The herd now started to follow the leader, some stopping to look aimlessly about and then continuing at the leisurely pace of someone with nothing important on their mind. One of the lovely beasts stared to browse its way directly towards Patrick's position when he saw the legs. Immediately behind the animal, his body hidden by the swell of the large belly, Patrick only had glimpses of Switch's legs. Too difficult to hit.

With about twenty yards to go the cow stopped, and swung its head round to look at the close attachment to it's tail. Patrick jumped up and bellowed, and dropped back to the ground. The cow wasn't really startled but nevertheless swung uphill away from the track and for a split second Switch was visible. Patrick fired twice. He heard the gasp and saw Switch fall, but he had no idea where he had hit him or how disabling it was. He lay still, again in the prone position, concentrating on the spot where Switch had gone down, but watching for any movement in the adjacent grass that might indicate that he was moving.

Suddenly Switch appeared coming out of the ditch by the roadside, almost at right angles to the direction Patrick faced.

'Hell.'

Patrick scrabbled onto one knee to bring the gun to bear as shots thudded into the clumps of grass around him.

Switch was close when he stumbled. The wounded leg did not hold and he dropped forward, supporting himself with one hand. As he regained his footing he peered upwards and fired at what, from his reduced elevation, must have been just a dark patch in the grass.

Patrick saw the slip, and despite the shots steadied himself. All he could see was Switch's snarling face and shoulders, and he fired. Once. Twice. Switch pitched forward and lay still.

Switch did not feel the shot that burst through his skull. His legs thrust and kicked again, and he lay still.

After a few moments watching the hut for other activity, Patrick raised himself to a crouch, and studied the black form lying on the grass ahead of him. It did not move. Patrick waited then slowly, very slowly, he stood up and walked over to the body. The bloody mess on the back of the head of the face-down man told him all he wanted to know, and without another glance Patrick checked that the hut was empty, then rejoined the track and continued up the hill.

Once again at the top of the rise he halted. Again he pressed himself hard against the rock face and looked down into the next bay. He recalled Karen point out 'Pulpit Rock', and the shelter it would provide. After only a few seconds Jimmy emerged from the shelter of the rock and started back up the hill towards Patrick. He was obviously going to determine the outcome of the shooting. He crouched as he walked quickly and did not see Patrick until he was upon him. As he looked up, gasped and instinctively reached for the shoulder holster, Patrick hit him on the side of the neck with the edge of his hand and he fell to the road. Patrick's foot crashed down hard on his shoulder blades and Jimmy flattened himself on the stony track.

'Stay very still. Hands on your head, and spread your legs. Wide!'

Jimmy made no sound; no effort to protest.

Patrick withdrew the small automatic from Jimmy's holster.

'You are lucky. You are still lucky. I am saving you for later. If you want to live don't move or you will be joining your friends, Bernie and Switch. Now sit against the rock over there.

Patrick directed him with a solid kick to the ribs, and then settled back against the rock face once more as Jimmy wriggled himself into a seated position.

He called out, 'Come along, Mark. This is the end of the story. If you are as important as you say, you are too valuable to allow yourself to be shot like a rabbit.'

The silence was broken only by the calls of the birds on their early morning foraging or as they homed in on their burrows after a night at sea.

Mark stepped cautiously out from behind the bulk of the large rock and came slowly along the track.

'Keep your hands where I can see them.'

Mark did not look afraid, almost confident.

Patrick did not miss the snarl of hatred from Jimmy, but as he looked he could also see fear in the younger man's eyes. He felt the pain surge in his groin. The temptation to shoot them was oppressive. He shook his head to clear his vision, kept himself hard to one side of the track and motioned Mark and Jimmy to pass on the other side.

'Now walk briskly, but keep your hands on your head.'

Like a scene from the war the small group made its way back past the body of Switch lying as though sunbathing in the warming air.

Mark glanced at the inert shape. 'Flat out again. I kept telling him he should lose weight. Very efficient. I presume that you dealt with Bernie also.'

'Yes. You should choose your associates more carefully. Sleazy bastards like Jimmy here are yellow in a crisis.'

Jimmy's hands raised fractionally from his head and then dropped back.

'Go on, Jimmy. Give me the chance. The first one will take your balls off. In fact I may just leave it at that. So go on.'

Mark sighed. 'Don't bother, Jimmy. It would spoil a beautiful morning, and make a mess of this lovely place.'

Patrick's eyes strayed to the south to the islands and the starkness of Mull just donning her morning coat to display the silvers and dusty greens of the shoulders of Ben More. The highland cattle looked up, only mildly interested, in the small group and up on the cliff the deer gazed down safe from any interruption of their morning ritual. The first pilgrims would be crossing the Sound of Iona bound for a day of legalised extortion. Who said masochism was unnatural?

Mark stumbled and Patrick's attention instantly returned to the backs of the two captives climbing the hill in front of him.

Tiredness was slowly overtaking him, and his thoughts went to Karen. *How will she react. Will she be too concerned about her husband now that he is close. Where is he?* For a moment he wondered about the Irish Rascal. He knew it was in the area. *Has it already arrived? Perhaps he has gone with the Irish.* For a fleeting moment he hoped he had, but he sensed that was much more likely to worry Karen than a face-to-face confrontation. *Will she still want him or will she see him as the person responsible for all of her problems?*

The beautiful bay of Gometra harbour again came into view as they approached the cottages, and Alan and Karen rose from the cemetery and made their way over to the track.

Once again his attention wandered. She looked so beautiful in the morning sunshine. Her hair glistened with a slight reddish tinge and her eyes sparkled as she approached.

Alan, who was no picture of beauty with dried blood over his forehead, nose and chin, smiled. 'Glad to see you're OK.'

'Thanks. I'm getting better by the second. How are you two?'

'We are fine. We both find this place so relaxing that it is easy to forget the problems.'

'A bit like toothache,' interposed Mark, 'And, by the way, I'm fine too.'

'You won't be when I get through with you,' retorted Patrick.

Alan, who had jogged off to the nearest cottage, had tucked the gun into the waistband of his trousers, and returned with a roll of brown adhesive tape. 'I would feel a whole lot happier if our friends were immobilised.'

Mark half turned towards Patrick. 'This really is quite unnecessary. I tried to explain to you that we are probably on the same side.'

Karen looked quizzically at Mark, 'And which side is that?'

'I know it is difficult when you have no experience of these things, but you should appreciate that there are times when governments have to sanction all sorts of activities to keep economies sound and to sustain allies.'

'I don't want to know what you are talking about. Does that include beating, rape and torture?

'I'm afraid it does, my dear. You people are just too naive. I regret that I have misread the situation, Pat, but you did not help.'

'Shut up, Mark. Just shut up, and get going.'

Patrick could see Karen was distressed, and the sparkle had gone from her eyes. He was desperate to put his arm around her and comfort her, and felt no jealousy when Alan did just that.

The deep boom of diesel engines at slow speed broke through the heavy, warm, morning air as the grey hull of the large launch entered the bay. Marines lined the deck although the ensign was blue and bore the portcullis of the Customs service.

As the small party made their way to the harbour all their attention had swung to the new arrival with its large rigid inflatable ready to launch. Even as the craft came to a stop alongside Fast Lady the launch and marines were on their way to shore whilst others jumped aboard the two pleasure craft.

Suddenly two Sea King helicopters crackled overhead, one disappearing to the west, the other to the east over Ulva.

As all of the eyes diverted skyward, Jimmy grabbed Alan's gun and held him with his arm around Alan's throat. 'Let's go, Mark.'

Mark's expression was of tiredness and disgust. 'There's no need for that, Jimmy. Give back the gun. I don't need you any more.'

The stunned expression on Jimmy's face gave way to one of befuddled understanding. He was on his own. 'Well, I might just fucking well need you. So move.'

Mark shrugged his shoulders and with a sideways glance at Patrick set off in front of Alan and Jimmy. Alan was now being dragged along behind Jimmy who had a firm hold of his hair. He was bent over as he tried to reduce the pressure on his hair but still provided a good shield; good enough to make any shot at Jimmy a risky one for Patrick. They quickly went from view along the track towards the small bridge to Ulva.

Patrick and Karen stood silently watching as they dropped out of sight.

At last he slipped his arm around Karen, but she looked up at him with a pleading expression. She had worked out that if Patrick wasn't trying to escape he must have known about the Navy. But Mark hadn't been trying to escape either.

'I'm not sure that I have the faintest idea what is happening, but it doesn't seem right just to let them get away.'

'They won't get away. Apart from the fact that these are islands, they will have to walk the whole length of Ulva before they get to a ferry or a boat and I think they will run into a welcoming party long before that.'

'What about Alan? I've known him for years. Jimmy is mad. He will kill him before they capture him. He doesn't deserve that.'

Patrick could sense her begging him to do something. He had relaxed. The tiredness was not creeping but bounding up on him. The moment seemed heavy, crucial, the look in her eyes an apocalypse.

'You're right. I'll get him.'

Karen threw her arms around him. 'Be careful. Thank you.' She sighed lightly as if considering the situation. 'I love you. Alan told me about Craig. I think I can live with that.'

He smiled and bent to gently kiss her forehead and lips, checked his gun and set off at a lope after the fugitives.

CHAPTER XXVII

SUDDENLY PATRICK felt light-headed, buoyant, the lassitude had vanished. He was happy! The crest of the hill arrived and he hesitated only long enough to glance behind to see Karen standing, in the now brilliant sunshine beside the golden seaweed, before he set off along the small inlet separating the two islands, his eyes searching the track ahead for signs of the others. He wasn't worried about Jimmy stopping or trying to lay an ambush, confident that Jimmy now had only survival and escape on his mind.

As he pressed on along the narrow track he had glimpses of Jimmy trying to prod Alan, who was now stumbling along ahead of him, and Mark into moving faster. Jimmy looked back and it was immediately obvious that he had seen Patrick, as he promptly prodded his two captives in the back. They all increased their pace slightly as they crossed the small bridge.

'Damn.'

Patrick realised that he had been seen and that at his present range there was nothing he could do. The light-headiness gone he stepped up the pace and was almost sprinting as he realised Jimmy might try some delaying tactic.

His concern was justified as he saw Jimmy pull Alan back to the small bridge and as he stood at the edge facing away from Patrick, Jimmy brought the gun down heavily on Alan's head. Alan pitched forward into the water. Jimmy turned, waved at Patrick and again prodded Mark into a near jog away from the small bridge and up the slope on to Ulva.

Patrick was now sprinting. The bruising of his groin was agony as he forced himself along as fast as he could. All he could think of was Karen's response if Alan was seriously hurt. *Will she believe I tried to save him?*

It took Patrick only around half a minute to reach the bridge and jump down beside Alan, who lay in the water, his face almost submerged. With a heave Patrick dragged him to the bank, grateful that, with the tide out, there was so little water in the narrow channel. He searched for a pulse. *Yes. Yes, there is a solid beat of a pulse.*

Is he breathing? No. No breath. Patrick quickly tilted back Alan's head, pinched his nose and, placing his mouth over Alan's started to resuscitate him.

After only a dozen or so breaths, Alan coughed, and coughed again and started to take deep breaths into his lungs. His eyes opened momentarily, and he smiled weakly.

Patrick winked at him.

'Wait here. I'll be back shortly.'

Patrick rolled him over onto his side, with his head resting on his arm as an added precaution, before clambering up the bank, and sprinting off up the hill after Jimmy.

As he reached the level moorland at the top of the slope he slowed as he rounded the corner. Ahead were the ruins of an old settlement, built where the land was flatter and there were some signs of past cultivation. Well ahead he could see Mark remonstrating with Jimmy. The fast pace was tiring Mark and his lack of fitness was slowing him, to Jimmy's annoyance.

Patrick cared little whether or not Jimmy shot Mark and summoned up an even greater effort to close the distance between them. They were shouting and as he got closer Patrick could see that Mark's face was scarlet with exertion.

As he ran on he was aware of Jimmy striking Mark and knocking him to one knee. As Mark's hands went to his head Jimmy kicked him, and Mark collapsed to the ground.

Patrick dropped onto one knee and took aim at Jimmy and stopped. The gun then swung to Mark and then back to Jimmy. Jimmy continued to rain kicks on Mark who was curled into a ball on the heathery turf. Patrick aimed over Jimmy's head, but did nothing. A hatred of them both overwhelmed him. *Let the bastards get on with it.*

How long he would have allowed the situation to continue he would never know, as two shots rang out; loud sharp shots, and Patrick followed Jimmy's gaze to the east. Just where another settlement of ruined houses was outlined against the skyline a group of armed men were strung out across the heather. Two knelt in front of the others, their automatic rifles pointing in Jimmy's direction.

Jimmy looked frightened, his head turning from side to side as if he were trying to see an escape route but, with the exception of the track and the drop to the sea, all other directions offered only rapidly rising moorland with almost total exposure. He suddenly darted away from Mark and back to the track.

As he took to his heels back the way he had come, he seemed to be oblivious to the presence of the kneeling Patrick. Not until he was very close, and Patrick arose in the middle of the track with his gun held at arms' length in both hands, did Jimmy stop in his flight. He looked confused and frightened. His gun arm dangled by his side and he made no effort to raise it. It was almost possible to feel sorry for him. He looked young at last.

'I think it is finished, Jimmy. Stop now before you make a big mistake.'

For a moment Patrick thought Jimmy was going to give in. His countenance brightened. A smile spread slowly as he looked straight at Patrick.

'Mark was right, wasn't he? He said you were one of the good guys. He said he was too. They never understand us, do they? We are really in the same team, aren't we? Right. You make a run for it. I'll hold them up.'

Patrick realised that Jimmy's mind was playing tricks, but before he could say anything Jimmy turned, took half a dozen steps towards the oncoming troops before stopping and looking over his shoulder at Patrick. 'Go on. You get away.'

He turned to face the advancing troops, raised the gun and fired continuously in their direction. Patrick saw as much as heard the reports from the soldiers, and watched as Jimmy staggered sideways like a drunk. The next shots spun him round to face Patrick, and as he collapsed two more shots bounced him off the road. Patrick did not need a close inspection to know that Jimmy was gone. There were too many wounds in the middle of his chest to make any survival possible.

The troops helped Mark to his feet and an officer approached Patrick. 'Major, sir. Are you alright?'

'Yes, thanks. Immaculate timing.'

Patrick turned away with a wave of his hand and took off at a fast jog towards the anchorage.

'For an officer to run like that there must be a woman somewhere around,' laughed one of the troops as they formed up on the track.

As he recrossed the bridge he checked his progress momentarily and noted that Alan has gone.

Patrick did not stop as he approached the marines coming from the harbour. They partially raised their weapons but realised he presented no danger and he ran past. The few minutes to the bay were interminable and the track felt bumpier. His ankles twisted on the small stones and he lurched as they dropped into the rain-made holes.

There was the bay. The grey powerboat. Wizard. Fast Lady. *Where is she?*

As he slowed to cross the intervening scrub and small boulders between him and the beach a tall man in a grey suit, and with a prominent scar on his left cheek, left the main group and stopped in front of him. 'Congratulations, Pat. We have accounted for everyone. How about you?'

Patrick ignored the proffered hand and looked wildly around. 'Where is she?'

'Oh, the lady. Right above you.'

Patrick turned and looked up the hill to see Karen and Alan seated on the grass leaning against the fence, both with large smiles on their faces.

'Talk to you later.'

Patrick suddenly felt the load vanish. His step over the rocks lifted and he almost flew up to the track side.

Alan was laughing as he watched Patrick slip and stumble on the seaweed-strewn rocks as he tried to hurry towards them.

'I don't know what you are laughing at. You look like Paddington Bear,' grunted Patrick.

Alan continued to laugh although the bandage around his head and down over one eye had indeed distorted his appearance somewhat.

'You can't talk. The way you ran along that road we thought you had found a pub. You looked like a drunk running for the last bus.'

Patrick plonked himself down beside Karen and gave her a big kiss. 'Great to see you.'

'Karen's eyes filled with tears. 'Oh God, I'm glad to see you. What happened along there. I heard so much shooting. Are they dead?'

'No. Mark is on his way back with an escort, although somewhat bruised. Jimmy is dead. He gave Mark a good going-over, but stopped short at shooting me. He seemed to think the troops were after me and decided to defend me. They shot him.'

He didn't quite know why he lied, but somehow softening Jimmy's image made sense. He felt it would reduce the hatred Karen must feel for him, help her to come to terms with things, but he didn't really know. This was foreign territory to him.

Karen cupped his face in her hands. 'I am pleased he did something right if he saved you for me.'

The relief they all felt was tangible.

Karen laughed as she pointed in a large sweep around the bay and hills. 'You have half the British Army here. You must be important.'

'Not this important. It has me puzzled too.'

Alan, who had been sitting trying to mind his own business and not intrude on the other two, could restrain himself no longer. 'What is this all about? I know we picked up drugs and the IRA were after them but how does all the rest fit in?'

'Later. I just want to rest and feel that sun.' He leaned back against the fence and appeared to close his eyes. He knew two of the grey men on the beach They were Joint Intelligence Committee, but there were two others, in naval uniforms, one of which was obviously not British, and he could hear snippets of a foreign language. It sounded like German, but it was slightly... Dutch! The same as the old labels he had seen on the boat.

The marines had returned and some of them had changed out of their combat gear and were wearing a naval uniform he did not immediately recognise, but he guessed it was Netherlands Navy too. He felt the need to know more. They were being ferried out to Fast Lady!

The sound of marching on gravel made Patrick visibly take notice as the army contingent arrived with Mark chatting vociferously, although Patrick smiled to note that he had not his usual upright bearing, and limped slightly. Jimmy had made an impression.

As they drew level Mark looked up, smiled and waved, before making his way down to the group on the shore. They all shook hands and an earnest conversation followed.

Patrick stiffened, stood and set off towards the group.

Karen watched. She sensed he was tense and Alan sensed it too. 'Trouble brewing, I think,' he mused.

'Yes. I think so,' agreed Karen.

Mark had walked to the water's edge to join two of the naval officers as Patrick approached the men in grey. Without any hesitation he marched straight up to them, grabbed the taller one by the shoulder and gesticulating in Mark's direction was clearly furious. The shorter man, with both hands raised in apparent supplication, was obviously trying to act diplomatically.

The scarred man stopped shouting in response and they all walked off along the shingle towards the old landing area. It was not possible to hear what was being said but Patrick was clearly still unhappy as he repeatedly gestured in the direction of the boats, Karen and Alan, and Mark. They turned to walk up the beach and were obscured from view but it was obvious that the discussion was far from amicable.

Karen stared up to hill opposite where two eagles were circling round and round.

'Did Craig have sex with that Irish woman?'

Alan was startled. Without warning the subject he had been dreading had been raised in as direct a way as possible. He hesitated.

'It's all right, Alan. You may as well know, if you haven't guessed, that I have fallen in love with Patrick, but just wondered why Craig went off again. I think I know.'

Thoughts flooded his mind. It was none of his business what his friends did. He shouldn't say anything.

Karen gave a slightly self-conscious laugh. 'It has happened before. It has all been going wrong for quite a while. I suppose it suited me to ignore it.'

Alan sighed, 'I don't really know. They were ashore alone and he certainly seemed besotted with her. He has acted strangely from time to time, but I don't really know.'

'It doesn't matter now anyway. Forget I said anything.'

As they watched, Patrick reappeared round the hill and stormed back along the shore with the two civilians in his wake.

Karen was perplexed, and stared hard at Mark.'That man has behaved like a beast and yet they are treating him like some sort of hero.'

'Patrick clearly does not think so. I think our man is the hero, and I think you believe that too.'

Karen smiled.

The tender from Fast Lady was on its way back to shore clearly making for Mark and the others. As Patrick reached them, Mark, smiling, detached himself from the group and walked up the shingle, hand outstretched, 'I told you we were on the same side.'

'Patrick stretched out his hand, 'Well, Captain, have a good trip.'

'Than — ' The sentence was not completed.

Patrick's hand had been suddenly withdrawn, and his clenched fist crashed straight into the middle of the big man's face. The crunch was satisfying and Patrick stepped back and clutched his bloodied knuckles in his other hand.

Mark had collapsed on one knee, and on top of the beating Jimmy had given him he was unable to respond. One of the officers grabbed Mark and arrested his fall, the other began to raise his gun, only to see the machine pistols of six soldiers pointing at him.

Patrick looked into the eyes of the foreigner. 'Clean that shit off my beach.'

He turned, clapped a hand on the shoulder of the nearest soldier, 'Thanks, mate,' and walked back to where Alan and Karen were standing, drawn to their feet by the sudden excitement.

'That didn't do our foreign relations policy any good,' laughed Alan.

'I see you have worked that bit out. No. I don't suppose it did, but I hadn't realised how much pleasure you can get from pain,' retorted Patrick as he nursed his rapidly swelling hand.

'Are you going to tell us what all this is about now?'

'Yes. I suppose you deserve an explanation.'

He stopped and stared out at the boats. Mark was visible in the wheelhouse and at the stern a Netherlands ensign fluttered gently in the breeze. As they stood in silence the big powerboat extricated itself from the other craft, made a sharp turn and motored slowly between the headlands. Clear of the rocks at the entrance the bow lifted slightly, the wake whitened and widened astern, the ensign streamed and the hull carved its way through the silver scales of the dark ocean. Away from Gometra and in the direction of the sacred Isle of Iona.

Troops were now arriving from the direction of the cottages and an officer was talking to the grey men. One broke off from the group and approached them, stopping in front of Karen. 'Mrs Burgess, I have been informed that our men have found your husband. He isn't in the best of condition but I am assured he will be OK. We have room in one of the helicopters and we will be taking him with us.'

'Thank you. Tell him to take better care of himself.' Karen could not bring herself to say 'Tell him I love him.'

'I will pass on your message.'

The suited man turned to Patrick. 'I know what you are thinking, Patrick. I have seen this type of situation before. I don't like it either but it happens. We control it or it controls us.'

'I can't view it like that,' responded Patrick. 'Can't believe it was worth all this.'

'The costs are much greater than this, I assure you. Have a rest. Get in touch in a week and we will see if we can find you something more rewarding. In the meantime, thank you. It's a dirty job, I know, but we do our best. You did all that could be asked of you.'

'We will clean up the . . . ' he hesitated, then continued, 'the debris on the way out.'

They shook hands, and as the grey man began to leave, he looked at Karen and Alan. Thank you both on behalf of your country. Oh, and your friend Mike is well. He was picked up by a fishing boat. We have had a hell of a job keeping him quiet. He knows the outline of the situation and has followed developments with us, so you should have a good time talking it over. In private though. I am sorry it all went so wrong.'

Patrick grimaced at the grey man's implication that it had all been a good day out and asked 'What happened to the Irish?'

'They were picked up by a boat we have under surveillance. Apparently they dumped the lady's husband as they left. Gave him a bit of a headache they did. Will you manage the yacht, or would you like me to leave some crew? Or we could get the yacht home for you and the cutter could take you all back to Ardfern if you like.'

Alan who was now looking grey and tired said, 'I don't think I'm up to sailing. Can I have a lift?'

'Of course. In fact if you head off with these men now you can have a helicopter ride in the other machine. With a body bag unfortunately.'

'That will do nicely.'

Alan embraced Karen, and shook hands with Patrick. 'Take care of her. She's a lovely lady. I'd like to meet you again some time. Life is never going to be dull with you.'

'I'll certainly look after her, and I would like to thank you. I couldn't have done it without you.' Patrick smiled. 'You'd make a good agent. We will meet again.'

'I think I'll give that idea a miss,' chuckled Alan, and without another word he joined the group heading off to the bridge. He did not look back.

'Well, that just leaves you two.'

Karen held Patrick's hand tightly. 'We will manage. In fact I am looking forward to the rest.'

'That's settled then. Take care and thank you again.'

The tall man turned and followed the group of soldiers who had already started back to the north-west.

CHAPTER XXVIII

T HE GREY HULL of the Customs launch with its accompanying Royal Marine crew had grumbled out of the bay; the helicopters had dipped into the bay before climbing rapidly to the east; and the peace and silence of the place surrounded Wizard as she bobbed on the ripples that swirled around the anchorage.

On the crag, the stag and its herd stood silhouetted against the skyline and looked down on the intruders; the eagles circled overhead and gannets, oystercatchers and redshank flew to and from the sea and seashore on their daily tasks. A seal swam slowly around the yacht, its head above water, stopping at the stern to stare at the two occupants as they sat entwined in each other's arms, sipping their Gordons and Schweppes tonic.

They had walked back across the island to the North Anchorage, past the cottages, through the herd of highland cattle, round the pulpit, past the teacher's house, the big house and the farmyard. They had seen frogs, a variety of sheep, stoat, eagles, deer, puff-ball mushrooms, heather, and gorse, and had been accompanied all the way by the pet goat. All of Scotland was there.

They gazed out to the Treshnish Isles, talked about the old monks who had lived there, reminisced about Iona and Columba, Staffa and Mendelsohn, and peered into the haze surrounding the islands of Coll, Staffa and in the far distance, Tiree. They walked, speaking little, laughing as the occasional stumble brought sharp reminders of what they had endured. Hand in hand they walked, shirts tied around their waists and marvelled at the glorious panorama, unbeatable anywhere in the world.

Afterwards, as they sat watching a small fishing boat picking its way around the rocks off the south-west corner of the island, Karen suddenly looked serious. 'You know you have to tell me what was happening. Why the Irish? Why the Dutch? How much did you know?'

Patrick sat silent for a few minutes.

'OK. I don't even now know the whole story. I doubt if any one

251

individual does, but for all our sakes I hope someone in the inner sanctum of the MoD or the Security Services does. On reflection, I am sure someone does. But it isn't the sort of person you would expect to know.'

'The government must know.'

'You would be surprised at how little the government knows. The Security Service accountability theoretically ends at the Prime Minister, but if you think about it you will appreciate that there are people in the Service who query even the activities of the PM. In other words the Security Services are responsible for monitoring the activities of the most senior individual with the power to check the Service. The Security Service, in effect, monitors itself.

'In fact it goes far deeper than that. The Service can and does act without reference on many matters deemed to be for the benefit of Britain. They justify it by maintaining that secrecy is essential.

'Unfortunately, the West of Scotland is moving with people who hold or have held senior positions in the grey suit team. If you think back just a short while you may recall the Scott Enquiry, and a variety of publications exposing the involvement of ministers and their families in illegal arms shipments. Names were named and yet nothing was done. It all died a death. A book written by a director of an armaments supplier actually named several of the Thatcher Government and even indicated how much money had been transferred to Tory Party funds offshore.'

'Why did the Labour Party let it all rest?'

'Well, they asked a few questions in the House but no real muscle was put into the investigation. You must ask yourself why. I think you will probably come to the same conclusion as me, that they too have a vested interest in these activities.'

Patrick sat silently for a few moments, before continuing.

'I know what you want to ask. If they were named so publicly why did they not go to law. I believe there are two possible answers. Firstly they have decided that although it was all true they had effectively nobbled any prosecution route with Public Interest Immunity Certificates and that sort of thing.

'And secondly because any attempt to sue would expose even greater scandals and corruption. They simply let sleeping dogs lie. For example. Do you recall the fuss?'

'Oh yes, but only vaguely.'

'There you are. They have won if respectable members of the public forget so quickly. What was picked up by Wizard was about 500 kilograms of heroin. I don't know the precise value, but let's just say millions. The heroin was payment for arms shipments to either Chile or China, probably for onward transmission to an even less desirable destination, and probably to a country with little or no resources.'

'Surely the government wouldn't take the drugs into Britain?'

'You may be right. I hope you are, and in this instance they would claim that the drugs were the property of the Netherlands. As you probably know the Dutch have the most liberal attitude to drug use in Europe. They will arrange to sell the heroin and the funds or at least a portion of them will, or perhaps I should say may, find their way back to the UK, after all sorts of commissions have been deducted. Don't ask me to whom. I would be afraid to guess.

'You can see that with this set-up the government can acknowledge what it feels will benefit it and ignore what doesn't. According to some reports the arms manufacturers will receive their payment from ECGD at worst and that means you and I pay.'

'ECGD?'

'Export Credits Guarantee Department. A type of insurance for exporters.'

'That explains the Dutch flag. Where do you and the Irish fit in?'

'Come on. Let's get back to the boat. I will tell you the rest then but right now I'd kill for a G&T.'

'Great idea.'

The ambling was over. They set off at a brisk pace with an occasional 'Ouch' from Patrick as he caught his foot in a grassy tuft, and very shortly they were paddling across the still water to Wizard.

Back on deck, Patrick looked into her eyes. 'I love you. Perhaps I shouldn't, but I do. I am sorry for all that you have gone through. Without all this I would never have known you. I can't work out why things happen this way but they do.'

'That's good news. I would hate to have fallen in love with someone who didn't love me. Fortunately we don't control how these things happen, although I think your grey man would like to. It was good to hear about Mike. He is a good man, and I know him well enough to know that he will shrug it all off and carry on as before. I am going to try to follow his example.'

Karen handed Patrick a glass with the mist of condensation coating the rim. 'I'm glad they kept the refrigerator on. I hate G and T without ice.'

'Now. I want you to finish telling me about why you are involved.'

Patrick rapidly swallowed the first drink and refilled the glasses, then sat back with his legs along the cockpit seat.

'I really shouldn't have been in on this sort of thing. I was with Army Intelligence for a number of years. In fact some of the lads you saw today were with me. We were in Ireland for quite a long time.

'I was born in Edinburgh and only my father was Irish, but I knew enough from regular family visits and my service there to enable me to infiltrate the IRA. It's a long story, but eventually my chiefs decided that it was becoming too dangerous and brought me out, back to the mainland where I was asked politely to transfer from the military side to the civil side of things and I was introduced to Mark. I won't bore you with the whole story but suffice to say that I was introduced to him at formal functions in the City as a businessman who could handle himself.

'The only thing about it is, I never really left Military Intelligence either, although I should imagine there will be some sorting out now!

'Mark was introduced to me as a major importer with something to hide. I was supposed to monitor it all. That is pretty ironic now as it is obvious that they knew all along what he was doing. He was doing it for us and the Dutch, and Lord knows who else. I must have just been there to keep tabs on him. I was told they didn't know who he was working with but I find that a bit hard to swallow.

'But that is when it gets interesting. One evening I had a call from a contact, an agent in Ireland, high in the IRA Command, who said they needed my help. I wasn't too sure but I said I would meet them to discuss it. It turned out that the pressure on the IRA to call another ceasefire was growing. The Sinn Fein faction felt they had made more progress during the ceasefire than had been made with all the mainland disruption, and the Labour Party had such a large majority that they could take a strong line with terrorism. A political presence was needed and the supporters of the IRA in the Labour Party were making comforting noises. They said that they did not see the break-up of the UK in the same light as the Tories. They had indicated that a ceasefire would lead to talks about, initially at least, greater autonomy for Northern Ireland. Even the IRA knew that it wouldn't be too many years before the nationalist vote in the North would be greater than the Unionist. They breed like rabbits those Catholics, you know.'

Patrick stopped short in mid flow. 'Oh. I am sorry. Are you Catholic?'

Karen laughed. 'No, but that was a bit of a faux pas for a spy, wasn't it?'

'Yes,' Patrick smiled. 'The main problem was lack of funds. Real money. The sort of money you need to run advertising campaigns; millions in fact.

'They had kept up a superficial contact with me and it was no secret who I worked for. Indeed Mark had a number of businesses which allowed him a reasonably high profile and my association with him was well known. In a nutshell, they wanted my help to hijack a major consignment of drugs. I had to inform them of the schedule and they would set up the rest.

'My bosses thought that was wonderful. Here was an opportunity to pick up senior officers of the IRA, in the act of attempting to import drugs. Although it wasn't intended to seek publicity, obviously if anything did go wrong it could be made public without any reflection on the other purpose of the pick-up. Indeed it could be projected as a coup for the Customs. There have been other ventures like this which have gone wrong. The Customs always end up doing the dirty work, and sometimes one of them is seriously injured, but just occasionally they get the success. There was a situation a bit like this on the east coast of Scotland not so long ago. Unfortunately a Customs officer was killed.'

'It is difficult to believe that the government would go along with this,' mused Karen.

'I can only repeat. You don't know the real government. Most important decisions are made in back rooms in Whitehall just like directors of companies used to have their important meetings away from their factories in the sixties so they didn't have the "Works Committee" members present when the important decisions were being made. That way all management decisions appeared to be with the unanimous support of the management team. The PM just wasn't good at working with the system. He couldn't keep his end of the bargain by keeping his team under control. Remember this sort of corruption runs through all levels of society. Even law lords aren't averse to keeping mum when they have a vested interest at stake.'

'I didn't have the whole picture until today, and even now I'm not sure I know all the ramifications. Anyway I set everything up: the transport system which was used by Mark and his associates, and the method of collecting the drugs. Sean and Mairread.'

'So that's her name. You knew her?'

Patrick looked for a reaction in Karen's eyes, but she seemed composed.

'Yes. I knew them from Dublin. I hadn't appreciated just how high up the command structure they were, but on reflection they always seemed to obtain answers to problems very quickly. They were a pretty ruthless pair. There was nothing they would stop at for "the cause".

'They made several pick-ups which were successful and eventually we had this big one coming in. A ship from South America which had been offloading in Copenhagen came round the North of Scotland and down the Minch. The packages were dropped on a shelf just south of Barra Head. They were sunk by weights connected to water soluble links, which would burst after a predetermined time and the packages were designed to float to the surface. Usually the pick-up was made during the day but occasionally the packs would rise to just below the surface and a pattern of small lights would identify the precise location. Sometimes the packs were deliberately left very deep and difficult to retrieve from a yacht, so a fishing boat would net them and very soon after would transfer them to a yacht. It all worked very well. With the Global Positioning System now so accurate this was relatively straightforward.

'There are so many yachts around the islands in the summer that it is difficult for even the fast boats that the Customs now have to keep in touch with them all.'

'Surely a boat sailing regularly would attract attention?'

'No. Exactly the opposite. Checks are made around all the boatyards and marinas, and the Customs know all the local boats. In general they are all crewed by genuine yachtsmen, but with so many people retiring early, the yachtsmen tend to be people with money or good pension provision, and much more often than in the past, yachts are sailing offshore for extended periods. Our boat was known and for a long time we got away with it. In addition there are so many charter boats now it is difficult to keep tabs on them all.'

'So what happened this time?'

'There was a tip-off that the yacht they had been using was under suspicion. I only knew that they had an alternative available, another vessel that sailed regularly in the area and was clean.'

'You mean this boat.'

'Yes, although I knew something was up when I was asked to get you away from home, I didn't know the details until we reached Liverpool. I mean that it was your boat. I reported what I knew about a large number of business people in the Newton Mearns area, but I didn't, at the time, know what was happening to the information.

'I thought I was reporting it to my civilian and military controllers, but I now suspect that it was going much further than that. I would like to think it was a tactical leak as the alternative means there is serious corruption at the very top of our Security Service.'

'Is that possible?'

'Yes. Everything is possible. On this occasion, the Irish were intending to meet up with the yacht, and transfer the goods to a fast powerboat and have them out of British territorial waters fast. This was to happen whilst Fast Lady waited off Jura for a signal saying the pick-up was completed. They expected the goods then to be transferred in a remote bay on Jura, in Corryvreckan, or West Loch Tarbert.'

'There aren't too many of them on Jura, and these were certainly good choices,' observed Karen, remembering wild and windy nights anchored in Loch Tarbert while southerly gales swept down from the sides of the Paps of Jura and sent the boat swinging wildly from side to side as it tried to free itself from its restraining anchor. Sleepless nights in a place she disliked intensely.

'Yes, that's correct. We have used it before. There are many possibilities from there dependent on where the consignments are going. Unfortunately a most unseasonable gale blew up just after Wizard had taken the consignment on board, and she was unable to punch her way south, being driven north, initially, as you know, to Eriskay.

'At the same time the Irish boat which could easily have reached them quickly was delayed with tanks full of dirty diesel and had eventually ended up at Ardfern to have the tanks drained and the fuel system cleaned out.

'After that it was a matter of trying to delay Wizard's meeting up with Fast Lady until the Irish were in the same area. I thought we wanted to get the people who would actually be on the Irish boat. A load of this value would bring out the top brass.

'The rest you know, more or less. I was stupid enough to believe we also wanted to nail Mark and his crew.'

'What happened to the Irish then? You didn't get them.'

'I think we probably did. You see, communications on the west coast are desperately poor. Mobile phone reception is more or less impossible, and we had "ears" in the sky picking up all the VHF transmissions from the boats.'

'What about the telephone calls?'

'We could monitor these too. The link to the coast station is also VHF.'

'Of course.'

'Well that's as much as I can tell you. I hope it's enough.'

Patrick watched the eagles now circling black against the dying sun. 'It's a lucky man who owns a heaven like this.'

'Yes, but I hope you noticed. Unlike the foreign owners, he is sharing it. Surely you saw the notices saying you are welcome to walk around the island. The only downside to this bay is that you can't see the sun set.'

'Yes, I did, and I'm pleased to hear that you don't consider the English to be foreigners. We could climb the hill to see the sun set.'

'I have a better idea,' smiled Karen. 'Give me a few minutes to organise the aft cabin and have a shower.'

'Yes. That sounds like a much better idea.'

Karen went below, and Patrick sat back listening to the evening call of the birds and watched the sky and sea slowly change colour from gold to silver to black as the sun eased itself over the far horizon; the last drop of gin was drained form his glass and he went below.

For many reasons their lovemaking was gentle and prolonged. Small butterfly kisses were spread all over bruises until at last lying facing each other, Karen's slim legs around his waist, Patrick eased himself into her and moved gently until they clutched tightly at each other and the surge of pleasure climaxed and subsided, and a blessed sleep overtook them.

Just south of Tiree a naval launch stopped a large white powerboat. Three men in plain clothes accompanied by armed ratings boarded the vessel, and two hours later returned to the launch which then headed west to the frigate just visible on the horizon.

The launch was almost back at the frigate when the last bubbles broke the surface and the bow of Irish Rascal sank below the darkening sea. No 'Mayday' call was heard and no search was mounted for the vessel. No-one on the launch looked back.

On board the frigate a ship-to-shore call was being made by a man in a grey suit. 'The last loose ends have been tied. Returning tomorrow. Goodnight.'

CHAPTER XXIX

KAREN HAD BEEN home for two weeks following an idyllic sail from the last scene of the trouble, visiting Fingal's Cave on Staffa before passing through the Sound of Iona, among the Torran rocks, down to Colonsay, to Gigha where they walked in the warm humid atmosphere of the gardens of Achamore House, maintained for many years on the proceeds of a nightcap, round the distillery at Craighouse on Jura and then finally back to Ardfern. David Wilkie at the yacht centre gave them a lift to Crinan to collect Patrick's car.

They spoke less and less as they approached Glasgow and after crossing the Erskine Bridge not a word was said until they drew up outside Karen's home.

'Can I give you a hand with your gear?'

'I think I can manage one holdall, don't you?'

'I think you can manage whatever you set your mind to. I will miss you. Will I see you again?'

'I don't know. I have a lot to think about.'

'Promise me you will let me know. Don't just disappear from my life.'

'What about you? How do I know where you will be at any time? Any relationship would be difficult with someone who is a spy.'

'You'd be surprised how mundane most of the security work is.'

Karen looked hard at Patrick, searching for something, she knew not what.

'We'll see. Thank you.'

She leaned towards him and kissed him lightly on his lips. 'Goodbye.'

She slipped out of the car and walked straight up the driveway to the front door, opened it and went inside without a backward glance. Patrick watched her go and drove off.

Craig had been at home when she entered. He still had a bandage round his head holding a pad in place at the back of his head. They hugged briefly and by some strange unspoken agreement nothing was said about the incident. Craig slept in the guest room.

*　　*　　*

About a week later they were sitting in the conservatory. It was a warm evening, humid after the afternoon rain with flashes of sunlight cutting through the light cloud coverlet. Both were looking out at the garden and talking about the way the new shrubs had established themselves.

'Where did Mairread go?'

Craig looked at Karen, an amazed look upon his face. 'How do you know her name?'

'It doesn't matter how I know. I just wondered what had happened to her.'

'Why should I know?

'Don't play stupid games. You released her from the cottage. You slept with her. I would have thought you would have heard from her by now. Have you?'

Craig hesitated for a short while. Alan had talked. He had expected him to. He had obviously told Karen everything. 'I haven't heard anything. And as for sleeping with her, you have read as much as me about hostage situations. I did what I had to do to stay alive.'

'Oh. Did Alan sleep with her too?'

'No. She didn't make him.'

'Make him. That's rich. I heard you were infatuated with her.'

'That was what she wanted. I just did what I had to.'

Karen stood up and walked to the window. 'That must be the first time any woman has forced you to do anything. Do you know the sort of things these people have done? Do you? Yes, you do, and you don't care. If a woman is prepared to drop her pants for you, you will fuck her regardless of who or what she is.'

Craig stood. He was crimson faced. 'Karen, stop it. You don't talk like that. I can't stand you speaking in that foul-mouth way.'

'What you can and can't stand is irrelevant to me. You wanted a neat presentable women to flirt with your friends and customers. One who wouldn't go too far. A near virgin, who could look attainable but kept it all for you. That wouldn't have been too bad. I wanted to keep it for you, but you wanted more. You wanted secretaries and anyone else you could find at the trade shows and exhibitions you went to. God knows why I put up with it, but I did. I believed it was right, that you couldn't help yourself, that it was right for the children.

'Well, it's finished now. All week I have waited for you to show an interest in us. All week I have waited for you to ask me about myself about the horrors I had to undergo. I waited and waited. You went straight to the spare bedroom. I didn't ask you to. You're guilt showed all the time. What's wrong. Don't you think you could get it up for me. I'd be amazed. You could get it up for a dead body.'

Craig, brows knitted, stared straight at Karen's back. 'I thought I should give you space. You seemed very distant.'

'After what we've been through, I would have thought that you would have wanted to comfort me, to throw your arms around me and show me you cared, but no, you guessed Alan had told me and instead of making a move to overcome the problem you just felt it would be easier if you stayed away from me. You wanted to wait to see if I would beg you to sleep with me. To see if I would beg you to come back to me after knowing you had been with another woman. Just like before.

'This time you are wrong. You have never ignored me before, even when you had been screwing your secretary, but this time you did. This time because you knew it had been spelled out to me that you did. You are just a bloody coward. I am not sure I don't wish that woman had kept you. She wasn't so stupid. She dumped you at the water's edge when she didn't need you any longer.'

There was a long silence, until Craig sat down again. He had never heard her like this. 'Where do we go from here?'

Karen turned from the window with tears in her eyes. 'We don't go anywhere. You get out. I now know what a man, a real man can do; do for others; do for his country, and yes do for me. You were so conceited, so full of yourself and what you saw as your problem, you didn't think to ask me how I coped.

'I came home intending that both of us should slowly get to know each other again, and try to forget the last few weeks. I knew we both had things to forget if we were to continue with the same life. You couldn't make the effort because you were too concerned about your own feelings. You didn't know how you would handle my reactions, and you wanted to avoid that. Even if we couldn't talk during the day you knew we would be bound to talk if we were in the same bed so you avoided that situation.'

Craig's voice rose to a high pitch. 'That isn't true. I was just shielding you.'

'From what? You didn't have any idea what I knew. You couldn't be certain I knew what you had done. I didn't give you any indication that I knew. You hadn't the guts to try. Or maybe you just didn't want to. It doesn't matter anyway. I don't want you here any more. If your lady calls make sure I can let her know where you have gone.'

Karen walked from the conservatory and upstairs to the bedroom where she lay quietly staring at the ceiling. Thoughts flashed through her mind. Mental pictures of the weekends spent before they married, with no money, a tiny boat and trying to make love on a minute double berth. The children tottering around the living room, John with an imaginary lawnmower making engine noises, and Susan riding her little bike along the narrow hall and straight into the corner of the wall. As images of friends, parties, holidays, and all the hard work spent together trying to keep calm while the business staggered fleeted through her mind she lay silent, until as the last glow of sun faded from the window and as shadows merged into the evening gloom she burst into tears.

CHAPTER XXX

S HE HAD DRIVEN PAST Patrick's house several times on her way to the supermarket and the gates had always been closed. She assumed that he had finished his business in the area and had been moved away. She still saw the delivery vans and the SEC still sent goods by them. One or two members commented that Patrick had not been at any meetings recently but not much was said as quite a number of the business people were away for extended periods.

The day after the confrontation with Craig the gates of Patrick's house were open. She stopped the car, reversed and then turned into the drive. When she reached the steps to the front door she stopped and sat for a while staring at the door. When nothing happened she got out and walked up to the door. She was shaking. The chimes respond to her push of the bell, and as there was no reaction she pressed again.

She didn't know whether or not she wanted to hear footsteps approaching the door but after the lack of response to the second pull her heart sank and she felt a chill hit her stomach. 'Damn. Damn. Damn. Damn.'

Karen turned and was looking down at the steps as she was about to return to her car when something made her look up. Leaning against the car, tanned and laughing was a man who had obviously been gardening. He held a large bundle of weeds in his hands, and his check shirt was unbuttoned to the waist. He was unkempt, with about two or three days growth on his face.

'You rat! You stood there and watched me going through hell and you said nothing.'

'You just looked so lovely, and my conceit was well pampered when I realised you really wanted to see me.'

With that Patrick threw the weeds all over the Golf and rushed forward to smother her with kisses.

'The door is open. Come in.'

'Yes, Mr Bond. I'm right with you.'

'No. Not Mr Bond, but not Patrick Dougan either. I think I should tell you my real name is . . . '